**"Who said I was a maiden?"
Gabby closed her eyes for a second,
allowing the sun to wash over her
face, the corners of her lips curving
up slightly into a smile.**

"You didn't have to say it," Alessandro said.
"I could feel it in your kiss." Or rather the lack
of it.

Her stomach sank down to her toes and she
opened her eyes again, the corners of her lips
falling. "Was it so terrible?"

Of course it hadn't been.

"Not terrible. Inexperienced. I could taste it on
your skin."

"That's ridiculous. Inexperience doesn't have a
flavour."

He grabbed hold of her arm again, turned her
to face him, drawing her closely toward him.
Rather than speeding up, this time her heart
stopped beating altogether.

He lowered his head slightly, then reached
up, sliding his thumb along the edge of her
lip. "Yes, Gabriell[a]
has a flavour. And
innocence and wil[d]
the taste of any of

The Billionaire's Legacy

A search for truth and the promise of passion!

For nearly sixty years
Italian billionaire Giovanni Di Sione has kept
a shocking secret. Now, nearing the end of his days,
he wants his grandchildren to know their true heritage.

He sends them each on a journey to find his
'Lost Mistresses'—a collection of love tokens
and the only remaining evidence of his lost identity,
his lost history…his lost love.

With each item collected the Di Sione siblings take
one step closer to the truth…and embark on a
passionate journey that none could have expected!

Find out what happens in

The Billionaire's Legacy

Di Sione's Innocent Conquest by Carol Marinelli

The Di Sione Secret Baby by Maya Blake

To Blackmail a Di Sione by Rachael Thomas

The Return of the Di Sione Wife by Caitlin Crews

Di Sione's Virgin Mistress by Sharon Kendrick

A Di Sione for the Greek's Pleasure by Kate Hewitt

A Deal for the Di Sione Ring by Jennifer Hayward

The Last Di Sione Claims His Prize by Maisey Yates

Collect all 8 volumes!

THE LAST DI SIONE
CLAIMS HIS PRIZE

BY
MAISEY YATES

First Published in Great Britain 2017
By Mills & Boon, an imprint of HarperCollins*Publishers*
1 London Bridge Street, London, SE1 9GF

© 2017 Harlequin Books S.A.

Special thanks and acknowledgement are given to Maisey Yates
for her contributon to The Billionaire's Legacy series.

ISBN: 978-0-263-92507-4

Printed and bound in Spain
by CPI, Barcelona

Maisey Yates is a *New York Times* bestselling author of more than thirty romance novels. She has a coffee habit she has no interest in kicking, and a slight Pinterest addiction. She lives with her husband and children in the Pacific Northwest. When Maisey isn't writing she can be found singing in the grocery store, shopping for shoes online and probably not doing dishes. Check out her website: maiseyyates.com.

Books by Maisey Yates

Mills & Boon Modern Romance

Carides's Forgotten Wife
Bound to the Warrior King
His Diamond of Convenience
To Defy a Sheikh
One Night to Risk It All

Heirs Before Vows

The Spaniard's Pregnant Bride
The Prince's Pregnant Mistress
The Italian's Pregnant Virgin

The Chatsfield

Sheikh's Desert Duty

One Night With Consequences

The Greek's Nine-Month Redemption
Married for Amari's Heir

Princes of Petras

A Christmas Vow of Seduction
The Queen's New Year Secret

Secret Heirs of Powerful Men

Heir to a Desert Legacy
Heir to a Dark Inheritance

Visit the Author Profile page at
millsandboon.co.uk for more titles.

To the authors that have brought me
countless hours of reading pleasure.
You inspire me.

CHAPTER ONE

IT WAS RUMORED that Alessandro Di Sione had once fired an employee for bringing his coffee back two minutes later than commanded and five degrees cooler than ordered. It was rumored that he had once released a long-term mistress with a wave of his hand and an order to collect a parting gift from his assistant in the following weeks.

There were also rumors that he breathed fire, slept in a dungeon and derived sustenance from the souls of the damned.

So, when his shiny new temporary assistant scurried into the room, with red cheeks and an apologetic expression, on the heels of his grandfather—who appeared neither red-cheeked nor sorry for anything—it was no surprise that she looked as though she was headed for the gallows.

Of course, no one denied Giovanni Di Sione entry to any place he wished to inhabit. No personal assistant, no matter how formidable, would have been able to keep his grandfather out. Age and severely reduced health notwithstanding.

But as his typical assistant was on maternity leave and her replacement had only been here for a couple of weeks, she didn't know that. She was, of course, afraid that Giovanni was an intruder and that she would be punished for the breach of security.

He saw no point in disabusing her of that notion. It was entirely possible she would spend the rest of the day deconstructing the meaning to his every glance in her direction. Likely, in the retelling, she would talk about the blackness of his eyes being a reflection of his soul, or some other such nonsense. And so, his reputation would darken even more, without him lifting a finger.

"I'm very sorry, Mr. Di Sione," she said, clearly out of breath, one palm pressed tightly over her rather unimpressive breasts.

He made a low, disapproving sound and raised one dark brow.

She was trembling now. Like a very small dog. "Should I go back to work, sir?" she asked, nervous eyes darting toward the door.

He waved his hand and she scurried back out much the same as she had scurried in.

"I see you're up and moving around," Alex said, not descending into sentimentality because his relationship with Giovanni didn't allow for that. With each returned Lost Mistress, Giovanni's health had recovered bit by bit.

"It's been a while since my last treatment, so I'm feeling better."

"Good to hear it."

"The way you acted toward your assistant was not overly kind, Alessandro," his grandfather said, taking the seat in front of Alex's desk somewhat shakily.

"You say that as though you believe I have a concern about being perceived as kind. We both know I do not."

"Yes, but I also know you're not as terrible as you pretend to be." Giovanni leaned back in his chair, both hands planted on his knees. He was getting on in years and, after seventeen years in remission, his leukemia had returned. At ninety-eight, Giovanni likely didn't have many years left on the earth regardless of his health, but it had certainly added a bit of urgency to the timeline.

The goal being to recover each and every one of Giovanni's Lost Mistresses. Stories of these treasures were woven into Alex's consciousness. His grandfather had been spinning tales about them from the time Alessandro was a boy. And now, he had tasked each of his grandchildren with finding one of those lost treasures.

Except for Alex.

He had been expecting this. Waiting for quite some time to hear about what part he might play in this quest.

"Maybe not," Alex said, leaning back in his chair, unconsciously mimicking his grandfather's position.

"At least you do not dare to behave terribly in my presence."

"What can I say, *Nonno*? You are perhaps the only man on earth more formidable than I."

Giovanni waved his hand as if dismissing Alex's words. "Flattery is not the way with me, Alessandro, as you well know."

He did know. His grandfather was a man of business. A man who had built a life out of nothing upon his arrival to America, a man who understood commerce. He had instilled that in Alex. It was how they connected. Where their minds met.

"Don't tell me you're feeling bored and you wanted to get your hands back into the shipping business?"

"Not at all. But I do have a job for you."

Alex nodded slowly. "Is it my time to take a mistress?"

"I have saved the last one for you, Alessandro. The painting."

"Painting?" Alex lifted a paperweight from his desk and moved it, tapping the glass with his index finger. "Don't tell me you were a great collector of clowns on velvet or some such."

Giovanni chuckled. "No. Nothing of the kind. I'm looking for *The Lost Love*."

Alex frowned. "My art history is a little bit faint at my advanced age, but the name does sound familiar."

"It should. What do you know about the disgraced royal family of Isolo D'Oro?"

"Had I known there would be a test, I would have studied before your arrival."

"You were given a very expensive education at a very high-end boarding school. I would hate to think my money was wasted."

Alex shifted, his hands still curled around the paperweight. "A school filled with teenage boys halfway across the world from their parents and very near a school filled entirely with teenage girls in the same situation. What is it you think we were studying?"

"This subject would have been *related* to your particular field of study. *The Lost Love* is a very scandalous piece of royal history. Though it was only a rumor. No one has ever seen it."

"Except for you, I take it."

"I am one of the few who can confirm its existence."

"You are ever a man of unfathomable depths."

Giovanni chuckled, inclining his head. "I am, it's true. But then, that should be a perk of living a life as long as mine. You ought to have depths and secret scandalous paintings in your past, don't you think?"

"I wouldn't know. My life primarily consists of long hours in the office."

"A waste of youth and virility in my opinion."

It was Alex's turn to laugh. "Right. Because you did not spend your thirties deeply entrenched in building your fortune."

"It is a privilege of the elderly to see things in hindsight no one can see in the present, and attempt to educate the young with that hindsight."

"I imagine it's the privilege of the young to ignore that advice?"

"Perhaps. But in this, you will listen to me. I want that painting. It is my last Lost Mistress. *My* lost love."

Alex looked at the old man, the only father figure he'd ever truly possessed. Giovanni had been the one to instill in Alex a true sense of work ethic. Of pride. Giovanni had raised him and his siblings differently than their parents had. After their deaths he had taken them in, had given them so much more than a life of instability and neglect. He had taught them to take pride in their family name, to take nothing for granted.

His son might have been a useless, debauched partyer, but Giovanni had more than made up for mistakes he made with him when he had assumed the job of raising his grandchildren.

"And you intend to send me after it?"

"Yes. I do. You spend too much time at work. Think of it as a boy's adventure. A quest to retrieve a lost treasure."

Alex picked up the paperweight again. It hovered an inch or so off the desk before he set it back down with an indelicate click. "I should think of it as what it is. A business transaction. You have been very good to me. Without your influence in my life I would likely be completely derelict. Or worse, some sort of social climber working his way through champagne and sunless tanner in South Beach."

"Dear God, what a nightmarish prospect."

"Especially as, by extension, I would be doing it with your money."

"Your point is made. I am a steadying and magnificent influence." The ghost of a smile that played across his grandfather's ancient features pleased him. "I need you to retrieve the painting for me. It took all of my strength to put my socks on and come down here today. I can hardly track across the Mediterranean to Aceena to retrieve the painting myself."

"Aceena?" Alex asked, thinking of what little he knew about the small island. With its white sand beaches and jewel-bright water, it was famous the world over.

"Yes, boy. Honestly, now I want a refund from that boarding school."

"I know where and what Aceena is, *Nonno*. But as far as I'm aware their primary attraction is alcohol and their chief import is university students on spring break."

"Yes. A hazardous side effect of beachfront property, I suppose. But also, it is where the D'Oro family has spent their banishment."

"On spring break?"

"In an estate, I'm told. Though I fear Queen Lucia's children have been on perpetual spring break ever since carving a swath of scandal through Europe. The queen lives there with her granddaughter. She was the rumored subject of the painting—" his grandfather paused "—and the last person to have it. So I've heard."

Alex wasn't a fool, and he didn't appreciate that the old man was playing him for one. Giovanni wouldn't send him off to Aceena because of half-heard rumors. And he would know full well who the subject of that painting was, had it been in his possession.

Leave it to Giovanni to have a portrait of a disgraced queen in his collection of lost treasures.

"You seem to know a great deal about the royal family," Alex said.

"I have some ties to Isolo D'Oro. I…visited for a time. There are…fond memories for me there and I carry the history with me."

"Fascinating."

"You don't have to be fascinated, Alessandro, you have to do my bidding."

Of course, if Giovanni asked, Alex had to comply. He *owed* him. Giovanni had raised Alex after the death of his parents. Had given him a job, instilled in him the work ethic that had made him so successful.

Without Giovanni, Alex was nothing.

And if his grandfather's dream was to see his Lost Mistresses reunited, then Alex would be damned if he was the weak link in the chain.

Enough suffering in his family was tied to his pigheadedness. He would not add this to the list.

"As you wish," Alex said.

"You're turning this into a clichéd movie, Alessandro."

"A quest for a hidden painting secreted away on an island by disgraced royals? I think we were already there."

CHAPTER TWO

"THERE IS A man at the door, here to see Queen Lucia."

Princess Gabriella looked up from the book she was reading and frowned. She was in the library, perched on a velvet chair that she privately thought of as a tuffet, because it was overstuffed, with little buttons spaced evenly over the cushion, and it just *looked* like the word sounded.

She hadn't expected an interruption. Most of the household staff knew to leave her be when she was in the library.

She pulled her glasses off and rubbed her eyes, untucking her legs out from underneath her bottom and stretching them out in front of her. "I see. And why exactly does this man think he can show up unannounced and gain an audience with the queen?"

She slipped her glasses back onto her face and planted her feet firmly on the ground, her hands resting on her knees as she waited for a response.

"He is Alessandro Di Sione. An American businessman. And he says he is here to see about...to see about *The Lost Love*."

Gabriella shot to her feet, all of the blood rushing to her head. She pitched sideways, then steadied herself, waiting for the room to stop spinning.

"Are you all right, ma'am?" asked the servant, Lani.

"Fine," Gabriella said, waving her hand. "*The Lost Love?* He's looking for the painting?"

"I don't know anything about a painting, Princess."

"I do," Gabriella said, wishing she had her journal on hand so she could leaf through it. "I know plenty about it. Except for whether or not it actually exists."

She had never outright asked her grandmother about it. The older woman was loving, but reserved, and the rumors about the painting were anything but. She could hardly imagine her grandmother engaging in the scandalous behavior required for *The Lost Love* to exist…and yet. And yet she had always wondered.

"Forgive me, but it seems as though knowing whether or not something exists would be the most essential piece of information to have on it."

"Not in my world."

When it came to researching genealogical mysteries, Gabriella knew that the possibility of something was extremely important. It was the starting point. Sometimes, collecting information through legend was the key to discovering whether or not something was real. And often times, confirming the existence of something was the *final* step in the process, not the first.

When it came to establishing the facts of her family's banishment from Isolo D'Oro, legend, folktales and rumor were usually the beginning of every major breakthrough. In fact, her experience with such things was leading her to odd conclusions regarding yetis and the Loch Ness monster. After all, if multiple cultures had rumors about similar beasts, it was logical to conclude that such a thing must have a grain of truth.

But until she was able to sift through the facts and fictions of her familial heritage, she would leave cryptozoology for other people.

"What should I do with our visitor, ma'am?"

Gabriella tapped her chin. She was inclined to have their visitor told that she and her grandmother were Not at Home, in the Regency England sense of the phrase. But he knew about *The Lost Love*. She was curious what exactly he knew about it. Though she didn't want to confirm the existence of it to a total stranger. Particularly when she hadn't established the existence of it in all certainty to herself.

She had to figure out what his game was. If this was just a scammer of some sort determined to make a profit off an elderly woman—and that was likely the case— then Gabriella would have to make sure he was never given entry.

"I will speak to him. There is no sense in bothering the queen. She is taking tea in the morning room and I don't wish to disturb her."

Gabriella brushed past the servant, and headed out of the library, down the richly carpeted hall, her feet sinking into the lush, burgundy pile. She realized then that going to greet a total stranger with bare feet was not the most princess-like act. She did quite well playing her part in public. A lifetime of training made a few hours of serene smiling and waving second nature. But when she was home, here in the wonderful, isolated estate in Aceena, she shut her manners, along with her designer gowns, away. Then unwound her hair from the tight coil she wore it in when she was allowing herself to be trotted out in front of the public, and truly let herself simply be *Gabriella*.

She touched her face, her glasses. She also didn't go out in public in those.

Oh, well. She didn't want to impress this stranger; she wanted to interrogate him, and then send him on his way.

She padded through the grand entryway, not bothering with straightening her hair or preening in any way at all.

He had already been admitted entry, of course. It wouldn't do to have a man like him standing outside on the step. And she could see what kind of man he was immediately as he came into her view.

He was…striking. It reminded her of an experience she'd once had in a museum. Moving through wall after wall of spectacular art before entering a small room off to the side. In it, one painting, with all of the light focused on it. It was the centerpiece. The only piece that mattered. Everything that had come before it paled in comparison.

The journey had been lovely, but this man was the destination.

He was like a van Gogh. His face a study in slashing lines and sharp angles. Sharp cheekbones, an angular jaw roughened with dark stubble. There was a soft curve to his lips that spoke of an artist with a deft hand. Who knew that after so much hardened and fearful symmetry there needed to be something different to draw the eye. There was a slight imperfection in his features, as well, one peak of his top lip not quite rising as high as the other. It gave a human quality to Alessandro that was missing from the rest of him. Those broad shoulders, muscular chest and slim waist covered by his severely tailored suit. Long, strong legs, feet covered by handmade shoes.

Yes, everything about him was formidable perfection.

Except for that mouth. The mouth that promised potential softening. That hinted at the fact that he was a man, rather than simply a work of art.

She blinked, shaking her head. That was a lengthy flight of romantic fantasy. Even for her.

"Hello?" She took a step deeper into the entry. "Can I help you?"

His dark eyes flickered over her, his expression one of disinterest. "I wish to speak to Queen Lucia about *The Lost Love*."

"Yes. So I was told. However, I'm afraid the queen is unavailable to visitors at the moment." She resisted the urge to push her glasses up her nose, and instead crossed her arms, trying to look slightly regal, though she was wearing black leggings and an oversize sweatshirt.

"So she sent…I give up. What are you exactly? The resident disaffected teenager? Ready to head out to a mall or some such?"

Gabriella sniffed. "Actually, I am Princess Gabriella D'Oro. So when I say that my grandmother is not available to see you, I speak from a place of authority. This is my home, and I regret to inform you that we have no space for you in it."

"Strange. It seems quite spacious to me."

"Well, things are organized just so. Quite a few too many American businessmen have been by of late. We would have to store you in the attic, and you would just collect dust up there."

"Is that so?"

"I fear you would atrophy completely."

"Well, we can't have that. This is a new suit, and I don't particularly want to atrophy in it."

"Then perhaps you should be on your way."

"I came a great distance to speak to your grandmother. This may surprise you, but I did not come to Aceena to engage in frivolity. But rather to speak to her about a painting."

"Yes, so you said. I regret to inform you there is no such painting. I'm not entirely certain what you heard about it…"

"My grandfather. He is…the collector. I came to see about purchasing the painting on his behalf. I'm willing to offer a generous sum. I imagine disgraced royals might not be in a position to turn such an offer down."

"Oh, we do just fine, thank you for your concern.

Should you like to make a donation to someone in actual need of your charity, I would be happy to provide you with a list."

"No, thank you. The charity was only a side effect. I want that painting. I'm willing to pay whatever the cost might be."

Her mouth was dry. It made it difficult to speak, and yet she found she also couldn't stop the flow of words. "Well, I'm afraid to disappoint you. While we do have paintings, we do not have that painting. That painting, if you weren't aware, might not even exist."

"Oh, I'm well aware that it's what your family would like the public to think. However, I think you know more than you're letting on."

"No," she said, and this time she did push her glasses up her nose. "I'm just a teenager headed out to the mall. What could I possibly know that you," she said, sweeping her hand up and down, "in all your infinite and aged wisdom, do not?"

"The appeal of Justin Bieber?"

"I'm not entirely certain who that is."

"I'm surprised by that. Girls your age love him."

"In that case, can I offer you a hard candy? I hear men your age love those."

She was not sure how this had happened. How she had wound up standing in the hallowed entry of her family estate trading insults with a stranger.

"I'll accept the hard candy if it means you intend to give me a tour while I finish it."

"No. Sorry. You would be finishing it on the lawn."

He rubbed his hand over his chin and she shivered, an involuntary response to the soft noise made by the scrape of his hand over his whiskers. She was a sensualist. It was one of her weaknesses. She enjoyed art, and soft cushions, desserts and lush fabrics. The smell of old books and the feel of textured pages beneath her fingertips.

And she noticed fine details. Like the sound skin made when scraping over stubble.

"I'm not entirely certain this is the tactic you want to use. Because if you send me away, then I will only circumvent you. Either by contacting your grandmother directly, or by figuring out who manages the affairs of the royal family. I am certain that I can find someone who might be tempted by what I offer."

He probably wasn't wrong. If he managed to find her parents, and offer them a bit of money—or better yet, an illegal substance—for some information on an old painting, they would be more than happy to help him. Fortunately, they probably had no idea what the painting was, much less knew any more about its existence than she did.

But they were wretched. And they were greedy. So there was very little that she would put past them.

Still, she was not going to allow him to harass her grandmother. Tempting as it was to keep him here, to question him. She'd been studying her family history for as long as she'd known how to read. Rumors about this painting had played a large part in it.

Part of her desperately wanted him to stay. Another part needed him gone as quickly as possible. Because of her grandmother. And partly because of the dry mouth and sweaty palms and strange, off-kilter feeling that had arrived along with him.

Those things defeated curiosity. He had to go.

"I'll chance it. Do feel free to meander about the grounds before you go. The gardens are beautiful. Please consider limitless viewing time on the topiaries a conciliatory gesture on my end."

The corner of his mouth worked upward. "I assure you, I have no interest in your…topiaries."

Something about the way he said it made her scalp prickle, made her skin feel hot. She didn't like it.

"Well, my topiaries are all you're going to get. Good day to you, sir."

"And good day to you," he said, inclining his head.

He sounded perfectly calm, but a dark note wound its way around his words, through his voice, and she had a feeling that somewhere within it was also woven a threat.

However, she didn't allow him to see that she had picked up on it. Instead, she turned on her heel—ignoring the slight squeak her bare skin made on the marble tile—and walked out of the entry without a backward glance, leaving him there. She fully expected a servant would show him out. Either that or she would have to have him installed in the attic. The idea of collecting a man like him and putting him in the attic like one might do to an old, rusted suit of armor amused her.

She let that little smile linger on her lips as she made her way down the hall, toward the morning room where her grandmother was having her breakfast.

"There was a man here, Gabriella. Who was he?" The queen's voice, wispy, as thin as a cobweb, greeted Gabriella as soon as she walked into the ornate room.

There was no sense asking how her grandmother knew about the visitor. She was never ignorant about the goings-on in her own household.

"An American businessman," Gabriella said, walking deeper into the room, feeling somewhat sheepish, yet again, about her bare feet.

Her grandmother was, as ever, impeccably dressed. The older woman made no distinction between her public and private persona. As always, her crystal white hair was pulled back into a neat bun, her makeup expertly done. Her fingernails were painted the same pale coral as the skirt she was wearing, her low, sensible heels the same cream as her blouse.

"I see," the queen said, setting her teacup down on the table in front of her. "And what did he want?"

"This is not something we've ever discussed before, I know, but he was…he was inquiring about a painting. *The Lost Love*."

Her grandmother continued to sit there, poised, her hands folded in her lap. Were it not for the subtle paling of her complexion, Gabriella would have thought she had merely been commenting on the weather. There was no mistaking her grandmother's response to what she had just said.

"But of course," Gabriella continued, "I told him that it has never been confirmed that there is any such painting. I told him it was nothing more than salacious rumor. And I sent him on his way. Though he may be meandering around the gardens."

Her grandmother turned her head to the window and Gabriella did the same. Just in time to see a figure in a dark suit pass by quickly before disappearing down the path.

Something in Lucia's expression shifted. "Call him back."

"I can't. I just… I just sent him away. That would be… Well, it would seem fickle. Plus, it's rather silly."

"You must call him back, Gabriella." When Lucia used that tone there really was no point in arguing. Still, Gabriella thought she might try.

"I don't trust him. I didn't want him to upset you."

"I need to know who he is. I need to know why he is asking about the painting. It's important." There was a thread of steel woven into her voice now, a command that Gabriella could not deny.

"Of course, Grandmother. I will go after him right away."

"For heaven's sake, girl, put some shoes on."

Gabriella nodded, turning and scampering out of the room, heading down the corridor toward her bedroom. She found a pair of easy slip-on canvas shoes, then continued to head out to the front door. It was firmly closed, the visitor nowhere to be seen.

She opened the door, heading down the paved walk, toward one of the gardens. He didn't exactly seem like the kind of person who would take her up on the offer of a garden tour, but she had to make sure. He might still be here.

Her grandmother had commanded an audience with him, and she would be darned if she would disappoint the older woman.

Her grandmother meant the world to her. Her parents had preferred a life of partying to that of raising children. Her brothers were so much older than her so she could scarcely remember a time when they had lived in the same household. As soon as Gabriella had been old enough to have a say in her own situation, she had asked to go to Aceena to live with Queen Lucia. The older woman had been more of a mother to her than her own had ever been, and she could deny her nothing.

She looked around, and she didn't see him. Of course he was gone. And she hadn't gotten any of his contact information, because she hadn't wanted it. She was annoyed. At him, at herself. But mostly at him.

She walked farther down the manicured lane, turned left at the first hedge, ran squarely into a broad back covered in very high-quality black fabric. She could tell the fabric was high quality, not just because of how it looked, but because of the way it felt squished up against her face.

She stumbled backward just as he turned to face her. He was even more arresting, even more off-putting, up close. He exuded… Well, he just exuded.

"Well, I see you were making use of my offer to tour the gardens."

He straightened his tie, the action drawing her eyes to his hands. They were very large. Naturally, as he was quite a large man. So really, they were nothing quite so spectacular. They were proportional. Useful. In possession of the typical number of fingers.

"No. I was skulking. I thought I might hang around long enough that I can try my hand at getting an audience with your grandmother later."

"That's quite sneaky."

"Sneaky is not typically a word I associate with myself, but I'll take it. Determined, I think sums it up."

"I don't see why you can't be called both."

"Whatever makes you happy. Why exactly are you looking for me?"

"It turns out…my grandmother wants to speak to you."

"Oh," he said, a slow smile spreading over his arrogant face. "I take it you're not the voice of authority when it came to your grandmother's desires, then?"

"I was trying to protect her. Surely, you can't fault me for that."

"Sure I can. I can fault you for anything I like."

She looked hard at him. It was impossible to tell if he was teasing. Impossible to tell if he had the capacity to tease or if he was deadly serious down to his bones. "Which, in a nutshell is exactly why I couldn't allow you to see her. You're a strange man. A stranger, I mean. You also don't seem very…sensitive."

"Do I not?"

She narrowed her eyes. "No."

"Well, I shall endeavor to work on that during the walk from the garden to where your grandmother is waiting for me."

Her lips twitched, but she wouldn't allow them to

stretch into a smile. "If you would be so kind as to do just that, it would be greatly appreciated."

"I live to serve."

She had no doubt he did *not*.

She led the way from the palace gardens back through to the estate; as they walked through the halls she kept her eyes on his face, trying to suss out exactly what he was thinking. His expression was neutral, and he wasn't nearly as impressed as she felt like he should be. The halls of the Aceena estate were filled with beautiful, classic art. Paintings, vases, sculpture. Really, he should be quite impressed.

She supposed that was the hazard with very rich men. It was hard to show them anything they hadn't seen before.

She had grown up in this luxury and she never took any of it for granted. There was always new beauty in the world to discover. It was why she loved art. Why she loved history. There were centuries of beauty stretching back as far as humanity had been in existence. And the future stretched before them, too. Limitless. Infinite in its possibilities. There was hardly a chance to get bored with anything.

Gabriella didn't see the point in jaded cynicism, though she knew some people found it a sign of intellectual superiority.

She just found it sad.

He was probably like her parents. Sensory seekers who were never satisfied with what was around them. Things had to be grand, loud, crowded. Otherwise, they could scarcely feel, could scarcely see.

Gabriella on the other hand needed very little to be entertained. A nicely appointed room, a good book. A lovely piece of art.

She appreciated small things. Quiet things.

She felt very sorry for those who didn't.

"She's in here," Gabriella said, pausing at the doorway.

He arched his brows. "Is she? What are you waiting for? Are you going to go in and announce me?"

"Well, very likely I *should*. I'm very sorry, I know you gave your name to the staff member who greeted you, but I seem to have forgotten it."

She was lying. Alessandro was his name, she remembered. But she didn't want him to think that he was so important he had taken up any space in her brain.

"Alex," he said.

"No last name?" she pressed.

"Di Sione."

"Should that name mean anything to my grandmother?"

He shrugged. "Unless she follows gossip about American businessmen, I don't know why it would. My grandfather made quite a name for himself both in the States and abroad, and I haven't done badly myself, neither have my various and sundry brothers and sisters. But I'm not certain why our names would matter to royalty."

"What is his interest in the painting?" Gabriella asked.

A brief pause. "He is a collector."

She didn't believe him.

Gabriella let out an exasperated breath. "Be cryptic if you must. But I'm sure there's more to the story than that."

Alex chuckled. "Oh, I'm certain there is, too, but you make a mistake if you think I know more than I'm letting on. I think you and I might occupy very similar positions in the lives of our grandparents."

"How do you mean?"

"We are subject to their dictates."

Shocked laughter threatened to bubble to the surface and she held it in check. She was *not* going to allow him to amuse her. "Well, regardless. Come with me."

She pushed the door open and stepped inside. Her grandmother was sitting in the same seat she had been in when Gabriella had left her. But she seemed different somehow. Not quite so tall. Slightly diminished.

"Grandmother, may I present Mr. Alex Di Sione. He is here to talk to you about *The Lost Love*."

"Yes," her grandmother said, gesturing for them to come deeper into the room. She turned her laser sharp focus onto Alex. "My granddaughter tells me you're interested in the painting."

"Yes," he said, not waiting to be invited to sit. He took his position in a chair opposite her grandmother, his long legs sprawled out in front of him, his forearms resting on the arms of the chair. He looked exceedingly unconcerned with the entire situation. Almost bored. Her grandmother, on the other hand, was tense.

"What is your interest in it?" she asked.

"I am acting on behalf of my grandfather." Alex looked out one of the floor-to-ceiling windows, at the garden beyond. "He claims the painting has some sentimental value to him."

"The painting has never been confirmed to exist," Queen Lucia said.

"I'm well aware. But my grandfather seems to be very confident in its existence. In fact, he claims he once owned it." His dark focus zeroed in on the queen. "He would like very much to have it back now."

Silence settled between them. Thick and telling. A fourth presence in the room. Gabriella noticed her grandmother studying Alex's face. She looked… She looked stricken. As though she was seeing a ghost.

"Your grandfather, you say?" she asked.

"Yes. He is getting on in years and with age has come sentimentality, I'm afraid. He is willing to pay a great deal for this painting."

"I'm afraid I can't help you with that," the queen said.

"And why is that?" he asked, a dangerous note in his voice.

"I don't have it. I haven't possessed it for…years."

"But the painting exists?" Gabriella asked, her heart thundering in her ears.

This was… Under any other circumstances, this would have been incredibly exciting. But Alex Di Sione was here and that just made it feel fraught.

"Yes," her grandmother said, her voice thinner, more fragile all of a sudden. "It is very real."

"Why have you never mentioned that before?"

"Because some things are best left buried in the past. Where they can no longer hurt you," the queen said.

"Do you have any idea where the painting might be now?" Alex asked, obviously unconcerned with her grandmother's pain.

"Yes, I know exactly where it is. Unfortunately, it's on Isolo D'Oro. One of the many reasons I have never been able to reclaim it."

"Where on the island is it?" he asked, his tone uncompromising.

"You wait outside for a moment, young man," the queen said, her tone regal, leaving no doubt at all that she had ruled a nation for a great many years and expected her each command to be obeyed without question.

And Alex didn't question it. Strange, since she imagined he wasn't a man who bowed to many. But at her grandmother's request, he stood, brushing the creases from his dress pants and nodded his head before he made his way out the door.

"You must go with him to find the painting," her grandmother said the moment he was out of earshot.

"Why?" Gabriella asked, her heart pounding in her ears.

"I…I should like to see it again. One last time. And because…because just in case, I shouldn't like for this man to be in possession of it if he is a fraud."

"I don't understand," Gabriella said, trying to process all of the information being given to her. "If he's a fraud in *what* way?"

"It isn't important."

"I think it must be quite important. We've never discussed the painting, but I've long suspected that it was real. I know…I know it was controversial. I know that it concerns you."

"Yes," her grandmother said. "At the time it was quite controversial. Evidence that…that the princess had a lover."

Her grandmother had been the princess then. Young. Unmarried. And it had been a very different time.

It was difficult to imagine her grandmother taking a lover. Difficult to imagine her doing anything quite so passionate or impetuous. She was the incomparable matriarch of the family. The figurehead so established, so steady, she might very well already be carved of marble, as she would now no doubt be in the future.

But if the painting existed, then she was the subject. And if that were the case, then of course it had been commissioned by a lover.

"I see," Gabriella said. "And…*did* you?"

Her grandmother let out a long, slow breath, raising her eyes to meet hers. In them, Gabriella could see so much. A wealth of sadness. Deep heartbreak.

Things Gabriella had read about, but never experienced.

"It is very easy when you are young, Gabriella, to lead with your heart instead of your head. You have seen this, time and again, with your parents. And they no longer carry youth as an excuse. This is why I have always told you that you must be in possession of your wits. It does not do well for a woman to lose her mind over passion. It doesn't end well. Not for us. Men can carry on as they see fit, but it isn't like that for women."

Gabriella nodded slowly. "Yes, I know." She thought of her brothers, who most certainly carried on exactly as they pleased. Of her father, who seemed to escape the most scathing comments. The worst of it was always reserved for her mother. She was a renowned trollop whose every choice, from her wardrobe to which man she chose to make conversation with at a social event, was analyzed, was taken as evidence of her poor character.

Gabriella knew this was true. It was just one of the many reasons that she had chosen to embrace her more bookish nature and keep herself separate from all of that carrying-on.

"Our hearts are not proper guides," her grandmother continued. "They are fickle, and they are easily led. Mine certainly was. But I learned from my mistakes."

"Of course," Gabriella agreed, because she didn't know what else to say.

"Go with him," Queen Lucia said, her tone stronger now. Decisive. "Fetch the painting. But remember this conversation. Remember what I have told you."

"I don't think there's any danger of my heart getting involved on a quest of this nature."

"He is a handsome man, Gabriella."

Gabriella laughed. "He's a stranger! And old enough to be… Not my father, *certainly* not. But perhaps a young uncle."

The queen shook her head. "Men like that have their ways."

"And I have my way of scaring them off. Please, tell me when a man last danced with me more than once at a social function?"

"If you didn't speak so much of books…"

"And weevils." She had talked incessantly about weevils and the havoc they played in early English kitchens to her last dance partner. Because they had been the subject of the last book she'd read and she hadn't been able to think of anything else.

"Certainly don't speak of that."

"Suffice it to say I don't think you have to worry about me tumbling into a romance. The only problem is… Why would he take me with him? Now that he knows the painting exists, and that it is on Isolo D'Oro, he'll no doubt have an easy enough time figuring out *where* it is. And I'm sure he'll have no trouble finding someone to impart what information they might have about it, for the right price."

"No," her grandmother said, "he won't."

"Why is that?"

"Because. Because *you* have the key. You're the only one who has the key."

Gabriella frowned. "I don't have a key."

"Yes, you do. The painting is hidden away in one of the old country estates that used to belong to the royal family. It is in a secret room, behind a false wall, and no one would have found it. So long as the building stands, and I have never heard rumors to the contrary, the painting would have remained there."

"And the key?"

Her grandmother reached out, her shaking hands touching the necklace that Gabriella wore. "Close to your heart. Always."

Gabriella looked down at the simple flower pendant that hung from the gold chain she wore around her neck. "My necklace?"

It had been a gift to her when she was a baby. A piece of the family's crown jewels that her mother had considered beneath her. So simple, but lovely, a piece of art to Gabriella's mind.

"Yes, your necklace. Did you ever wonder why the bottom of it had such an odd shape? Once you get into this room, you fit this into a slot on the picture frame on the back wall. It swings open and, behind it, you will find *The Lost Love*."

CHAPTER THREE

TRULY, HIS GRANDFATHER had a lot to answer for. Alex was not the kind of man accustomed to doing the bidding of anyone but himself. And yet, here he was, cooling his heels in the antechamber of a second-rate country estate inhabited by disgraced royals.

If he were being perfectly honest—and he always was—one royal in particular who looked more like a small, indignant owl than she did a princess.

With her thick framed glasses and rather spiky demeanor it did not seem to him that Princess Gabriella was suited to much in the way of royal functions. Not that he was a very good barometer of exceptional social behavior.

Alex was many things, *acceptable* was the least among them.

Normally, he would not have excused himself from the room quite so quickly. Normally, he would have sat there and demanded that all the information be disseminated in his presence. Certainly, Queen Lucia was a queen. But in his estimation it was difficult to be at one's full strength when one did not have a country to rule. In truth, the D'Oro family had not inhabited a throne in any real sense in more years than Princess Gabriella had been alive.

So while the family certainly still had money, and a modicum of power, while they retained their titles, he did not imagine he would bring the wrath of an army down on his head for refusing a direct order.

However, he had sensed then that it was an opportune moment to test the theory of catching more flies with honey than vinegar.

He did so hate having to employ charm.

He had better end up in possession of the painting. And it had better truly be his grandfather's dying wish. Otherwise, he would be perturbed.

The door behind him clicked shut and he turned just in time to see Princess Gabriella, in her fitted sweatshirt and tight black leggings, headed toward him. She was holding her hands up beneath her breasts like a small, frightened animal, her eyes large behind her glasses.

That was what had put him in the mind of her being an owl earlier. He did not feel the need to revise that opinion. She was fascinating much in the way a small creature might be.

He felt compelled to watch her every movement, her every pause. As he would any foreign entity. So, there was nothing truly remarkable about it.

"Well, my princess," he said. "What have you learned?"

"I know where the painting is," she said, tucking a silken strand of dark hair behind her ear before returning her hands back to their previous, nervous position.

"Excellent. Draw me a map on a napkin and I'll be on my way."

"Oh. There will be no direction giving. No napkin drawing."

"Is that so?"

She tossed her hair and for a moment he saw a glimmer of royalty beneath her rather dowdy exterior. And that was all the more fascinating. "No. I'm not giving you directions, because *I* have the directions. You are taking me with you."

He laughed at the imperious, ridiculous demand. "I most certainly am not."

She crossed her arms, the sweater bunching beneath them. "Yes, you are. You don't know how to get there."

"Gabriella, I am an expert at getting the information I want. Be it with money or seduction, it makes no difference to me, but I will certainly get what I need."

Her cheeks turned a rather fetching shade of pink. He imagined it was the mention of seduction, not bribery, that did it.

"But *I* have the key," she insisted. "Or rather, I know where it is. And trust me when I tell you it is not something you'll be able to acquire on your own."

"A key?" He didn't believe her.

"And the…the instructions on how to use it."

He studied her hard. She was a bookish creature. Not terribly beautiful, in his estimation. Not terribly brave, either. Intensely clever, though. Still, the lack of bravery made it unlikely that she was lying to him. The cleverness, on the other hand, was a very large question mark.

It made her unpredictable.

This was why he preferred women who were not so clever.

Life was complicated enough. When it came to interactions with the female sex he rather liked it simple, physical and brief.

He had a feeling his association with Gabriella would be none of those things and that only set his teeth on edge all the more.

"I do not believe that you have the key, or rather, have access to it that I cannot gain."

"Okay, then. Enjoy the journey to Isolo D'Oro without me. I'm sure when you get there and find that you hold nothing in your hand but your own—"

"Well, now, there's no need to get crass."

She blinked. "I wasn't going to be crass. I was going to say you hold nothing in your hand but your own arrogance."

He chuckled. "Well, I was imagining you saying something completely different."

"What can I have possibly—?" She blinked again. "Oh."

He arched a brow. "Indeed."

She gritted her teeth, her expression growing more fierce. "Crassness and all other manner of innuendo aside, you are not gaining access to the painting without me."

"Right. So, you know where it is, and you clearly possess the key. Why not go without me?"

"Well, it isn't that simple. I am a member of the D'Oro family. And while technically I can return to the island because I am only of the bloodline, and I never ruled, gaining access could still be a problem."

"I see. So, how do we play this? Wealthy American businessman on a vacation takes a beautiful…" He paused for a moment, allowing his eyes to sweep over her, not hiding how underwhelmed he was by the sight. "A beautiful princess as his lover?"

"Absolutely not!" She turned a very intense shade of pink, and he found himself captivated by the slow bleed of color beneath her skin.

"You have a better suggestion?"

"I want to prevent scandal. I want to bring the painting back here with as little fanfare as possible. I don't want you making a big production of things."

"And I assure you I will not. This is for a private collection and has nothing to do with causing embarrassment to the royal family."

She worried her lip between her teeth. "I don't trust you."

"Excellent. I wouldn't trust me, either."

"Excellent. No trust." Her cheeks were getting redder.

This time, he figured it was from frustration. "I want to go with you. But I don't want to cause a scene. I can't cause a scene. You have no doubt seen the kind of scandal my parents create in the headlines with their drug use, affairs, separations, reconciliations… The press would love to smell blood in the water around me and I just can't chance it."

An evil thought occurred to him and it made him smile. "Well, if you don't wish to go as my lover—"

"I don't!"

"Then I'm afraid you'll have to come as my assistant."

"No one will believe that I'm your assistant. I'm a princess." She lifted her little nose in the air, dark hair cascading over her back like spilled ink. Now she did indeed look every inch insulted royalty.

"What do you typically look like when you go out and about? I imagine it isn't like this," he said, indicating her rather drab trappings.

"I don't go out frequently. But when I do I have a stylist."

"Your glasses?"

"I normally wear contacts."

He nodded slowly. "Princess Gabriella D'Oro. I *have* seen pictures of you—it's only that I would never have recognized you in your current state. The difference is remarkable."

He had an immediate picture in his mind of a glossier, more tamed version of the woman in front of him. Sleek and, actually, quite beautiful. Though not remotely as interesting as the version of Gabriella that stood before him.

She waved a hand. "Between professionally fitted dresses, undergarments to hold in all undesirable lumps and bumps, makeup to cover every flaw, false eyelashes, red lips…I'm scarcely the same person."

"A good thing for our current situation." He regarded her for a longer period of time. "Yes, that will do nicely.

You will come as my assistant. With your hair just like this. With your glasses. And with some horrible pantsuit. No one will ever believe you are Princess Gabriella. No one will look twice at you. Certainly not close enough to identify you. That eases any and all problems we might have with the press, with the local government and with scandal."

He could see that she was fuming, *radiating* with indignity. He quite liked it. He didn't have a lot of time. He certainly didn't have *extra* time to stand around negotiating about keys and directions with a silly girl.

So she would come. It was no difference to him either way.

"That is a ridiculous idea," she said. "Anyway, I've never traveled. I mainly stay here in the estate."

"Curled up on a cushion reading a book?"

She blinked. "What else would one do on a cushion?"

"Oh, I can think of several things."

"Drinking tea?"

"No. Not drinking tea."

Her expression was a study in confusion. It was almost cute. Except that he had no interest in bookish virgins.

She was...naive. Young. For a moment he was concerned about how young. "How old are you?"

She sniffed. "I'm twenty-three. You can stop looking at me like I'm some sort of schoolgirl."

"*Cara mia*, you are a schoolgirl to me."

"How old are *you*?"

"That is none of your business."

"Am I to respect my elders?"

He laughed, he couldn't help it. Rare was the person who poked back at him. He rather enjoyed having fun at other people's expense, but they didn't dare have it at his.

His secret was that he found it rather entertaining just how afraid everyone seemed to be in his presence. His formidable reputation afforded him a great deal of enjoyment. Though the fact that he took pleasure in making people quake in his presence was likely why he had so few friends. Not that he minded.

He had sycophants, he had business associates and he had mistresses. He had no room in his life for anything else. Nor had he the desire for them.

Unfortunately, he also had family, and with them came obligations. Family was, after all, how he found himself here now.

"Then it is decided. You will be my personal assistant, a college student, doing a work experience program. Traveling with me to Isolo D'Oro to take in some of the local culture and scenery while I negotiate a business deal."

"I'm supposed to be your…intern?" She was positively incandescent with irritation now.

"Yes. Of course, Gabriella is a little bit posh for that. How about Gabby? It has a very nice ring to it. Don't you think, *Gabby*?"

"I hate being called Gabby."

"But I'll wager you hate scandal even more. So, Gabby my assistant you will be, and we will not create any of it."

She frowned, her dark brows lowering, disappearing behind the thick frame of her glasses. "If you're going to be this exasperating for the entire journey I can see it's going to be a problem."

"I don't plan on being this exasperating for the entire journey." She breathed out a sigh of relief. "I plan on being at least twice as exasperating."

Her eyes flew wide. "And why is that?"

"Oftentimes I find life short on entertainment. I do my best to make my own fun."

"Yes, well, I live in an estate with an old woman in her nineties. I make a lot of my own fun, too. But typically that involves complicated genealogy projects and a little bit of tatting."

"Tatting?"

"You can never have too many doilies. Not in a house this size."

He arched a brow, studying her face to see if she was being sincere. He couldn't get a read on her. "I will have to take your word for that."

"Don't you have doilies?"

He lifted his shoulder. "I might in one of my residences. I can't say that I ever noticed."

"I could make you some. No one should have a doily deficiency."

"God forbid." He turned and began to walk away from her. "Aren't you going to show me to my room?"

"Excuse me?" she asked.

"Aren't you going to show me to my room?" he repeated. "We will leave early tomorrow morning for Isolo D'Oro. I don't see any point in my staying elsewhere. You have a great many rooms in the estate. And they are replete with doilies, I hear. Which means you should be able to accommodate me."

He turned his most charming and feral smile in her direction. Usually women shrank back from them. Or swooned.

She did neither.

"I did not invite you to stay. And it's particularly impolite of you to invite yourself."

"It wasn't particularly hospitable of *you* to not invite me. I will put aside my pique for the sake of convenience, and a more companionable journey tomorrow. Now," he said, his tone uncompromising. He excelled at being uncompromising. "Be a good girl and show me to my room."

CHAPTER FOUR

"WHAT IS THIS?"

Gabriella came out of the bedroom positioned toward the back of his private jet. She was wearing her glasses, as instructed, her dark hair pulled back into a ponytail. She was also newly dressed in the outfit he had gone to great lengths to procure for her before his plane had departed this morning for Isolo D'Oro. Well, one of the palace servants had gone to great lengths to procure it. He had taken a rather leisurely breakfast during which he had checked his stocks and made sure that things were running smoothly back at his office in Manhattan.

"Your costume, Gabby," he said.

Had she been an owl he was certain that at the moment her feathers would have been ruffled. "It isn't very flattering."

"Well, neither was the sweatshirt you were wearing when we met yesterday. But that did not seem to stop you from wearing it."

"I was having a day at home. I had been sitting in the library reading."

"Naturally."

She frowned. "What does that mean?"

"You look like the type. That's all."

She shifted slightly, her frown deepening. "Yes, I sup-

pose so. But I'm not entirely lacking in vanity. This..."
She indicated the black dress pants, tapered closely to
her skin—much more closely than he had anticipated—
and the white blouse she was wearing, complete with a
large pin that should have looked more at home on her
grandmother than on her, but managed to look quite styl-
ish. "This is not the kind of thing I'm used to wearing in
public."

She didn't look like a princess—that much was true.
But the outfit was not actually unflattering. The outfit
was very nearly fashionable, albeit in a much lower-rent
way than she was no doubt used to looking.

"What exactly is the problem with it?"

"The pants are very tight."

"Their most redeeming feature in my opinion."

He was rewarded with another of her blushes. "I do not
like to draw attention to my body."

"Believe me when I tell you this, Gabriella. You do not
have to do anything to draw attention to your body. The
very fact that it exists does draw attention to it." He found
it was true even as he spoke the words. He had not readily
noticed her charms upon his arrival at the estate yesterday, but she was certainly not lacking in them. Her figure
was not what was considered attractive these days. There
was no careful definition of muscles earned through long
hours in a gym. No gap between her thighs.

She was lush. Soft. Average-size breasts that were remarkable if only because breasts always were, a slender
waist and generously rounded hips. Hips that were currently
being flaunted by the pants she was complaining about.

"Oh. Well. That is... Was that a compliment?"

"Yes. It was a good compliment."

"Sorry. I'm not used to receiving compliments from
men."

He found that hard to believe. She was a princess.

Moreover, she wasn't unattractive. Usually one or the other was enough. "Do you ever leave the estate?"

"In truth, not that often."

"That must be your problem. Otherwise, I imagine you would be inundated with compliments. Sincere and otherwise."

"Why is that?"

"Because. You have quite a few things men would find desirable."

"Money."

"That is certainly one of the things. Though right now you could easily pass for a personal assistant. Which is exactly what we are going for." He took a seat in one of the plush armchairs and picked up the mug of coffee he had poured himself earlier.

"What are the other things?"

"Your body. And its various charms. I thought I made that clear."

She frowned. He expected her to…well, to get angry. Or shrink up against the wall like all bookish virgins should do. Instead, she walked through the plane and took the seat opposite from him, crossing her legs at the ankles and folding her hands in her lap. "You're very blunt."

"Yes. I find it frightens people. Which I very much enjoy."

"I'm not certain if I'm blunt in quite the same way you are. But I do tend to say whatever pops into my mind. Often it's about something unrelated to the situation. That also seems to frighten people. Men specifically."

"The reason you don't receive many compliments?"

"My mother always told me to keep conversation to the topic of the weather. But we live on an island. Unless a hurricane or tsunami is threatening, the weather isn't all that interesting."

"That's the point. A great many men prefer their women to be dull on the inside and shiny on the outside."

"You among them?"

He chuckled. "Oh, I am *chief* among them."

She tilted her head to the side, a rather bemused and curious expression on her face. "Why is that?"

"Why is what, *cara mia*?"

"Why do so many men prefer their women to be quite the opposite of what one should prefer in a person?"

"Because. Those sorts of men, myself included, don't want women for sparkling conversation. They want them for one thing, and one thing only."

She sighed, a rather heavy, irritated sound. "I imagine you mean sex."

He was momentarily surprised by her directness. Not that directness shocked him in any manner; it was simply that this kind of directness coming from *her* was shocking.

"Yes," he said, not seeing why he shouldn't be equally direct in return.

"Predictable. I suppose that's why my mother is able to skip through life behaving so simply. She's a prime example of what you're talking about. Someone who is all sparkle and shine. My father no longer even possesses any shine. But I imagine in his case it's the promise of money and an eventual payoff that bring women into his bed."

"That sounds quite familiar to me."

She studied him, a confused expression crossing her face. "But—and I'm speaking in a continued metaphor— you seem to be *quite* shiny."

He laughed. No one had ever characterized him as shiny before. "I wasn't thinking of myself. It's true, I have my own set of charms that bring females into my bed. Money. Looks, so they tell me. But in this case I was thinking of my parents."

"Oh?"

"Yes. It sounds very much like they would have been friends with yours."

"Do your parents enjoy drugs, wild affairs and questionable fashion sense?"

He laughed, but this time the sound was bitter. "They liked nothing more. In fact, they loved it so much it killed them."

She seemed to shrink in her seat, the regret on her face pronounced. "Oh. I'm sorry. I should not have made light of it. Not without knowing your background."

He picked up his clear mug of coffee and turned it until the light coming from outside the plane window caught hold of the amber liquid, setting it ablaze. "One *must* make light of these things. Otherwise, it's all darkness, isn't it?"

"Some things are only dark, I fear."

He shrugged, taking another drink. "They don't have to be."

"How did your parents die?"

The question struck him. She genuinely didn't know. But then, it stood to reason. She'd had no idea who he was when they had first met. Rare was the person who didn't know his entire family history before introducing themselves to him. She was an odd creature. And her cleverness was *still* off-putting. But he found small pieces of her to be a breath of fresh air he hadn't realized he'd been craving.

"They died in a car accident," he said. "They were having one of their legendary fights. Fueled by alcohol, drugs and a sexual affair. Basically, all of their favorite things combined into one great fiery ball of doom."

"Oh. That's awful."

"Yes. I suppose it is. But I was very young. And not much a part of their lives." He did his best to keep the memories of that night from crowding in. Snowy. The roads filled with ice. His parents shrieking obscenities. And a small boy standing out in the cold, looking lost and lonely. "I find them a tragedy. A cautionary tale. I might be a bit jaded, but I'm not a total libertine. I suppose I have their tragedy to thank for that."

She nodded, as though she completely understood what he was talking about. He had no doubt she had little experience of libertines outside the pages of a book.

"If it weren't for my parents," she said, her words coming slowly, "who knows how I would be? It is their example that has kept me so firmly planted in the estate in Aceena. It's their example that has caused me to crave a quieter existence."

That surprised him. It seemed she *did* understand. At least a little bit better than he had guessed she might. A little bit better than most.

All of his siblings had started life with the same parents he had, and yet he had been the only one affected in quite this way.

His twin brothers were hellions. They were playboys who lived their lives entirely as they saw fit. At least, they *had* been before their respective *true loves* had come into their lives.

But always, they had lived with much more passion than Alex ever had. Even now that they had settled down, they continued to live with more passion and emotion than Alex would ever consider.

"Everything makes much more sense if you see life as a business," he said, speaking the thought before he had decided he would.

"Do you think so?"

He nodded. "Yes. Business is sensible. Everyone is in it to make money. That's the bottom line. Because of that, everyone's motives are transparent from the beginning. They're going to serve themselves. Sometimes favors are traded. Contracts are drawn up, terms are met."

"A bit more clear-cut than people," she said.

"I've always found it slightly strange that divorce is much easier than breaking a business contract. If people took marriage as seriously as they took business deals, the world would be a different place." He leaned back in his chair. "Of course, you could go about metaphorically hopping into bed with other partners after taking on exclusive deals with another. But you would quickly lose your credibility, and your business with it. It wouldn't serve your bottom line. Personal relationships are much more murky. There is no common bottom line. I find that disturbing."

"I see what you're saying," she said. "I hadn't thought about it that way. But then, I suppose it's because I don't have a head for business."

"What is it you have a head for, Gabby?"

She bristled at the nickname. "Books, I suppose."

"What sorts of books?"

"All sorts."

His eyes narrowed. "You said you liked genealogy."

"Yes. I do. I'm very interested in my family history. I find it completely fascinating. I believe that history contains truths. I mean, history goes beyond what's been published in the media. What the press reports…that isn't real history."

"I suppose the granddaughter of some of the world's most infamous disgraced royals would feel that way."

She lifted her shoulder, an unconscious gesture she seemed to do a lot. She had a very delicate frame; whether in glasses or ill-fitting clothing, that couldn't be denied. She was like a strange, old-fashioned doll.

He was rather disturbed by the part of him that felt compelled to lean in and pull her from the shelf, so to speak.

"I suppose I would," she said. "But that isn't why I'm doing this. I quite like the idea of uncovering the truth, in an unbiased fashion."

"And so you study your family history."

"Yes."

Her eyes had grown brighter when the subject was introduced. Strangely, he found he quite liked it. It was very interesting to make conversation with a woman about something other than shallow topics. And in this instance, it had been quite easy. Was she truly so different?

It made him wonder if the women he conversed with were actually as shallow as he imagined or if they thought *him* to be shallow. Strange that it should matter to him at all. It shouldn't. Not when he purposefully kept those interactions as meaningless as possible.

He kept a wall between himself and others, using all manner of methods, and limited conversation with his lovers was one of those methods.

It didn't matter what he thought of them. It didn't matter what they thought of him. It only mattered how it felt when they were in bed.

"You will find this trip back to your homeland fascinating, then."

He wanted to try out a bit more of that excitement. He wondered what it must be like, to possess that level of enthusiasm. God knew he no longer had the ability. He had seen what happened with passion. Had seen it firsthand when his parents were killed, lost forever in a storm of twisted steel and broken glass. He had no desire to be a part of anything like that. He led with his mind. He had relationships that were mutually beneficial for both parties involved.

They never ended in screams and accusations of infidelity. No. He always gave his women a gift, made sure he complimented their beauty, lied about how diverting he found their company and promised to cherish their time together always and to remember them fondly.

He never did.

The moment they walked out of his bedroom he forgot their names. He simply didn't possess the capacity to care about people with any real depth. At least, people outside of his family.

He couldn't see the value in it. He could only see the cost.

"I expect it will be wonderful. My grandmother has told me stories about the old family estates. About the palaces. But I've never been to see them myself. All I've ever seen are old, faded pictures."

"Why exactly was the royal family expelled from the country?"

"Oh, there are a great many rumors of unfair taxation. Of my great-grandfather being a tyrant. Greedy. But I'm not entirely convinced. And certainly, that isn't my grandmother's take on the situation. Regardless, there was an uprising and the family had to escape in the dead of night. They're lucky to have escaped with their lives. Most royal families don't make out quite so well during violent depositions."

"You speak the truth there."

"I think I'll be the first in my family to set foot on Isolo D'Oro since then. It's probably a good thing that I'll be incognito."

"Probably."

She smiled, her whole face brightening. It was like watching light shift over the ocean. The color moving from slate gray to a brilliant blue. "This is all a bit like a good adventure story, don't you think?"

It reminded him of something his grandfather had said. About the whole thing being like a boy's adventure. Why were people eternally attempting to excite him about something that felt like little more than a menial task?

"I consider it an errand," he said, lifting his glass to his lips again. "One that I intend to do and do well, because as

I said, I believe in business. In fairness. I owe my grandfather and I am determined to repay him. But that's it."

His dry response doused her smile and he cursed himself. "Well, I think anything can be considered an errand with the incorrect mind-set. And anything can be a game if you purpose for it to be."

"All I need is a spoonful of sugar?"

She smiled. "It couldn't hurt."

"No, I suppose it couldn't." The plane began to descend, and Alex could see the scenery below growing larger. Could begin to make out the whitecaps of the waves on the bright water. "You had better buckle yourself, Princess. We are about to arrive in Isolo D'Oro. And that is the last time you will be called *Princess* for the foreseeable future."

CHAPTER FIVE

GABRIELLA WAS STUNNED by the view spread before her. Her grandmother had told her how beautiful her homeland was, but she hadn't been prepared for the true splendor of it.

The city that she and Alex were staying in was filled with ornate, old-world architecture, the Mediterranean Sea spread out before it like a gem. It was a glorious mixture of old and new. High-rises being built in a new section of the city, dedicated to bringing much needed commerce to the nation. While the old historic districts remained unchanged.

She wanted to go out and explore. She did *not* want to cool her heels in the grand hotel suite that Alex had installed them in. But Alex had insisted that he had some work to do, and it would not do to have her wandering around the country by herself.

She supposed that she could defy him on the matter, but she honestly had such limited travel experience that she didn't feel terribly inclined to do that. She was much more likely to stick close to the large American businessman acting as her escort, as she had a feeling he would be a little bit more accomplished at guarding her physical safety than she would.

Not that anything about Isolo D'Oro seemed menacing, but stories of how her family had escaped under threat echoed in her mind. It wasn't something she could simply forget.

"How are your impressions so far?"

Alex chose that moment to come out of his bedroom. He had discarded his suit jacket, his white shirt unbuttoned at the collar, revealing a wedge of tan skin covered with just the right amount of dark chest hair.

She questioned that thought the moment it entered her mind. What on earth was the appropriate amount of chest hair, and how was she so certain that he was in possession of it? It wasn't as though she was an expert on men's chests or the quantity of hair on them.

How strange that she was putting so much thought into his.

"It's lovely," she said, turning her focus back to the view, and resolutely away from his chest.

"I'm glad you think so."

She studied him closely. "Are you?"

He smiled and the impact of it felt like a punch in the chest. He was an irritatingly large presence. His every movement set the hairs on her arms on end, his shifting expressions creating a seismic reaction in her internal organs.

"No," he said. "I don't actually care what you think. It just seemed a polite thing to say."

She looked at him, unable to get a genuine read on him. "I can't decide whether or not I'm amused by you," she said.

"I believe the general consensus of me is that I'm *horrifying*."

"Hmm. Really?"

"My reputation precedes me in all corners of the earth. I'm known to be quite hard. Demanding. A perfectionist in areas of business. Sometimes scarcely human. Some say that if you cut me, I would, in fact, not bleed."

"Well, that is ridiculous. Because everybody bleeds," she said.

"For such a clever creature, you are alarmingly literal."

"It is ridiculous," she insisted. "All of it. Obviously you're human."

His smile only grew broader. "*Is* it obvious? I feel it isn't to many. But then, I find that amusing and don't do much to dispel the idea that I might be some kind of monster."

"Why?"

He walked across the small living area, heading back toward the bedroom he had just come out of and pushing the door open. "Coming?" he asked.

Her heart slammed against her rib cage. "What?"

"You asked a question. I thought you might want to hear the answer. But I have to go into my room to get my jacket and retrieve my tie."

She scrambled after him, feeling a little bit silly that she had somehow read something *else* into those words. Of course he wasn't asking her to come into the bedroom for...well, anything that might be done in the bedroom.

She wasn't the kind of woman who invited seduction. And she was genuinely fine with that. Someday, she would find a man. A suitable man who would make a suitable match. Possibly a minor role. Or someone who moved in high European society but who also liked books and dusty libraries. Yes, that. Most likely. Definitely not an American businessman who took joy in tormenting others with his dry sense of humor and seemed to regard her love of reading and research with the kind of curiosity one usually reserved for a bug under a microscope.

"You want to know why I enjoy keeping others at a distance?"

"I am curious, I admit," she said.

She was also surprised that he was even pretending he

was going to give her an answer. After all, if he truly enjoyed keeping people at a distance, why would he disclose any information that might bring the two of them closer together? It didn't make sense.

"I like the freedom it affords me," he said. He opened up the closet and pulled out a jacket and a tie. Both black, exactly like the ones he'd worn earlier. Though she had a feeling they were a different set than before. "When people fear you they tend to defer to you. That ensures I get my way most of the time."

"What are they afraid you'll do?"

"I don't know." He began to button his shirt collar. "That's the most amusing part. For all the rumors of my misdeeds, I have yet to actually throw anyone in a dungeon. Neither have I ever sucked anyone's blood. However, my legend looms large, and who am I to argue with that?"

"I don't think I have a legend. Well, obviously I don't, as you had never heard of me when you arrived at the estate."

He lifted a shoulder as he looped the tie around his neck. "But then, you had never heard of me, either, *cara.*"

"True enough. But I'm rather cloistered there at the estate. There are a great many things I haven't heard of."

He arched a dark brow. "Does your grandmother not have Wi-Fi?"

"Yes, we have the internet. It's just that I don't often make use of it."

"And why is that?"

"It's very disconcerting to know you could log into a news website at any time and your family is the headline. I just…" Her stomach twisted just thinking about it. "I prefer to avoid it. My brothers… Well, they're as rich as you are. Just as ruthless. Libertines, as you put it earlier. My parents are worse. At least my brothers have some good qualities to redeem them. They are amusing. When they want to be. And they're quite nice actually. To me. Their ex-mistresses would tell you a different story. But even if they've earned it...even if parts of it are true...I don't really enjoy seeing what the media has to say about my family."

"No," he said, his voice softer all of a sudden. "You prefer to gather facts."

"Yes. Exactly that."

"You like to control the story."

She shook her head. "No, it isn't about me controlling a story. I want to know the truth."

"That's a lie, Gabby. You like to control the story. You like to hear it first. You like to decide what is done with it. You want to make sure that you are able to collect the information at the speed in which you can process it. You like to ensure that you are the one who gets to form the first opinion. There isn't anything wrong with it. But it is the truth."

She felt as though he'd run her through with a scabbard. It hurt terribly and made her feel exposed. As though he'd seen down deep into parts of her she'd never even examined before.

And the only reason it felt that way was because...it was true.

"Why is it you seem to think you know me so well?" she asked.

His dark eyes leveled with hers. "I recognized something of myself in you. On that same topic, I'm never entirely certain whether or not you amuse me."

She looked down, clasping her hands together and picking at her thumbnail. "Not very many people find me amusing. I think they find me boring."

"Now that, I can't imagine. You are the farthest thing from boring. In fact, I find that to be one of your foremost negative qualities."

She frowned. "Why would being entertaining be a negative quality?"

"Because I *like* boring women. Boring women are easy to sleep with and forget about. Boring women are the best kind."

A rash of heat broke out over her skin, color flooding her face. "I'm not going to sleep with you so my...*interestingness* shouldn't be a problem for you."

He chuckled. "I wasn't making an offer."

Shame washed over her. Of course he wasn't. Of course he hadn't meant that. But she was still talking and she couldn't stop herself. "When I do make room in my life for that sort of relationship, I will most definitely be pursuing a man closer to my own age who has interests in common with my own."

"Oh, right. I forgot. We have quite the generational gap between us."

"It's prohibitive. We won't even like the same music."

He chuckled softly. "But you don't like popular music. You like classical music."

This statement infuriated her, because it was true, too. Just like the last one. Was she somehow telegraphing her private thoughts via her eyeballs?

"And what sort of music do you like?" she asked.

"Classic rock." He smiled. "You're right, it isn't to be. We're too different."

"Ah, well, just allow me to get the broom and dustpan so I can sweep up the pieces of my broken heart."

"I would, but we haven't the time for such carrying-on. We have a meeting."

She blinked rapidly. "We do?"

"Yes. We have a meeting with the prime minister of Isolo D'Oro."

"But... When?"

He raised his hand and looked down at his wrist, at the

watch he wore that no doubt cost more than some people's yearly salary. "In about ten minutes."

She took in his perfectly pressed appearance. The sharp white shirt, and the rest, all an inky black to match his hair and eyes. He was like a dark angel come to life in Armani. And she was…well, she was wearing polyester pants.

"Wait a second! That isn't fair. You had a chance to change your clothes. I'm still wearing the same thing that I was wearing on the plane."

"Which is perfect. Because you are my assistant, not a lover. Not a princess." He reached back into the closet and pulled out a garment bag. "So, in the next ten minutes, I would like you to make sure that you put this out for the hotel staff. The jacket I was wearing earlier. It needs to be cleaned."

She sputtered. "I'm going to meet the prime minister of Isolo D'Oro in these ridiculous skinny…pants…whatever they are. And now I have to do your menial chores?"

"Well, Gabby, had we decided to go with the story that you were my current mistress I would have draped you in silks. As it is, I'm going to have to drape you in my dry cleaning."

She sniffed. "You don't have to enjoy this so much."

He chuckled, a darkly amused sound. "Oh, yes, I absolutely do have to enjoy this. As I told you before, I'm accustomed to making my own fun. And I'm finding this quite unexpectedly fun."

CHAPTER SIX

THE TROUBLE WITH meeting politicians was that they always came with an unreasonable amount of security detail and other various hangers-on. Of course, there were a few paparazzi, as well. But Alex knew that the prime minister was the quickest way to gaining access to the various historic sites they would *need* access to in order to find *The Lost Love.*

Most of the dining room had been cleared in preparation for his arrival, and it was almost entirely empty except for the three of them, seated at a table in the far corner.

When the man had finally arrived at the hotel restaurant a good fifteen minutes after he had said he would, he had spent an age pouring over the wine list and finding things disappointing.

Immediately, Alex found him insufferable. A pale man with a weak chin who clearly thought his time was precious, but had thought nothing of keeping Alex and Gabriella waiting. Or of insulting the hotel staff with comments about the wine, while not bothering to make a formal introduction.

Alex made it a point not to telegraph any of his irritation to the other man. As soon as the wine had been selected, Alex turned his focus to the business at hand.

"Alessandro Di Sione," he said, extending his hand. "It's good to meet you, Prime Minister Colletti. This is my assistant, Gabby. A university student doing a bit of work experience. She's come with me to help me on my mission."

"And what exactly is that?" asked the prime minister, leaning back in his chair, his arms behind his head.

"I've become somewhat of an avid art collector of late. I heard that the collection here on Isolo D'Oro is beyond price. I'm interested in acquiring some pieces. Particularly those that belonged to the former royal family because of the...significance of the time period."

"A historian *and* an art enthusiast?"

"Absolutely," Alex said.

The other man smiled. "Which sorts of art are you most interested in?"

Alex hesitated. His grandfather was right. He probably *was* owed a refund on that expensive boarding school education.

"Portraiture primarily," Gabriella interjected. "Oils on canvas, mostly. Though I know that there are some excellent marble busts. And also some paintings that depict the scenery. Some wonderful depictions of farms? I have heard tell—I mean, Alessandro has told me. He is quite enthusiastic about the painting of the geese."

The prime minister laughed. "Yes. One of my favorites. I don't think I could part with it."

"Everything has a price," Alex said.

"Some things."

"Either way, we would be very interested in seeing the collection," Alex continued.

"And I am happy to show it. The palace is home to the art collections of the royal family, so you'll find whatever you like there. But I'm curious. You're currently in charge of a vast shipping company, is that correct?"

Now, the other man was speaking Alex's language. Alex leaned forward, suddenly feeling much more interested in the interaction. "Yes, I am."

"I might have need of your services. The entire country might. It would be interesting to see if we can come to some sort of agreement."

"Yes, that *would* be interesting," Alex said.

It was suddenly clear why Prime Minister Colletti had been so eager to meet with them. Money. Alex's very favorite language.

"Well, but we're here to study art," Gabriella protested.

"A good businessperson learns to multitask early on, as you will learn when you discover more about the world," he responded.

She said nothing to that, but he could tell she wanted to kick him under the table.

"Wonderful," the prime minister said. "It just so happens that I'm having an open house party at the palace. Celebrating fifty years of independence for Isolo D'Oro."

He could feel Gabriella quivering with rage, and for once, not all of it was directed at him. He reached beneath the table and quickly squeezed her hand. A warning.

What he hadn't anticipated was how soft her skin would be. How smooth.

He withdrew his touch quickly, keeping his focus trained on the prime minister.

"I would very much like to have you attend the party," the other man was saying. "Your assistant is welcome also. That way, you can see some of the art, a bit of the architecture and we can also discuss the possibility of a business partnership."

"That sounds perfect," Alex said, thinking it sounded anything but. A house party. Out in the country. It sounded like an awful costume drama. All they'd need was for the butler to murder somebody and for an elderly lady detective to show up and try to solve the crime.

"Excellent. We will discuss business over the next week. And until then we will just enjoy the dinner."

CHAPTER SEVEN

STANDING IN A hotel room and looking down at the magnificent views of Isolo D'Oro had been a magical moment for Gabriella. But it hadn't truly hit her until the limousine sent by Prime Minister Colletti rolled up to the grand estate that this was her *home*.

At least, in heritage. These magnificent, sprawling grounds should have belonged to her family. The beautifully appointed house with the magnificent stonework around the windows, the grand pillars and the arched doorway had been property of the royal family once. Until they had been driven out, banished from the nation that was in their blood.

For centuries, her ancestors had ruled. For centuries, they had inhabited these walls, walked through the gardens. Now, her grandmother couldn't even return to fetch a painting that held value to her that went far beyond money. Far beyond the attached history.

That was what struck her so hard, so deeply, as she walked through the front door, as they were led through the halls to the quarters in which they would be staying. This wasn't just history in the broad sense of the word. This was *her* history. Her family history. The blood of her ancestors might as well be in the stonework. Babies had been born here, the elderly had died here. Her people. Her ancestors.

It felt very personal. Almost painful.

And yet, at the same time, her heart felt swollen. She felt so connected to this place around her that it emboldened her. Filled her with a sense of confidence. Of belonging.

She had never felt so right before. As if this place was woven through her, a part of her she hadn't known she'd been missing.

All of that lasted for a spare few moments before they were shown to a magnificent suite with a small room off to the left. The tiny quarters belonged to her, the proximity of her room to Alex's of course intended to allow him easy access to her when he might need her to...assist him with whatever she was meant to be assisting him with.

Once the staff who had ushered them in was gone, Alex smiled. "It is comforting to know that if I have need of your services, you will be nearby," he said, looming large in the small doorway of her humble living quarters.

Her cheeks flamed. She knew that he didn't mean it in any kind of lecherous way, but for some reason her body insisted on interpreting it that way.

"After all," he continued, "you are my assistant. And I may well be in need of some *assistance* in the middle of the night."

She gritted her teeth, well aware that her cheeks were glowing an incandescent pink. He could not be in denial about her thoughts. And she had a feeling that now he was just trying to wind her up.

"In case you need a glass of milk?"

"Yes." A wicked smile curved his lips. "I do often enjoy a glass of *warm milk* in the middle of the night. I find it helps me sleep."

"I'll be sure to give it to you early. The middle of the night for someone your age is what…eight o'clock?" She almost regretted taking that cheap shot. *Almost*. If only because it revealed the fact that she found him very disconcerting.

"Yes," he said, arching a brow. "Do bring it to me along with my vitamins."

Drat him. He wasn't even perturbed by that.

"I will do so, as you have requested, sir."

"I like that," he said, his voice a low rumble that rolled through her like thunder.

He had the ability to touch her, all through her body, without ever getting near her, and she couldn't quite understand how he managed it.

She wrenched her focus from him and looked around the modest room. Really, it wasn't bad. Everything was clean, and elegant. The walls were a mint green with white molding adding texture to them. There was no art in this room, but there was a lovely view of the gardens. And that, in her estimation, counted as art.

Alex moved away from the door and she followed him through, not quite sure why. She only knew that he seemed to draw her to him, like he was pulling her on a string.

She was too fascinated by it to fight it.

In contrast to her room, Alex's was sumptuously appointed. The walls had dark wood paneling and a great deal of classical art. There were floor-to-ceiling windows, but she couldn't tell what the view might be because the rich, velvet drapes were drawn over them. Then, in the back corner, there was a large bed with lots of fabric hanging from the ceiling, promising to seclude the sleeper from any unwanted light or noise.

"I don't think they've redecorated since the turn of the century. Last century," Alex said.

"Yes, I suppose this is all original. But that's part of the charm."

"Do you think? I find your perspective on things quite fascinating. You are a romantic."

She frowned. She had never thought of herself as a romantic before. She didn't think he was right. "I'm rather more invested in fact than fancy."

"So you say. But you are always delighted by the beauty around you. There is nothing terribly practical about beauty. And it isn't absolute. One person can find something beautiful when someone else finds it wholly unremarkable. Similarly," he said, speaking slowly, his dark eyes lingering on her in a manner that left her feeling hot, that left her feeling like he had touched her, "one can look at something every day for quite some time and never notice the beauty of it. Then suddenly, one day it might become beautiful to them. Beauty is strange that way. It hides in plain sight."

She swallowed hard, not quite sure why she felt like she was on fire. "I suppose the reverse is also true. Beauty can be obvious. And as it proves itself to be nothing more than pale vanity it can lessen."

"Speaking of your mother and father?" he asked, the question bold and insensitive.

She supposed he was entitled, as she had been rather bold and insensitive herself when they had discussed his parents. "Yes. Does it remind you of yours, as well?"

"Very much."

"All right, I will concede then that maybe you're correct about me. I do like art. I do like frivolous things. Just not…the same kinds of frivolous things as some in my family."

"There is nothing wrong with enjoying the frivolous. I'm not even sure I would call it frivolous. Many people would argue that it is the beauty around us that makes life rich, don't you think?"

She nodded slowly. "I do agree. My life is very quiet compared to most people in my family. Really, it's very quiet compared to most people in my age group, I know. I live with an old woman and I suppose my habits are more reflective of hers than the average twenty-three-year-old. But I like it. I like to read. I like to listen to the sound of the rain on the roof. I like to watch the drops roll down the windowpane. I enjoy the quiet. I enjoy art for all that it doesn't tell us. For the fact that it makes us think and draw our own conclusions. I suppose I enjoy genealogy for the same reasons. We have to extract our own meaning from what we see before us and, from there, guess what the truth might be."

"A very interesting way of looking at it," he said, his tone different now.

"Is that how you see things?"

He shook his head. "I do not have much time for art. Or for books. Or for sitting and listening to the rain."

Her heart sank. "Oh. I thought… By the way you were talking…"

"I've lost the ability to appreciate beauty in the way you seem to. But it doesn't mean I don't appreciate your perspective."

"I suppose you are too jaded."

"Yes," he said, his tone taking on a rather black quality. "I suppose I am a bit too jaded. But then, living the sort of life I have, opulence all around me, my every whim, my every desire, so easily serviced, I don't know how I could be anything but."

"I've had a similar experience, don't forget."

"Yes, you seem to have practiced the art of self-denial a bit more successfully than I have."

"I don't consider it denial."

"Another of your virtues, I'm certain."

She frowned, walking slowly past him, pacing the length of the room, the marble floor clicking beneath her low-heeled shoes. She studied the paintings on the walls, depictions of the scenery around them. During another time. During other seasons. "My parents have indulged in everything imaginable, and yet, they still live life with a fair amount of excitement and passion. I want nothing to do with it. It looks exhausting. Dangerous. Selfish. But…for all their sins they aren't jaded. I feel they enjoy their excess, or they wouldn't continue in it. For you… You seem very bored. And I wonder why that might be."

"I think perhaps the problem with my life, Princess, is that I have seen where the road ends. There is desperate poverty in this world. Tragedies. And I know that there are those who believe that if they simply had one more *thing*, a little bit more money, they would find happiness. But my parents had everything. They had wealth. They had family. They had beauty. Sex, drugs and alcohol in every combination. They had everything. And they were never satisfied. They never stopped searching. They were hungry, always. When they should have been full. It was that continued searching that took everything beautiful they had in their lives and twisted it beyond reason. They had marriage. They had children. And yet, they went out and had affairs. My father made a child with another woman. A child that he never acknowledged. A child whose existence only hurt everyone involved. When you have so much, and yet you have no satisfaction. When you have so much and yet you must continue going until you destroy it all, I can only conclude that there was no happiness to be found in any of it. Not really. And so, I suppose having seen the end my parents came to I have trouble putting much hope in any of the things around me."

"You think it's pointless."

"I don't think it's pointless or I would have thrown myself off a building by now. I think there are aspects of life to enjoy. There is music I like. I enjoy my work. I certainly enjoy my money. I quite enjoy sex. But I'm not certain the satisfaction is to be found. I'm not certain that happiness is a thing that truly exists."

"That all sounds quite…hopeless."

"Maybe it is. Or maybe that's why I choose to take things in life with a healthy dose of cynicism. There are worse things, I should think."

"I think that there's happiness. I don't think that life is quite so meaningless as all that."

He lifted a broad shoulder and she was drawn to the way he moved. He was like a big cat, a predator. Lying in wait for his prey to make the wrong move. The one that would trigger the attack.

She had to wonder if she was the prey in this scenario.

"We all have our coping mechanisms," he said. "You have chosen to try and find satisfaction in the opposite things. While I have decided that I won't find whatever magic cure my parents were looking for within life's various debaucheries."

She paused in her pacing, turned to face him. "Do you think you'll find it anywhere?"

"I have my doubts."

"Do you believe in anything? Do you believe in love?"

He only looked at her, his dark eyes a bottomless well. "No."

"But you're here for your grandfather. Surely—?"

"I believe in fairness. I believe in faithfulness. I believe in keeping my word. As I told you before, I am a man who believes in business."

"Follow your head and not your heart, in other words."

"My head is the only thing I trust."

She let out a heavy sigh, looking back toward her bedroom. It was going to be strange, sharing such a close space with him. Last night in the hotel suite had been strange enough, but there had been a living area between their two bedrooms. This felt…rather more intimate. She should think nothing of it. It should be…nothing. That he was a man and she was a woman shouldn't matter because they wouldn't be engaging in any…man/woman things.

But it still felt strange.

"Then maybe you could use that very large head of yours to figure out how we'll find the painting in this enormous palace?" Her uncertainty, the fluttering in her stomach, made her feel cross.

"I could, I suppose." He tapped his chin as though he were thinking very hard. "The easiest thing to do would be to take a tour. It's likely the hiding place would be revealed to us during it."

"Sure. If only we could arrange that."

"Well, there will be tours. The biggest thing is that we can't turn the pockets of the place out, then leave with a valuable work of art. We have to appear to have come for reasons of business and pleasure. We have to stay. Anyway, I sincerely intend to work up some sort of trade agreement, so we will stay until the last evening party."

"There are parties?"

"Every night. He emailed me a PDF of the itinerary. Very helpful," he said, his tone dry. "But I think we should make sure to stay until the last party. Four days. Then we go. Easy."

Nothing about it sounded easy to her, not at all. To exist in this fishbowl playing a part she didn't know the lines for.

"Are you tired?" he asked. She had to wonder if he'd seen her sag beneath the weight of everything just as she felt it.

"Yes," she said, suddenly feeling exhausted down to her bones. That surge of strength, of certainty that she had felt when she first walked in, was gone now. Now she just felt wrung out. It was strange that coming to this place was so emotional. But it was. Enduring it all with this man who was so…intense, so very *present*—it only added to it.

"Perhaps you should get some rest. There is going to be a gathering tonight with the guests at the party. Appetizers and the like."

She frowned. "What am I supposed to do about that? I can't very well fix myself up. Here people know that I'm Princess Gabriella. Or they'll at least suspect."

"Then you won't fix up."

She scowled. "I like very much how this farce isn't damaging your vanity in any way."

"All of this was your choice, *Princess*. I for one am happy to create a bit of scandal. What do I care if the world thinks I've taken you to my bed? I don't care. Not at all."

"Yes, that is a charming perk of being male. You don't have to worry about rumors of your sexual promiscuity."

He chuckled. "I would guess you've never had to much worry about rumors regarding yours, either."

That goaded her pride. She didn't like him being quite so certain about that. "Perhaps I'm just discreet."

"Oh, I have no doubt that you are. You seem to me to be the very soul of discretion."

She sniffed. "I am. For reasons you should well understand."

"Go rest up. Then put on your armor of discretion and ready yourself for the party tonight."

CHAPTER EIGHT

AT THE MOMENT, no one would suspect Gabriella was a princess, as she was doing an excellent impersonation of a potted plant. She was all but hugging the back wall, dressed in a rather understated pencil skirt and a cream-colored top, complete with a single-string pearl necklace. Her dark hair was partly down, the front pulled back by a clip, the large glasses still fixed on her face.

She looked exactly as an assistant should. And yet, Alex found himself irritated by it.

The other women in the room were dressed in bright colors, saucy cocktail dresses designed to aid in the flaunting of their figures. Their hair expertly styled. And they were certainly not hanging on to the wall. He found that he wanted to see Gabriella without her glasses. That he wondered what it might be like to get a good look at her large, brown eyes. That he might like to see her full lips painted red.

And he knew he would like to see her figure in something designed to flatter it.

He would never be a very great appreciator of art, but he was certainly an appreciator of the female form. And as such, he would simply like to see this one done up with a bit more finesse. That was all. All that discussion of beauty had been on his mind.

She wasn't talking to anyone, rather she seemed to be closely regarding the paintings on the wall. More than that, she seemed to be examining the molding, the floor, the baseboards, the wallpaper... She seemed to be having an entire love affair with the house.

Though he imagined that was to be expected. This was her ancestral home. She had never been here.

He imagined that must bring up all sorts of thoughts.

His family was originally from Italy, and he lived in America. But he had never felt displaced. Giovanni had often told him stories of how he had come to the US, how he had worked his way up from nothing to become one of the most successful men in the nation. Alex enjoyed going to Italy, but he supposed the point of it all was that he could. Yet, while in a technical sense Gabriella *could* have come to Isolo D'Oro, there would have always been a block of some kind. Her family hadn't left of their own accord. They had been banished. It was an entirely different circumstance. One that was quite heavy. And it seemed to be hitting her with its full impact.

"Alessandro Di Sione, right?"

Alex turned to his left and saw a shimmering blonde regarding him with her bright blue eyes. Now *this* was a woman who had taken great pains to flaunt every aspect of her beauty to its greatest advantage. The entirety of her potential was on display before him. There was nothing to wonder about. Nothing at all.

Except perhaps how she would look naked.

Though he had seen enough women naked to be able to guess. He studied her for a moment. He was so confident with his estimation of the size of her breasts without the cleavage-enhancing bra, of the color of her nipples based on her coloring in general, that he found he ultimately wasn't even curious.

"My name is Samantha," she said, smiling grandly,

both realizing she'd lost him before she'd ever started. "I've followed your business exploits with great interest recently."

The way she said *exploits* left him in little doubt that it wasn't his business she had been paying attention to.

"Oh, have you?" he asked. "Perhaps you could tell me about them. I rarely pay attention myself."

She laughed, a high, sharp sound that shot down his spine like an arrow before ricocheting back up to the base of his skull. She touched his arm, leaning in closer. "I didn't know you were funny. I had heard you were frightening."

"Boo," he said.

She laughed again and he fought to keep from cringing.

He flicked a glance across the room at Gabriella, who was watching this interaction between himself and Samantha with what appeared to be great interest. She was now literally standing next to a potted plant, her hand closed around a leaf, her posture rigid.

He couldn't begin to guess what she was thinking. Couldn't begin to guess much of anything about her.

With Gabriella there were a great many unanswered questions.

"Really, we must make more time to get to know each other over the course of the week," she was purring now, all but arching into him like a very needy cat.

"What exactly brings you to the party?" he asked. He didn't care what her answer was. Not in the least. His attention was split between her and the little dark-haired woman with glasses standing against the wall. But he didn't think she noticed. She was far too involved in the performance she was putting on with him.

And he was too busy regarding Gabriella to listen to what she had to say. Which was a shame, really, for Samantha at least. He had a feeling she was putting her full effort into this. An intended seduction, or whatever nonsense she had in her head.

Strange, because in most circumstances he would be more than willing to take her up on the unspoken offer. But not now. He wasn't sure what it was. Perhaps the little bespectacled witch had cast a spell on him. He smiled ruefully, dimly aware that his companion Samantha had likely taken that smile as her due. And of course, it was actually owed to Gabriella.

Very strange. She wasn't the kind that revealed itself immediately. It was more like the sun shining through the trees as you drove down the highway. He would catch flashes of golden light before it faded away again into the darkness. But it was there. And when it struck him directly it was so intense, so brilliant, that it stopped him where he stood.

His eyes caught hers and held for a second before she looked down sharply, obviously embarrassed to have been caught staring at him. He felt no such embarrassment over being caught staring at her.

Then, suddenly, she scurried from the room, hugging the wall as she made her way to the exit.

"Excuse me," he said to Samantha. "I'm very sorry. I have to go."

He wasn't anything of the kind.

He set his drink down on a table as he left, exiting out the same door Gabriella had. He saw her turn left at the far end of the corridor, and he continued on down that way. Maybe she was just headed to the bathroom. Most definitely he didn't *need* to be following her. That didn't seem to stop him.

He had known from the beginning that it was her cleverness he would find to be trouble. He was not wrong.

Had she been boring he would never have chased her

out of a crowded room while being talked to by a busty blonde.

But no, she did not have the decency to be boring.

She had to be interesting. She had to like books. And she had to explain things to him in funny, intricate ways that he would normally find incredibly arduous.

He was angry at her. And with each step he took he felt angrier. Because he was Alessandro Di Sione. He did not pursue women into empty corridors. But then, he also didn't go around hunting for old paintings, either. It was a week of strange happenings. It was entirely possible he should just embrace it.

He saw her head out one of the glass double doors and into the garden, and he followed suit. He said nothing as he walked along behind her in the darkness, heading down a gravel path through the garden. He wondered if she had any idea where she was going or if she was just following some sort of impetuous instinct.

She was a study in contradictions.

Quiet, and yet also very loud. She swore that she was practical, and yet he could sense that she was so much more than that. She was sensual. She enjoyed tactile pleasures. Visual pleasures.

He thought back to the way she had eaten dinner last night. How she had lingered over her wine. The way she had nibbled slowly at the fresh bread on her plate, and the appreciative sound she had made when she'd bit into the dessert she had ordered without hesitation.

There was no doubt about it; she was not an entirely practical person.

Damn her for being so fascinating.

The path curved, feeding into a clearing surrounded by hedges. At the center was a stone bench and he imagined that there were a great many flowers planted at various levels throughout. It was dark, so he could see nothing.

Nothing but great inky splotches, breaking up the pale gravel.

Gabriella took a seat on the stone bench, planting her hands on either side of her.

"I do hope you have room on your bench for two," he said, moving closer to her.

She gasped and turned toward him, her wide eyes just barely visible in the dim light. "What are you doing out here?"

"Stopping to smell the roses?"

"You were deeply involved in a conversation when I left," she said.

"Oh, yes. That. Remember our discussion about boring women?"

"Yes."

"She was one."

Gabriella laughed softly; the sound lifted high on fragrant air, mixing with the scent of flowers and winding itself around him, through him.

"How terribly tragic for her. At least she is beautiful."

"I suppose," he said. "Though I don't think she knows she's boring."

"I guess that's a compensation for the dull."

"Such a comforting sameness."

She scuffed her toe through the gravel. "It wouldn't be so bad."

"I don't know about that. I think you would find it excruciating."

She shifted, and he couldn't make out her face in the darkness. "Do you think so?"

"Yes. I am completely certain that Samantha does not do genealogy in her spare time."

"A loss for Samantha, then. But points to you for remembering her name."

"I was only just speaking to her five minutes ago.

I might be shameless, but my shamelessness has its limits."

"Does it? You were talking to her like you were interested. But you looked…very bored."

"Did I? Perhaps I was simply looking down Samantha's dress and that's what my expression looks like in such situations."

"Unless you find breasts boring I don't think that's the case."

He laughed. He couldn't help it. He was shocked by the forthright statement. He felt he should know better than to be shocked by her small moments of honesty at this point. It was another of her contradictions.

She should be mousey. She should be timid. She should be utterly out of her depth with a man such as himself. And yet she handled everything he threw at her with aplomb, and never passed up an opportunity to shock him, which he would have said under any other circumstance was impossible.

"People are the same. Everywhere you go," he found himself saying as he walked over to the bench where she sat. "May I?"

She nodded slowly. "Sure."

He took a seat beside her, an expanse of empty stone between them. "These parties are the same."

"No, they aren't," she said. "How can they be? I once went to a gala at the most incredible castle. It was medieval and all the stonework was original. There was a chapel and I left the party to go explore—it was incredible. This place…it's full of my family history. I've studied it in books. But…being here is different. Books can't prepare you for the reality of something. It can only hint."

"I suppose to get all that out of a party you have to appreciate art, architecture and history."

"And you don't."

"I was mainly speaking of the people."

Of women who were looking to attach themselves to a man of wealth and status for short amounts of time. Of men who stood around touting their successes as they grew increasingly red-faced from alcohol and a lack of taking a breath during their listing of accomplishments.

"Yes, well. Places might have to be experienced in person to be fully understood. But books are better than people. In a great many ways."

"Is that so?"

"Yes. It's all written out in front of you, and even if you don't know what's going to happen…at least it's all there. Very certain. People aren't certain."

"I disagree. People are predictable. They want pleasure. They want to be important, to feel good. They want money, power. There are a limited number of ways they can go about obtaining those things. I find people extremely bland."

"I guess I just don't possess the insight you do," she said, sounding frustrated. "They don't make much sense to me at all. Those things they call pleasure…the things my parents do…they don't make them happy, do they?"

"And now our conversation circles back around," he said, pressing his palm flat on the bench, the stone cool beneath his touch. "So you live through books?"

"To an extent."

"Adventure stories?"

"Yes."

"Romance novels?" He was leading her now. Because he couldn't guess at her response. She was the one person who surprised him, and he found he wanted to keep being surprised.

She cleared her throat. "Uh. Not so much. The, uh, masculinity is all a bit…*rampant* in those."

"As one in possession of masculinity that might be considered rampant, I'm not sure what the issue is."

She sputtered, followed by a strange coughing sound. "I don't even know what that means," she said.

"You were the one who coined the phrase, not me. I think it's fairly self-descriptive. And I find well suited to me. A kind of masculinity that can't be contained."

"I think it makes it sound like a weed."

"A virulent one."

"I just...I don't find any of that relatable."

"Of course not. You don't possess rampant masculinity."

"I meant *romances*."

"I see," he said, something goading him to continue pushing her. To see where this conversation would go. He couldn't guess at her game. Couldn't read any calculation on her face, and not simply because of the darkness that shrouded them. "What exactly is it you find unrelatable?"

She paused for a moment, and when she spoke again, her voice was muted. "Well, he always finds the wallflower interesting, doesn't he?"

"Who?"

"The hero. He finds the strange girl fascinating. Wants to know more about her. Men don't. For the record, they *never* do. As you said, they like women boring. *You* like them boring. Or at the very least, they don't like them weird. Plus, there's all that racing heart, sweating palms business. Aching body parts."

"Your body parts don't...ache?"

She growled, a small feral sound. "That's horribly embarrassing."

"You're the one who brought us here," he said, lying. He had led the entire thing for just such a moment. "You can't get mad at me for building off it."

"I can get mad at you for whatever I like," she said, sounding completely regal again.

Silence settled between them. Finally, he spoke again. "We are, by the way."

"You are what?"

"We are fascinated by the wallflower. At least, I was tonight."

"You were not. You were bored."

"I was bored by the businessman who couldn't stop telling me about his portfolio. I was bored with Samantha. And I did not look down her dress. But you… You're the one person in that room that I couldn't predict. That I couldn't figure out. I had to follow you when you left the room because I had no idea where you were going, or what you intended to do. Very few people surprise me, Gabriella, but you do."

"I'm not sure how I feel about that. I'm not here to surprise you. I'm not really here to do anything to you. I'm just supposed to find that painting, which of course we haven't done yet. And I…I'm playing secretary to you and having to face the kinds of social situations I would rather eat a handful of bees than contend with."

"Well, don't eat a handful of bees. It sounds incredibly unpleasant."

"These kinds of things are unpleasant. Even more so when I look like this. At least when I have my team of people making me look…polished… At least then people are fooled for a few moments. Right now, my outside kind of matches my inside."

"Why is that a problem?"

"I just told you."

"I don't think that's all of it."

She shifted next to him. "I don't know. When I'm in costume—so to speak—at least when people reject me they're rejecting this strange version of me that isn't who I see in the mirror every day. Princess Gabriella is something I put on when I go out. But otherwise, I'm just me. And right now, it feels very much like all of those people out there ignoring me are rejecting real pieces of me."

"No one is rejecting you. It's my fault for having you come here as an employee. You are definitely being treated as such." He found that he felt a little bit contrite about the situation. And he was never contrite.

"That's my own set of issues, I suppose. I don't make very much sense, Alex. That's the real problem. I want to be left alone. I want to be anonymous. But… Not always. Not every time. Just once it would be nice to have a handsome man look at me and cross the room to be by my side."

"I'm not entirely certain whether or not I'm handsome, at least not by your standards, but—" he paused "—you're the one *I* crossed the room for tonight, Gabriella. Take that as you will."

Silence fell between them and she placed her hand flat on the bench, a few inches separating their fingertips.

"I suppose you did," she said, her voice unsteady.

"I could have had her," he said, speaking of Samantha. "But this was where I wanted to be."

"You're quite confident in yourself," she said, her voice trembling.

"Brought about by predictable patterns. I told you, people don't surprise me."

"I wish I had that confidence. I wish I wasn't so afraid."

She had no reason to be afraid. And in that moment he hated a world that bestowed so much confidence on the terrible and unworthy—on her parents and his. And robbed it from the truly unique.

He lifted his hand, placing it over hers, and feeling

every inch a bastard for doing it. She was vulnerable, and by touching her at the moment he was taking advantage of her.

He wasn't sure whether he cared or not. He was accustomed to dealing with people who moved in common circles to himself. People who saw the world much as he did.

Gabriella was an entity unto herself. She was not an experienced woman. She didn't know this game.

Why are you even bothering to play the game with a woman you thought plain only forty-eight hours ago?

He didn't have the slightest idea.

He was equally confused by the idea that he had ever found her plain. She clearly wasn't. Not in the least.

"I find you impossible to predict," he said again.

"Is that… Is that a compliment?"

He was trying to process her words, but most of his brainpower was taken up with relishing the velvet softness of her hand beneath his. She was so warm to touch after the cold stone of the bench. So very much alive.

How long had it been since he'd had a woman? He couldn't remember. Because it was irrelevant. Whoever the woman was, whenever she was, she hadn't been Gabriella.

Gabriella, who seemed to be her own creature.

"Why are you touching my hand?" she asked.

"Because I want to. I have never seen much use in denying myself the things that I want."

"There are a host of reasons for self-denial," she said. "We both know that."

"Oh, I am better trained than my parents ever were. My desires don't come from errant passions. I'm a logical man."

"There is nothing logical about you touching my hand."

He moved his thumb slowly over her knuckles, stroking

her. "No, I suppose there isn't. I suppose there is nothing logical at all in this."

There wasn't. He was touching her now, but it could never be more than that. Alex had few scruples, it was true. But he had some. He had limitations on his behavior, if only because he had seen what it was like when people didn't. His parents had cared for nothing.

He preferred life to be a series of business transactions. He only entered into transactions with people who had a similar amount of resources. He wasn't the kind of man who swooped in and killed off dying companies. Wasn't the type to offer seed money to a start-up. It just wasn't his way. He preferred everything equal. In terms both parties understood.

It was the same with his sexual liaisons. He had no interest in despoiling innocents. No interest in corrupting a girl who barely understood what desire was.

His stomach tightened, his body hardening at the thought. Calling him a liar.

Well, perhaps his body *was* interested, but that didn't mean he would act on it.

He had spent all of his life endeavoring to become a better person than his mother and father. To learn from the mistakes of that fateful night.

A little bit of errant arousal was hardly going to change that.

But still, he didn't move his hand.

"I think you're like me," she said, her words small, soft. "You say that you're logical. That you like business transactions. You play with people. You toy with them. You were doing it to Samantha back in the drawing room. You had no intention of ever taking her up on her offer, did you?"

"No. I didn't."

She shifted slightly beneath his touch and a surge of warmth shot from their point of contact straight down to his gut.

"But you let her think you might," Gabriella continued, her voice soft. "Right now, you're touching me and we both know that you'll never—"

She didn't get the chance to finish the sentence. Whether it was the challenge in her voice, the bold statement that he would *never*, or the softness of her hand beneath his, he didn't know.

Whatever the reason, he halted her words with his mouth against hers, kissing her hard, hard enough that he hoped it would make the wallflower bloom. That it would show she wasn't that wrong.

It was everything else.

But she was so warm, so soft, he forgot his goal almost immediately as it entered his mind.

She froze beneath his lips, her body stiff, rigid. She didn't return the kiss, rather she simply sat, motionless, shocked. She was soft. Indescribably so.

He moved away from her, his heart pounding heavily, his shaft as hard as iron. How long had it been since the simple meeting of mouths had had such a strong effect on his body? Since he was fifteen, sixteen? Perhaps never.

She hadn't even parted her lips for him. Hadn't softened beneath him. Hadn't succumbed in any way, and yet he felt as though he had just conquered the world.

"I should have taken her up on her offer," he said, his voice rough, gasping. "I should have wanted her. I should be upstairs in my room, or in her room, having sex with her now. But I'm not. I didn't want her. I wasn't even tempted. No matter how much we might like it to be, desire isn't logical. Which means, at the moment, neither am I."

He stood up from the bench, needing to put as much

distance between them as possible. He turned away from her, and even knowing he shouldn't, he spoke again. "All I know is that tonight I just wanted to cross the room to be with the wallflower."

CHAPTER NINE

HE'D KISSED HER. It was all she'd been able to think about last night, lying in bed with her lips—her *body*—burning.

It was all she could think about the next day, too. Which was ridiculous because they were on a tour of the stables. Which were fascinating from a great many angles—historical and equine.

But she was prickly and distracted. From exhaustion. From the heat of Alex's body next to her, from the night spent not sleeping.

Her jacket was itchy, too. Which didn't help. It was a pleasant day, warm and dry, the air blowing in off the sea. And she was wearing a jacket because Alex had said it was secretarial and that it was important she appear so because of reasons she had now forgotten since she had a bead of sweat running down the center of her shoulder blades.

Also she was still thinking about the kiss.

Ahead of them, one of the prime minister's employees was extolling the virtues of the groundskeepers, and the brave servants who had saved the facilities and all the horses during a fire that happened a hundred years ago.

"This is boring," Alex said, his lips brushing her ear as he leaned in to whisper to her. It sent a shiver down her neck, down her arm, caused heat to pool in her stomach.

She took a breath, realizing when she inhaled a healthy

dose of his masculine scent that it had been a mistake. "Excellent," she said, taking great pains to keep her voice crisp. "A chance to see The Alessandro in his natural habitat."

"Are you observing me for a nature guide you are working on?"

"Rampantis masculinitis," she said, smiling slightly.

"Characterized by?" he asked.

She looked up at him, at the wicked glint in his eye, and she quickly looked away again.

The tour group had gone on ahead of them, and she had only just noticed that their pace has slowed dramatically. He'd acted like this was done with last night. Like he'd realized what a bad idea it was to encourage all of this...this stuff between them. But he was back in fighting form this morning.

He was deliberately keeping her back from the group. Keeping them both separate.

This really was like watching a nature show. The predator had separated the weaker gazelle from the herd. And after last night, she knew beyond a shadow of a doubt that she was the weaker gazelle.

"What are we doing?"

"I told you," he said, his smile turning wicked. "I'm bored. Anyway, it wouldn't do to have you acting skittish around me, or to have me avoid you. You are my assistant, Gabby, not a bookish princess who all but forced herself into a treasure hunt with a stranger."

She looked ahead of the group, then looked up at him, at his dark, glittering eyes. There was an air of good humor about him, but there was something else, too. A base note that ran beneath it that spoke of danger, excitement.

She should turn away from it. She should have learned from last night. From letting him get too close.

She didn't. She hadn't.

"The painting," she said, her voice hoarse.

"Is not out here in the stables," he said. "I had hoped that we would tour the house today so we might get an idea of its location."

"Well, we can do a little bit of exploring on our own."

"I would like to do it during the day. I'm not sure where our host gets to during the daylight hours. He certainly isn't parading us about. But once the sun goes down, and the brandy comes out, he does seem to reappear."

"So, you think we should look for it at night?"

He lifted his shoulder. "It lowers the risk of running into him in the halls if we know he's socializing. It's either that or we tell him what we're after. But I have a feeling the cloak and dagger might be necessary. I told you, I'm willing to pay for the painting, but my fear is that he won't want to part with it when he understands what it is. That isn't an option. Money might be no object, but failure is unacceptable."

She nodded slowly. "Why do you want the painting so badly?"

"Because my grandfather wishes to have it. And I owe him a debt, I told you that already. He wants it—I will see he gets it."

She studied his expression. She could see that he had no attachment to the painting. He must love his grandfather. That she was certain of. Because Alex was not the kind of man who did anything that he didn't want to do. Only a few days in his presence and she was certain of that.

"What does it mean to him?" she asked.

"I'm not entirely sure. But there is a story…" He looked away from her, stared off toward the horizon line. "He has always told us this story, from the time we were children. About coming to America with nothing. He had eight objects that were dear to his heart. Objects that he had to sell slowly over the years to save himself from ruin. They were…they were very special to him. He often referred to them as his mistresses. Items that held sway over his heart. I don't know why. I don't know if it was because of their value, because of their beauty or because of their connection to another person. Regardless, these eight objects were the most important thing that Giovanni Di Sione possessed."

"The painting is one of them," she said.

"Yes. I was the last grandchild he asked. The rest have either been found or are being found by my siblings."

"But I don't understand how your grandfather could have come into possession of the painting."

"There are a great many possibilities. He could have bought it at an art auction of some kind, could have bought it off a merchant. And of course, your family could have bought it back and brought it to this house for safekeeping after the fact. I doubt there's any kind of serious connection."

She suspected that he didn't doubt it at all. She was beginning to suspect that there was some sort of connection between his grandfather and her family. And seeing as Alex wasn't stupid, she imagined he saw it, too.

"Or," she said, "he knew my grandmother."

"I'm certain your grandmother would have said something when she heard my name. At the very least, she might have thrown me out."

"What would throwing you out accomplish? As you pointed out, you didn't need either of us to retrieve the painting, not really. You're right, you could have flashed a little gold at my mother and you would have had all the information you needed."

"True. But still, I don't think there is much point in spinning a fantasy out of any of it. I know my grandfather. He is a good man. He raised us after our parents died. And before they died, he was our most stable influence.

I've always cherished my time with him. He treasures his grandchildren. In a way that our parents never did. We were very lucky to have him. We are lucky to have him still. But I know we won't have him much longer. And that's why…"

"You need the painting." She looked up at the clear blue sky, blinking against the sun as the cool sea breeze ruffled her hair. "You love him very much."

He paused. "He's family. Of course I feel a great deal for him."

She smiled slightly, trying not to laugh at him, since she knew he wouldn't appreciate it. "Alessandro, I think you might have a heart."

He arched a brow and looked toward her. "Don't say that too loudly. We can't have any rumors about that getting around."

"Why? Would it destroy your reputation for being a monster? I have ample evidence that you aren't bad."

"Oh, really? Give me a few examples."

She sighed, letting out a breath and starting down a path that led back toward the estate, winding through a row of hedges that had bright pink flowers on them, little explosions of color against the dark green. She kept her eyes on those blossoms. A welcome distraction from Alex and his persistent presence.

"Well, you haven't breathed fire once since I met you."

"I've been taking antacids. It helps with that."

She laughed, the sound pulled reluctantly from her. "Okay, I haven't seen you gnawing on the bones of any villagers, either. In fact, I don't think any villagers have gone missing since we've arrived on the island."

"That's because I only eat royalty," he said, giving her a rather meaningful look.

She directed her gaze back to the flowers. "Also, you don't sleep in a coffin."

He reached out, grabbing hold of her arm and stopping her in her tracks. "How is it you know where I sleep? Have you been watching me?"

A rush of heat traveled up her arm from the point of contact with his hand and she blushed furiously. "Of course not. Even if I had looked into your room, you would have been shrouded behind the velvet curtains."

"Maybe I have a coffin behind them."

"I doubt it."

"All right, so maybe you have caught on to my secret. I'm simply a man."

"One who is going out of his way to help his grandfather. I think you might have a heart *and* a soul."

"My heart is hard as a rock and my soul is ever so slightly charred from walking through life's fires, but I suppose they're still there."

"You also didn't…" She looked away from him, regretting the words even as she began to speak them, but finding she was unable to stop them. "You didn't take advantage of me last night. You could have. Had you wanted to."

"I have no interest in taking advantage of maidens," he said, his voice hard.

Oh…oh, of course he didn't.

It dawned on her. Suddenly. Horrifically.

Of course he didn't have an interest in maidens. In her. Whatever madness had possessed him last night when he'd kissed her, it hadn't been attraction. Men like him simply weren't attracted to women like her.

To him, she was barely a woman. She was little more than a girl, and he made that very clear. Of course, she had made a similar number of comments about his age, and she didn't truly think he was old.

"I don't think you're old," she said, feeling the need to clarify it suddenly.

"Oh, that's excellent. I guess I won't dip into my retirement account just yet then."

"You're thirty-six?"

"Yes."

"See? Not even middle-aged."

He laughed. "Not even… You're a minx. Do you know that?"

She blinked, her heart suddenly beating faster. Stupid heart. He didn't want her. He didn't even like her. "I'm not trying to be."

"I'm sure that's true."

"You can let go of my arm now," she said, looking down at where he was still hanging on to her.

"What if I told you I didn't want to?"

"I would ask you why. And then I would ask you what good could possibly come of it."

Her heart was pounding so hard now she could barely hear herself speak. If he couldn't hear her heartbeat she would be surprised.

"You're right. There is no point. As I already told you, I'm not interested in defiling any maidens this week."

She pulled herself out of his grasp and continued on down the path. "Who said I was a maiden?" She closed her eyes for a second, allowing the sun to wash over her face, the corners of her lips curving up slightly into a smile.

"You didn't have to say it," he said. "I could feel it in your kiss."

Her stomach sank down to her toes and she opened her eyes again, the corners of her lips falling. "Was it so terrible?"

Of course it had been.

"Not terrible. Inexperienced. I could taste it on your skin."

"That's ridiculous. Inexperience doesn't have a flavor."

He grabbed hold of her arm again, turned her to face

him, drawing her closely toward him. Rather than speeding up, this time her heart stopped beating altogether. He lowered his head slightly, then reached up, sliding his thumb along the edge of her lip. "Yes, Gabriella, inexperience absolutely has a flavor. And on your lips, there was also innocence and wildflowers. I did not mistake the taste of any of that."

He released his hold on her, put distance between them, and she still couldn't breathe any easier.

"You didn't taste like anything," she said.

"That's because you didn't taste me."

Prickles crawled up her back like an army of ants and she hunched her shoulders up around her ears, lowering her head and continuing on toward the estate.

"Suddenly, you don't seem to like honesty very much," he said.

"Suddenly, you're a bit too honest. You said—"

"I am bad at behaving, and I am terrible at restraint. Tell me you didn't like kissing me, and I won't bring it up again."

It would be easy to lie. All she had to do was open her mouth and tell him that she didn't like kissing him. That should be an easy thing to do. It should be a simple thing to make her lips form those words. But right now everything felt stuck. The words lodged in the center of her throat, curled up into a little ball, refusing to budge.

She said nothing; she just kept walking on ahead.

If he was triumphant over her silence, he didn't let on.

He was the one who broke the silence and it felt like a definite checkmark in the loss column for her.

"The party tonight is formal," he said, "everyone is going to be in their finest."

She let out a heavy sigh. "Except for me. In fact, I may skip this one and just sit in my little servant's quarters with a crust of bread and some cheese."

"That's quite dramatic. I think we could at least get you some fresh bread."

"There isn't any reason for me to go. Actually, I might be able to roam the halls a little bit if I stay behind."

"Hospitality has been extended to both of us. And I'm concerned about angering the host."

"Is that because of the painting or because you want to do business with him?"

"Everything is about business. I have an opportunity to increase my success while I'm here and I'm definitely going to take it. I don't want to do anything to compromise that. I certainly won't allow *you* to compromise it."

"Well, I don't want to be embarrassed."

"You didn't let me finish. The party tonight is a masked ball. That means everyone will be wearing masks."

"Thank you," she said, her tone flat. "I actually got that from the title *masked ball*."

"Just making sure."

"Well, there is still a problem with that."

"What's that?"

"I left my ball gown and my elegant face mask in my other luggage."

"I might not be royalty, *cara mia*, but I am a billionaire. I could acquire white tigers in the space of a couple hours if I wanted to. A gown and a mask will be no trouble at all."

"What if I would rather have the white tigers?"

"Your room is too small."

"They can sleep in my bed."

"I'm not getting you white tigers. It would only spoil you. Plus, then everyone would want one."

She couldn't stop the laugh that escaped her lips. She had no idea how he managed all of this. How he managed to make her feel hot, frustrated and amused in the space of only a few seconds. It was some kind of strange witch-craft she had never encountered before.

"Fine."

"*Fine* to the gown and the mask?"

She let out an exasperated sigh. "Would it matter if I said no, Alex?"

Suddenly, his voice seemed to be coming from closer behind her, his low, sensual tones skimming along her skin. "Not especially. If I had to I would go into your room myself and act the part of your valet."

"You aren't suggesting you would dress me?"

"I confess I have much more experience undressing women than I have dressing them. But I might be willing to make an exception."

It was official. She was going to burst into flame.

She had lied when she'd told him she didn't read ro-mance novels. She did. Secretly. And while she pretended to snicker at them from behind her hand, the truth was she was fascinated. She had always been curious to know if at-traction like that existed. If it was possible to look at some-one and feel like they were touching you. Like it would be too much if they did. Like you would die if they didn't.

She knew it did now. And she knew it was the kind of intensity that fiction simply couldn't prepare you for.

His lips had barely skimmed hers last night and she had felt like the moon and stars had fallen from the sky and scattered around her in the garden, leaving the world upside down, glittering all around her, rather than in the distance.

But it didn't matter. She wasn't going to lose her head over him. That was the last thing she had told her grand-mother. That she would not allow him to seduce her.

Her grandmother had warned her away from this kind of thing in vague terms, and when the subject of the paint-ing had come up, just before they'd come to retrieve it, it had become clear to Gabriella why. Her grandmother had been wounded by a man such as this. One who was powerful, handsome.

One she was not meant to be with.

Quite apart from the fact that Gabriella couldn't imagine a future with a man like this, one who didn't believe in love, or commitment, she was a princess. And even if she didn't have a throne she would be required to make a certain kind of marriage.

It would not be to an Italian American businessman who had no pedigree. That just wouldn't do.

She blinked, trying to get a hold on her thoughts. The last thing he needed to know was that she was thinking about sex or marriage in connection with him.

"Well, there's no need for you to dress me. I will dress myself. But tonight we need to try and look for that room my grandmother spoke of. We need to try and find the painting."

"I agree with you. I think tonight might be the time we change the nature of this farce, don't you?"

"What do you mean?"

"I mean, we have established that you are nothing more than my assistant. No one suspects that you are Princess Gabriella D'Oro, and no one has any reason to. Tonight you will be wearing a beautiful dress, and your face will be covered by a mask keeping you from being recognized… When we slip away together a little bit early, it will hardly be suspicious. At least not if I have been holding you in my arms a little bit more closely than I have for the previous nights."

"What are you suggesting?"

"Tonight, you will play the part of my lover, Gabriella. There will be no scandal, and it will be the perfect excuse for us to slip away."

Her throat was dry, her heart pounding so hard she

was afraid it might gain enough momentum to tumble up her throat and come spilling out of her mouth. "But I..."

"You don't know how? You don't know how to play the part of doting lover?"

Her cheeks flamed. "I have no worries about that. I can more than handle you, Alessandro."

"You see, when you say my full name like that, I become convinced that you are a bit more nervous than you let on."

"And when you take on that dry tone, I begin to suspect that you are a little bit more off-kilter than you like to let on. Perhaps it is *you* having a difficult time figuring out how you will play the part of my lover. But don't worry, I will be wearing a mask. So my looks shouldn't put you off."

"Did my kiss last night not prove to you that I don't find you unattractive?"

"The only thing your kiss last night proved is that you very much like playing games. But I don't like being the subject of them."

A man like Alessandro would never want a woman like her. With her large glasses and ill-fitting clothing—the only thing she had ever worn in front of him—her face devoid of makeup, he would never look twice at her.

Likely, he had seen her as a challenge, and he had set out to conquer her. Because that's who he was.

Well, she refused to be conquered.

"I have no problem playing the part of your lover tonight, Alex," she said, keeping her tone frosty. "But do not get any ideas about making it real. I understand what manner of man you are. I understand what motivates you. I am a source of amusement to you, as you have made very plain. I will not allow you to amuse yourself with my body."

Filled with a new sense of dignified rage, she stormed

toward the estate. She had no idea why she was reacting this way. Had no idea why she hadn't seen all of this before. Had she truly imagined that he had been attracted to her? That the kiss had been genuine? That the rake had gone after the wallflower?

She was as much a fool for a beautiful face as her grandmother had feared.

As much a fool as anyone in her family was. Perhaps that was the curse. Her grandmother had fallen prey to a man. And had her heart broken by him. Her mother threw herself in front of men as though she were a willing victim and they were an oncoming train. Only to find herself tangled, destroyed, after each affair. Chipping away pieces of her marriage, pieces of herself.

Perhaps, in spite of all her attention to avoid such emotions, Gabriella should have truly known better.

She rushed through the estate, heading toward her room. Once safely inside, she closed the door and locked the connecting one between her room and Alex's. She would have to face him tonight. Tonight, she would have to pretend that she was his lover. She would need to fortify herself to cope with that.

She sat on her bed, breathing hard, anger, *hurt*, rising up inside of her.

But with a few breaths came clarity.

The only solution here would be to take control of the situation. Alex saw himself as above temptation, she knew that. He only gave in when he chose to. And of course, he didn't want her.

But tonight, she would *make* him want her. She would. She would turn the tables.

He would be the one left unsatisfied. He would be the one who didn't sleep because he was burning. But she would never give in to him. She would make him want her, and then, she would turn away.

She flopped backward onto the bed, a smile crossing her lips. She was incredibly satisfied with this new plan. With this vision for the future that put her much more in charge of things than she'd been previously. Yes, last night she had momentarily lost her head over Alex. And there were a few moments today when she had done so, as well.

But it would not happen again. If anyone was going to lose their head tonight, it was going to be him.

CHAPTER TEN

ALEX HAD BEEN dimly aware of the fact that Gabriella was a princess. He had originally fooled himself that she was not attractive, but now was exceedingly aware of the fact that she was beautiful. But what he had not realized was that, even behind the little gold mask that covered her eyes and part of her nose, her regal bearing would shine through.

What he had not realized was that, even with most of her face covered, her beauty would be undeniable. What he had not realized was that, in a designer gown that clung to her generous curves, she would be a temptation he was not sure he had the strength to resist.

He hadn't realized that manner of temptation still existed for him.

Her dark hair was left loose, styled in dark curls, full lips painted red, the only part of her face that was visible. Her dress was a bright blue, the neckline high, covering more of her golden skin than he would like. But it hinted at a figure more spectacular than he had thought it could be. It clung to her hips and thighs before flaring out at the knee and billowing about her feet.

She was, in truth, a much more elegant creature than he had ever imagined. It was like looking at a stranger, and yet someone familiar at the same time.

Then she took a step forward, turning her foot sideways, and tripping slightly on her heel. "Drat!" she said, straightening and fussing with the bottom of her dress.

He smiled, because there was the Gabriella he had grown to know over the past few days.

"You look beautiful," he said, the compliment rolling effortlessly off his tongue. She did look beautiful. She was *more* than beautiful.

"You don't have to say things like that," she said.

His chest tightened. He had wounded her earlier, and he bitterly regretted that. Still, he wasn't entirely certain it was bad if she didn't truly believe him attracted to her. He would never be like his father. He would never be the sort of man who simply took what he wanted without considering the feelings of others.

As a young man he had fixated on that little boy standing outside of the manor that night, the bastard child of his father who'd caused the car accident that killed his parents.

He had spent a great many years blaming that little boy. Hiding that little boy's existence. Something he bitterly regretted later on in his life. Something he had done his very best to make right. But it had been too late. Nate's life had been broken beyond recognition. Rejected by the only family he might have had, because of his birth.

Alex had brought Nate back into the family's life when his grandfather had needed a bone marrow transplant and no one else had been a match. He hadn't regretted it, but he and his half brother had never made much of a relationship with each other.

As an adult his memory of the events of that night had expanded. Not just to his mother, and her distress. Not just to the boy. But to the other woman, who was equally broken. Who had been brought into his father's web somehow, who had born his child and received no support. Yes, more and more he thought about her. He thought about every single person who had been damaged by his father's selfishness. By his unchecked lust.

The more the years passed, the more he realized his father was the villain.

Alex was a great many things, but he refused to become that manner of monster.

And that meant he would never touch Gabriella. She was so very different than anyone he'd ever known. So untouched by the ugly things in the world. She had seen the way her parents had behaved, and she had managed to retain a kind of simple, open view of the world he could never remember possessing. She had retained her hope. He would be damned if he were the one to take that from her.

One thing was certain, while he might be able to give her physical pleasure, he would never be able to offer anything beyond that. Nothing more than pain.

His family was stuck with him. The damage to Nate was done.

He would extend that damage no further.

"Shall we go to the ball, Cinderella?"

He extended his hand and she looked at it as though it might bite her. "If I'm Cinderella," she said, keeping her hands fixed firmly to her sides, "does that make you my fairy godmother?"

"Never. Fairy godmothers are endlessly giving. They live to bestow gifts with no hope of receiving anything in return." He smiled. "I'm not so selfless."

"And what exactly do you hope to get in return for your gifts?"

"I'm getting it. Right now. As I told you, you look beautiful."

He could see pink color bleeding beneath her skin, spreading outside the edges of the mask, revealing her blush to him. Reviewing the pleasure she took in his compliment. "And you... You look like the Phantom of the Opera."

He touched the white mask on his face. "That's kind of the point."

"Except you aren't hideously scarred."

"My scars are metaphorical in nature."

"The same can be said for most of us, I suppose. Though scarring is kept to a minimum when you spend most of your time in the library."

"I knew my lack of a library would become problematic one day."

"Right now, the only problem we have is a lack of a painting," she said, gently steering the conversation back to the reason for all of this.

She was good at that. He was losing the plot. Completely. For a moment he had forgotten that he had a goal that extended beyond dancing with her tonight. A goal that went past seeing her in this gown and that mask.

Time moved a strange pace here. It was slower. Being away from his phone, his desk, being outside of his world, was doing strange things to him. He wasn't entirely certain he disliked it.

"Then I suggest we get a move on. The painting will wait for no man. Except it has done exactly that for the past fifty-plus years."

This time, she did take his hand. And he was the one tempted to pull away. From the heat. From the silken quality of her touch. He didn't. He was the experienced party. The touch of a woman's hand against his should not be cause for any reaction whatsoever.

He knew that. Repeated it over and over as he led her from their quarters down the long hall and toward the ballroom.

No matter how committed he was to understanding it

on an intellectual level, he could not convince his body to agree.

So he did his best to concentrate on the feeling of his feet making contact with the marble floor. One step, then another. When he focused on that, the burn, where her skin made contact with his, lessened.

A bit.

They approached the doors to the ballroom and two elegantly appointed staff, not wearing masks, opened the double doors for both of them. "I feel like I should bow," he said, leaning in to whisper the words in her ear. "But at my age it might be bad for my back."

She looked up at him, dark eyes glinting from behind the mask. "Stop that."

"But it's so much fun."

She rolled her eyes and he led her into the ballroom where couples were already dancing. "This room... It's amazing," she said, looking about them at the high, painted ceiling before her eyes fell to the pale walls, made ornate by sconces and crisp white molding.

Nothing about the designer dresses the other women were wearing. Of course not. Gabriella preferred art and architecture. Always.

"Gabby," he said, drawing her attention back to him. She didn't look nearly as annoyed as she typically did when he used the nickname. She looked... There was something strange in her expression. Something he feared he understood. Something he wished he hadn't seen. "If you keep staring at the walls with more admiration than you afford me no one will believe it when we slip away."

He led her deeper into the ballroom, toward the dance floor, and her attention drifted from him as she continued to stare at the walls, at the art, probably at particularly historically significant dust motes, knowing her.

"That could be a problem," she said, distracted.

"Yes. One I will correct."

He chose that moment to pull her into his arms, into a closed hold. Her attention snapped back to him. "What are we doing?"

"Dancing," he said as he led her into the first step.

"So we are," she said, one hand caught up in his, the other resting on his shoulder.

She curled her fingers in a fist, as though she were afraid to touch him too much so she needed to minimize the amount of skin making contact with his jacket.

"I feel tonight we might be very rude."

"Will we?"

"Yes. We should socialize with everyone. You should approach the women and ask them who they are wearing and I should try and forge as many business connections as I possibly can with everyone in attendance. But I'm not going to. And neither are you. Because tonight we are only going to look at each other. We are only going to stay for the minimum amount of time and we're going to make the world believe that I could not wait one more moment to have you in my arms."

He could feel the breath leave her entire body, could feel her limbs go stiff. "I'm in your arms right now."

"No. Not like this. It would be different."

"How?" she asked, her voice a hushed whisper, her dark eyes full of fear, curiosity and excitement.

"It would be different because we would be alone. Because if there was nothing around us but all of these beautiful walls and I were to take you into my arms you would know that there were no limits to what might happen next. Everything would be different. It would be quiet, there would be no music. Only our breathing. The air around us would be different."

She swallowed visibly. "That's what…that's what everyone will think is going to happen?"

"Yes. By the end of this dance no one will be in any doubt that the moment I have you alone we will not be discussing art, let alone looking at paintings."

He drew her closer as the music changed, not releasing her between songs, but rather continuing to sway gently with her. "But we are," she said, "looking at paintings."

"Of course," he said, never taking his eyes from her. "Touch my face, Gabriella."

"Wh-what?"

"I want you to lift your hand from my shoulder, and rest your palm against my face. I want you to take your fingertips and trace my jaw, down to my chin, then bring your hand to rest on my chest."

"Why?" she asked, her expression almost frantic.

"It's for the painting." He ignored the dull beating of his heart—it was for a lot more than that. That reminded him there were other ways to do this.

She obeyed his command, even while her expression remained frightened. Soft skin made contact with his face, the light drift of her fingertips along his cheek, down his jaw and then, just as he had told her to, she brought it to rest against his chest. He was certain that she could feel his heart, beating hard beneath her palm.

He never took his eyes off hers as he slipped his arm slowly from around her waist and reached for her wrist, curling his fingers around it and drawing her hand to his lips, pressing a kiss to the center of her palm.

"That wasn't... You didn't..."

He released his hold on her, raising his hand to capture her chin between his thumb and forefinger. "I suppose I didn't. How many 'Hail Marys' do you suppose I have to say to atone for that?"

"I don't know," she said, her voice raspy, scraped raw.

"It has been longer than I care to remember since my

last confession. But for you, I would gladly get on my knees."

Gabriella straightened, as though bolts of lightning had just shot straight down her spine, as though she had been hit with a thought so real, so strong, it had manifested itself physically. "You're very good at empty flirtation, Alex." She moved her arm around his neck, placing her fingers on his skin. "I wonder what might happen if you had to make good on any of your promises."

"Why don't you try to hold me to them, Gabriella?"

"Say something real," she said, moving closer to him, slowly, as though it were taking great effort for her to move nearer to him, as though it took everything she had in her to keep herself from running away. "You've been playing a game with me from the moment we met. So now, if you want this to go on, I want you to tell me something and I want you to say it without that mocking gleam in your eye, or that wicked curve to your mouth. I want you to be real for one moment. Just one."

"And what do I get in return?"

"Whatever you want."

He could tell that the words had left her lips before she had given them her full permission. He could also tell that she wished she could call them back.

"A very dangerous gift to offer to a man like me."

"I have no doubt." But, to her credit, she didn't rescind the offer.

"A real kiss for a real confession," he said, "it's only fair."

"All right," she said, her words breathless.

"You are beautiful," he said, keeping his gaze locked with hers. He kept his grip on her chin tight, didn't allow her to look away. "Quite apart from this quest, this game, apart from…me. The fact that no one has ever told you before, or at least has never made you feel it before, is a crime unspeakable in its cruelty."

She blinked, relaxing in his hold. "I...I don't know what to say. No one has ever... No one has ever said anything like that to me."

"You were very angry yesterday. I... The way that I dealt with you was wrong. I hurt you. It was not my intent. You are sweet, Gabby. I am a man who licks the sugar off sweet things and leaves them discarded. But even if I shouldn't say this, I want you to understand that while we might be here putting on a show for others, while I may have confessed to you my boredom with life, the attraction I feel for you is separate from that."

She took a deep breath, her eyes fluttering closed, and then, her hands still curved around the back of his neck, she stood up on her toes and pressed a kiss to his mouth. It was quick, short, but he felt branded by it. Was certain that she had left a crimson stain behind from her lipstick, but something deeper than that. Something permanent.

"Now," he said, "I think it's time for us to excuse ourselves."

Gabriella had failed in her objective. And she wasn't entirely sorry about it.

She was supposed to seduce him. She was supposed to flip the tables on him. But from the moment she walked out of her room wearing that dress, she had felt like putty. Particularly when he looked at her, with all that heat and masculine energy radiating from him. He certainly looked like a man not entirely indifferent to what he saw before him.

And that, she supposed, was the variable she hadn't counted on. The fact that coming close to seducing him might seduce her right back.

Then there had been the touching. Her touching his

face, him kissing her hand. She had felt very much the frustrated mouse in the paws of a cat that wasn't really hungry, just looking for amusement.

That was when she'd remembered herself. When she'd realized she was failing at her own objective. And so she had tried a different approach.

Yet again, he had come out on top. She had turned to nothing more substantial than spun sugar when he complimented her, then she'd nearly lost her nerve when she'd kissed him. Then she nearly dissolved when his lips had touched hers.

She was not a very good seductress. That was just the truth.

But…it turned out she was eminently seducible. Beautiful words from a beautiful man that touched her down deep beneath her clothes, beneath her skin, changed everything around inside of her. Made her forget to protect herself.

The wing of the palace they were in now was completely empty of guests or staff, it seemed. Everyone was in the ballroom, or on the other side of the house wearing a path between the kitchen and the ballroom.

"Come with me," he said, wrapping his arm around her waist and moving at a brisk pace toward a set of double doors at the end of the corridor.

She did. Because this was the game. Because there was nowhere else she wanted to be. And after tonight it was over. This hunt. This flirtation. Whatever it was.

The only flirtation she'd ever had in her life.

The thought made her want to cry. Sit and weep in the middle of the corridor. But she couldn't do that because they were on a painting quest.

She hoped it took all night.

That they could spend the whole evening wandering through vacant halls on a quest, and if he never touched her it would be okay. It would be okay as long as she was walking with him.

Are you that easy? A few compliments and you're ready to melt all over him like butter.

Yes. She was.

But the strange thing was, she knew Alex now. And she knew that what he'd said in the ballroom was real. What she didn't know was what it meant for him, for them, and for the ticking clock that was winding down to midnight, when the enchantment would break and Cinderella would go back to being a bespectacled bookworm beneath his notice.

He opened one of the doors and slipped through the crack, bringing her with him, before closing it behind him.

"Do you suppose he has some kind of security camera system?"

"Not that I've noticed," Alex said. "And believe me, I've been keeping my eye out. But he has no reason to think that any of the guests are going to make off with the art. And we're not going to make off with any of the art that he knows about."

"A fabulous technicality."

"Speaking of technicalities, I want my kiss," he said, turning to her, his expression suddenly hard, like granite.

The breath rushed from her body. "I kissed you," she said. "Already, I mean."

"You kissed me in front of everyone else. You wanted real words for me, and I want a real kiss from you. That kiss always had to happen for the two of us to excuse ourselves from the ballroom. I want one that isn't inevitable."

"Is that so?"

"Though I'm beginning to wonder if a kiss between the two of us was always inevitable."

She laughed, a shaky, breathless sound. "Since when? Since you first walked into my grandmother's house when

I was barefoot and in my glasses?" She wished it were true. She wished he had.

"Yes."

"That doesn't make sense."

"It doesn't. You're right. Nothing about this makes sense." He was the one who closed the distance between them, who reached out and curled a lock of her hair around his finger before letting it fall free. "I'm not certain it matters."

"It should."

"There are a lot of *shoulds* in the world, Gabby. But they very often become *shouldn'ts*. There isn't much to be done about it. Except perhaps do the one thing that feels right."

She didn't know if this felt right. No. It didn't feel right. It felt wrong. Very, very wrong. But she still wanted it. That was the thing.

She took a sharp breath, taking a step in toward him, pressing her hand to his chest. She looked up at his eyes, hard and dark, his expression still mostly concealed behind the mask. She flexed her fingers, scrunching the stiff white material of his shirt, then smoothing it again, relishing the feeling of his heat, his hardness, beneath the fabric. He was so different than she was. She had never truly fully appreciated just how different men and women were. In a million ways, big and small.

Yes, there was the obvious, but it was more than that. And it was those differences that suddenly caused her to glory in who she was, what she was. To feel, if only for a moment, that she completely understood herself both body and soul, and that they were united in one desire.

"Kiss me, Princess," he said, his voice low, strained.

He was affected.

So she had won.

She had been the one to make him burn.

But she'd made a mistake if she'd thought this game had one winner and one loser. She was right down there with him. And she didn't care about winning anymore.

She couldn't deny him, not now. Not when he was looking at her like she was a woman and not a girl, or an owl. Not when he was looking at her like she was the sun, moon and all the stars combined. Bright, brilliant and something that held the power to hold him transfixed.

Something more than what she was. Because Gabriella D'Oro had never transfixed anyone. Not her parents. Not a man.

But he was looking at her like she mattered. She didn't feel like shrinking into a wall, or melting into the scenery. She wanted him to keep looking.

She didn't want to hide from this. She wanted all of it.

Slowly, so slowly, so that she could savor the feel of him, relish the sensations of his body beneath her touch, she slid her hand up his throat, feeling the heat of his skin, the faint scratch of whiskers.

Then she moved to cup his jaw, his cheek.

"I've never touched a man like this before," she confessed.

And she wasn't even embarrassed by the confession, because he was still looking at her like he wanted her.

He moved closer, covering her hand with his. She could feel his heart pounding heavily, could sense the tension running through his frame. "I've touched a great many women," he said, his tone grave. "But at the moment it doesn't seem to matter."

That was when she kissed him.

She closed her eyes and leaned forward, pressing her lips to his, her heart thudding against her chest so wildly she could hardly breathe. She felt dizzy. She felt restless. She felt…everything.

It was the most natural and comfortable thing in the

world to be in his arms. And also the most frightening. The most torturous.

She felt as though she'd come home, as though she'd finally found a place to rest. One that was hers and hers alone. But it wasn't enough. And it never would be. His suit and her gown put too many layers between them.

Her title and his lack of one.

His age and experience coupled with her relative youth and inexperience.

Thirteen years. Thousands of miles. Lord knew how many women.

An unbridgeable divide, but one that was reduced to nothing as she stood here, tasting him. Savoring him. Holding him.

There was no space between them now. None at all. They were both shaking, both needing, both wanting.

She curled her fingers into a fist, holding him tightly as she angled her head. Then she jolted when he parted his lips, his tongue tracing the seam of her mouth, requesting entry.

She couldn't deny him. Not now. Possibly not ever.

He wrapped his arms around her, enveloping her, holding her close. One hand pressed between her shoulder blades, the other sliding low, just low enough to tease the curve of her buttocks without actually going past the line of impropriety.

Her world was reduced to this. To his hands, his lips, his scent. His every breath. If they had come into this room for anything other than the kiss she didn't remember it.

If there was anything beyond this room, this moment, this man, she didn't remember it, either.

They parted slowly, so different from that kiss in the garden. This felt natural, even though she regretted the end. They were both breathing hard, both unsteady. She lifted her hand and touched his cheek, felt the rasp of his whiskers beneath her palms, drank in the sight of him. What she could see of him that wasn't covered by the mask, anyway.

"We should look for the painting," she said, knowing she sounded dazed.

Her lips felt hot. Swollen. She wondered if they looked different, too. She couldn't possibly have any lipstick left on them—that was certain.

"Painting?" he asked, the corners of his mouth turning up.

"Yes," she said, her tone dry. She cleared her throat and started to walk toward the back wall. "She said there was a painting in one of the rooms, and only I could open it…"

"The key," he said.

"Yes. I'm good at keeping secrets, it turns out. All those years of not having very many people to talk to, I guess."

She reached beneath the neckline of her gown and fished the necklace out, holding it up in front of her.

"The key," he said, his tone slightly different than it had been a moment earlier.

"Yes. It fits into a frame. She said it was scenery. Of a farm."

"There's a lot of that here."

"I know," she said, moving closer to the far wall and examining the different scenes in front of her. "They really do like their geese," she muttered as she moved down the row, examining the frames, looking for any evidence that one might not be a typical picture. "There are some farm scenes in here, but nothing quite like what my grandmother described. I feel like this is the wrong room. The sorts of farmhouses my grandmother described were from a slightly different era. They predate these more modern houses."

"Do they predate the geese?"

"There were always geese, Alex," she said, enjoying the way his words played off her own. A thrill the way their lips worked together, even when they weren't touching.

"Then let's keep looking," he said.

He took hold of her hand and another thrill shot through her as he led her from the room and back down the hall. He opened another door.

"What sorts of paintings are those?" he asked.

She looked in, her heart pounding hard due to the excitement. Sort of. Mostly it was the proximity of Alex.

"Cityscapes," she said, "it won't be here."

They continued through a room filled with the portraits of royals, and one with scenes of the beach. Finally, they opened up a door to a room with a wall lined with paintings of farms. Pale, rosy cheeked children with animals, thatched roof homes and, well, more geese.

"It would be here," she said, "I'm sure. So now…we just have to figure out which. Which painting looks different? Which one might be a false front?"

Alex squinted looking around the room. Then his posture went straight as though a realization had shot through him like a lightning bolt. "Here," he said.

She turned to look at him. He'd stopped in front of a painting with a farmhouse, and a young girl in front of it. His fingertip was pressed into the corner of the frame.

"What is it?" she asked.

"There's a small…a notch here in the corner. Look."

She moved over to where he was and her mouth fell open, her fingers trembling as she held the charm on the necklace out in front of her. "I think…I think this is it," she said.

He moved aside and she stepped forward, pressing the back of the necklace into the notch and pushing it in. The frame popped away from the wall about two inches and Gabriella stood back, bringing her necklace with her.

She stared at the picture for a moment, then looked over at Alex. "Well, now I'm nervous," she said. Her stomach was flipping over, her hands sweating. She was…excited. But terrified. If the painting was there…who knew what would happen. If it got out and it created more waves for her family it would be disastrous. She would never be able to salvage their reputations. Not even with a more complete and fair history compiled.

But if it wasn't there…

She had wondered about the painting for so long. If it was real. And now they knew it was real and the possibility of seeing it…

Alex swung the painting open and revealed a large rectangle behind it, set deep into the wall, covered in burlap.

"Oh," she breathed, "that could be…I mean, it probably is…"

Alex reached out and grabbed hold of the burlap, drawing it down to reveal the painting underneath.

"Well," she said, "you kind of took the drama out of it."

"You don't think this is dramatic enough?" he asked.

It was. Even without fanfare. Because lowering the burlap had revealed what could only be *The Lost Love*. It was a woman, sitting in front of a vanity, hands in her dark curls as she gazed into the mirror. She was naked, her bare back on display, the suggestion of her breasts in the reflection of the mirror. She was seated on a cushion, the curve of her bottom visible.

It was…provocative, certainly. But beautiful. And hardly the salacious, distasteful scandal the press had insinuated it might be so long ago.

"And this is why…" she breathed. "This is why we search for the truth. There's nothing… There is nothing filthy about this. Nothing wrong with it."

"I'm inclined to agree. But then, I am a fan of the female form."

She turned to look at Alex. "I only mean that the media made it sound as though revealing this photo would be detrimental to my grandmother's reputation. Certainly…" She looked back at the painting. "Certainly, it suggests that she was intimate with the painter. It is not a standard sort of portrait that one might sit for. And someone in her position was hardly ever going to pose nude. Plus… There's something… There's something more here than you see in a portrait that simply contains a model. The painter was not detached from the subject. I can feel it in every brushstroke. There's so much passion."

Her fingers reached out to the corner of the painting, where the artist's initials, *B.A.*, were faintly painted.

"Or," Alex said, stuffing his hands in his pockets, "he was a very good painter."

"It was more than that, Alex."

"It makes no difference to me. My job is simply to bring the painting to my grandfather."

Gabriella frowned. "Why does your grandfather have more of a claim to this than my grandmother? It's her in the painting."

"Yes, it is. But my grandfather owned this painting at one time. He will be willing to pay whatever price is fair. It was not your grandmother's dying request, but it is his."

"We will bring it back to Aceena. She wants to see it. At least give her that."

"I can't be away from work indefinitely, Princess," he said.

She looked at him, unable to make out the finer points of his expression behind the mask. "Please. Let's bring it back to her."

He regarded her closely for a moment. Then he nodded slowly, moving over to where the painting was, extending his hand and brushing his thumb along the edge of the canvas. "It is very beautiful. In fact," he said, looking away from the painting and back at Gabriella. "It reminds me a bit of you."

Her face heated. "I don't look anything like that."

"You certainly do. Beautiful. Lush."

"I don't."

"This painting is not the view of the subject. It's the vision of her admirer," he said, his dark eyes locked on to hers. "For that reason, I would say that I'm in a much better position to evaluate it than you."

"You're not my lover," she said, the word sweet and thick like honey on her tongue.

"No," he said, his tone taking on a wistful quality. "I'm not."

"How are we going to get this back to our room?"

"Very quickly," he said.

He took the portrait out, covered it with the burlap again and quickly closed the original painting.

She moved forward and pressed her necklace deeply into the notch again to lock it just as before.

"If he truly had no idea this painting was here, he will have no reason to believe it isn't mine," Alex said. "Of course, carrying a rather large canvas through the house may arouse suspicion. I doubt I could convince him I was simply taking the painting out for a walk."

"Then we had better hurry," Gabriella said. "Everyone else is still occupied in the ballroom."

"And thank God for Prime Minister Colletti's devotion to having a good time."

They walked to the double doors that led back to the corridor. Alex opened the first one slightly, peering out into the hall to see if anyone was there. "It looks clear," he said.

She nodded, and they both slipped through the outside, closing the gallery door tightly shut behind.

It was ridiculous. Alex was wearing a suit that was rather disheveled, they were both masked and now Alex was also carrying a piece of art.

If anyone saw them, they would likely imagine they had simply had too much to drink.

They walked down the hall quickly, then they rounded to the left and froze. Up against the wall was another couple engaged in the very thing Alex had wanted the rest of the party to believe *they* were engaged in. The man had the woman pressed tightly against the wall, her hands held over her head while he kissed her again, his other hand roaming over her curves.

A flash of heat wound itself around Gabriella, her entire body ready to go up in flames at the sight of it.

What would it be like to have Alex unleash his passion on her like that? To have him press her up against the wall. To have him touch her like that.

The scene before them highlighted just how circumspect he had been.

For some reason, she was disappointed.

"Quietly," Alex whispered as the two of them continued behind the amorous couple. The woman's eyes were closed, the man's back to them, and they were able to walk along behind them without detection. They hurried through the halls, the rest of which they found empty. Not stopping until they reached their rooms.

"Excellent," Alex said, closing the door tightly behind them. "I will pack this away, and if anyone looks through my suitcase I will say that I acquired it elsewhere during our travels. There is no reason for them to think otherwise."

Gabriella shook her head, laughing—a husky sound.

"I never imagined in my wildest dreams that I would be involved in an art heist."

"Does it not belong to your family, Gabriella?"

"I feel it does," she said.

"Then it's hardly a heist."

"Still. I've done quite a lot today that I never imagined I would."

Dancing with him. Kissing him. Being called beautiful. Now it was ending. This was the end of it all. She didn't care about stealing the painting. She cared about the mission being over.

"I have to say the same, Gabby, and I did not think that was possible."

She wasn't even irritated this time when he called her Gabby. No one else called her that. It was a name that only came from Alex. And she decided that there was something she quite liked about that. Whether it was because it kept this entire event separate from her real life, or because it made all of this feel special.

She was desperate to feel like it was special to him.

"I'm glad you found it diverting."

He laughed. "Oh, I found it more than that."

He took his mask off then, reached up and loosened his black tie. There was something about that look. That rakish, disheveled look that made her heart beat faster. That made her limbs feel weak. That made her stomach tighten.

Of course, it was the same when he was perfectly pressed, the same when he had a mask over his face. It was the same no matter what.

"We will leave tomorrow," he said.

"What reason will we give?"

"I will tell him that urgent business has come up in the States. I think I have done enough to secure a deal with the prime minister, and I managed to get what I came for. All in all, quite a successful trip."

Gabriella couldn't help but laugh. "Almost too successful. I keep expecting guards and hounds to descend upon us."

"Nothing like that, I think. I'm not sure this painting is truly valuable to anyone other than our grandparents."

Gabriella blinked, pulled up yet again by the link between Lucia and Giovanni. "Yes. It's very strange, that."

"Not especially."

"A bit."

"Only if you like romanticizing things. And I do not."

She rolled her eyes. "How very surprising."

He paused in front of her, a strange expression passing over his face. The left side of his lips curved slightly upward as he studied her. He moved forward and her breath caught in her chest.

He reached out, tracing the edge of her mask before lifting it slowly. He pulled it away, the soft brush of his skin against hers enough to make her feel like she was on fire. "So very beautiful," he said, his words hushed.

She waited for him to lean in. Waited for him to kiss her again. But he didn't. He simply stood, looking at her, not touching her, not making a move to close the distance between them.

She wished she were brave. Brave enough to touch him. To lean into him. To recapture what had happened in that empty room.

"Goodnight, Gabriella," he said finally, his words summarily dismissing her, stealing her chance at bravery.

She cleared her throat. "Goodnight, Alex."

She turned and walked into her bedroom. She felt very much like she had missed something. Like she had left a very important piece of herself behind.

She blinked hard against the stinging sensation in her eyes, did her best to breathe around the rock that had settled on her chest.

They would leave tomorrow. They had completed their objective. Tomorrow, she would be back on Aceena. Back with her grandmother. And everything would return to the way it was.

CHAPTER ELEVEN

EVERYTHING HAD GONE smoothly during their escape from Isolo D'Oro, and it continued to go smoothly upon their reentry into Aceena. Alex would have been surprised, but things tended to go smoothly for him, so he saw no reason this should be different. Except for the fact that everything about it felt different in a million small ways he could not quite quantify.

Well, there was one thing that he could name. Gabriella. He ignored that thought as they walked into the hall at the D'Oro estate.

He had the painting under his arm, the rest of their bags being handled by the staff. Gabriella was walking along beside him, wearing a pair of plain pants and a button-up blouse, her very large glasses returned to their usual position. And somehow, even with all of that, he saw her no differently than he had last night. She was fascinating, beautiful, irresistible. But here he was resisting. Overrated, in his opinion.

"We must bring this to my grandmother as quickly as possible," Gabriella was saying, the animated tone of her voice never failing to stir something inside of him.

She cared about so many things. Dusty books and history and the people around her. It made him ache. Made him wish he could still feel like that. Feel in ways he hadn't since he was eleven years old.

They were directed by the staff to the morning room, where her grandmother was taking her tea.

"Grandmother," Gabriella said, the word sounding more like a prayer than anything else. As though Lucia were Gabriella's salvation, her link back to the real world.

He still didn't feel linked to the real world. The shipping company was back in New York, along with a great many of his real-world concerns. Somehow, over the past week, his life had started to revolve around a painting, and giving compliments to the woman that stood before him.

"Is that it?" Lucia asked, gesturing to the painting that Alex held, facing away from her.

He nodded slowly.

"May I?" she asked, her voice suddenly hushed.

He handed the painting to her, careful not to reveal too much of it. He had seen it, but he felt the need to allow her to experience this at her own pace. In somewhat of a private fashion.

He watched the older woman's face, watched as she placed her fingertips over the painting, her dark eyes filling with tears. "I can see," she said, her voice trembling, "I can see how much he loved me. It is there. Still."

"Who?" Gabriella asked.

"Bartolo. His name was Bartolo. An artist. And I...I did not think there was any way I could sacrifice my position for love. But I'm old now, Gabriella. And I look at this and I see just how deep his feelings were. And then... Then we were thrown out of Isolo D'Oro, anyway. I asked myself every day what the sacrifice meant. I married a man who was suitable. I rejected the one who was not. For what? For a kingdom that crumbled. Seeing it again... Understanding... His love was more than I deserved. He did not deserve one so faithless as myself."

Gabriella's hands were folded in her lap and she was wringing them as though the queen's words were causing her great distress. "Grandmother, of course you did what you had to do. You did what you felt was right."

She sighed slowly, sadly. "It is all any of us can do, I'm afraid. But when your best isn't good enough it galls particularly with the sharp clarity of hindsight."

"I hate to cause you any further pain, Your Highness," Alex said. "But—"

"But your grandfather wants this painting returned to his possession," Lucia said, her tone grave.

"Yes. There are few things in his life that he prizes beyond money. Beyond anything. This painting is one of them. And though I can't tell you why, though it must seem strange as you are the subject of the painting, I can only tell you that it is an old man's greatest wish to have this again."

A tear rolled down her cheek, and Alex felt shamed by the emotional display for some reason. Shamed by how jaded he was, by how little credibility he gave to love and emotion when he saw such depth of it before him.

"Of course he can have it," Lucia said, her words shocking Alex down to the core.

"I will pay whatever you ask for it. He's prepared to compensate you handsomely."

She placed her hand over the painting again. "I don't want money. I *want* him to have it."

Alex met her gaze and nodded slowly. "He will."

Gabriella looked over at him, her expression filled with concern. "He isn't going to make a scandal with it?"

Alex shook his head. "No. My grandfather has no interest in scandal. He has no need for money."

Gabriella didn't ask if he was telling the truth. Something about that warmed his chest in a way that he wasn't certain he deserved.

"You must stay with us tonight, Alex," Lucia said.

His heart slammed against his breastbone. Denial was

on the tip of his tongue. He shouldn't stay. He should go.
But he was in no position to deny the older woman anything. "If you wish."

"And I do have a condition on giving you the painting."

Everything inside of him stilled. "Do you?"

The older woman nodded. "Gabriella shall go with you.
She will help deliver the painting. Acting as an ambassa-
dor for our family."

"If you wish," he said again.

He had been desperate to escape Gabriella. Her tempting mouth, her soft touch. Nothing good could come of the
attraction between them. Ever. Acting on it—more than
they already had—was simply not an option. He would
leave her untouched.

But in order for him to honor such a vow, he would need
to get a good deal of distance between them.

This was not conducive to that goal.

He had honorable intentions, but he was a flesh and
blood man. His spirit was willing but his flesh was very,
very weak where she was concerned.

Still, he could not refuse.

"Of course," he said.

"Excellent," the queen said, "I will have some of the
staff show you to your room. In the meantime, I would
like to spend some time with my granddaughter."

Gabriella looked at the clock. It was nearly midnight, but
she was still sitting awake in the library. Her conversation with her grandmother was playing over in her mind.

Lucia had been talking of an old love, of honor and duty
perhaps not being everything. Of how her heart still ached,
all these years later, when she looked at the painting.

It was so very strange for Gabriella, to hear her prag-
matic grandmother speaking of love. They had spoken of

it before, but always Lucia had been cautionary, because she had spoken of its loss.

Now, though…she said when she looked at that painting it made her feel so full. It made her realize all the beauty she had carried with her thanks to that ill-fated affair.

Made her realize she could never truly regret loving Bartolo, though she had not spent her life with him.

In addition to that, Gabriella's nerves were slightly frazzled with the idea of going to New York. More specifically, going with Alex.

It meant an extension on their time on Isolo D'Oro. More time just to be near each other. Circling around the larger things that neither of them were prepared to embrace.

She wanted it. She wanted more time with him. But she wasn't sure they should have it.

Things were… Well, they weren't normal between them. She had been looking forward to getting away from him, and now it appeared that wouldn't be happening. Of course, as much as she had been looking forward to there being some distance between them, she had also dreaded it.

The idea of going back to life as it had been before. As though she had never met him, as though they had never spent a week on Isolo D'Oro together. As though he had never called her beautiful, as though they had never kissed… The very idea of that was painful to her. Sat in her chest heavily like a leaden weight.

Which was probably the most telling sign that she didn't need to get away from him.

She stretched out on her tuffet, raising her arms, her hands balled into fists. She looked back down at the book she'd been reading and rubbed her eyes. It was a history book that focused on the art and culture of Isolo D'Oro. She had thought to look at it with her newfound real-life take on Isolo D'Oro to see if it might enhance it. Mainly, she had just sat there staring at the pages. Imagining the countryside. Being there, standing in the sunshine with Alex. Sitting in the garden with him, basked in moonlight as he tasted her. Touched her.

The door to the library opened and she startled.

Alex was standing there looking dashing, like a hero from a historical novel come to life.

He was wearing a white shirt open at the collar, the sleeves pushed up past his forearms. His hair looked as though he'd been running his fingers through it. He looked... Well, he looked like temptation personified.

"I thought I might find you here, Gabby," he said.

Her stomach did a little flip at his use of her nickname. "Yes, I do like the library."

She took her glasses off and rubbed at the bridge of her nose before putting them back in place.

"You look tired," he said.

"I am. But I couldn't sleep. I don't see how I could with everything that's happening tomorrow. New York. I've never been."

"I feel much the same."

"Why? Are you so anxious to get back to your real life?"

"No," he said, his tone dry. "That isn't the problem. It isn't fantasies about work that have me tossing and turning."

"If it isn't fantasies of work, then—" Her eyes clashed with his, the meaning of his words suddenly sinking in. "Oh."

"It would be better if you were not coming with me, Gabriella," he said, his tone full of warning.

She nodded slowly. "I have no doubt that's true."

"Doing what's right is incredibly tiresome," he said, walking deeper into the room, moving to sit in the chair across from hers. "And yet, it is the only thing that separates us from our parents, is it not?"

She nodded mutely.

"And I have to separate myself from them," he continued, his voice rough.

"You have," she said. "You're nothing like them at all."

"I have a half brother," he said, the words hitting her in a strange way, taking a moment for her to untangle. It seemed like a change of subject, and yet she knew it wasn't. Not really. "I found out about it when I was eleven years old. My father had an affair, as I told you before."

"My parents have had many," she said slowly.

"Affairs were nothing new," he continued as though she hadn't spoken. "But a child... My mother was incensed. He was humiliating her. Bringing shame upon her. Causing the world to believe she might not be desirable."

Gabriella tried to force a smile. "My mother screams a very similar refrain once every few months."

"This was different," Alex said. "I heard the altercation. It was Christmas. Snowing. Outside, the house had white lights strung all over it. As though they were trying to tell the world that we were normal. That we were a happy household. But inside... There were no lights. There was no tree. There was no happiness. And out there... My father's mistress brought her son. He was not much younger than I was. Ten, maybe. She stood out there screaming at my father, their son by her side. Telling him that he had to acknowledge him. My father refused. I...I looked out there and I saw him. And I knew exactly who he was. I told no one. My father drove off in a rage, my mother with him, as they tried to escape the scene. Tried to get away from his mistress. This monster of his own making. That was the night they were in the accident. It was the night they died. And the only people left alive who knew about Nate were his mother, himself and me. I told no one. I kept my half brother a secret."

"Oh, Alex, what a terrible burden."

"What a terrible burden I put on *him*. A child. But I was so angry, Gabby. I blamed him. He was what they were arguing about. And so…I chose comfort over truth. I chose to do what was easy, not what was right. Had I been any sort of man…"

"You weren't," she said, her chest tight. "You were a boy."

He shook his head, lowering it. "Not so much a boy." He looked younger when he said it. She felt like she could see him, as he'd been then. Young and trying so hard to be brave. To uphold the honor of his family in the only way he knew how.

"Yes," she said, her throat aching. "You were."

"He was entitled to that money. To come to the funeral of his father. To be acknowledged. I robbed him of that. Until we needed him. When my grandfather needed a bone marrow transplant I let everyone know about Nate's existence. He was Giovanni's only hope, you see. I…I cannot forgive myself for those things, Gabby. I cannot. They reveal that underneath everything I have tried to fashion for myself I am nothing more than my father's son. A man who uses people. A man who thinks nothing of putting others through hell in order to preserve his own comfort."

"That isn't true, Alex."

He curled his hand into a fist. "Yes, it is. There's a reason I'm telling you this."

"What's the reason?"

"Because I need you to understand. I need you to understand that I'm not a saint. That while I make a habit of practicing restraint, in the end I will only fail. In the end, I will reveal myself to be nothing more than what my blood has dictated I should be."

"We're more than blood, Alex, don't you think?"

"Are we?"

"You said yourself your grandfather took care of you. Your father is his son."

"In which case I have to ask myself if it was my mother. If some people are destined to drag down those who they love. Just another reason to stay away from me."

Her heart thundered, and she felt dizzy. He was so convinced he was toxic. And that was why they couldn't… She wasn't even entirely sure what they *couldn't*. Knew only that he was saying they couldn't, and she knew whatever it was that she wanted to. "But what about what I want?"

"You don't know what you want."

She blinked. "Of course I do. I'm a grown woman, Alessandro. You don't know what I want more than I do."

He got out of the chair, dropping to his knees so that he was down in front of her. He lifted his hand, brushing his thumb over her lower lip. He looked raw. Desperate. And she had to close her eyes, all of her focus going to that slow, sensual touch. "Gabriella, I have seen so much more of the world than you have. Believe me when I tell you that I know what you *should* want. What will keep you safe."

"No," she said, shaking her head.

"It cannot happen," he said, and she wasn't sure if he was telling her or himself. "I cannot kiss you again," he continued. "If I did, I would only sin greater."

She opened her eyes, looked down at him. At the creases on his forehead, the deep grooves that bracketed his face. Those lines made him all the more devastating. Without them, he would be too beautiful. But those lines—the evidence of years lived—gave him texture. Took him from mere beauty to devastating.

She ached. For him. With need for him. "All sins can be forgiven, can't they?"

"Not all, Gabby. My life—my childhood—is a testament to that. Some sins cause damage that is irreparable. That wound so deeply they will never heal. Ask my half brother about that. I would tell you to ask my parents, to ask my mother, but she's dead."

"But, Alex... If we both want each other..."

"You don't even know what it means to want, Gabriella."

Her chest felt tight, her eyes stinging with unshed tears. "That isn't fair, Alex, you don't get to tell me that I don't know what desire is when you're the one who showed it to me. When you're the one who made absolutely certain that I learned what it was."

"I have already hurt you." He shook his head, his tone filled with regret. "I would not like to do it again."

"Then don't." She was on the verge of begging for something she had never imagined wanting with this much ferocity.

"I won't."

"Must you be so honorable? Must you choose this moment to be a man of your word? To be sincere?"

He nodded slowly. "If there is any moment where I must choose it, it is this one."

She slid out of her chair, joining him on the floor. She took his hands in hers, leaning forward, touching her lips slightly to his. "But if you didn't?" she asked, her mouth brushing his as she spoke the words.

He reached around behind her head, sifting his fingers through her hair and drawing her head back slightly, his dark eyes intent on hers. "If I did not, Gabby," he said, his special nickname for her sending shivers along her spine. "If I didn't, then I would lean in and I would kiss you, more deeply than you kissed me just now."

"What else?" she asked, knowing she would burn for this. Past the point of caring.

"I would run my tongue along the line of your top lip before delving inside. I would taste you. So deep and long neither of us would be able to breathe. We wouldn't want to breathe."

She was shaking now, trembling with need. "Alex," she whispered.

"I would pull your T-shirt up over your head, so that I could see you," he said, resting his palm on her stomach, his touch scorching the material of her shirt. "So that I could feel how soft your skin is." He left his hand there, his other still buried deep in her hair. "Then I would remove your bra. Get a good look at those beautiful breasts. They are beautiful. *You* are beautiful. I have said it many times to you now, but I need you to understand how true it is. It is the deepest truth I know, Gabriella. Your beauty. As real as the night sky."

Tears filled her eyes and she made no move to wipe them away.

"I would trace your breasts with my tongue," he continued, "before moving down to kiss your stomach. Then I would strip off your pants, your underwear. For a moment I would just…look at you. I would be afraid to blink for fear that I would miss a moment of that beauty. I would taste you, tease you, touch you, until you were sobbing in my arms."

Gabriella closed her eyes, going still beneath his touch, focusing all of her attention on the pressure of his hand against her stomach, on the erotic words that were flowing from his mouth and over her like heated oil. "What then?" she asked.

"Oh, my darling, I would send you to the moon and back. I would make you scream with pleasure. Then, and only then, I would enter your body, slowly. I would be as careful with you as possible. But I fear it would not be as careful as I ought to be. Because by then…then I would be desperate for you. Beyond thought. It is important that I make you scream before that, because I will not last long once I'm buried deep within you."

She let her lips fall open, her head drawn backward. "Yes," she said, the word a sigh.

"It would be heaven," he said, his voice a hoarse whisper. "To feel you all around me. You would be so tight, so hot and wet. For me. Only for me, Gabby. It would only be for me."

"Of course," she said. "It would only ever be for you, Alex."

She found herself swaying forward, her heart beating so quickly she thought she might faint.

Suddenly, Alex released his hold on her, standing up and putting as much distance between them as possible in one fluid movement. He was breathing hard, and she could see the press of his arousal against the front of his slacks. Could see that what he said was true. That he wanted her with a ferocity that he could not deny. That he would in fact love nothing more than to do everything he had just said.

And she wanted it. So badly that it echoed inside of her. An empty, aching need that only he could ever fill.

"We cannot, Gabby," he said.

"Why?" she asked, the word torture.

"Because I have committed so many grave sins already. I have hurt so many people. Gabriella, I will do nothing but hurt you. And it is the last thing on earth I want to do."

That was why she let him go. That was why she didn't press. Because of the desperation in his voice. Because of how much he wanted to turn away from this. Because of how difficult it was for him. She would not add to his torture. Not after what she knew about him. Not after what he had told her about his parents, about his brother.

So she did nothing but nod slowly. Did nothing but

watch him turn and walk out of the room all the while she sat there, shaking.

She felt cold suddenly. Where before she had only been hot.

She thought back to an earlier conversation they'd had as she sat there on the floor of her library, shivering. She had told him that one was much less likely to get scarred if they stayed in here. She almost laughed. Because she would never forget this. His words, his touch, was branded into her, a scar that would never heal. One that she had acquired—of all places—on the library floor.

It had been her place. The place she had always felt safe. Her refuge.

But it was his now. Irrevocably.

She was afraid it was the same for her.

CHAPTER TWELVE

GABRIELLA AVOIDED HIM for the entire plane ride. He supposed he couldn't blame her. He didn't know what he had been thinking. Confessing those things to her. Saying those words to a virgin.

To a woman that he could never touch. Not any more than he already had.

So, he had allowed her to avoid him. On the plane, then again in the car as she had stared out the window, gazing at the unfamiliar city skyline. And he had watched her reflection in the window, uncaring about the buildings that had become so familiar and mundane to him. New York City failed to enthrall him. What fascinated him was seeing them through her eyes. Wide and glistening as she took in everything around her, her mouth open slightly. Her lips looked so soft. He would give a good portion of his fortune to kiss them again.

He continued to think about her lips as they arrived at his penthouse in Manhattan. Normally, after this much time away from work he would go directly into his home office and set about catching up. But tonight… Tonight it simply didn't appeal.

The first thing he did when they arrived was set the painting up in the living room, taking a step back and looking at it for the first time since they had taken it from Isolo D'Oro.

"It's beautiful," Gabriella said, looking around the space, then at the painting. "All of this. I can't quite believe that I'm here."

"Yes," he said in agreement. But he didn't mean the view or his penthouse were beautiful. He meant her. Always her.

So then he looked at the painting to avoid looking at her. Close study of Gabriella's features could only lead to ruin. He had been so taken with the woman in the painting upon first viewing that he hadn't noticed much of the surrounding objects. For the first time he noticed that everything on the table of the vanity was painted in loving detail. That it was all very purposeful. The woman was wearing a necklace, the reflection of which could barely be seen in the mirror. Emeralds, and white diamonds. On her finger, almost entirely concealed by the tumbling locks of her dark hair, he could just make out the hint of a ring. There was a box, ornate and beautiful, certain to contain more jewelry. A tiara, set next to a beautiful bracelet. His breath caught, and he took a step closer. There was a book set on the vanity, as well.

That meant…

He moved closer still, scanning the surface of the table. Yes. There they were. A small pair of earrings.

"The Lost Mistresses," he said.

"What?" Gabriella asked.

"This is all of them. The artifacts my grandfather sent us after. They are all in this painting. The painting is the last one."

He turned to look at Gabriella. She was staring at him, her dark eyes wide. "What does that mean?"

"It means that I don't think you're being fanciful when you thought there might be a deeper link between our grandparents."

"But the painting… It was by someone called Bartolo."

"I know. But there is something. At one time your grandmother was in possession of every one of these objects. They were the dearest things to my grandfather's heart at another time."

"Alex…"

At that moment, Alex's phone rang. It was his half brother, Nate. Things were better between the two of them in recent years, but they had never been close. It surprised him that the other man would call him for anything.

"I have to get this."

Gabriella watched Alex as he paced out of the room, his phone pressed to his ear. It was strange to be here. In his house with him. Not domestic—because she doubted anything with Alex could ever feel domestic—but intimate. Of course, he hadn't stayed in the room with her to take his phone call. A stark reminder that they didn't really share much about their lives.

She looked back at the painting, looking closely this time at the objects in it. Alex's grandfather was Giovanni Di Sione. As far as she knew he had no connection to the royal family. No connection to Isolo D'Oro. If not for this painting… On its own it was coincidental. Combined with these other objects…

Alex came back out of the room he had just gone into, his dark jacket on, his expression purposeful. "I have to go out. I will be back as soon as possible. You can help yourself to any of the food in the fridge. Or any of the alcohol."

"You don't have a library. What am I supposed to do?" She was only half teasing.

"You'll have to watch a movie, *cara mia*."

She did her best to keep busy while Alex was gone. But one hour turned into two, which turned into three. Then four. Before she knew it she was dozing on the couch, feeling rather sulky, and a little bit concerned. She should have asked him for his mobile number. So she could at least make sure he wasn't lying dead in an alley somewhere.

And once that thought was in her mind, she couldn't shake it.

Surely Alex was dead in an alley. Or if not dead, perilously close to bleeding out onto the cracked concrete sidewalk.

The idea made her stomach hurt. It was also ridiculous. Still, now that it had taken root, there it was.

She walked across the expansive living area and opened one of the bedroom doors to reveal a large bed with a black bedspread. She frowned. Not quite sure which room belonged to Alex. She opened the door next to it and saw another bed that looked almost exactly the same.

She let out an exasperated sigh and walked deeper into that room, letting her fingertips trail over the lush bedding. She was tired. She hadn't unpacked any of her things since she wasn't sure which room she would be staying in. She had changed into her sweats to get a bit more comfortable but she wasn't going to go hunting for her pajamas.

She sat on the edge of the bed, bouncing slightly on the mattress before lying back. She looked over at the clock, the glowing blue numbers showing that it was well after midnight.

She suddenly had a thought that was even more disturbing than the idea of Alex dying in an alley. Maybe he was out with a woman. Why else would he stay out all night? If the issue wasn't that he couldn't make it home, then he wasn't here because he didn't *want* to be home.

The only reason she could think that a man would want to stay out all night was if he was with a woman.

He might be doing the things with her that he wouldn't do with Gabriella. Acting out those words he'd said to her, so deeply erotic. As if he'd woven a fantasy together that was spun with a desire called up from the very depths of her soul. Desire not even she had realized she possessed.

She hated whoever the other woman was. A woman who would—even for a night—capture *all* of Alex's attention. Not just a piece of him.

Not just his smile, or the glint in his eye. Not just his rough, perfect voice, or promises he could never keep. But his body. No barriers between them.

She would touch him everywhere, this mystery woman. Her hands beneath his clothes, learning secrets about him Gabriella would never, ever know.

She burned. She didn't know that jealousy would burn from the inside out. Scalding her. Making her feel raw and restless and angry. She had never been jealous before.

There had never been a man before.

She had been too busy burying herself in dusty books. Wrapping herself in a blanket of safety, insulated by the shelves of her library. By the family estate.

Protecting herself from more rejection.

What she'd said to him had been true. Her own parents didn't truly want her. Didn't really choose her. It was difficult to believe that anyone else would. She was invisible. That was the best case scenario. The worst was that she was in the way.

She swallowed hard, closing her eyes tight and curling her knees up to her chest.

The next thing she knew, she heard heavy footsteps coming into the room. Her eyes snapped open, locking onto the clock. It was after three now.

She was on her back, moving into a sitting position. "Alex?" she asked, her heart thundering heavily.

"Gabriella?" Her name sounded strange on his lips. As though he were convinced she was some sort of apparition.

"Yes. Is this your room? I should have investigated

further, but I…" *Didn't want to.* She couldn't very well finish that sentence.

Couldn't tell him that a part of her had been hoping this was his room. That she would encounter him later.

Shortsighted. As well as a little bit creepy. Shortsighted mainly because she was still wearing her sweats, which was hardly the official uniform of seduction.

"You were asleep," he said.

"Yes. I fell asleep waiting for you to come back. I thought maybe you were dead." Her other concern hit her, cold and hard. Obviously he wasn't dead, but he could very well still have been having sex. "Were you with a woman?"

He let out a heavy sigh and sat down on the edge of the bed. "No. Would it have bothered you if I was?"

"That's a stupid question. Of course it would have." She saw no point in playing coy. She was sleepy, and cranky, and a little bit gritty behind the eyelids. She was in no state to play coy.

He shifted his position, lying down beside her, and her breath caught. There was still a healthy expanse of mattress between them, but still. "It was my brother. My half brother, Nate. I told you about Nate."

"Yes, you did."

"He found the ring. It has an inscription on it. *B.A.*"

"Bartolo," she said.

"Probably. They are the same initials on the painting, Gabriella. They were his. *She* was his, just like your grandmother said. But it's more than that. I know that my grandfather had to start over when he came to America. And I wonder just how completely the new beginning was."

"You think he was my grandmother's lover." His suspicions mirrored her own. It made sense. There just didn't seem to be another way someone could possess all of the same objects that appeared in the painting. More than that, it was her grandmother's reaction to everything. The fact that she had seemed to want Giovanni to have the painting. "She knows," Gabriella said. "She figured it out before we did."

She thought back to the way that her grandmother had looked at Alex when he'd first come into the room at the estate in Aceena. "I bet you look like him," she said. She couldn't see him now; she was staring through the darkness, looking in his direction, barely able to make out his silhouette against the dark bedspread. "I mean, like he did."

"I guess that's why she let me take it in the end."

"They loved each other. They couldn't be together because she had to marry royalty. My grandfather." Suddenly, her throat felt tight, painful. "The artist... Bartolo... he did love her very much. I know. You can see it. It must've killed him to part with those things."

"Not quite. He's still very much alive. For now. It wounded him to part with them. I wonder if he thinks seeing them will return some of his strengths."

"It isn't the objects he needs," she said, her voice wistful.

"You are right." He reached across the distance between them, drawing his fingertips slowly across her cheek. She closed her eyes, tried to fight the tears that were welling in them.

"It is a tragedy, Alex. To think of that. Just think of how much they loved each other all those years..."

She could see her life suddenly, stretching before her. Bleak and lonely. She realized that she could never marry a man who didn't incite fantasy in her. Down to her very core. That she couldn't possibly ever marry a man who understood art the way she did, or appreciated books, or had a library. That she couldn't marry a man who was closer to her age and experience or didn't think of her as an owl. Because that man wouldn't be Alex.

It was Alex for her. Now and always. Forever.

She realized now that maybe she had not been protecting herself so much as waiting for this. For him. For the kind of desire that reached down deep and took over your soul. For the kind of desire that went well beyond common sense. The kind that didn't care if heartbreak lay down the road. Even if it was a short distance away.

She thought of the way her grandmother had spoken of Giovanni—because she was certain that Giovanni and Bartolo were one and the same—of the fact that no matter the heartbreak she could never regret their time together, and it made her tremble. She wasn't certain if she was that strong. To grab hold of an experience while giving no thought to the pain that the consequences might cause.

It was the kind of thing she had been avoiding all of her life. Being like her parents.

But they don't do anything because of love. It's because of selfishness.

Her chest felt like it had cracked open. Of course. That was the difference. Action was always empty, dry, when there was no love. There had been a time when her mother had kissed her good-night before going off to a party, but the gesture had been empty. And the proof was in the fact that now that Gabriella was an adult neither of her parents ever spoke to her. Those goodnight kisses could not be a happy memory, not now that she could see them so clearly for what they were. The proper motions that her parents went through in order to salve what little conscience they had.

This…this had nothing to do with going through the motions. Had nothing to do with doing the right thing. It was just…need.

Alex was a man so far removed from the world. Everything in it seemed to move around him. And he seemed to exist in it untouched.

She wanted to touch him. Not just his skin, but beneath it. She wanted to reach him down deep where his heart beat. Wanted to heat him from the inside out, warm his blood, his soul.

Mostly, she just wanted everything he had promised her back in the library. When they parted, the wound would linger. No matter what happened now. If he was going to leave a scar, she wanted it to be such a scar. So deep, so affecting, it would never heal.

She inched toward him, reaching out and placing her hand over his cheek, mirroring his action.

"Gabriella," he said, his voice a growl, warning.

She didn't listen to it.

She leaned forward, claiming his mouth with hers, kissing him as though she had a right to do it. As though she knew how.

She knew that he would recognize her limited technique, because she had learned it from him. It was all she knew. So when she traced the seam of his lips with her tongue, she was keenly aware of the fact that she was plagiarizing his earlier kiss. But if he was aware of it, he didn't show it. He was still beneath her touch, completely motionless. But he hadn't pushed her away.

They parted, her hand still resting on his cheek. She could hear ragged breathing filling the space between them, but couldn't tell if it was his or hers. Both.

"Gabriella," he said again, "you have no idea what you're asking for. No idea what you're doing."

She pressed her forehead to his, the tips of their noses touching. "I want to make love. I know what that is, Alex. Sex. I've never wanted it before. Not in a specific sense. But I do now."

"I can't offer you anything. I won't make you any promises, because I will only break them."

"Maybe."

"Certainly."

"Well, tomorrow the sky could fall, or I could get hit by a bus—"

"It won't, and you won't."

"You don't know that. We don't know anything beyond right now. I saw my grandmother's face. I know there was a lot that she regretted. But I don't think she ever regretted being with Bartolo." She knew that these words were tantamount to admitting that she felt more for him than simple attraction, but she couldn't bring herself to care.

"I am the worst of sinners. I condemned my half brother to a life lived outside of the family. It was me who stood in his way. Made him feel like he could never be close to us. He told me that tonight. It is on me, Gabriella."

"Alex—"

"I carry the blood of my father. Weak selfishness that I've worked a very long time to overcome. So believe me when I tell you I will regret nothing of what happened here tonight. My nobility is nothing more than a construct. There is no conviction behind it. But you, Gabriella, you, I fear will regret this."

"Maybe. Tomorrow. But not now. And the only thing we have for sure is now."

A feral sound rumbled low in his chest and he shifted positions so that he was over her, his arms braced on either side of her shoulders.

She locked her leg over the back of his calf, an action designed to hold him prisoner even though she knew it wouldn't be truly effective. Still, she wanted him to know that she wanted him here. Desperately.

"Alex," she said, his name a prayer on her lips. She bracketed his face with her hands, looking at him, trying to see what he was thinking, even through the darkness. "Don't you know how much I want you?"

He tensed, pulling away from her slightly. Her heart hammered hard in her chest, clawing at her like a small beast.

"Alex," she said his name again, ready to beg him if she needed to.

He flicked on the light. The way it illuminated his face cast the hollows of his cheekbones into darkness, adding a tortured quality to his features.

"If I'm going to sin, then I'm going to do it with my eyes open," he said. "If I'm going to have you, then I'm going to look at you while I do it."

She breathed a sigh of relief, sliding her hands around to the back of his neck, holding him to her. "I'm glad."

"You won't be. Gabriella, I am too old for you, too jaded, too tired. I can offer you nothing. It's a strange thing to realize that. I am a billionaire. I have more money than I could ever spend in a lifetime. I have all of these things. And for a great many years that has been good enough. I have had whoever I wanted in my life when I wanted them. I have had ultimate control over my own reputation. Wielding it like a sword when I needed to. But none of that helps me here. None of that helps with you. It is…insufficient, and I am a man who is not used to falling short."

"You have yourself. That's all I have to offer. That has to be enough."

"Tonight it will be."

Alex lowered his head, kissing her deeper, harder, than he had before. A restless groove in the pit of her stomach spread through her entire body. Like a creeping vine that took over everything in its path. Winding itself around her limbs, around her throat, making it impossible for her to breathe. Binding her to Alex in a way that was so intense, so permanent, she knew that parting from him would be so much more painful than she'd imagined it would be.

But she wouldn't stop. Even knowing that, she wouldn't stop.

This time, he did not keep his hands still. He did not simply press his palm to her stomach. He let himself explore her body, his fingertips skimming her breasts before he took one firmly in hand, sliding his thumb over one hardened nipple. She gasped, arching against him, her entire body alive with sensation.

"This is a gift I don't deserve," he said, his tone fractured and reverent.

She couldn't speak, but if she could, she would have told him that she was the one receiving a gift. So many lonely, isolated years. So much hollowness inside of her. She had hidden herself away to avoid being hurt again. To avoid more rejection. The neglect of her parents had been enough. And when she went out, she put on a mask. She didn't let anyone see both parts of herself. Princess Gabriella never messed with Gabriella as she was day to day. She didn't give anyone the chance to reject who she really was. But Alex had it all. Held it all in the palm of his hand as surely as he held her body. And he was here. He was touching her. Pouring out all of this attention, all of this care, onto her.

It was so beautiful she could barely breathe.

He pushed her shirt up over her head, baring her breasts to him. She had taken her bra off when she had put her sweats on, and now she was relieved. One less barrier between the two of them. She didn't want anything standing between them. Didn't want any walls up whatsoever. She wanted to give him everything—her body, her soul—and no matter how foolish she knew it was, she couldn't stop that desire that roared through her like an untamed animal.

It would end in heartbreak. It would end in destruction.

But when she was old, she would look back and she would have this moment. She would have Alex. And she knew without a doubt that giving in to pure, true love was something she would never regret.

She had no idea how this moment had happened. How this woman in this bed, in this man's arms, was the same woman she had been only a week ago.

She was changed. She was new. Already, he had changed the world for her. Lifted the veil so that she could see the colors more clearly, feel pleasure more keenly, feel desire sharp like a knife's blade sliding over her skin.

It was painful, incandescent and magical all at once.

He made quick work of her sweatpants and underwear, leaving her completely bare to him, his dark gaze filled with hunger, a desire that couldn't be denied, as he took in the sight of her body.

"Gabby," he said, her name a whispered prayer. "I never thought I appreciated art. But this... You. You are every bit of beauty a painter has ever tried to capture onto canvas. The fields, the mountains, all of the smooth female skin that has ever been painted in an attempt to show some of the glory that is here on this earth. They fall short. It all falls short of you."

Her heart felt so full she thought it might burst. How was this real? How was this man saying these things to her?

It was inconceivable that she might be enough for this man.

That he was afraid that he might not be enough for her. That he was apologizing for the lack of what he had to give.

It didn't make sense. It didn't make sense at all.

But she reveled in it. Accepted it. Took it as her due for so many years of feeling like she was less than.

"I need to see you," she said, her voice a hoarse whisper she barely recognized.

"Not yet," he said. "Not yet."

He lowered his head, kissing her neck, kissing a trail along her collarbone, and down to the swell of her breasts. Then he shifted, taking her nipple into his mouth, sucking it in deep before tracing it with the tip of his tongue. The pleasure that sparked along her veins was shocking, white-hot and almost terrifying in its intensity. There was so much more to making love than a simple caress, and still, this had nearly burned her to the ground. How would she survive at all?

She wouldn't. Not the same.

Nothing passed through the fire and came out the same. But at this point, she didn't want to. She wanted to be changed. By him. Irrevocably, eternally.

He continued his exploration, peppering kisses over her stomach, encircling her belly button with the soft stroke of his tongue before traveling downward. "You see, *cara mia*, were I to take my clothes off, I would not be able to resist sinking inside of you. And you deserve more than that. You deserve for me to take my time. As I told you in the library, once I'm very deep within you I will not be able to hold myself back. And so, your pleasure must come first. Now."

He gripped her hips, drawing her toward his mouth, her thighs spread wide as he pressed his lips to the center of her need. A short, shocked scream escaped her mouth as he lavished attention on that sensitive bundle of nerves with his tongue, as he tasted her, slowly, deeply. He shifted again, pressing his finger against the entrance of her body as he continued to lavish pleasure on her with his mouth. The invasion was foreign, but it felt good.

He added a second finger, stretching her slightly this time, the vague painful sensation drawing her out of her reverie, but only for a moment.

Before long she grew accustomed to that, pleasure

mounting inside of her again as he established a steady rhythm, working his hands and tongue in time with each other. She felt need, tension, gathering in the pit of her stomach like a ball of electricity, scattering outward, sending shocks along her system as it continued to build an intensity. So hot, so bright, she felt like she might burst with it.

And it did burst. Rolling over her in waves unending, unfathomable in its depth. She gripped the bed covers, trying to use something to root her to the earth, anything. Because without it, she feared that she would lose hold of herself entirely.

He rose up above her, kissing her deeply, her own desire a musky flavor on his tongue. "Are you all right?" he asked, his chest rising and falling with the effort it took for him to breathe.

"Yes. More than all right. I'm... Alex, I didn't know it was like this."

"What did you think it would be?" His words slurred as though he were drunk.

"I didn't know. Because I didn't know it would be you."

"Does it matter *so* much that it's me?" She sensed a rawness behind that question, a vulnerability.

"That's the only thing that matters."

He growled, kissing her again as she grabbed hold of the edge of his button-up shirt, undoing the buttons as quickly as possible. She spread her hands over that broad expanse of chest. His hard muscles...that perfect sprinkling of chest hair that reminded her just how much of a man he was. How different they were. It was heaven to touch him like this. To finally have the promise of that glorious body fulfilled, in her hands. She pushed the shirt from his shoulders and threw it over the side of the bed, running her hands down his back, exploring the intricate musculature there. She parted her thighs, arching against him, feeling the evidence of his arousal against where she was wet and aching for him already. She should be satisfied, after what he had just done for her. She found she was far from it.

"I need you. How can I need you this badly after all of that?" she asked, her voice trembling.

"I would tell you that's sex, *cara*. I would tell you that's desire. But it is not sex or desire in any way that I know it. I do not shake for want of being inside of a woman. You make me shake. You make me feel as though I won't be able to breathe until I have you. Until I'm joined to you. What witchcraft is that, Gabriella? You must tell me."

"How can I? I'm just a virgin. You are supposed to be wise. You're supposed to be the one teaching me."

"How can I? When I feel you have so much to teach me." He kissed her gently as his hands moved to his belt. She could hear him undoing the buckle slowly and a shiver of anticipation ran through her. She helped him push his pants and underwear down his narrow hips and he sent them over the side of the bed to join the rest of their clothes. She could feel him, feel his hot hard length, pressed against her heat.

"I want to see you," she said, her voice husky, unrecognizable to her own ears. "I've never seen a naked man before."

He straightened, a dull slash of red coloring his cheekbones. "So many honors I don't deserve, Princess."

He sounded tortured, and at any other time she might have felt sorry for him, or wondered why. But not now. How could she feel sorry for him when she was too busy exulting in this triumph for herself?

He was perfect. Masculine beauty depicted in sculpture could never have prepared her for Alex.

Marble was cold, lifeless. It might show the shape of a man, but it didn't show the vitality. His life, his strength.

It was everything and more. His broad shoulders, perfectly defined chest and washboard stomach, bisected by a line of hair that ran down to his very evident desire was enough to take a breath away.

He was so very...large. Thick. Part of her was made nervous by that, the other part marveled at the glory that was in front of her. The glory that would be hers.

"You're right," she said, her words hushed.

"About what?"

"You are in possession of very rampant masculinity."

He laughed, the sound tortured. "I only hope that it isn't too rampant for you."

"It's just perfect for me. How can it be anything else?"

He dropped forward on his knees, between her thighs, his hands on her shoulders. She looked up at him, her heart pounding heavily.

"You're beautiful," she said.

"And you are more than I deserve," he said, kissing her, wrapping his arm around her waist and drawing her body hard up against his as he pressed the head of his arousal against the entrance to her body.

She winced slightly, bracing herself for his invasion. It hurt. But she wanted it. There was no question. Even as he pressed forward, and she stretched around him, trembling as he joined their bodies together, she didn't want anything else but this. It was desire so perfectly and beautifully realized, the fulfillment of fantasy. Not because it brought pleasure. But because she was joined to him. Because they were one. Even though it hurt.

And when he thrust deep within, completing their joining, there was no pleasure to be found at all. Not in the physical sense.

But her soul felt alive. Complete. For the first time.

And as the pain slowly began to fade and the pleasure

began to build again, she felt so full with it that she could scarcely breathe.

Desire was a wild, needy thing inside of her. She wanted it to be satisfied. Needed it to be satisfied. And yet at the same time she wanted this to go on forever. Wanted to prolong the moment where she would reach her peak. Because once that happened it was the end. Of this perfect moment where they were joined. Connected. Where they were one with each other. The desire to cling to him, to cling to this, was doing battle with the desire to find completion. Ferocious, intense. She didn't know which one would win. Didn't know which one she wanted to win.

"Gabby," he said her name. Just her name.

Gabby would always belong to him. Only to him. The very idea of someone else saying it made her ill.

His teeth scraped the edge of her collarbone, the small slice of pain mingling with the pleasure, drawing her back to earth, making her feel so acutely aware of everything. So perfectly in tune with her body, and his.

She could feel his building pleasure along with hers. Could feel how close to the edge he was as his muscles tensed, as his control frayed.

She opened her eyes, determined to watch his face. Determined to watch this man who was everything she was not. Hardened, masculine beauty. Experienced. World-weary. She would watch him as he felt the same thing she did. As they experienced this storm of pleasure on the same level. It reduced them, this desperation, reduced them down to their souls. To ravenous, needy things that had nothing beyond this moment, this common need.

It was how Princess Gabriella D'Oro, recent virgin and definite bookworm, met with Alessandro Di Sione, rumored fearsome monster and a man who claimed to have a hardened heart. How they not only met, but understood each other. Spoke in perfect words that each other alone could understand. How had she ever thought they were different? How had she ever looked at him and seen a gulf they couldn't bridge? They had. She was closer to him now, in this moment, than she had ever been to another person in her life.

It was powerful, fearsome, awe-inspiring. These needs that only the other could meet. That only the other could inspire. A hunger only he could arouse and satisfy.

"Alex," she said, arching against him, the source of her pleasure meeting his heart and body as he thrust deep within her. A shower of sparks rained over her, pleasure breaking over her like an electrical storm, flashes of light blinding brilliance behind her eyes. She closed them, but only for a moment. Then she forced them open again, watched his face as he, too, gave himself over to this thing between them. She watched as that face, that face that could have been carved from granite, softened, the lines on his forehead shifting, a look of pure pain and desperation contorting his features as he growled his release, his entire body trembling as he spilled himself deep inside of her. She held him, as pleasure continued to rack his frame, as aftershocks kept moving through her in an endless wave.

They were connected in this. This pleasure. This moment.

And when it was over they simply lay there, entwined in each other. Breathing together.

She knew that Alex would feel regret later. Because no matter what he said he wasn't a monster. She had to wonder why he was so desperate to convince not only others, but himself, of the fact that he was.

She knew it came down to his fear that he would become like his father. She knew enough about him to understand that. But she also knew him well enough to understand it would never be him.

He had made some mistakes in his life with his family, but he had been a young man. Barely more than a boy. She had made far fewer mistakes. If only because she interacted with less people. Life wasn't as difficult when you hid from it.

He looked at himself and saw nothing but a potential monster and he was dedicated to forcing others to see the same.

She knew better.

He was so dry. So funny and brilliant. He cared. Very deeply. For her, for everyone else around him. He pretended he didn't. The way he looked after his grandfather, the pain that laced his voice when he spoke of his half brother and his past treatment of him, the way he had taken such great care with her, told an entirely different story than the narrative Alex had spent so many years carefully constructing.

He had only given when she had pushed. And both passed the point of resistance. He had never pressured her for anything, and she knew without a doubt that he never would have.

He was a hero in her eyes and yet he insisted on casting himself as the villain.

She wished, more than anything, that he could see himself through her eyes. That he could see himself clearly. She would make it her mission to change his thoughts on himself. She would.

No, it wouldn't change in a moment. No matter how much she might want to. She was going to have to show him, over time. Show him the man he really was. But in order to do that she would have to stay with him. Leave Aceena. Convince him to attempt to make some kind of relationship with her. He had arrangements with women, he had said as much. Why couldn't he have one with her?

Eventually…he would have to see that they were good

together. Her thoughts were spinning, her entire body humming. There was so much going on in her brain. But she had never been good at letting things rest. She was always trying to solve the problem. Always trying to get down to the truth. To figure out the source of the problem so that she could stamp it out.

Unfortunately, there was no history book she could look at to conduct a simple study on Alex.

She would have to study him in person. Not a hardship, really.

"You're very quiet," he said.

"Thinking," she said honestly.

"About?"

She bit her lip. She could hardly tell him that she was plotting ways to convince him to love not only her, but himself.

"You're very good in bed," she said, rather than telling him the exact thoughts that were on her mind. That was what her body was thinking about, anyway. "Granted, I have no one else to compare to, but I can't imagine there are very many men who exceed your skill."

"It isn't about skill, Gabby." He brushed her hair out of her face, his body still entwined with hers. "This is chemistry."

A burst of warmth fired up in her heart, then fizzled out just as quickly. It was more than that. For her, it was so much more than that.

She would show him. She would find a way. After a lifetime spent hiding away she knew one thing for certain. After standing in the light with Alex, she would never retreat back into the shadows.

CHAPTER THIRTEEN

ALEX HAD CALLED himself ten kinds of villain since that first night he had taken Gabriella to bed. Of course, it had not stopped him from taking her to bed every night since. She was everything he had fantasized she might be. Beautiful, soft. And her enjoyment of study had come into play in some erotic and interesting ways he had not imagined. She was very thorough.

She had explored his body as though he were an ancient text she was attempting to pull meaning from.

No one had looked that deeply into him and his secrets in…ever. He was stone people built legend around. But no one ever looked beneath to see the man. And he'd kept it that way. For a reason. Several reasons.

He found it hard to keep Gabby at that same distance. Found it hard to even want to keep her at a distance.

She was soft and beautiful, and more generous than she should be. And he spent late nights not only exploring her body, but lying next to her, skimming his hands over her bare curves while she read passages from favorite books to him, and did her very best to educate him about art and other things he didn't care about in the least.

But he liked hearing the words on her lips. Enjoyed the way they poured over him like warm honey, soothing him in a soul-deep way he hadn't imagined possible. Mostly because it was easy to imagine he didn't have a soul.

Because a man who had kept his own half brother a secret, who shared the blood of the most selfish, pleasure-seeking bastard on earth, could hardly have regular human emotions. Could hardly feel softness, tenderness, for a beautiful woman he had nothing in common with.

Could hardly be soothed to a soul he didn't have.

But with Gabby things felt different. Possible. Ridiculous, since he was a billionaire and *everything* was possible. He could have small mammals on jet packs delivered by noon if he wanted. One princess shouldn't make anything feel more possible.

Still, it was the word that came to mind, whether it made sense or not. Well, there were other words, but none of them were appropriate.

He hadn't ever cared about anything like that before, but with her he did. He couldn't afford to care, and he needed to get back to work. But until he dealt with his grandfather, the painting and his family, he couldn't.

Fortunately, they were meeting today. Gabriella would come with him; she would be part of passing the painting to his grandfather, as her grandmother had asked. And then she would go home.

The thought shouldn't make it feel like a knife's blade had been slipped beneath his skin and twisted.

"Hi, Alex," she said, coming out of his bedroom right then, dressed in nothing but a T-shirt. His T-shirt. And what would have been cliché on another woman was new on her. As though he'd never before seen it. As though no woman had ever slipped her lover's T-shirt on over her luscious curves after an evening of passion.

Gabby was an original no matter what she did. Perhaps because she was his, and only his. Because no other man had touched her, no other man had kissed her. He'd never been with a virgin before. Maybe he was just archaic enough for it to matter.

He hadn't thought he was. But then, he hadn't thought he had a soul, either.

"Good morning, Gabriella," he said, lifting his coffee mug to his lips.

"So, we meet with your family today?" she asked, her dark eyes liquid, hopeful for some reason. Perhaps she was ready to be rid of him. Ready to go back to Aceena.

But last night she had not sounded like a woman ready to be rid of him.

"Yes. Soon. You'll have to get dressed in something other than that."

She smiled, and it was a little bit wicked. On that innocent mouth that he had trained to do such sensual things, it was another Gabby original. "You mean I can't wear this to go and meet your family?"

The way she said those words. Meeting his family. They did something to him. Grabbed hold of something down deep inside of him and twisted hard. He was torn between an intense longing and a fierce need to reject the desire.

He cleared his throat. "It would probably be best if you are wearing pants of some kind when I introduce you to my grandfather."

"Because I would shock him?" She seemed rather pleased by the thought.

"Because he would steal you away from me."

"No one could do that, Alex," she said, crossing the distance between them and kissing him on the cheek. "But I will get dressed."

She turned and walked back out of the room and he was left wondering what the hell had just happened here. What was happening in his life? Gabriella seemed to be happening. And far from being the harmless little bookworm she had seemed to be when he first met her at the door of the estate in Aceena, it appeared now that she was a rather intense bespectacled whirlwind.

Today all of the Lost Mistresses would be reunited again, would be with his grandfather. He had helped make his grandfather's last wish come true. He would focus on that. What happened beyond today? Well, what happened beyond today would be what was necessary. Gabriella returning home was necessary. Gabriella getting as far away from him as possible before he did even more damage was necessary.

Damage was all he would do. It was all he was capable of. She would only need to ask Nate to know that was true. Would only need to ask every other woman who had ever passed through his life. Every one of his siblings he had been distant with, emotionally unavailable to.

The idea of Gabriella returning home should fill him with nothing more than a sense of completion. He could get back to his real life. Get back to the running of his company, could forget treasure hunts for lost paintings and art lessons and owlish eyes.

Instead, he felt as though his chest was full of lead.

But he had spent the past thirty-six years ignoring his feelings. He saw no reason to start engaging with them now.

He didn't often make his way to the Di Sione family estate. As far as he was concerned it held nothing but ghosts from his past. Too many memories of what it was like to be a lonely little boy who just lost his parents. An angry, fearful eleven-year-old who had hidden the existence of a half brother to protect a man who didn't deserve protecting.

He shook off the thought as he walked through the grand entry, determined to shed every last one of his memories and feelings like mud on his boots with each step he took.

He could hear Gabriella following behind him, her footsteps timid on the marble as she did so. He was carrying the painting, making his way into the family sitting room, scarcely feeling prepared to face not only his grandfather, but his assorted siblings.

When he walked in, every eye in the room landed on him, the painting he was carrying and the woman who was trailing behind him. He couldn't remember the last time they'd all stood in one room.

Hell, Dario and Dante were standing beside each other. The identical Di Siones finally speaking again after years of discord.

Everyone gathered here in this room, united in this mission for Giovanni. This would have been impossible before. Before the quest Alex had been so quick to mock.

Nate, who he had always had the most challenging relationship with, was here, too, with his pregnant lover. And when Alex looked at him…he didn't feel the weight of his failure, of his guilt. Not anymore.

Now he wondered. Wondered if it had ever truly been about these artifacts, or if they had been searching for a different kind of treasure all along.

"What's the matter with all of you?" he asked, his tone sardonic. "Have you never seen a painting before? Or a woman?"

Giovanni stayed seated, his dark eyes trained on Gabriella. And Alex knew that his grandfather was seeing the same spark of resemblance in Gabby as Lucia had seen in him.

"It has been a very long time since I have seen such a painting," his grandfather said slowly. "Or," he continued, looking at Gabby, "such a woman."

Gabriella looked up at him, her eyes searching. All of this was confirming what they both already suspected, but Alex was eager to hear the story from his grandfather's own lips. "There is not only a woman in this painting,"

Alex said. "The mistresses are here, as well." He turned, standing the painting up on the mantel.

His siblings were no longer looking at him, but at the painting.

"I sense there is a story here, *Nonno*," Alex said, his voice hushed. "And I can't imagine you sent all of us on a worldwide scavenger hunt only to keep the truth hidden from us forever."

Giovanni rubbed his chin, his expression thoughtful. "You are right there, Alessandro. I had no intention of keeping you in the dark forever. Nearly a century is long enough for a man like me, to live, to hold on to his secrets."

"Well, I expect you to live a few more years," Alex said, knowing that such a thing was highly unlikely, but hoping to speak it into existence, anyway.

"From your lips to God's ears," Giovanni said. "But in the event the Man upstairs is busy, too busy to hear such a pronouncement, I suppose I should speak my piece now. You may have begun to suspect that Giovanni Di Sione is not my given name. I was born Bartolo Agosti."

"The letters *BALDO* on the jewelry…" Dario said.

Giovanni smiled.

"The inscription on the pieces I gave to Lucia… Bartolo Agosti, Lucia D'Oro. When I came to America I reinvented more than simply my fortune. I did not just recreate my wealth, I recreated my legend. I was born on Isolo D'Oro. The son of a wealthy family. My brother and I often played with a little girl in the gardens of the palace. It was a simple time on the island. The royal family was in no danger and they moved about freely, mixing with those who were beneath them, playing in the sunshine. I was one such child who was far beneath the princess, though I was titled. I still wasn't a prince—never destined to be a king.

"My friendship with that little girl became much more. As we grew, so did our feelings. But sadly for Lucia and myself, while spending a few amusing hours in the garden together was acceptable, it would not make for an acceptable marriage. I knew that things between the two of us had to come to an end. I knew that she had to take up the mantle of her destiny, not take up a life with a man such as myself. But before we parted, I wanted to paint her. I wanted to paint her with the gifts that I had given to her—tokens of our affection. I wanted to show her that no matter what I said, no matter how things ended, I wanted her to be able to look at this painting and see how I loved her.

"But in the end, when I told her we could not be, when I told her she had to marry the man her parents had selected for her, she was angry. She gave everything back. All of the gifts. Including the painting. I kept them, the only pieces of my Lucia that I retained. I kept them until I was forced to part with them. Part with them or starve. But the painting…I sent it back to her. I never knew what she did with it. I never heard from her. Never found out if her husband intercepted it, if her family kept it from her. But I wanted her to look at it again. With distance between us, with years between that heartbreak, I wanted her to look at it and understand that what I did was not because I cared so little for her. But because I cared so very much."

He turned his focus to Gabriella.

"Tell me, my dear. Did your grandmother have the painting?"

Gabriella's expression was so soft, so caring, her dark eyes nearly liquid. "She did. When the family was banished from Isolo D'Oro she had to leave it. But she hid it. She held on to it. She knew just where it was, and when she saw it…"

"She saw it again?"

"Yes. Before we came here to New York. We returned to Aceena and showed it to her. It was her one request. She wanted you to have it back, but she wanted to see it first. She cares, Bartolo," Gabriella said, using Alex's grandfather's real name, a name he had doubtless not heard for years. "She cares so very much."

"And that, right there, is a gift that supersedes all of this."

"That's nice, Grandfather. So you send us on a field trip around the world to find your trinkets and all you needed was emotional reassurance the whole time," Dario said, his tone dry. "If I had known that, I might have simply purchased you a nice card."

"God knows you needed a diversion, Dario. I also reunited you with the mother of your child and the love of your life." His grandfather snorted. "You could perhaps say thank you."

"I could." But he didn't.

He did, however, step back and take hold of Anais's hand, stroking his thumb over her knuckles.

That was, for Dario, as much of a sincere gesture as would likely be demonstrated.

"It's strange," Giovanni said, "but I expected a greater sense of completion. Upon seeing everything together I thought perhaps I would feel a sense of resolution. But they are simply things."

"Perhaps you were waiting for a person. Not an object."

Everyone turned toward the sound of the thin, elderly voice coming from the doorway of the sitting area. It was Gabriella's grandmother, Lucia. The older woman was slightly stooped, but still, her bearing was regal. She was dressed in a deep purple that complemented her olive skin and dark eyes. And though her hair was white, though her skin was aged, it was undeniable that she was the woman in the picture. Not so much because of the resemblance she bore, but because the love that shone from Giovanni's eyes matched the passion in the artist's brushstrokes.

Giovanni stood, the move slow, labored. It was clear that he stood on unsteady legs, but in spite of the difficulty, he began to cross the room, closing the distance between himself and his long-lost love.

"I have a feeling we could have saved ourselves a lot of work if we had simply gone and fetched her in the first place," Dario said.

But they regarded each other cautiously, and then Lucia stretched out her hand and curled her fingers around Giovanni's, squeezing them gently. "Bartolo," she said, her voice thick with tears.

"It has been too long."

To everyone's surprise, Lucia laughed. "I would say an excess of fifty years is most definitely too long to be parted from the love of your life."

"I hope very much that there was love in your last fifty years regardless," Giovanni said.

Lucia nodded slowly. "There was. There is. But that doesn't mean yours wasn't greatly missed." She looked around the room, at all of Giovanni's grandchildren. "And I see there has been a great deal in yours."

"Yes, there has been. But I never released the love I have for you. I simply made room for more."

"I think we have a great deal to discuss, Bartolo," Lucia said. "Don't you?"

"Yes. I think we do."

He looped his arm around hers, and the two of them made their way slowly out of the room. The siblings looked at one another and, for once, no one seemed to know what to say.

But it was a strange thing, the realization that they were all in the same room. Nate included. They were all here together, united by their grandfather's quest to bring closure to the long-ago love affair.

If Alex were a sentimental man at all, he might even say that love had brought them together.

Gabriella would say that. Probably the moment they were alone.

It was a strange thing to him that he felt he could anticipate the sort of thing she might say. He couldn't recall ever feeling like that about anyone before. Couldn't recall ever thinking he was certain about the feelings of the person standing beside him. Though something about Gabriella felt ingrained in him, intrinsic to his system. He could guess at her thoughts, emotions and opinions as easily as he could guess at his own. Potentially easier.

"Alex," Gabriella said, "can we talk?"

It wasn't exactly what he had anticipated her saying, but she wanted to talk because she was having some kind of reaction to the scene between their grandparents. And that he had figured out. For some reason, he drew comfort in his ability to recognize and anticipate Gabriella's moods. Which wouldn't matter at all when she went back to Aceena. Not at all. It wasn't as though they would keep in touch. Wasn't as though they would exchange fluffy texts with emoticons like modern-day star-crossed lovers.

"Of course," he said, placing his hand on the small of her back and leading her from the room, ignoring the questioning gazes of his siblings as they followed their progress.

"Gardens?" she asked.

"Not a gallery?"

"I like gardens. And galleries. And libraries. I contain multitudes."

He laughed. "Yes, you do. You are large indeed. In a very small way."

She inclined her head, smiling at him. Her expression

was impish, but there was something serious behind her dark eyes, and it filled him with a sense of foreboding. Yet another ridiculous thing, because there was nothing that Gabriella could possibly say to him that was worth feeling a sense of foreboding over. He had never felt foreboding in his life.

"This way," he said, leading her down the long corridor that would take them to the back doors and out to the garden. "I'm not sure it's as spectacular as the grounds in Aceena. But they'll have to do." He pushed the French doors open, then stood like a footman, his hand outstretched, indicating that Gabriella should go ahead of him. She did. And he took great joy in watching her walk out into the sunshine, the rays of the sun shining over the glossy dark waves of her hair. She was a bright, shiny, beautiful thing, a thing that he could not hope to possess. Not with all of the money that he had in his bank account. Not with all the power and influence he wielded. Because it would take something else to hold on to a woman like Gabriella, something he simply didn't have. Something he couldn't even identify. And if he couldn't identify it, how could he hope to obtain it?

This was a foolish line of thinking. He was fine. He had been fine until his grandfather had sent him on the fool's errand to collect the painting. This was Giovanni's happy ending, at ninety-eight, and it had nothing at all to do with Alex. Alex would go back to the way things were. Alex would go back to life without Gabby. That was as it should be. And he should want nothing else.

She walked over to a stone bench that was positioned just in front of a manicured hedge and took a seat, drawing one delicate, manicured finger over the hard, cold surface. Then she looked up at him. "It's a very sad thing that our grandparents had to wait half a century to find each other again."

"But a very happy thing that they have each other again, yes?"

"Yes. It is very happy."

"And as they both said, they did not lack for love in their lives."

"Yes. You're right. But don't you think…considering what they said, considering the evidence…that they never forgot each other? That their feelings for each other never lessened? That what they shared was different? They reserved a special place inside of them that was never replaced by anyone else. Not by the people they married, not by their children, not by their grandchildren. I believe that they both had happy lives. But I also believe that what they shared between each other was unique. I believe that it was special in a way that nothing else was. And I believe—"

She swallowed hard, looking up at the sky, curling her fingers around the edge of the bench and planting her feet firmly on the ground.

"I believe that there is such a thing as true love. Real love. The kind that people write sonnets about, the kind that makes people paint. That makes them sing. Like a real 'I have one half of the magic amulet, and you have the other half and they can only be complete when they're together' kind of love. I just saw it in there."

He felt cold inside. And it had nothing to do with the clear, frostbitten December day, and everything to do with the words that were spilling out of Gabriella's mouth.

"What is the point to all of this, Gabriella?"

"I think…I think that we might have that. Because it doesn't make sense, Alex. None of this makes sense. We don't. We should have nothing in common. Nothing to talk about. Attraction might be one thing, sexual compatibility another. But there's more than that. I have never felt more like myself than when I'm with you. I thought, all this time, that I needed to find someone who is like me. That I needed to find someone who would keep me safe, the way I had kept myself safe. But that isn't it at all. I don't want to be safe. I want to be with you." She laughed. "I guess it doesn't really sound right. It isn't like I think you're going to put me in danger…"

"No," he said, the word coming out of his mouth, heart tortured. "You are exactly right. I am going to put you in danger. I already have. It's evidenced by the fact that we're having this conversation. You should not feel these things for me, Gabby. I made it very clear that what we had was physical, and only physical."

"Yes," she said, her voice sounding hollow, as though he had already eviscerated something essential inside of her. "I know you did. Then things changed for me. I thought it wasn't entirely impossible that they had changed for you."

"And that is where our differences are a problem. You are innocent. And for you, all of this is new. So of course things have changed. And I can understand why you might have thought they would change for me. But you have to understand that nothing about this is original to me," he said, directly combating his earlier thoughts. Because he needed to. For himself, not just for her. "I have conducted more of these relationships than I can count. And there is absolutely nothing unique about you."

She blinked furiously, tears glittering in her beautiful eyes, and he wanted nothing more than to wipe them away. But he had put them there, so he forfeited the right. "But you didn't… If I wasn't different, then you would have had me the moment you wanted me. I don't think you would have held me on the floor of the library and used your words to—"

"That's the thing, Gabby, you don't think, because you don't have any idea how this works. When a man wants to seduce a woman he appeals to her in any way he can.

I'm not above pretending to be a much nicer man than I am. I was seemingly honest with you," he said, the words cutting his throat on their way out. "I told you about my fearsome reputation, but then I treated you gently. I made you feel like you were different. What better way to seduce a virgin? But I never wanted your love, darling girl. I only wanted your body."

"Why are you saying this?"

"Because it is time I told the truth. The moment you started spouting poetry I knew this had to be over. It was one thing when I thought you were going to quietly return to your home country the moment the painting was delivered. Clearly, you had other designs. And I don't have any interest in prolonging this farce."

She closed her eyes, a single tear trailing down her cheek. "That wasn't the farce. *This* is."

"Gabriella," he said, his voice hardened, harsh. "I told you the sort of man I am. I deal in business. In exchanges. We exchanged pleasure. That's all there is for me. Beyond that? I kept my own brother a secret to try and protect the reputation of my father. A man who was debauched beyond reason. That's the sort of thing I stand in defense of."

"No. You say that. You're determined to make sure that I and everyone else think you're a monster. Why? What are you hiding?" She opened her eyes, meeting his gaze directly, and anger was replacing the sadness that had been there only a moment ago.

"That," he said, "is my deepest, darkest secret, *cara mia*. I am hiding nothing. The water is just as shallow as it appears from the surface. Nothing is running deep here."

"I understand that you need to believe that, Alex. I understand that it's what you need everyone else to believe. What I don't understand is why."

He spread his hands. "There is nothing to understand. That is the simple, tragic truth of me. My legend is far more interesting than I will ever be. Stories of me being a monster. Of being heartless, and cruel. The simple fact is I'm self-serving. There is nothing intricate to figure out. I do what makes me money. I do what brings me pleasure. Those are my motivations. Those are my actions. Women, the media, they like to pretend that there is something else beneath all of that. I am no more interesting than my father and mother ever were."

"No," she said, her voice a whisper. "You said you didn't want to be like him."

"I said a lot of things. Don't believe them. I believe this. It's over, Gabriella. The painting is delivered, our grandparents are reunited. They can keep their true love. I will keep my money, my varied sex life and my freedom. You can go back to your books."

"Alex," she said, her voice broken, a plea.

It stabbed him, made him feel like he was being scraped raw from the inside out. This was for the best. He had to end it. He had to end it with the kind of finality his grandfather had ended things with Lucia. But he would leave no painting behind. He would leave no trail of bread crumbs for Gabriella to find her way back to him eventually.

What he did, he did for her best interests. For her future. She really would find a man who was better than him. She thought, right now, that he was more exciting than the intellectual, nice man that she would ultimately end up with, but in the future she would see that she was wrong. She would understand that she needed someone companionable, someone stable, someone who would give her everything that she deserved and more.

She was emotionally scarred by parents who had been so much like his own. And he would do nothing to continue that scarring. To continue that pain. Removing himself now was the kindest thing, even though it didn't seem like it now.

"You were right," he said, knowing that the death knell to all of this was on his lips even now. "The rake never ends up with the wallflower. He crosses the room for her, Gabby, every time. Because she's needy. Because she's vulnerable. Because she's a challenge, a change in flavor to a jaded palate. But he doesn't end up with her. He doesn't end up with anyone."

And then he turned, leaving her standing in the garden, leaving her breaking to pieces behind him, while his own chest did the same.

It was so very like Giovanni and Lucia. But with one major difference. There would never be a time in Alex's life when he stood in a roomful of his grandchildren and told this story. Because there would be no grandchildren for him. There would be no other woman, no wife.

It would be up to his brothers and sisters to carry on the bloodline, because he would not.

He would leave nothing behind. Not his tainted blood, not any Lost Mistresses.

Without him, Gabriella would be free to have love in her life. She would not hold on to him.

He wasn't worth it.

CHAPTER FOURTEEN

GABRIELLA WAS IN a daze. She had been ever since Alex had left her sitting out in the garden at his grandfather's estate. Now, she was staying at the estate. She had stumbled into the house some two hours later and found her grandmother, who was of course planning on staying and reacquainting herself with Giovanni, and spending as much time with him as possible with the remaining time he had.

She should feel happy for them. Part of her did feel happy for them. But so much of her was broken, smashed into tiny pieces. Tiny, aching pieces. That made it difficult to feel wholly happy for anyone or anything.

She wasn't entirely certain she would ever take a full breath again, much less crack a full smile.

It was seriously dramatic, but she felt seriously dramatic.

She would like to think of Alex as her first love. Her first heartbreak. But with each and every beat of her heart the word wasn't *first*, it was *only*. Her only love. Her only lover. The only man she would ever want, the only man she could ever possibly need.

She was hurt. But she was also angry at him. Because no matter what he said she knew that there was more to him than this. She knew that he hadn't seduced her, tricked her, just for a little bit of sport. He felt something for her, and she knew that. The fact that he was so cruel when he'd abandoned her earlier today was proof enough of that.

He talked about being like his father, but she knew that people like their parents were not intentionally cruel. They were simply self-seeking. When he had been confronted with his half brother he had preferred to ignore the situation.

This was different. His reaction was different. Yes, she knew he had a reputation for being a monster, but she had also never seen it in action.

Still, even knowing that something deeper was going on inside of Alex, it didn't mean this didn't hurt. Because while she had confidence that he had feelings for her that went beyond the physical, she had no confidence that they would be able to resolve it.

Though there was something wonderful in finding a belief in true love because of the reunion of their grandparents, there was also something sobering about the fact that it had taken them more than fifty years to come and find each other. She didn't want to wait fifty years for Alex.

She flopped backward onto the bed, groaning loudly. She closed her eyes, letting her lips part, imagining that Alex was here. That he was leaning in, about to kiss them. She let her imagination drift. To the way that he touched her. The way that he held her.

She might have been a virgin, but she wasn't an idiot.

She opened her eyes, sighing heavily.

There was a knock on the door and Gabriella rolled onto her side, her head on her arm. "Come in," she said, not quite sure why she was allowing anyone entry when she felt like day-old crusty bread.

When the door opened, Gabriella straightened. It was her grandmother. "Hello, Gabriella," the older woman said, walking into the room slowly.

"I trust everything is going well?"

Lucia smiled. "Better than."

"I'm glad."

"I know Bartolo's health is not as good as it might be, but I am more than happy to devote time to caring for him."

Those words, so gentle, so serene, shook something inside of Gabriella. It made her think of Alex again. She would do that for him. She would care for him. She didn't need the whole world in return; she only needed what he could give. At least for now. If he hadn't sent her away she would be willing to be patient. She didn't need him to throw rope around the moon and lasso it, didn't need him to pull it down for her. He was the moon all by himself. The idiot.

"Gabriella," her grandmother said, her tone gentler now. "Is there something you wish to tell me?"

"Alex," she said, because she knew that would be enough.

"I did warn you," the older woman said, her eyes soft, no condemnation in her voice.

"I know you did. Unfortunately, Alessandro was a bit more persuasive than you are."

Lucia laughed then. "They always are. I have some experience with that, as you may know."

"Yes. I know."

"And sometimes they push us away because they think they are doing what's best for us. In truth, while I know Bartolo believes I was angry at him, I was angry at myself. I knew what he was doing that whole time. He was trying to play the part of nobleman. He didn't want me to be denied anything he considered my birthright. Didn't want me disowned by my family. But I have always felt that I should have fought harder. Always wondered what would have happened if I would have told him no. If I would never have let him get away with hurting me to save me."

The truth of her grandmother's words resonated inside of her. Because it was what she had imagined Alex might be doing. Of course, she was too afraid to hope. Maybe he simply didn't want to be with her. "How do you know?"

Her grandmother took a step forward, patting her on the hand. "You don't. Not unless you go ask. Take it from someone who spent half a century wishing she would have asked—it's worth the risk. Pride does not keep you warm at night. Pride won't smile at you every morning, day in day out, with ever deepening lines as the years pass. Pride is very cold comfort, Gabriella."

Lucia straightened and walked back out of the room, closing the door softly behind her. Gabriella thought of the way Alex had looked at her before leaving her in the garden earlier. Of the painful words he'd spoken, designed specifically to inflict the deepest wounds on her.

Her grandmother was right. There was no room for pride. Her pride could go straight to hell, but she would keep her love for Alex.

She had spent a great many years hiding. Trying to prevent herself from being rejected ever again, the way her parents made her feel rejected. But all that had ever gotten her was a dusty library. She was done with that. She would have her dusty library and her man.

It was suddenly clear. She'd been doing her family's genealogy for years. Trying to uncover the mysteries of the past, to shine a light on history and events lived by other people. She used it to hide.

But there would be no more hiding. She could no longer pin everything on the past. She had to make her own life. Her own history.

She stood up, vibrating with determination. Alessan-

dro Di Sione might think he was the most fearsome creature to roam the earth. But hell had no fury like Gabriella
D'Oro when she was scorned. And she was determined
to show him that.

CHAPTER FIFTEEN

ALEX WAS CONTEMPLATING the merit of filling his bathtub with whiskey and seeing if he could absorb the alcohol straight through his skin. Anything to dull the roar of pain that was writhing through his body, the pounding in his temples, the bone-deep ache that had settled down beneath his skin and wrapped itself around his entire being.

Drinking had proven ineffective. It wasn't strong enough. He could still see her face. Could still see the way she looked at him. Wounded, impossibly hurt, as he had done what he had thought to be the noble thing.

Was it the noble thing? Or are you simply a coward?

That question had been rattling around in his brain for hours, settling like acid in his gut and eating away at his every justification.

And once it had been introduced, he couldn't shake it. Was he protecting her? Or was he protecting himself? She had been very open about the fact that she had hidden away from the world, choosing to protect herself from further rejection because of the way her parents had treated her. Like an incidental. Like she didn't matter.

And he had…

Hadn't he hidden away from the world, too? Behind the facade of being a dragon, of being a soulless monster. Keeping everyone at a distance. Most especially the half brother who had been there that terrible night. Who had been wound around that most painful event.

The thought was enough to take his breath away. To realize that his own actions had been born not of a need to keep control, but out of fear. It ate away at the very foundation of who he believed he was. He thought himself strong. He thought himself in total command.

Now he wondered if he was still a boy, hiding from difficult feelings. Difficult decisions. Concealing the existence of the truth so that he didn't have to face it. Just as he had done with Nate.

But what life could she have with him? What did he offer to Gabriella? He knew what she did for him. She gave him hope. She made him see art, made him see beauty. With her, he experienced softness, hope, in a way that he hadn't done in his entire life. Yes, he knew exactly what she offered him, and he feared that all he had to offer her was his endless, dark well of neediness. Left open the night his parents died. It held nothing but fear, nothing but anguish, and those things consumed, they didn't give.

Suddenly, the door to his apartment swung open. He had to wonder for a moment just how much he'd had to drink, because there stood Gabriella, the light from the hallway illuminating her with a golden halo around her dark hair, making her look like an angel standing in the middle of hell. His own personal hell. As though she had come to raise him from perdition.

And he desperately wanted it to be so.

How was it that this young innocent could reduce the jaded playboy like himself to such a needy, desperate thing? How was it that she had reached inside of him and scraped him raw? He should have had all the control here. She should be the one in pain because he had ended things. And he should be able to move on as he had always done. And yet, he couldn't.

"Gabby," he said, the word raw and rough as his insides.

"You don't get to call me that," she said, sweeping into the room and slamming the door behind her. "Not unless you intend to fix what you did."

"My list of sins is long, Gabriella. You have to be more specific."

"The small matter of lying to me and breaking my heart." She crossed her arms, her proud chin tilted upward, her small frame vibrating with rage. "I understand. It took me a while, because I had to dig beneath my own pain to understand, but I do. You're afraid. Just like me. And just like me you are protecting yourself."

Hearing the words from Gabriella's lips made it even harder for him to deny. He had suspicions about his own behavior, but they were just that—suspicions. Gabriella knew him. And he trusted that. She had an intelligence about emotions, the kind that he could hardly lay claim to.

"But we can't do that anymore," she said. "It isn't worth it. What do we get for it? Years of wishing we were together? We can be what we're expected to be. We can be safe. No, Alex, I shouldn't be with you. I'm a princess. And I should be with a man who is at the very least a member of nobility, or failing that, not a complete and total dissolute playboy. You should be with a woman who is sophisticated, who has a tough outer shell and a lot more experience than I have. But that is what we want. We want each other. Because you're my deep love, Alex. The other half of my amulet. The one that I'll never forget. You are the hole in my soul, the one that I have carried from the day I was born and I wasn't even aware that it was there until the moment I met you."

Her words echoed inside him, rang with truth. It was the same for him. He knew it was the same for him.

"How?" He swallowed hard. "How do we just forget everything else?"

"I figure it's either that or we forget that we love each other, Alex. And I would so much rather forget my pain. I would so much rather forget my fear. I would rather forget that on paper we don't make any sense and just remember that I love you. In the end, doesn't that sound easier?"

His chest seized tight, his breathing becoming labored. "I'm not sure if there's anything simple about love, Gabriella."

"Maybe not. Maybe I'm living in a fantasy. But… Oh, Alex, how I would love to live in this fantasy with you. I know you think I'm young and silly—"

"No," he said. "I don't think you're silly. I think you are magically unspoiled by all of the things that have happened to you in your life. I think you are a gift that your parents didn't deserve, that they didn't appreciate. I think that you are a gift I don't deserve."

"Well, what's the use in being a gift that no one wants?"

He felt like his chest was going to crack open. "I do want you. I do. But…I am…a thousand years too old for you. A thousand ways too corrupt. Wouldn't you rather be with a different man?"

"No," she said, the word so simple, with no hesitation. "No one else made me want to come out of the library. I liked small things. Quiet things. And what I feel for you… it isn't quiet or small. It's big and loud and it rings in my ears, in my chest, and it terrifies me. But I want it still. I was so caught up in the fact that the rake could come after the wallflower that I didn't stop to think how amazing it was that I came out of hiding for you. Alex, the fact that I want you is a miracle in and of itself. I'm not sure you appreciate that."

He laughed, but there was no humor in the sound. "Believe me, I do."

"Well, so do I. I love you. And I'm sorry if that isn't sophisticated. I'm sorry if it wasn't supposed to happen.

But it did. And it's the most amazing, wonderful thing. So much better than hiding away. Please, come with me. Away from the guilt. Because I know you still feel guilty. But you were a boy. You have to forgive yourself."

He nodded slowly. "I do. Because you're right, I was a boy. But I'm not a boy now. I'm a man. Still, I was hiding like one. And it has to stop, Gabriella. You are right. I was very dedicated to the idea that I was a monster. Convincing you, to convince myself. Because I'm a very convenient hiding place. That mask was the best thing I had. It kept everyone away. But... I don't want that anymore. I thought that it made me strong. I convinced myself that I was turning away from the way my parents lived. Cutting myself off from that kind of reckless behavior, keeping myself from poisoning other people in my life. But I wasn't afraid for others. I was afraid for myself. But you are right. Living without you would be far worse than learning to let go of all this."

He took a step toward her, cupping the back of her head and gazing down into her dark eyes. "If you will have me, after all the things I said, after everything I have done, both before and since I met you, then I would be very honored if you would... I suppose I can ask you to marry me, can I?"

"No," she said, causing his heart to sink. "You can't. Because you haven't said you love me yet."

"I thought that was implied."

"Not good enough. I like art, I like poetry, I like books. I like all of the beauty laid out before me."

He felt a smile curve his lips upward. "My face isn't enough?"

"It's a start. But I need the words."

"I love you, beautiful Gabby."

"Really?" she asked, tears filling her eyes. The good kind of tears. The kind that made his chest ache and his whole body shake at the wonder of it. "Even though I'm not boring?"

"Most especially because you aren't boring. Because you are clever. Because you teach me things—about the world and about myself. I want to spend the rest of my life holding you, touching you, being with you. I want your lips to be the last lips I ever kiss. And your heart to be the only one I ever hold. And in case you missed it the first time, I love you."

She smiled, the kind of dreamy smile he had never dared hope to be on the receiving end of. The kind of dreamy smile he hadn't even known he ever wanted to be on the receiving end of. Amazing the things that his princess was teaching him. "That's better."

"Now can I propose to you?"

"You really want to get married, Alex?"

"Yes. Because that's what you deserve. Forever. All in. And…I still feel like there are things inside of me that I'll have to work through. I'm afraid that I'll take too much from you."

"Never. Maybe you will sometimes. But then, there will be other times when I take too much from you. We're not in half-and-half. We are all in. Forever. When you need to be carried, Alex, I'll carry you," she said, taking a step forward and resting her palm on his cheek. "And I know that when I need to be carried you'll carry me. That's what love is. It gives. We know what it looks like when people take, when they consume and do only what pleases them. But that isn't us. It isn't this."

"If I falter, Gabriella," he said, grabbing hold of her chin with his thumb and forefinger, "promise me you'll put me back on the path."

"You have my word."

"I can't paint you, Gabriella. I can't show you the way

that I see you. I can't explain it to you in terms of art, and really, I'm not all that good with poetry."

"Lies. You're wonderful with it."

"I'm really not. So I'll just say it plain, and honest. I love you. From now until forever."

"That's really all I need."

"No white tigers?"

She tapped her chin, as though she were considering it. "I wouldn't say no to a white tiger."

"Well," he said, "I may not be able to accommodate you there. But how about a white Christmas wedding?"

She smiled, throwing her arms around his neck and stretching up on her tiptoes to give him a kiss. "That sounds just about perfect."

EPILOGUE

A WEDDING BETWEEN a billionaire and a princess really was an amazing thing. Mostly because when titles and money were thrown around it became surprisingly easy to throw things together in only a couple of weeks.

The entire family came to help Gabriella and Alessandro celebrate their love. Love was always beautiful, but there was something particularly beautiful about watching Gabriella and Alessandro joined together. It wasn't simply the ring she wore on her finger, or the tiara she wore in her dark hair, nor was it the earrings that glittered in her ears. It was the love that radiated between them, the strange sort of symmetry evident there.

Giovanni had to wonder if their family blood was simply destined to love a D'Oro. If there was something ingrained on a soul-deep level that was inescapable. If so, he was glad of that. As he sat, watching his beloved eldest grandson pledge his life to the granddaughter of the woman he had always loved, he felt a sense of absolute completion wash through him.

Though he imagined that had something to do with the woman sitting at his side. Queen Lucia, his true lost mistress, finally returned to him. It was a miracle.

And it didn't matter how many years he had left to his name, because he knew they would be the happiest years yet. And he imagined there were very few people who could claim such a thing.

At his appointment last week the doctors had told him he was doing well, something no one had ever expected to happen at his age. They also told him he was healthier than should be possible. That he was a miracle. He wasn't entirely certain that he was a miracle, but there were certainly miracles all around him. Each and every one of his grandchildren, settled and fallen in love. Nate, brought into the family in a real and true way. Alessandro healed from the wounds left behind by his parents.

And Lucia by his side.

Yes, as he looked around the family estate, lushly decorated for Christmas, glittering with lights, ribbon and boughs of holly, he couldn't help but think that the miracle had nothing to do with him at all.

The miracle was, and had always been, love, available for anyone who would reach out and take it.

And though it was late in his life, he was taking it now.

He took Lucia's hand in his, just as Alessandro pulled Gabriella into his arms for a kiss. He looked at Lucia and saw that her eyes were fixed to the painting hanging in the great room. Perhaps scandalous in some ways, but then, when it came to the Di Sione family, it was difficult to say what was scandalous and what was simply everyday business.

"I love you," he said, squeezing Lucia's hand.

She took her eyes away from the painting and looked back at him, offering a slow smile.

"I can see that. I can see it clearly."

* * * * *

**"I'll return to my original question,"
Maggy said. Not politely. "Who the hell
are you, and why do you care if some
barista in a photograph looks like an
old, dead queen?"**

Reza drew himself up to his full height. He looked
down at her with all the authority and consequence
that had been pounded into every inch of him all his
life—even when his own father had failed to live up
to the crown he now wore himself.

"I am Leopoldo Maximillian Otto, King of the
Constantines," he informed her. "But you may call me
by my private family nickname, Reza."

She let out a sharp, hard sound that was not quite a
laugh, and thrust his mobile back at him. "I don't
want to call you anything."

"That will be awkward, then."

Reza took possession of his phone, studying the
way she deliberately kept her fingers from so much
as brushing his, as if he was poisonous. He was a
king, not a snake. The way this creature dared to
treat him—*him*—with such disrespect baffled him,
but did nothing to assuage that damnable need that
still worked inside him. She confounded him, and he
didn't like it.

But that didn't change the facts. Much less what
would be gained by presenting his people with the
lost Santa Domini princess as his bride.

He met her gaze. And held it. "Because, one way or
another, you are to be my wife."

Wedlocked!

Conveniently wedded, passionately bedded!

Whether there's a debt to be paid,
a will to be obeyed or a business to be saved…
She's got no choice but to say, 'I do!'

But these billionaire bridegrooms have got another
think coming if they think marriage will be that easy…

Soon their convenient brides become the object
of an *inconvenient* desire!

Find out what happens after the vows in

The Billionaire's Defiant Acquisition
by Sharon Kendrick

One Night to Wedding Vows
by Kim Lawrence

Wedded, Bedded, Betrayed
by Michelle Smart

Expecting a Royal Scandal
by Caitlin Crews

Trapped by Vialli's Vows
by Chantelle Shaw

Baby of His Revenge
by Jennie Lucas

A Diamond for Del Rio's Housekeeper
by Susan Stephens

Bound by His Desert Diamond
by Andie Brock

Look out for more **Wedlocked!** stories
coming soon!

BRIDE BY
ROYAL DECREE

BY
CAITLIN CREWS

First Published in Great Britain 2017
By Mills & Boon, an imprint of HarperCollins*Publishers*
1 London Bridge Street, London, SE1 9GF

© 2017 Caitlin Crews

ISBN: 978-0-263-92507-4

Our policy is to use papers that are natural, renewable and recyclable
products and made from wood grown in sustainable forests. The logging
and manufacturing processes conform to the legal environmental
regulations of the country of origin.

Printed and bound in Spain
by CPI, Barcelona

USA TODAY bestselling and RITA® Award–nominated author **Caitlin Crews** loves writing romance. She teaches her favourite romance novels in creative writing classes at places like UCLA Extension's prestigious Writers' Program, where she finally gets to utilise the MA and PhD in English Literature she received from the University of York in England. She currently lives in California, with her very own hero and too many pets. Visit her at caitlincrews.com.

Books by Caitlin Crews

Mills & Boon Modern Romance

Castelli's Virgin Widow
At the Count's Bidding
Undone by the Sultan's Touch
Not Just the Boss's Plaything

One Night With Consequences

The Guardian's Virgin Ward

The Billionaire's Legacy

The Return of the Di Sione Wife

Wedlocked!

Expecting a Royal Scandal

Secret Heirs of Billionaires

Unwrapping the Castelli Secret

Scandalous Sheikh Brides

Protecting the Desert Heir
Traded to the Desert Sheikh

Visit the Author Profile page
at millsandboon.co.uk for more titles.

To anyone, like me,
who dreamed they were really a princess…

CHAPTER ONE

THERE WERE FEW things Maggy Strafford liked less than scrubbing the coffee shop floor—or really any floor, for that matter. Dental surgery. The stomach flu. Any and all memories of her unfortunate childhood in foster care. Still, there she was on her hands and knees, dutifully attacking an unidentifiable sticky patch on the hardwood floors of The Coffee Queen in the tiny, tourist-rich hamlet of Deanville, Vermont, just down the road from one of the state's most famous resorts. Because it was her job as the most recently hired barista on this, the first night the owners had trusted her enough to close up shop.

And for once in the bumpy carnival ride that had been her life since she'd been found by the side of the road as a feral child with no memory of where she'd come from, Maggy was determined to keep her job. Even if it involved scrubbing unidentified sticky things off the floor of a coffee shop in almost the middle of nowhere, Vermont.

She scowled when the bell on the door rang, announcing the arrival of one more coffee-obsessed tourist who couldn't, apparently, read the closed sign she'd flipped over on the glass. Or spare a glance inside to see all the chairs flipped up on the tables, clearly indicating the shop was closed for business. Or notice Maggy herself, there on her hands and knees on the floor, obviously not manning the espresso machine.

"We're closed," she called out as a blast of chilly winter air rushed in, swirling around her and making her wish she hadn't stripped off her thick sweater to do the end of day wipe down. She did not say, *which you can see right there on the door, assuming you can read*, because that kind of knee-jerk, snotty response was the Old Maggy. New Maggy was kinder and gentler. And had thus been steadily and gainfully employed for the past five months.

With that in mind, she summoned a smile as she tossed her sponge back into her bucket with enough force to make the brown water slosh alarmingly. She hated smiling on command. She wasn't exactly made for customer service and never had been, as her spotty employment record attested. But New Maggy knew better than to share her real feelings with anyone, especially not the customers, and who cared how rich and correspondingly annoying they were. Her real and inevitably prickly feelings were her personal business and best kept hidden away if she wanted to keep her current, surprisingly okay, situation. Which she did. So she aimed all her teeth at the door when she looked up.

And her half-assed smile toppled straight off her face.

Two heavily muscled and stern-faced men in dark suits that strained over their physiques strode inside, muttering into earpieces in a language that was definitely not English. They paid Maggy no mind whatsoever as she gaped up at them, moving swiftly past her where she knelt on the floor with a certain brisk efficiency that made her stomach flip over. In warning and a little bit of panic. She knew she needed to jump up and deal with them somehow, which her ingrained fight-or-flight monitor suggested meant running the hell away rather than confronting either one of them.

She braced herself to do just that.

But then another man walked in, flanked by two more muscle-bound goons with earpieces and cold, grim eyes. And giant, ugly handguns on their hips. *Guns.* The obvious security detail peeled off, each one taking a position at one of the front windows, all dark suits, hard gazes, and grim, bulging arms.

The man in the center took another step or two inside the coffee shop and then simply stood there, gazing down at Maggy as if he'd anointed himself the new messiah.

Maggy was no particular fan of arrogant men. Or men at all, if she was honest, given the less than stellar examples she'd encountered over the years, particularly in the foster care system. But she found her usual defense mechanisms—those being her smart mouth and her willingness to wield it first and ask questions later—seemed to have fled her completely.

Because the man standing there above her as if there was a sound track playing the "Hallelujah Chorus" as he did so was…something else.

He stood as if it was commonplace for him to find all sorts of people on their knees before him. As if, in fact, he was faintly bored that there was one more person at his feet. She should have loathed him on sight.

Instead, Maggy's heart slammed against her ribs—and didn't stop. She told herself he was nothing special.

Just another man, and an evidently pompous one at that. Obviously, ridiculously, eye-rollingly wealthy like so many of the people who descended on this little après ski town in the winters. They were a dime a dozen here, leaping in and out of their gleaming four-wheel-drive monstrosities and blinding people with their lazy, too-white smiles. They draped themselves over all the best tables in the town's restaurants, jacked up the prices in all the village's boutiques with their willingness to purchase T-shirts for upwards of a hundred dollars, and cluttered up the coffee shops with their paragraph-long orders of joyless fake drinks.

This guy is nothing special at all, Maggy assured herself, still gazing up at him as if this was a church and she'd taken to her knees to do a few decades of a very specific sort of rich man rosary on a dark winter evening. *This guy is interchangeable with all the rest out there.*

But that was a lie.

He was extraordinary.

Something seemed to *hum* from him, some intense power or perhaps that sheer *certainty* that seemed stamped into his very bones. It was more than simple arrogance. It was more than the tanned faces, white teeth, and high-end vehicles idling by the curb that the others in this town assumed made them demigods. It made it hard to look away from him, as if he claimed all the light in the shop—in the town, in the whole of New England—for himself. And he wasn't exactly hard to look at, she was forced to concede. He wore dark trousers and boots that Maggy could tell at a glance cost more than the fancy SUVs the usual tony ski bums drove. He wore one of those expensively flattering winter coats that exuded upper-class elegance and deep masculinity at once. He was tall, and not just because she was still kneeling. He had wide shoulders and the kind of rangy, offhandedly athletic physique that suggested he spent a lot of very hard, very physical time catering to his own strength and agility—a notion that made her stomach flip again, and this time, definitely not in warning.

But it was his face that was the real problem.

He was not a blandly attractive, run of the mill rich guy, like all the rest packed into Deanville at this time of year in their designer ski togs and indistinguishable store-bought tans. Not this man. His face was too relentlessly and uncompromisingly masculine. Too harshly male. He had a nose like an old coin and a hard, stern, unsmiling mouth that made a shocking, impossible heat uncurl, low and insistent, deep in Maggy's belly. If she was honest, lower than that. His gaze was the color of a hard rain and much too shrewd besides. It seemed to kick up some kind of electricity as he aimed it at her, as arrogant and aloof as it was ruthless.

And he stood there with that gray gaze trained on her as if he was used to nothing less than adoration from all he surveyed. As if he expected nothing less from Maggy.

"Who the hell are you?" she demanded. It felt like self-preservation. In that moment, she didn't care if she was fired for her tone. She didn't care if that meant she got behind on the rent of her shabby little room again. She didn't care what happened, as long as the raw, fierce *thing* that swept over her didn't take her down with it.

"That is perfect, of course," the man said, in a dry tone that made it clear that it was no such thing. "Crude and disrespectful at once. My ancestors turn in their graves as we speak." His voice was rich and deeply cultured, his English spiced by the hint of something else entirely. Maggy loathed the part of her that wanted to know what that *something else* was. Needed to know it, even. The man only gazed down at her, a faint frown marring the granite perfection of his dark, arrogant brow. "Why are you blonde?"

Maggy blinked. Then, worse, lifted a hand to the hair she'd dyed blonde three days ago because she'd decided blonde made her look more approachable than her natural dark chestnut color.

Then she went a little cold as his implication settled deep in her gut.

"Why are you watching me?" she demanded. Not in any sort of approachable manner, because there was friendly and then there was freaked out, and she was already a little too close to the latter. "Are you a stalker?"

There was a slight noise from the goons behind her at the counter, as if they'd reacted to that, but the man before her merely moved one of his index fingers. That was all. He was wearing the sort of buttery soft leather gloves she'd be afraid to touch with her rough hands and he merely lifted one finger. And that was that. Instant silence.

"You do not know who I am."

It wasn't a question. If anything, it seemed like an indictment.

"You do realize," Maggy said slowly, sitting back on her heels and wondering if she could use her bucket and sponge as some kind of weapon if things got serious here, "that anyone who asks that question is basically outing themselves as a giant, irredeemable douche."

His brow rose as if he had never heard the term. But there was no question, as his gray eyes glittered, that he recognized it as the insult it was.

Maggy had the strangest notion he was unused to insults altogether. And perhaps astonished that she dared change that. It meant he was even more of an untouchable rich guy than she'd already imagined—but she couldn't figure out why recognizing that made her a little breathless.

"I beg your pardon." His voice was dark. It rolled through her, making that breathless feeling worse and her chest feel tight besides. "A *douche*? Is that what you called me?"

She tipped her chin up in that way a battalion of counselors and former employers had told her was aggressive, and pretended not to notice the emphasis he put on that last word.

"The coffee shop is closed," she said flatly. "Please gather your goon squad and go and in future? Maybe take a moment or two to consider the fact that marching around with a pack of armed men with potential steroid problems isn't necessary when you're after a cup of coffee."

The man did nothing for a moment but gaze down at her, his dark eyes assessing in a way that washed over her and left strange goose bumps in their wake. Then he thrust his hands into the pockets of his trousers, widening his stance, in a manner that should have looked more casual. But didn't.

"Tell me," he said in that same commanding voice that seemed to resonate deep inside of her. "Do you have a small birthmark behind your left ear? Shaped like a lopsided heart?"

Maggy felt cold. As frigid as the winter air that had rushed inside when they'd arrived.

"No," she said. Though she did. And it took every bit of self-possession she had not to reach up and run her fingers over it.

He only studied her, his austere mouth flat. "You are lying."

"And you're creeping me out," she retorted. She clambered up and onto her feet then, aware again of an instant reaction from the goons—and, again, the way the man in the center stopped them with the faintest wave of one finger. "What is this? What do you want? I'm guessing it's not a Mexi-mocha soy latte with an extra shot."

"Is your name Magdalena, by any chance?"

Maggy understood then that this man already knew the answers to the questions he was asking. And it hit her like a kick to the belly that he was asking at all. It made the hardwood floors seem to creak and slide beneath her feet.

"No," she lied again. She couldn't have said why she was halfway to panicked, only that she was. "My name is Maggy. It's not short for anything." She pulled her phone from the back pocket of her jeans and clenched it tight in her hand. Maybe she even brandished it at him a little. "And if you don't leave right now, I'm calling the police."

The man didn't smile. His mouth looked as if perhaps he never had. Still, there was a silver gleam to those hard rain eyes of his, and her breath got tangled somewhere in her throat.

"That will be an exercise in frustration for you, I am afraid," he said as if he wasn't the least bit threatened by the notion of the police. Almost as if he welcomed it instead. "If you wish to contact the local authorities, I will not stop you. But it would be remiss of me if I did not warn you that doing so will not achieve the results you imagine."

Maggy couldn't have said why she believed him. But she did. It was something about the way he stood there, as if he was used to being mistaken for a very well-dressed and granite-hewn statue, and was about as soft himself.

"Then how about you just leave?" she asked, aware that her lips felt numb and that her stomach felt…weird, the way it kept flipping and knotting and then twisting some more. And meanwhile that place behind her ear where her birthmark sat seemed to be much too hot. As if it was lit on fire. But she didn't dare touch it. Not in front of this man. "I want you to leave."

But this man in all his haughty, brooding ruthlessness wasn't listening to her. She'd stood up and he was clearly intrigued by that. He let those shrewd gray eyes travel all over her, and the worst part was that she had the childish urge to cover herself while he did it. When really, what did she care if some weird guy stared at her? She didn't wear skinny jeans and tight thermal long-sleeved T-shirts that fit her like a second skin to admire her own figure.

Yet somehow, she got the impression he wasn't staring at her ass like all the other rich guys had when she'd worked down the street in one of the village's bars and they'd been after a little bit of local flavor in between ski runs and highly public divorces.

"It is uncanny," the man said, his voice lower now

and something like gruff. "You could be her twin, save
the brazenly appalling hair."

"I don't have a twin," Maggy snapped, and she could
hear that there was too much *stuff* in her voice then. The
way there always was anytime some stranger claimed
she looked *just like* their niece or friend or cousin. When
she'd been a kid, she'd gotten her hopes up every time.
But she was a lot older and whole lot wiser now and she
recognized these moments for what they were—throw-
away comments from people who had no idea what it
was like to have been thrown away themselves. "I don't
have anyone, as a matter of fact. I was found by the side
of the road when I was eight and I can't remember a
single thing from before then. The end."

"Ah, but that only proves my theory," the man said,
something hard, like satisfaction, gleaming like silver
in those eyes of his.

He pulled off his leather gloves as if it was part of
an ancient ceremony. Maggy couldn't have said how
he managed it, to somehow exude all of that brooding
masculinity and yet be standing there doing nothing
but *removing a pair of gloves*. He wasn't sacking the
walls of a city or performing some athletic feat, no matter how it echoed around inside of her. When he was
done—and when she was busy asking herself what on
earth was wrong with her that she should find a man's
strong, bare hands *illicit*—he pulled out a smartphone
from his pocket, much larger and clearly more high-
tech than the one she'd gotten recently when she'd felt
so flush after her first month of regular paychecks here.
Her fingers clenched hard on hers, as if she was embarrassed by her own phone, and she shoved it in her
back pocket again. He swiped his screen a few times

and then offered it to her, his face impassive. Though through it all, his gray eyes gleamed.

Maggy stared at his shiny, top-of-the-line smart-phone as if it was a wasp's nest, buzzing a warning straight at her.

"I don't want to look at that," she told him. Because he was overwhelming and he didn't make sense and he was *too much*. And she was being smart not to let him reel her into anything, the way she'd always had to be smart, because it was that or be a victim. But that didn't explain the sudden, hollow sensation deep inside her. "I want you to go. Now."

"Look at the picture, please."

He didn't sound as if he was really asking. He didn't sound as if he ever *asked*, come to that. And she noticed he didn't promise that he would leave her alone if she looked as ordered, either.

So Maggy had no idea why she reached out and took the damned smartphone from him, making absolutely certain not to touch him. Or why the faint glint of approval in his stern gray gaze…did something to her. She swallowed hard and looked down at the smartphone in her hand, still warm from its close contact with his skin. Which should absolutely not have made her fight back a shudder.

Maggy focused on the screen in her hand. And then froze.

It was a picture of a woman.

She was standing somewhere beautiful, all gleaming lights and old stone, and she was looking back over one bared shoulder with a wide smile. Her dark chestnut hair was swept back into some kind of complicated bun and she was wearing the sort of dress real people never wore, long and sleek and seemingly threaded through with diamonds to match the bright strands draped around her neck.

If Maggy didn't know better, she'd have said it was a picture of her.

"What is this?" she whispered, aware as she did that her heart was pounding at her. That her stomach knotted so hard it hurt. That her head ached, hard and strange at her temples. "Who *is* this?"

The man before her didn't move a muscle. He didn't lift one of his powerful fingers. He didn't do anything, and yet there was something about the way he watched her then that took over the whole world.

"That is Serena Santa Domini." His voice was cool, and yet she was sure there was something like satisfaction in his voice, threaded in deep, like stone. "Better known as Her Majesty, the queen of Santa Domini, who died twenty years ago in a car crash in Montenegro." His gray eyes flashed with something Maggy didn't understand, dark and sure, but it hit her like a wallop all the same. "I believe she was your mother."

Reza Argos, more widely known and always publicly addressed as His Royal Majesty, King and Supreme Ruler of the Constantines, was not a sentimental man.

That had been his father's downfall. It would not be his.

But either way, there was no doubt that he was a king. That meant there was no room for the maudlin trap of sentiment, especially in a country like the Constantines that prided itself on its *correctness* with, it was true, a certain intensity that suggested a number of unpleasant undercurrents. Like all the whispers about his father's longtime mistress, for example, that no one dared mention directly—especially not after the way his father had died. Not that anyone said *suicide*, either. It was too messy. It hinted too strongly at the darkness beneath the Constantines, and no one wanted that.

It was all unpleasant history. Reza focused on the present. His trains ran on time. His people paid their taxes and his military zealously maintained his borders. He and his government operated transparently, without unnecessary drama, and in the greatest interests of his people to the best of his ability. He did not succumb to the blackmail of a calculating mistress and he certainly did not risk the whole country because of it. He was nothing like his father. More than that, the Constantines were *nothing* like their closest neighbor, the besieged Santa Domini, with its civil and economic crises these last thirty years.

Unsentimental attention to detail on the part of its rulers was how such a small country had maintained its prosperity, independence, and neutrality for hundreds upon hundreds of years. Europe might rage and fall and rise again around them, but the Constantines stood, a firm guard against encroaching darkness and Santa Dominian refugee crises alike, and no matter how grim and worrying it had all been these last three decades.

His father's descent into cringe-inducing protestations of *what the heart demanded*—followed by what might well have become a constitutional crisis had it not been stopped before the blackmail had truly ripped apart the kingdom—did not count. Since very few people knew how bad it had all gotten outside the royal family and the most highly ranked ministers.

Reza had held his tiny alpine country together since

his ascension to the throne at the tender age of twenty-three following what had been widely reported as his father's sudden heart attack, as the latest in a long line of monarchs from the House of Argos. The Constantines was a small country made up of two pristine valleys high in the European Alps. The valleys were connected by a vast, crystal blue lake, bristled with picturesque villages and plump, comfortable banking concerns, and were bordered on all sides by crisp snowcapped mountains and luxury ski resorts.

The Constantinian people liked the kingdom as it was. Untouched. A legacy of a bygone era, yet with all the comforts of the present day. That their longtime ally and closest neighbor, Santa Domini, had suffered a violent military coup when Reza was a child, had lost its exiled king and most of its royal family when he was eighteen, and had strewn out refugees seeking escape from the harsh military government all this time made Constantinians…upset.

Reza did not particularly care for the fact that his reign was often characterized as "rocky," purely because he'd had to spend so much of it handling his neighbor's messes and making up for his father's adulterous yearnings, the blackmail that had nearly brought the kingdom to war, and the suicide he'd had no choice but to conceal from the public lest all the rest of it come out, too. He'd handled that necessary lie. He'd handled his furious, spiteful mother. He'd even handled his father's awful mistress. It was unfortunate that no one outside his inner circle knew how much he'd handled. But things were looking up. Next door in Santa Domini, the usurper, General Estes, was dead. The rightful Santa

Dominian king's restoration to the throne had changed his country and calmed the whole region.

If this woman in front of him was the lost, long presumed dead Princess Magdalena as he suspected she was, that changed everything else.

Because Reza had been betrothed to the Santa Domini princess since the day of her birth. And while he prided himself on his ability to live without the mawkish sentiment that had brought down his father and led him straight into an unscrupulous woman's hands, he suspected that what his people truly wanted was a convenient royal fairy tale with all the trappings. A grand royal wedding to remind them of their happy fantasies about what life in the Constantines was meant to be was just the ticket. It would generate revenue and interest. It would furthermore lead to the high approval ratings and general satisfaction Reza's grandfather had enjoyed throughout his long reign. Contented subjects, after all, rarely plotted out revolutions.

He opted not to share the happy news with his prospective bride just then.

The woman before him shook slightly as she stared at the picture on his mobile. He'd expected joyful noises, at the very least, as he'd imagined anyone standing in a second-rate resort town undertaking menial labor might make upon learning she was, in all likelihood, meant for greater things than her current dire straits. Or a celebration of some kind, particularly given the circumstances under which he'd found her. On her hands and knees, scrubbing the floor like the lowest servant. Her hair like brittle straw around her bony shoulders, making her look even more pale and skinny than she already was.

Wearing the sort of fabrics that looked as if they might set themselves alight if they rubbed together.

Her mouth as foul and crude as the rest of her.

This, then, was his long-lost queen. The fairy-tale creature he would use to beguile his people and secure his throne, all rough, red hands and that sulky, impertinent mouth. He supposed he would have to make the best of it.

And if there was some part of him that was pleased that he could not possibly be in any danger from this creature—that she was about as likely to beguile him as was the exuberant potted plant in the corner—well. He kept that to himself.

She raised her gaze to his again, her eyes a deep, rich caramel that he found he couldn't read as he wished. He watched the curious way she set her frail shoulders and lifted her stubborn chin. As if she wished to hold him off physically. As if she thought she'd have a chance at it if she tried.

On some level, Reza was deeply appalled she might ever have had reason to lift a finger to protect herself. He was almost entirely certain that she was the lost princess of Santa Domini. *His* princess. A blood test would merely confirm what was obvious to the naked eye, as the family resemblance was astonishing. And the lost princess of Santa Domini, the future mother of the kings of the Constantines, was not a scrubbing woman. She was not this…hardscrabble washerwoman persona she'd concocted over the past two decades.

He told himself that he should find it in him to be sympathetic. If he was correct in his assumption about what had happened, she'd been granted a strange mercy indeed—but that made it no less merciful.

"I don't have a mother," she told him, without the faintest shred of deference. Or any hint of manners. And Reza admired her spirit, he supposed, even if he deeply disapproved of its application. "And if I did, she certainly wasn't the queen of anything, unless maybe you mean welfare."

Reza ignored that, already trying to work out how he could possibly take this…fake blonde sow's ear and create the appropriately dignified purse, one worthy of being displayed to the world at his side.

She had the bones of the princess she clearly was. That was obvious at a glance. If he ignored the tragic clothes, the questionable hair, and the decidedly un-refined way she held herself, he could see the stamp of the Santa Dominis all over her. It was those high cheekbones, for a start. The sweet oval of her face and that impossibly lush mouth that was both deeply aristo-cratic and somehow carnal at once. She was an uncivi-lized, hungry sort of skinny, a far cry from the preferred whippet-thin and toned physique of the many highborn aristocratic women of Reza's acquaintance, but she was evidently proud of the curves she had. He could imagine no other reason she would have gone to such trouble to wear her cheap clothing two sizes too small.

What Reza could not understand—what curled through him like smoke and horrified him even as it sent heat rushing through him—was how, when he had no worries at all that she could access his heart no mat-ter who she was, he could possibly want her in any way. This…renovation project that stood before him.

And yet.

It had slammed into him the moment he'd walked into the shop and it had appalled him unto the depths of his soul. It still did. He was the king of the Constantines. His tastes were beyond refined, by definition and inclination alike. His mistresses were women of impeccable breeding, impressive education, and all of them were universally lauded for their exquisite beauty, as was only to be expected. Reza did not dabble in shallow pools. He swam deep or not at all.

The woman he'd intended to make his queen, until he'd seen this creature before him now in a photograph ten days ago, was appropriate for him in every possible way. The right background. Unimpeachable bloodlines dating back centuries. An excellent education at all the best schools. A thoughtful, spotless, and blameless career in an appropriate charity following her graduation. Never, ever, so much as a breath of tabloid interest in her or her close friends or anything she did. Not ever.

The honorable Louisa had been the culmination of a decade of hard searching for the perfect queen. He hadn't imagined he'd ever find her until he had. Reza still couldn't entirely believe that he was here, across an ocean from his kingdom and his people and the woman he'd intended to wed, hunting down a crass, ill-dressed creature who had already insulted him in about seventeen different ways. It offended him on every level.

As did the fact that every time she lifted that belligerent chin of hers or opened her mouth to say something indelicate if not outright rude, the most appalling need washed through him and made him…restless.

His Louisa had been crafted as if from a list of his desired specifications for his potential queen, and yet he had never, ever felt anything for her beyond the sort of appreciation for her lovely figure he might also feel for, say, a pretty bit of shrubbery or an elegant table setting. Reza was the king of the Constantines. The state of his garden and the magnificence of his decor reflected on him. On his rule. On his country. So, too, would his choice of bride.

His feelings, appropriately, were that all of these things should be beyond excellence. And that sort of distant admiration was the only feeling he intended to have for his queen, as was appropriate. Unlike his father's disastrous affair of the heart.

"Perhaps you failed to understand me." He waited for the princess's unusual eyes to meet his and gritted his teeth against his body's unseemly reaction to her. It would be one thing if she were dressed like her mother had been in that picture. If she looked like the princess she obviously was instead of a castoff from *Les Misérables*. What was the matter with him? "Ten days ago my aide returned from a brief location scouting expedition in the area."

"A location scouting expedition." She echoed his own words in much the same way she'd said the word *douche* earlier, and he liked it about as much now as he had then. "Is that fancy talk for *a trip*?"

Reza could not recall the last time any person had managed to get under his skin. Much less a woman. In his experience, women tended to fling themselves into his path with great enthusiasm, if impeccable manners befitting his status, and if they found themselves on their knees, it was for entirely different reasons. He opted not to share that with her. Just as he opted not to share that he'd been planning an engagement trip to ask Louisa to become his queen in appropriately photogenic surroundings. He had not been at all interested in America for this purpose, but his enterprising aide had made a case for the enduring appeal of the New England countryside in winter and the smallish hills they called mountains here.

"I saw you in the background of these pictures." He eyed her brash, blond hair, looking even less attractive in the overhead lights the more she tipped her head back to glare unbecomingly at him. In the pictures her hair had swirled around her shoulders, feminine and enticing, the dark chestnut color suiting her far more. It had also made it abundantly clear whose child she was. "The resemblance to Queen Serena was uncanny. It took only a phone call or two to determine that your name matched that of the lost princess and that your mysterious past dovetailed with the time of the accident. Perfectly. It seems too great a coincidence."

Again, her chin tilted up, and there was no reason at all Reza should feel that as if her hands were on his sex. He was appalled that he did. Until tonight, his desires had always remained firmly under his control. Passion had been his father's weakness. It would not be his.

"I don't have a mysterious past," she told him. Her caramel-colored eyes glittered. "The world is filled with bad parents and disposable kids. I'm just one more."

"You are nothing of the kind."

She folded her arms over her chest in a show of belligerence that made him blink.

"I'll return to my original question," she said. Not politely. "Who the hell are you and why do you care if some barista in a photograph looks like an old, dead queen?"

Reza drew himself up to his full height. He looked down at her with all the authority and consequence that had been pounded into every inch of him, all his life, even when his own father had failed to live up to the crown he now wore himself.

"I am Leopoldo Maximillian Otto, King of the Constantines," he informed her. "But you may call me by my private family nickname, Reza."

She let out a sharp, hard sound that was not quite a laugh and thrust his mobile back at him. "I don't want to call you anything."

"That will be awkward, then."

Reza took possession of his mobile, studying the way she deliberately kept her fingers from so much as brushing his, as if he was poisonous. When he was a king, not a snake. How this creature dared to treat him—*him*—with such disrespect baffled him, but did nothing to assuage that damnable need that still worked inside him. She confounded him, and he didn't like it.

But that didn't change the facts. Much less what would be gained by presenting his people with the lost Santa Domini princess as his bride.

He met her gaze then. And held it. "Because one way or another, you are to be my wife."

CHAPTER TWO

"I GET IT," Maggy said after a moment. The word *wife* seemed to pound through her like an instant hangover, making her head feel too big and her belly a bit iffy, and if there were other, stranger reactions to him moving around inside her...she pretended she didn't notice. "Someone must have put you up to this. Is this some new reality show? *The Cinderella Games*?"

Reza—as the other six hundred names he'd rattled off, to say nothing of the title he'd claimed, were apparently not fit for daily use—blinked in obvious affront.

"Allow me to assure you that I have not, nor will I ever, participate in a *show* of any kind." He managed to bite out his words as if they offended him. As if the very taste of them in his mouth was an assault. Then he adjusted the cuffs of his coat in short jerks of indignant punctuation. "I am a king, not a circus animal."

Maggy found that despite never having seen a king in all her life, and having entertained about as many thoughts about the behavior of monarchs as she did about that of unicorns and/or dragons, she had no trouble whatsoever believing this man of stone and consequence was one.

"I'll make a note that you're not a sad, dancing elephant." Somehow, she kept from rolling her eyes in the back of her head. "Good to know."

"I suggest you look it up," he said, very much as if she hadn't spoken. Maybe for him, she really hadn't. It was entirely possible that a king simply wasn't aware that anyone else spoke at all. He nodded toward her hip, and the phone she'd stashed in her back pocket. "Pull up an image of the king of the Constantines on your mobile. See what appears. I think you'll find that he resembles me rather closely."

And Maggy opted not to explore why the certainty in his voice shivered through her, kicking up a commotion in its wake.

"It doesn't matter what comes up," she told him, careful to keep that shivering thing out of her voice. "I don't care if you're the king of the world. I still need to clean this floor and lock up the shop, and that means you and all your muscly clowns need to go." When he only stared at her in cool outrage, she might have smirked a little. Just a little. "You're the one who mentioned a circus. I'm only adding to the visual."

"What an extraordinary reaction." His gray eyes were fathomless, yet still kicked up entirely too many tornadoes inside of her. And his voice did strange things to her, too. It seemed to echo around inside of her. As if *he* was inside of her—something she was better off not imagining, thank you. "I have told you that it is highly probable you are a member of one of Europe's grand, historic royal families. That you are very likely a princess and will one day become a queen. My queen, no less. And your concern is the floor of a coffee shop?"

"My concern is the lunatic in the coffee shop with me, actually," she managed to say, fighting to keep her voice even. Because she knew, somehow, that if she allowed herself to feel the reaction swelling inside of her, it might take her right back down to her knees. And not by choice this time. "I want you to go."

He studied her for what seemed like a very long time. So long she had to rail at herself to keep from fidgeting. From showing him any weakness whatsoever—or any hint that she was taking him seriously when she wasn't. She couldn't. Princesses? Queens? That was nothing but little girl dreams and wishful thinking.

If there was one thing Maggy knew entirely too much about, it was reality. Cold, hard, grim, and often heartbreaking reality. There was no point whining about it, as she knew very well. It was what it was.

"Very well," he said after what seemed like a thousand years, and was that…*disappointment* that washed through her? Had she wanted him to keep pushing? She couldn't have. Of course she couldn't have. "If you feel you must continue with these unpleasant tasks of yours, then by all means." This time he waved a hand, and it was even more peremptory and obnoxious than his previous partially raised finger. It made her blood feel so hot and so *bright* in her veins that she flushed with it. With temper. And she was certain he saw it. "Don't for one moment allow your bright future to interfere with your menial present circumstances."

Maggy had wanted to hit quite a few people in her time. That was what happened when a girl found herself on her own and entirely alone in the world at eighteen, when the foster care system had spit her out. She'd found herself surrounded by bad people and worse situations in places where violence was the only reasonable response to pretty much anything. Still, she'd scraped by and she'd survived—because what was the alternative?

But she wanted to hit this man more. She even did the math as she eyed him there in front of her. His four goons would likely object to any manhandling of their charge, but she was closer to him than they were. She was sure she could land a satisfying punch before they flattened her. She was equally sure it would be worth the tackle.

She didn't know how she kept her hands to herself.

"I appreciate your permission to do my job." Maggy was not, in fact, anything remotely like appreciative. "Here's a newsflash. Even if you are a king, you aren't *my* king."

She watched, fascinated despite herself, as a muscle worked in his granite-hewn jaw, indicating the impossible. That this man of stone and regal airs was having his own set of reactions to her.

To *her*.

There was absolutely no reason she should feel that as some kind of victory when she didn't *want* to win this. Whatever this was.

"You will dine with me tonight," he told her, in the manner of one who was used to issuing proclamations and, more, having them instantly obeyed.

Maggy let out a short, hard laugh. "Um, no. I won't be doing that. Tonight or ever."

Reza only gazed back at her, and she told herself she was imagining that little suggestion of heat in his stern gaze. That she was a crazy woman for imagining it. That he was a *king*, for God's sake. That she shouldn't care either way, because it was her own, personal law that she didn't do complications of any kind.

And there was no pretending a man who pranced around calling himself a king in a coffee shop wasn't one giant complication, no matter how harshly compelling that fierce face of his was.

"Then I am happy to remain where I am," he told her after another long, tense moment.

"Until what?" She shook her head, then shoved a chunk of her hair back behind her ear. "You convince me that this insane story is true? I already know it isn't. Princesses don't go missing and end up in foster care no matter how many little girls wish they did. You're wasting your time."

"You cannot possibly know that until you take a blood test."

"Oh, a blood test? Is that all?" Maggy bared her teeth at him. "You can expect *that* to happen over my dead body."

He smiled then. And it was devastating. It…did things to his face. Made it something far closer to beautiful than any man so hard and uncompromising should ever look. It should have been impossible. It was certainly unfair. Maggy's mouth went dry. Parts of her body she'd stopped paying any attention to outside of their sheer biological functions prickled to uncomfortable awareness.

Oh, no, she thought.

"Let me tell you how this will go," Reza said softly, as if he knew exactly what was happening to her. As if he was pleased it was. "You will give me a blood sample. You will sit and eat a decent dinner with me tonight not only because I wish to get to know you, but because you look as if you haven't eaten well in some time. If ever. The blood test will confirm what I already know, which is that you are Her Royal Highness Magdalena of Santa Domini. At which point, you will leave this menial existence that is beneath you in more ways than it is possible to number and is an insult to the blood in your veins. And then, among other things, you will assume your rightful position in your brother's court and in the line of ascension to his throne."

She'd opened her mouth to protest his snide reference to her menial life, not to mention his idea that she was some wayward waif who'd never eaten a meal, but got caught on that last bit.

Maggy's heart seemed to twist in her chest. "My brother?"

And she knew she gave herself away with that. There was no chance this overwhelming man didn't hear the breathiness in her voice. The longing for that life so many people took for granted. A life with family. With *people* who were as much hers as she was theirs, whatever that looked like. The kind of life she'd never had—and had taught herself a long time ago to stop wishing for.

"Yes," Reza said. His harshly regal head canted to one side, though he kept his gaze on hers. "Your brother. He is the king of Santa Domini. Previous to his coronation, he was rather well-known as one of the world's greatest and most scandalous playboys. If you have been in the vicinity of a tabloid newspaper over the past twenty years, you will have seen a great deal of him, I'd imagine. Too much of him, I would wager."

Her hands felt numb. With some distant part of her brain, it occurred to her to think that was a strange reaction. That pins and needles should stab at her fingers as if her arms had fallen asleep when they hadn't.

When, despite what was happening here, she was very much awake.

"Cairo," Maggy whispered. Because even she knew that name. Everybody knew that name. She'd seen his pictures all over every magazine in existence for as long as she could remember, because there was nothing else to do while standing in line in sad discount supermarkets stocking up on cheap staples but look at pretty people doing marvelous things in exotic places. "Cairo Santa Domini."

Reza inclined his head. "The one and only. He is your brother. As someone who saw him in person not long ago and is now looking at you, I must tell you that there is absolutely no doubt that you are his blood relative."

Maggy shook her head. She took a step back and only stopped because she had nowhere to go, with his henchmen looming back near the counter. "No."

She didn't know what she was denying. Which part of this madness. Only that it was crucial to her sanity—to everything that had kept her upright and grimly moving forward all her life no matter what got thrown at her—that she keep doing so.

But his dark gaze was much too knowing on hers. She was sure he could see far too much. And the fact he could—that he seemed to have no problem whatsoever seeing straight through her when no one else had ever come close—shook through her like a winter storm, treacherous and dark.

"This will not go away, Princess," he told her, very matter-of-factly. And he didn't shift that gaze of his from hers. "Nor will I. And you can be certain that if I recognized you, so, too, will someone else."

"I think you're overestimating the amount of time

people in your world spend looking closely at people in mine."

Again, a curve of those stern lips, and she wasn't equipped to deal with that. She couldn't process it. She could only feel the way it flushed over her, like another kick of temper when she knew full well it wasn't that. She might not have felt anything like it in recent memory, but she knew it wasn't anything close to *temper*.

"You're decades too late," she threw at him. She didn't know where it came from. Or, worse, she knew exactly where it came from. That dark little hollow place she carried around inside of her that nothing ever filled. And she couldn't seem to stop herself once she'd started. "Everyone dreams they're secretly a princess when they're ten. Especially in foster care. But I'm over that now. This is my life. I made it, I'm happy with it, and I'm staying in it."

"Come to dinner with me anyway," he ordered her, and there was something about the way he said things as if they were laws instead of requests that, oddly, made her want to obey him. She had to lock her knees to keep from moving toward him. She, who was famous for her attitude problems and inability to follow the orders of people who were *paying* her to listen to them. What was *that*? "You can consider it a date."

Maggy assumed he was joking. Because he had to be joking, of course. No one asked her for dates, even roundabout ones like this one. She had *stay the hell away from me* stamped all over her face, she was pretty sure.

And the few times anyone had actually mustered up all their courage and asked that scrappy Strafford girl on a date, it had not been a king.

Not that she'd independently verified this man was who he said he was.

"I would rather die than go on a date with you," she told him, which was melodramatic and also, in that moment, the absolute truth.

Again that slow, coolly astonished blink of his, as if he required extra time to process what she'd said to him—and not, she was quite sure, because he didn't understand her.

"How much money can you possibly make in this place?" he asked.

"That's rude. And it's none of your business. Just like everything else about me is none of your business. You don't get to know everything about another person simply because you demand it or send your little minions to dig it up."

"By minions, am I to assume you mean my staff?"

"If you want to know things about someone, you ask. You wait to see if they answer. If they don't, it could be because they don't want to answer you because your question is obnoxious. Or because they think you're a random creepy guy who showed up with his personal collection of armed men after closing time to say a whole lot of crazy things, suggesting you might be delusional. Or that you won't go away no matter what you are. Or in my case, all of the above."

That muscle in his jaw clenched tight. "Consider dinner with me an employment opportunity." When she only stared back at him, that muscle clenched tighter. "An interview for a position, if you will."

"A position as what? Your next little piece on the side? While I'm sure competition for that downward spiral is intense, I'll pass. I prefer my lovers, you know, *sane*."

She knew she'd gone too far then. Reza went very, very still. His gray eyes seemed to burn through her. Her pulse took off at a gallop and she had to order herself to keep breathing.

"Be very careful, Magdalena," he advised her, his voice low and stern and still, it wound its way through her like a wicked heat. "I have so far tolerated your impudence because it is clear you cannot help yourself, given your circumstances. But you begin to stray too far into the sort of insults that cannot and will not be tolerated. Do you understand me?"

Maggy understood that he was far more intimidating than he should have been, and she was fairly hard to cow. She told herself it didn't matter. That she was as numb as she wished she really was, head to toe, except for that wildness deep in her core that she wanted to deny was there.

She rolled her eyes. "You don't have to worry about tolerating me. And I really don't care if you do or don't. What you do have to do is go."

He let out a breath, but she knew, somehow, he wasn't any less furious.

"I have already told you the only way that will happen and I am not in the habit of repeating myself. Nor am I renowned for going back on my word. Two things you would do well to keep in mind."

And Maggy thought, to her horror, that she might explode. And worse, do it right in front of him. Something was rolling inside of her, heavy and gathering steam, and she was terrified that she might break down in front of this granite wall of a man and humiliate her-self. *Ruin* herself.

She didn't know him. She didn't *want* to know him. But she knew, beyond a shadow of a doubt, that she couldn't show any weakness in front of him or it would kill her.

"Fine," she gritted out at him, because when there were no more defensive plays to make, offense was the only way to go. She'd learned that the hard way, too, like everything else. "I'll have dinner with you. But only if you leave right now."

And then she wished she could snatch the words back the moment she'd said them.

Reza didn't smile or gloat. He didn't let that stark, hard mouth of his soften at all. And yet there was that silver gleam in his gaze that kicked at her anyway and was worse, somehow, than the gloating of a lesser man. Or it hit her harder, anyway.

He merely inclined his head. Then he named the fanciest resort within a hundred-mile radius, waiting until she nodded.

"Yes," she bit out, letting her sharpness take over her tone because it was much, much better than what she was afraid hid beneath it. "I know where it is."

"I will expect you in one hour," he told her.

Expect away, idiot, she thought darkly.

But she made herself smile. "Sure thing."

"And if you do not appear," Reza said quietly, be-cause apparently he really could read her like a very simple book, "I will come and find you. I know where you live. I know where you work. I know the car you drive, if, indeed, that deathtrap can rightly be called a car at all. I have an entire security force at my beck and call, and as the sovereign of another nation, even one who is flying under the radar as I am here, I am granted vast diplomatic immunity to do as I please. I would suggest you consider these things carefully before you imagine you can plot your way out of this."

And he turned on his heel before she could come up with a response to that. Which was good, because she didn't have one. His men leapt to serve him, flanking him and opening the door for him, then swept him back out into the night.

The cold air rushed in again. The door slapped shut behind him, the echo of the bell still in the air.

Maggy was breathing too hard. Too loud. And she couldn't seem to operate her limbs.

So she made herself move. She sank back down to her knees and she scrubbed that damned sticky area like her life depended on it. And only when she was finished, only when she'd mopped the rest of the floor and dealt with her bucket in the utility room in the back, did she pull out her own phone again.

She looked at it for a long moment. Maybe too long.

Then she pretended she was doing something, anything else as she opened up her browser and typed in *king of the Constantines…*

And there he was. Splashed all over the internet. On the covers of reputed newspapers and all over their inside pages. In image after image. She saw articles about his childhood. His education at Cambridge. His coronation following his father's sudden heart attack and the war he'd wrenched his country back from in the months that followed. That same harsh face. That same arrogant brow. That same imperial hand waving here, there, everywhere as he gave orders and addresses and spoke of this law and that moral imperative and the role of the monarchy in the modern world.

It was him. Reza was exactly who he'd said he was.

Which meant that there was a very high probability that she was, too.

And this time, when Maggy went back down on her knees on the floor, it wasn't because she was in a hurry to get back to cleaning it.

It was because for the first time in her entire life, when she'd learned how to be tougher than tough no matter what, her knees failed to hold her.

CHAPTER THREE

By the time Maggy walked into the gaspingly precious and markedly high-class resort and spa, set in all its grand timber and soaring glass splendor some miles outside of Deanville at the foot of the local mountains, she'd done a great deal more research.

She'd gone home after locking up the coffee shop and she'd crouched there on her single bed in her narrow little room with her phone to her face, taking an internet crash course on the life and times of the Santa Domini royal family. And everything she'd discovered had made her…a little bit dizzy.

Could this be real? Could she have a history after all these years of being nothing but a blank slate? Would she finally discover how and why she'd been left by the side of that road twenty years ago? Was it possible that the answer really, truly was something like one of the many silly and fanciful stories she'd made up when she was a girl to explain it away?

She'd spent a lot of time and energy back then trying to explain to herself how and why she'd ended up the way she had. The possibility that she'd been a kidnapped princess had featured heavily in the rotation of the tales she'd told herself when she'd still had a little foolish hope left. After all, it was a much better story than the more likely one—that whatever adults had been responsible for her had abandoned her because they couldn't care for her or didn't want that kind of commitment any longer. For whatever depressing reasons adults would have to make such decisions. A few came to mind as more likely than finding out she was a misplaced princess. Substance abuse, for example. Mental illness. Poverty. She could take her pick and they all ended the same way: a sad eight-year-old girl on the side of a road with no memory of how she'd gotten there.

But that wasn't the sort of story Maggy had wanted to tell herself back then. Princesses won hands down every time.

"Don't get your hopes up," she'd snapped at herself, there in her rented room in an old, converted Victorian that had likely seen its better days when Vermont was still more or less one big farm.

She'd scrolled through pictures of the queen, the king. She'd taken great care not to think the word *parents*. Or the other, more personal words that indicated the kind of close relationships she'd never had with anyone. *Mother. Father.* And she'd sucked up her courage and taken a long, close look at the princess who had supposedly died in that car accident twenty years ago. She'd stared at that little girl's face, not sure what she saw when she looked at it. Or what, if anything, she *should* see. There was no sense of recognition. There was… nothing inside of her. No spark, no reaction. There was simply the picture of a little girl lost years ago.

And then she'd studied the many, many pictures of and corresponding articles about Cairo Santa Domini. He was once the most scandal-prone royal in all of Europe. Now he was the beloved king of the country he'd taken back from the military everyone seemed to assume had not only wrested control of his kingdom thirty years ago, but ten years after that had engineered that car accident in Montenegro to take out the exiled king. And in so doing, had killed everyone in the Santa Domini royal family save King Cairo himself, who had been in boarding school in the United States at the time.

He was potentially her only living family member.

It was possible, after all this time and a life lived entirely on her own in every conceivable way, that she *actually had* a living family member.

Maggy had felt as if she might be sick.

She'd thought a lot about simply getting into her junky old car and driving absolutely anywhere Reza—who it seemed really was the king he'd claimed he was no matter how little she wanted that to be true—was not.

But in the end, she hadn't done it. She'd thrown on the only dress she owned that was even slightly nice and she hadn't gone to too much trouble with the rest because he'd made his feelings about her appearance pretty clear. And then she'd driven herself over to the upscale resort instead of out west toward California. And yes, she had to sit in her car in the frigid parking lot until her hands stopped shaking, but that was between her and her steering wheel and the close, hard dark all around.

Maggy prided herself on the toughness she'd earned every day of the past twenty years, having had no one to depend on but herself. Ever. That meant that no matter how she felt—in this case, about as far from *tough* as it was possible to get without actually dissolving into a sea of tears, which she never allowed herself and certainly not in public places—she'd pulled herself together and climbed out of that car, her shaking hands be damned. She'd wanted answers to questions she'd stopped asking years ago. It was a little bit surprising *how very much* she wanted them, so long after she'd decided wondering about such things only made her weak. And how, with only the slightest provocation—if that was what she could call the appearance of an actual king in The Coffee Queen on Main Street—all those same old questions flooded her.

Making her realize she'd never really gotten over wondering who she was or where she'd come from the way she'd assured herself she had. She'd simply stuffed her urge to ask those things way down deep inside, where none of that could leak out into her daily life any longer. The way it had when she'd been much younger and much, much angrier about her lot in life.

When she started across the chilly, icy parking lot, well salted to make certain the wealthy people who could afford to stay here didn't slip, break their heads open, and then fail to pay their astronomical bills, she was caught for a moment in the dark grip of the cold night. It seemed to tumble down around her and she took as deep a breath as she could stand of the sharp winter air, tipping her head back so she could see all the far-off stars gleaming there above her.

Always watching. Always quiet, always calm. No matter what darkness was engulfing her, the stars shone through.

By the time Maggy made it to the front door of the resort, that great, raw thing inside of her that felt like the sort of sob that she'd rather die than let free had subsided a bit. Just a bit. But it was enough to keep her hands from shaking.

A hotel employee with a clipboard and a walkie-talkie waited for her in the slick, self-consciously rustic lobby of the hotel, a serene smile on her face, as if she and Maggy had already met a thousand times before. Maggy was certain they had not.

"If you'll follow me, Ms. Strafford," the woman said warmly. Maybe too warmly, Maggy thought, when greeting a complete stranger. "I'll take you where you need to go. Mr. Argos—" and there was specific emphasis on that name "—is waiting."

On any other night Maggy would have asked a few follow-up questions. Demanded to know how this woman knew who she was at a glance, for a start. But something told her she didn't want to know the answer to that question. That it would involve the word *appalling* again. And while Maggy felt her self-esteem was strong enough to withstand the snotty comments of an uninvited king in her coffee shop, there was no point testing that theory here, in the sort of five-star hotel broke girls like herself normally gave a wide berth.

Instead, she let the woman lead her back outside and into a waiting hotel shuttle, clearly set aside for her use. She didn't ask any questions then, either. She only settled into the seat she was offered in the otherwise empty vehicle and stared out the window, trying to keep her eyes on the stars as the shuttle wound its way out into the depths of the property, deep into the woods and halfway up the mountain. It stopped there. Maggy glanced out to see a guardhouse and gates, and heard many short bursts of noise on multiple walkie-talkies before the shuttle started to move again.

"It's only a few moments more," the woman from the hotel told her, still smiling so happily.

Maggy practiced smiling like a normal person. It was a skill she'd never mastered, given how little cause she'd had to go around smiling at random people. Or at all. In her experience, anyone who wanted her to *act friendly* and who wasn't paying her to do so was best avoided altogether. It felt awkward and wrong, as if she was *doing something* to her cheeks. She was relieved when the woman looked back to the shuttle driver instead.

Gradually, Maggy realized they were on a long driveway. It climbed farther up the steep incline in a corridor of evergreens and ghostly birch trees, then stopped beneath a towering palace of a house done in more timber and even more dramatic glass. It sprawled over the mountainside as if it had been placed there by divine intervention instead of the resort's developers.

She wasn't the least bit surprised that this was where Reza was staying.

And when she walked inside the soaring entry hall that must have commanded views over most of New England in the sunlight, she was equally unsurprised to find a battalion of servants waiting for her as if she'd strolled into Buckingham Palace.

Not that she'd ever been anywhere near Buckingham Palace. But she'd seen as many pictures of the British palace in the supermarket tabloids over the years as she had of Cairo Santa Domini and his exploits.

After her coat was taken and she'd been greeted approximately nine hundred times by uniformed staff members who pledged to attend to her every need, whatever those might be, Maggy was led off into the house. Each room she walked through was more impressive than the last. Here a library of floor-to-ceiling books and dark leather armchairs pulled close to a crackling fire. There what appeared to be a games room, with a pool table and a chess table and stout cupboards likely filled with every board game imaginable, if she'd had to guess. A large living area, ripe with comfortable couches and deep, thick rugs set out before the glass windows and an outside deck with views over the valley. A closer, more intimate den, with wide armchairs and enveloping sofas and the sort of wall of closed wood cupboards she figured hid television equipment.

Only when she'd walked for what seemed like miles was she finally delivered into a final room. This one was as magnificent as the rest. It featured cozy log walls and architecturally significant windows. There was a stone fireplace and a small seating area arranged around it, and in the center of that area stood a small table set for two.

Maggy stared at that intimate little setup for so long, her heart doing strange things in the back of her throat, she forgot to look around at the rest of the room.

"Do not tell me you have never seen a dinner table before."

His voice was dark and perhaps slightly amused. She jerked her head away from the table and the fire and there he was, standing near a small, personal bar, where he'd clearly just poured himself a drink.

Reza Argos. His Royal Majesty, the king of the Constantines.

Her heart went wild. She felt her pulse rocket through her, making her strangely aware of her temples, her neck. Her wrists. Her sex. Her hands felt numb again, and twice as shaky, and she couldn't tell if it was the

insane circumstances or if it was just him. His gaze
was gray and steady on her, and that made it worse.
That made it…dangerous in ways she was afraid to
consider too closely.

It had been one thing when she'd thought he was a
crazy person, there in the coffee shop. It had been easy
to keep her wits about her. But now she knew who he
was. And that seemed to make everything feel…pre-
carious.

"They buried that princess," she blurted out.

Because if she waited, she was afraid she wouldn't
dare ask. She was afraid of too many things, suddenly,
and they all had to do with his harshly fierce face and
those elegant hands. And the truth was that she *wanted
things*—and that, more than anything else, made her
chest feel tight and jittery. Maggy hadn't made it this
far by wanting things she couldn't have. She'd learned
better. And yet here she was anyway.

"With her parents," she continued when Reza only
gazed back at her, his gray eyes glittering as if he was
trying to read her. "I can't possibly be a person whose
body was recovered from an accident site, legally identified, and then very publicly laid to rest. No one can,
but especially not some random foster care kid on the
other side of the world."

"A very good evening to you, too." His dark voice
was reproving. And something else that moved in her,
deep and low.

Maggy told herself she could not possibly have cared
less what *moved in her*. And that she shouldn't feel it—
or anything—anyway.

"Oh, I'm sorry," she said. Or really *seethed*. "Did
you think I was here for my health? You told me a huge,

ridiculous fairy tale of a story earlier. If it's the lie it seems to be, I'm out of here."

Reza swirled the amber liquid in his crystal tumbler and eyed her over the top of it.

"*A* body was found, yes," he said, his tone cool. "It was said to be the princess's, but then, the entire royal family was identified by members of the very military who had ousted them. There is no telling who lies in those graves. But until now, aside from a few conspiracy theorists in dark corners of the internet, no one had any reason to doubt it was exactly who General Estes's government said it was."

"So in this conspiracy theory, the king and queen are alive, too?" Maggy did nothing to keep that scoffing note out of her voice. "And, what—are currently wandering around aimlessly, disguised as homeless people in Topeka?"

His regal brow rose in affronted astonishment. Or whatever the kingly version of that was, and what pricked at Maggy was that she felt that, too. Everywhere, as if his expression was specially calibrated to work inside her like a flush of heat. She shoved that weirdness aside.

"Topeka?" he echoed. As if she'd said *chlamydia*.

"It's a city. In Kansas."

Reza blinked. Very slowly. She understood that it was deliberate. It was how he indicated his displeasure. That, too, made her feel entirely too warm.

"And Kansas is one of your states, is it not?"

She practiced her smile. "Do you need me to give you a geography lesson?"

He didn't quite sigh. He seemed to grow taller and stormier at the same time, and somehow more formidable. He was wearing a dark suit that was unlike any suit she'd ever seen a man wear in her life. Calling it a *suit* seemed like an insult. It was molded to his tall, solid form, *doing things* to his broad shoulders and making it impossible to look away from all his lean, hard muscles and the planes of his well-cut chest.

"I understand that I must treat you as I would any stray, wild creature I happened upon," he said, almost musingly, his voice calm and light, though his hard gaze gleamed silver. "Your instinct is to bite first. It is no doubt how you survived this ordeal unscathed."

His gaze swept over her, from the top of her head where she'd clipped back her hair in what even she knew was a sad attempt at the sort of hairstyles she'd seen the queen wearing in those pictures to her shoes, which were the black stiletto heels she'd been required to wear during her brief tenure as a cocktail waitress last year. His gaze rose again, taking in every detail of her stretchy little black dress and making her feel as if she was stripped naked, before he found her gaze again.

"Relatively unscathed, that is," he amended.

And that was a different kind of heat then. The scorching reaction to the way he looked at her and then the slap of the insult. Maggy hated both versions. She had to order herself not to clench her fists. Not because she didn't want to hit him; she did. But because she didn't want him to have the slightest idea how much he got to her.

She had no idea how or why she knew that would be the death of her. Only that it would. And that she had to do whatever she could to avoid it.

"Two things," she managed to say, keeping the various rioting factions inside of her at bay and her voice as chilly as the winter night pressing against the windows. "First, I'm not a raccoon. It might surprise you to learn that I don't really like being compared to one. And second, is an insult called something different when it comes out of the mouth of a king?"

His mouth pressed into a hard line, and he set his glass down on the bar with a sharp *click*. He crossed the room in an easy step or two, which wasn't an improvement because then he was *right there*. Too solid. Too tall. And much too close.

He gazed down at her, his gray eyes like a storm, and she couldn't understand that. Why *he* seemed as if this was hard for *him* when it had so little to do with him. He was a messenger, nothing more. He wasn't the one who'd been discarded.

You don't know that you are, either, she snapped at herself.

But then everything stopped. Inside her. Out in the world. Everywhere.

Because he reached out his hand and he touched her. *He touched her.*

He fit his hand to her cheek gently. Very gently. As touches went, it was innocuous. Maggy had fended off far more intimate grabs at her person as a matter of course when she'd worked in that cocktail bar.

But this was Reza.

And everything changed.

His palm was hot. Hard. It molded to her jaw while his fingers brushed into her hair, then ran over that spot behind her ear where her birthmark lay. As if he knew exactly where it was. As if he knew exactly who she was. And something burst open inside of her. She'd never felt anything like it. It exploded wide-open, then rolled through her, sensation rocketing from her cheek to her limbs. She felt herself shake. Worse, she knew he could feel it.

She told herself to jerk away from him. But she didn't. She couldn't.

Her eyes were too wide. His were too gray.

"It is called an insult either way," he said quietly, and she thought she heard an echo of that impossible explosion in his dark voice. She was sure of it when he dropped his hand and adjusted the cuff of his jacket and the crisp white shirt beneath it. "But most people, of course, would pretend it was a bit of flattery instead, simply because it came from me."

What Maggy wanted to pretend was that her heart wasn't racing. That the lopsided heart behind her ear didn't seem to burn like a brand because he'd touched it. That she didn't feel trembling and silly and ridiculously vulnerable. That there wasn't that ominous prickling behind her eyes, and that deep in her core, she wasn't melting and much too soft.

But she couldn't quite get there. She took a deep breath instead.

"It must be nice to be king," Maggy said after a moment, and the funny thing was that there was no edge in her voice then. As if she'd forgotten to try to play the angles here. As if his touch had smoothed them all away, making her feel safe when she knew she wasn't. "I bet no one tells *you* that you need to modify your tone and attitude or you'll be out of a job."

His lips quirked. "Certainly not. No one would dare."

And suddenly, Maggy didn't care if she looked weak. She needed to put space between them. She needed to keep his hands away from her, because she didn't know what she might do with her own. She stepped back and she didn't care how silver that gleam in his eyes was.

"Come," he said then, and she didn't like that. The way his voice was so rich and warm, as if it was as much a part of the fire that crackled in the stone fireplace as it was of him.

Get a grip, she ordered herself.

He ushered her to one of the seats at that intimate table before the fire then, and everything got awkward as he held her seat. Or maybe she was the awkward thing here, while she could still feel his hand against her skin like a new tattoo, a red-hot pulse of sensation. She didn't let herself look at him. She sat down and was *aware* of him all around her, looming and compelling, as he pushed her closer to the table. It was such an odd, old-world sort of gesture, she thought as he took the seat opposite her. There was no reason at all she should feel so…fluttery.

She was absurdly glad that there was now a table between them.

As if responding to some secret signal, a breath after Reza sat down the doors to the room opened and their dinner was wheeled in by more uniformed servants. As they bustled about the table, a different man appeared at her side. This one wore a dark suit and a diffident smile, and held what looked like medical supplies in his hands.

"If I could take a quick sample, Ms. Strafford," he murmured, but his gaze was on the king.

Maggy's eyes flew to Reza's. Too much silver and too much hard gray beneath it. Yet Reza only gazed back at her, his mouth an unsmiling line.

"Do you want to know?" he asked quietly. "I think

you already suspect the truth. I know I do. But this is how we know for certain."

That question echoed inside of her like a drum, loud and low and long.

Did she want to know? He'd offered her this lovely little fairy-tale explanation for her life earlier this evening. A mere handful of hours ago. But she'd risen to meet it, armed with twenty years of her own secret fairy tales to choose from, rattling around inside of her and making all of this feel a whole lot more fraught with peril and meaning than it should.

Do you want to know?

Maggy told herself—sternly—that she wanted to confirm the fact that she was not Magdalena Santa Domini. That the only reason she was here was to prove him wrong, and it had nothing at all to do with that scraped-raw hollow deep inside her, that unleashed sob she refused to let out. That it had nothing to do with a lost little girl, tossed aside like so much trash, who had waited her whole life to belong somewhere.

That she was not a fairy-tale princess. That she'd gotten over imagining otherwise a long time ago. That there was nothing wrong with reality and who cared that once upon a time she'd wet her pillows every night with too many tears for too many fantastical stories that never came true.

She told herself she'd exorcised that little girl a long time ago. And that this, right here, was a way to make sure she never came back—because that little girl was dangerous. She didn't know any better than to *want* with abandon.

Maggy refused to meet Reza's gaze then. She ignored the little voice inside of her that warned her not to do this, no matter what might come of it. And then she held out her arm and let the smooth-faced man draw a vial of her blood, as quickly and efficiently as the other servants tended to the plating and presentation of the food.

That was it, then, she thought as the man gathered up his supplies, bowed slightly to the king, and took his leave. The answer was coming at her whether she liked it or not. Like a train.

"When will we know?" she asked. Despite her best attempt to keep from saying anything.

"Shortly." Reza's gaze was still on her, she could feel it. She kept hers on the edge of her heavy silver fork. More precisely, *one of* her heavy silver forks. "I've assembled a makeshift laboratory in the solarium."

That didn't surprise her at all. "Of course you have."

Maggy stared down at her plate as a first course was set there before her, not sure what it was and also not at all sure she could eat anything anyway. She told herself that was what happened when she had a needle stuck in her body three seconds before dinner, but she was fooling no one with that, least of all herself. She felt…outside herself. Turned inside out. Exposed in a way that didn't make sense, when this man had no more idea who she really was than she ever had.

The feeling only got worse when the staff retreated, leaving them alone in a bright little room that seemed to shrink tight around them.

"It is a country paté," Reza murmured, sounding remote and polite. As if he was commenting on the weather. "Locally sourced, I imagine."

Maggy blinked at her plate, then at him. And knew before she opened her mouth that she shouldn't. That there were too many vast, unwieldy things rocking around inside of her and making her…not quite herself. But that didn't stop her.

"I don't understand the point of this. You said you wanted to get to know me, which we both know isn't true. You don't want to know *me*. You have some fantasy about a lost princess. And I didn't agree to eat—" she wrinkled up her nose "—whatever this is."

"Your palate is likely far more refined, I am sure."

"My palate is basically Cheetos and beer," she retorted, which wasn't exactly true. She also enjoyed ramen. "Does that dilute royal blood? If so, I'm afraid you're not going to get the answer you want."

She had the impression he was clenching his teeth again, though she couldn't actually see it. Only that same muscle in his freshly shaved jaw, calling attention to the harsh perfection of his decidedly regal face.

But when he spoke, his voice was smooth. Calm. "I notice that you seem to have accepted both that I am the king I claimed I was and that you, too, might indeed be Magdalena Santa Domini."

Maggy wouldn't have called the feelings sloshing around inside of her just then *acceptance*. She shrugged, hoping to mask them a little.

"You're either the king of the Constantines or a very good impersonator," she told him offhandedly. "And I'm not sure an impersonator would go to the trouble or expense of renting out this ridiculous place for the sole purpose of conning a broke coffee shop barista." She considered that a moment. "I can't see any reason why anyone would bother conning me."

Again, she saw that mix of affront and astonishment all over his regal face.

"I am delighted that I have distinguished myself in

some way from those charming individuals who clamber about in places like Times Square, dressed up as some or other famous fictional character. For tips." He cut something on his plate, too precisely, as if *tips* was a filthy curse word. But then he looked at her instead of putting his food into his mouth, and she had the impression that edge in his voice made a far better knife than the one he held. In that hand of his she could still feel on her jaw. "The generations of monarchs who preceded me to the throne of the Constantines would no doubt be pleased that a son of the House of Argos has not been mistaken for a street corner hustler with a traveling act."

Maggy felt as if she was sitting on an earthquake, not a chair with a high, solid back. As if the more she pretended the whole planet wasn't shaking there, directly underneath her, the more it actually tore through her, shifting whole continents and ripping up the ground.

"I don't want to talk about country paté or my clothes or wild animals," she managed to say, her voice as edgy as his had been, if somewhat less precise. "You said a lot of things in the coffee shop today."

"I did."

"What happens…"

"Eyes on me, if you please. Not your plate."

Her gaze rose and met his of its own accord. As if she had nothing to do with it—because if left to her own devices, Maggy knew she would have ignored that order. Especially when she was lost in all that intent gray, focused on her as if nothing else existed.

And she couldn't believe she was going to ask the question. She couldn't believe that after all this time she was going to take so little care of herself when it most mattered—when she most needed to protect what little was left of her that could still be hurt. But she couldn't seem to keep herself from it.

"What happens if the blood test says what you think it will?" she asked, because she couldn't seem to help it.

And once again, she could see intense satisfaction all over him. It made him seem bigger. Harder. More dangerous than she thought a king ought to seem, especially when he wasn't doing anything but sitting there on the other side of a few fresh flowers and a couple of dramatic candles.

"Once your identity is verified it becomes a question of how and when to announce yourself to the world."

"You mean to Cairo Santa Domini." She frowned at him when he didn't respond, though he kept that hard, intent gaze of his trained on her. "Surely you would tell him first. If it turns out he's actually…" She couldn't say the word. But then she worried not saying it was more telling, so she forced it out, ignoring how it felt in her mouth. "If he's family."

"Of course," Reza said after a moment, but she wasn't sure she believed him. "But there are one or two matters to attend to before placing you in the spotlight your brother seems to roll around with him wherever he goes. It is a very bright spotlight, I must tell you, the sort that brings all manner of things out from the shadows. It is a decidedly relentless glare."

Maggy couldn't bring herself to worry about spotlights, of all things. She thought Reza meant that figuratively, but who knew? He was a real, live king. Cairo Santa Domini was also a real, live king. For all she knew, real, live kings traveled with actual physical spotlights wherever they went, as part of their entourages.

She concentrated on the other part. "Matters? What matters?"

Reza leaned back in his chair and studied her for a moment. She was caught by the forearm he'd left on the table, strong and hard, a hint of the excessively masculine watch he wore peeking out from his cuff. It was outfitted with enough inset gadgetry to man a space shuttle, she thought. Or, hell, operate a spotlight or two if he needed one.

"I do not wish to insult you, Magdelena."

"Maggy," she corrected him, but without the heat she should have summoned, mostly because she...liked that version of her name in his mouth. *Any* version of her name, for that matter.

Idiot.

He appeared not to hear her anyway. "But the fact remains that you have spent the past twenty years in a situation that can only be called somewhat suboptimal."

"I can think of a whole lot of other things to call my 'situation.'" She let out a short laugh. "None of them polite."

He inclined his head in that way of his that made her want to scream. And also maybe reach her own hand out, across the table, and touch his.

Obviously, she did nothing of the kind. Because that was *insane*.

"You will be the subject of intense scrutiny." He tapped one of his long, tapered fingers against the tabletop, as if to a beat in his head only he could hear. "It will make the coverage of your brother all these years seem mild in comparison. You cannot underestimate the draw such a story will have."

Maggy tried out one of those smiles again. "Everybody likes a princess."

"But that is the issue, of course." His stern mouth curved slightly, and she had the strangest notion that he was trying to be kind. "Not everyone will, and not in the same way. Particularly not a long-lost princess who has suddenly emerged fully grown to claim her place in the world with all its attendant privileges. And those who do not care for a princess who rises from the dead will attack you however they can. They will dig into your life here. They will rip you to shreds in the papers. They will use any ammunition they can find to shame you."

"Why?"

His gaze was matter-of-fact. "Because they can. Because they are paparazzi scum who love nothing more than tearing things down however possible. Because it sells." He shrugged. "You can pick any reason you like, but the manipulation of public sentiment will be the same."

Maggy swallowed. "In case you're wondering, you're not really selling this."

She reached out for her water glass and was horrified to see her hand was shaking again. She dropped it back to her lap and only frowned when Reza poured her a glass of wine instead and set it before her. Wine, she thought, would not help this situation at all. It would blur everything and complicate it far too much.

And God knew she'd never manage to keep her hands to herself with a glass or two of wine in her.

The fact that notion made her feel something like seasick didn't make it any less true.

"Never fear," Reza said as he sat back in his seat.

"You have a secret weapon that will make all of this child's play."

This time her smile came a little more easily. "Do you mean my biting wit? Or maybe you mean my famous charm. Both known as weapons in their way, you're right."

His gray eyes gleamed silver in the candlelight. "I mean me."

CHAPTER FOUR

"You," Maggy said, sounding as resoundingly un-impressed as ever, which might have dented Reza's confidence somewhat had he not been, for all intents and purposes, bulletproof. He was the king of the Constantines. He'd learned from his father's mistakes and the collapse and war Reza had narrowly avoided. His confidence was unassailable. "You are my secret weapon."

"No need to fall all over yourself to thank me," Reza said drily. "It is but one of my many royal duties to aid a lost princess in her time of need."

Her captivating eyes narrowed. "Let me guess. You run a royal princess rescue and travel the world, collecting princesses wherever you roam and then holding adoption events on Saturdays."

Reza found himself paying far too much attention to her impertinent mouth, and not only because of the astonishing things that came out of it. He ordered himself to raise his gaze to hers again.

"I have always been good with strays, Magdalena," he told her, his voice low, and he was sure he could see goose bumps prickle over the exposed skin at her neck-line. He liked that far more than he should when she was such an unrefined little thing, scrappy and sharp. "It is always about letting them know two things."

"Wait. I know this one." Her gaze flashed with something too dark for simple temper. "Something about how you're a mighty king. And then something else about how, in case anyone missed it, you're a mighty, mighty king."

He had no idea why, instead of igniting his outrage the way it should have done and would have done with anyone else, her arch tone and the matching look on her face made him bite back a wholly unexpected surge of amusement instead. Reza didn't know whether he was baffled by her behavior—or at himself. Both, perhaps.

"One," he said, as if she hadn't spoken, because that was clearly the safer course, "that they are safe at last. And two, that it is far better to have me as an ally than an enemy."

"I bet that goes over really well with the average puppy," Maggy murmured, as disrespectfully as ever. "It must make potty training a breeze."

And it occurred to Reza then, as they sat there on opposite sides of the small table and Maggy's guarded caramel gaze was fixed to his as if she was expecting an attack at any moment, that he was unused to participating in interactions with women when he didn't already know the outcome.

Such things simply never happened, not even back when he'd been at Cambridge and had enjoyed the illusion of slightly more freedom while his father had run the country toward ruin. He'd still had guards who made sure no one ever got too close to him or approached him without permission, especially any women he might have wanted to meet. And even then, he'd been too conscious of the responsibilities that waited for him and his own father's *do as I say, not as I do* expectations of his behavior to risk something that could end up in tabloid photographs and appalling tell-alls.

As a sitting monarch—and the son of a father who had bent the rules because he'd allowed himself to get into a position where he could be blackmailed in the first place—Reza obviously could not date. He could not participate in anything remotely like a date, in fact. In the years before he'd been seriously looking for an appropriate queen, he'd had to find his women a different way entirely, as there could be no chance meetings for a man in his position. No happening upon a bar or whatever sort of place single people congregated. No accidental meetings of the friends of his friends, given that no one appeared in his presence without both permission and a thorough vetting. Reza's advisers presented him with thick dossiers detailing any woman deemed appropriate for his notice. He sifted through them when he was of a mood until he found any who appealed to him. When he did, arrangements would be made to meet privately, usually at dinners like this one or with a careful selection of very old friends who proved indisputably loyal and discreet.

But the women in question, vetted or not, had ample time to decline the invitation to meet with him before they ever set foot in any room where he might appear. Refusals were not common, of course. Still, they happened every now and again. Reza was a powerful and public figure forever bound to his country first. Some women didn't wish to put themselves into that kind of fishbowl, and how could he blame them?

The ones who did, the ones who met him in artfully

arranged places like this one far away from the eyes of the world, were always sure things. Give or take a bit of artful flirtation and the appropriate amount of flattery on his side and awe on theirs, if they sat down with him, they were his.

His lost princess, however, was nothing like a sure thing. She had thus far ignored every reference he'd made to the fact they had been betrothed years ago and, beyond that, made no secret of the fact she did not exactly respect him or even note his eminence. These things were remarkable enough. But more than that, Reza found the unusual sensation of being in some suspense about what might happen here made him... restless.

Maggy sat before him as if she wasn't the least bit intimidated by him—still. When she'd clearly discovered that he was exactly who he'd said he was. It pricked at something in him, that her disrespect hadn't eased in any way. The truth was, he'd expected her to have a full personality shift into the sort of overawed obsequiousness that usually marked his interactions with other people. Especially because she was the only living human who had ever insulted him to his face. He'd imagined this woman would be even more determined to smooth things over with him now that she knew his identity.

That she did not appear to care in the least what he thought of her seemed to stroke him, like hot hands all over his body.

Which was not acceptable. At all.

"What exactly do you want to do to me?" she asked, snapping him back to the dinner at hand.

And for a moment Reza was entirely a man. Not a king. Another sensation that was entirely new to him, and threw him into his father's territory. *I am as much a man as I am a king*, his father's voice echoed in his head. It should have appalled him. Yet he was focused much too intently on her lush mouth, not to mention all the things he'd like to do with that mouth—

Enough. This was neither the time nor the place. This wasn't who he was. He'd made certain of it.

But his body was not paying the slightest bit of attention to his cool, rational mind. It wanted her.

He wanted her.

Not as the queen he'd been promised since her birth, though he wanted that, too. But as a man.

Reza had absolutely no idea what to do with that. Of course, it was not his emotions. Not with a woman who still looked like a servant. Though the fact it was something far more earthy didn't exactly thrill him.

"Because I have to tell you," she was saying, utterly unaware of what was happening to him as far as he could discern, and thank God for that, "as amusing as it is to be compared to an entire zoo's worth of rescue animals, I'm going to go out on a limb and say that, probably, I don't want to do it. Whatever it is."

He was relieved—to an unseemly degree—when the doors opened again and his staff swept in, trading out one course for the next with brisk efficiency. He ordered himself under control, and for the first time in a life dedicated to his duty and the necessity of projecting a great calm whether he felt it or not, he wasn't sure he could manage it.

What the hell was happening to him? Was he genetically predisposed to repeat his father's great folly? He would not allow it. He could not.

Reza glanced up when the door did not close behind

the waitstaff, to see his own personal aide waiting there. Something pounded in him, hard and triumphant. Because this was a formality. He was sure of it.

"Do you have a result?" he asked his man.

He was aware of the way Maggy stiffened in her seat across from him. And more curious, the fact she didn't turn around to look toward the door. She kept her eyes on the plate before her and her hands in her lap. He was certain that if he looked more closely, she'd have balled them into fists. But he kept his gaze trained on the man at the door instead.

"It is a match, sire," the man said, as Reza had known he would since the moment he'd seen that picture of Maggy ten days ago.

He nodded his thanks and his dismissal at once. His blood seemed to roar through him, making him hard and focused and *needy* in a way he didn't quite understand. He was not a man who *needed. A good king does not need the things a man does*, his mother had always told him. The memory set Reza's teeth on edge. He was a king who had all that he needed, thank you. He'd never felt anything like this in his life.

But he kept his voice cool when he spoke, amazed that it, too, was far more difficult than it should have been.

"Congratulations, Princess." He waited for her to look at him, but she didn't. He studied the elegant line of her neck that no cheap black dress could obscure. There were centuries of good breeding right there in her still form. And she would be his queen. All of him—man and king alike, not that he'd ever found there to be much difference between the two before tonight—exulted. "You are, as expected and now beyond any shadow of doubt, Magdalena of Santa Domini."

Naturally, *this* woman did not swoon. Or carry on in any way. Or even seem to react to the news that must surely have been near enough to magic or a lottery win after so many years of hardship and toil. She took a breath that was slightly deeper than any she'd taken before, that was all. Then she raised her head.

There was no joy there on her lovely face. No gleam of victory or relief. Her caramel gaze was flat. Blank.

Reza found her fascinating. And that was the trouble. He had wanted women before, in appropriately discreet ways. He had enjoyed their company, but mostly that was because every woman he'd ever encountered— especially in private—had dedicated herself to entertaining him until the inevitable day he lost interest. He hardly knew what to make of this, that his lost betrothed was about as enamored of him as she was of the table they sat at, and made no attempt to hide it. And while all his previous mistresses seemed to blur together in his mind, this princess who called herself Maggy and sat there before him with badly colored blond hair and a dress that could most charitably be called beneath her station...was not blurry at all. If anything, she was the only thing in sharp, intense focus.

He only just repressed the urge to shake his head, as if to clear it.

"What if there's been a mistake?" she asked.

"There is no room for error," he told her. He found it was preferable to discuss concrete facts than it was to interrogate himself about the strange things happening inside of him tonight. "For various security reasons, samples of many royal families' blood are taken and stored. One never knows the circumstances under which one's identity or paternity might be called into question. A sample of yours was given to my family when our betrothal contracts were executed. Your blood tonight has matched it." He studied her proud, intent face. "There is no mistake."

He watched, drawn to her in a way he chose not to analyze just then, as she reached up and rubbed behind her ear with one finger. Touching that birthmark that marked her, the same way he had earlier.

Again, he expected a reaction. And again, he was disappointed.

Maggy only swallowed, as if against a constriction in her throat, but when she spoke her voice was smooth. "What happens now?"

Reza needed to get ahold of himself. If only because it was unacceptable to imagine any scenario in which the king of the Constantines was the *less* composed person in a room. In any room.

"First, you must look the part," he said, forcing himself to concentrate on the practicalities. Not this madness that was sweeping through him, rendering him a stranger to himself. When he had known exactly who he was and all the contours of the life he would lead from the day of his birth, and had never deviated from that knowledge in all his life. Especially when it came to matters of the flesh, after his father's terrible example.

Uncertainty did not suit him. It horrified him, in fact. Deeply.

Maggy's unreadable eyes were fixed on him. "You said I already look like the late queen. Problem solved."

He noticed she did not refer to Queen Serena as her mother, but he tucked that away. "I'm afraid it is not your bone structure that the paparazzi will focus on."

"Oh, wait." Her caramel gaze turned hostile then. But

not surprised. "What you're trying not to say is that I don't look like a princess. I probably look like a cheap townie who's had to work her ass off to get anything she has, no matter how crappy it looks to visiting royalty. Because guess what? That's who I am."

Reza did not quite sigh. "I cannot imagine any reason the phrase *cheap townie* would exit my lips," he told her. He eyed her mutinous expression. "And certainly not as a description of the woman I am contracted to marry."

"I don't know why not," she retorted. Once again sliding right past their betrothal. Reza found that fascinating, too. What he didn't know was if that was because he was interested in what she tried to ignore—or if his ego was a bit stung by the continuing proof that this woman was the only one alive who, apparently, wasn't transported into a froth of joy at the idea of marrying him. He had the lowering suspicion it was the latter, especially as Maggy kept going, her voice hard. "You weren't quite this shy or retiring back in the coffee shop. Hit me with it. I can take it." She lifted her hands, palms up, but didn't shift her gaze from his. "Tell me all the ways I'm defective. I dare you."

Reza was not used to direct challenges. Much less outright dares. And he was certainly not used to such displays from those who ought to have found his very presence nothing short of miraculous. Worth gratitude, at the very least—but he shoved that aside. That was most definitely his ego talking. The inbred arrogance he'd been born with. He was self-aware enough to recognize he had both in abundance. What he didn't recognize—and did not care for one bit—was this uncontrolled, dark thing he couldn't identify as it swelled in him. It was as if with her, he truly was nothing but a man.

From one breath to the next, he couldn't decide if that was unforgivable or intriguing.

Nonetheless, he took that dare.

"That false color in your hair does not suit you," he told her, keeping his tone even, because he was a king, not a common lout. He did not attack those weaker than him, or in need of his aid. And no matter the mouth on her, his lost princess was very much both. He needed to keep his heavier artillery to himself. "And only partly because it is inexpertly applied. But the rest is a cosmetic matter, easily handled. A question of more appropriate clothing. Garments made to flatter your particular figure rather than off some bargain rack somewhere. Some tutoring in deportment, so you might comport yourself in a manner more in line with your heritage. Perhaps even some time in a spa to tend to your general air of exhausted desperation."

"It must be some spa," Maggy replied darkly, "to combat twenty years of poverty and loneliness. Will a massage do the trick, do you think? Or will I need something a little more theatrical to get the stink out, like some of those hot stones?"

"You asked me to tell you these things and I thought you could take it. Did you not say so?"

"This is me taking it. I didn't promise I'd be mute." She pressed her lips together for a moment. "Anyway, I don't care about cosmetic things. This might be hard for you to comprehend, but for some people, primping is pretty far down the list."

"That is all very well for a coffee shop drone in the middle of nowhere." He lifted his shoulder, then dropped it. "But we are no longer speaking of that woman. We are speaking of a princess who will return from the dead and find herself in the center of intense public scrutiny."

"You mean me. Not a random, theoretical princess. Me." Maggy shook her head. "And let me tell you something about me, since you're so interested. You can't pretend the last twenty years didn't happen, no matter what a blood test says. *I* certainly can't."

"Do you wish to be ridiculed?" he asked her quietly. "Do you imagine you will enjoy snide tabloid articles about your inability to attend to your own grooming? You didn't care for it when I called you a wild animal. Will you like it when the tabloids screech that you are a feral creature more deserving of a wilderness habitat than a palace?"

She looked as if he'd thrust his fork into her jugular, and he didn't much care for the sensation.

"These are realities you must consider now. Who you are is essentially meaningless. It is who you let them see that matters." He waved a hand at her dress, obviously mass-produced, which hugged her figure in a way that would have rendered his own ruthlessly correct mother pale with horror. Reza found that the man in him appreciated the close embrace of all that cheap, stretchy black material more than he wished to admit. "You cannot simply throw on any old thing and step out in it."

"This is the only dress I own," she said, her tone a frozen thing. "I apologize if it offends you. Had I known that I'd be having dinner with a mighty king, I might have made a trip to the mall."

He placed it then. She almost sounded as if he'd hurt her feelings. He couldn't imagine how.

"I am not insulting you," he told her, frowning. "I am trying to prepare you for what will come. You will need to plan your appearances very carefully, as you will no longer be a private citizen. You will represent the crown."

"As its ungroomed, trailer trash face in a cheap black dress. The poor crown. What if I tarnish it?"

Something inside of him turned over, surprising him.

"Do you think you are the only one who finds these boundaries and necessities absurd?" he bit out at her, and the fact he was shocked by the flare of his own temper should have kept him from continuing. But it didn't. "Insulting, even? Let me assure you that you are not. But there are things that matter more than your feelings."

"So far," Maggy said softly, "it seems that everything matters more than my feelings."

"You can, of course, be the sort of royal beloved by the tabloids for different reasons," Reza said, his tone grim. "There are any number of blue-blooded tarts who fall in and out of Spanish clubs and make fools of themselves at so-called 'edgy' parties in Berlin. The brightest beaches in the Côte d'Azur have dark and desperate shadows where many an heiress loses her way, usually quite publicly. This is always a path that is open to you, if you wish it. You would hardly be the first princess to choose hard partying over hard work."

"Yes," she said, her words a bare whisper, though her caramel eyes were fixed to his and glittered hard with something much darker—something he felt like an echo deep inside of him, and he didn't like it at all. "My goal in life is to be an international whore. It seems like such an upgrade."

Heat seemed to rise in the air between them, electric and impossible. Reza did not want to imagine this woman as any kind of whore, international or otherwise. Or perhaps the truth was, now that she'd said it, he was having trouble thinking of anything else except how much he'd like to descend into a few depths with her. And what the hell did that make him?

"The choice is yours." He sounded darker than he should have. Grittier. "I, personally, prefer a more respectable approach, but then I have been the ruler of the Constantines since I was twenty-three. There was no time for me to make a name for myself in all the wrong ways."

Maggy folded her hands in her lap and Reza suspected it was to keep them from shaking. And if so, he wanted to know if it was anger or some other emotion that worked in her—like maybe some faint echo of the things he felt inside himself that were causing far too much of a commotion. She sat tall in her seat, and he wondered if she knew how very regal she looked while she did it. Or if it was something innate in her. As if her very bones had been calling out her true identity all this time, if only someone had thought to look in the back of beyond and on the wrong continent.

"But nothing you're telling me is about me, really," she said after one long moment dragged into another. She held his gaze and there was no pretending he didn't still see the challenge in her eyes. In the proud tilt of her chin. It was as novel as it was astounding. "You didn't come all this way with a lab in your back pocket because you were concerned about *me*. This entire thing is all about you."

"I beg your pardon?"

That particular tone of his usually ended conversations and led straight to abject apologies and groveling. Maggy didn't appear to hear it—much less heed it. She looked at him with challenge all over her face and not a single trace of anything like respect.

"You don't care what kind of princess I am. You care what kind of queen I might make you, in the unlikely event I actually ever marry you."

Reza paid no attention to that roaring thing in him that was eating him alive. He focused on her, making no attempt to hide the full force of his intent. His need. His royal will that had so far gone uncontested in every way that mattered.

She might be something different than what he was used to. He might find her far more fascinating than was wise or good. She might seem to speak to a part of him he hadn't known was there and didn't like at all— as it seemed a bit too close to the sort of nonsense that had made his father a weak, sentimental, and ultimately dangerous man behind the mask of the decent enough king he'd been before the end. But that didn't change the fact that he would get what he wanted.

He always did.

"You are Princess Magdalena of Santa Domini," he told her. "It is not your choice whether or not to marry me, I'm afraid. It is your destiny."

Maggy didn't feel like a princess. She felt turned inside out. It stood to reason she didn't feel like anybody's *destiny*, either.

Especially not his. No matter what that blood test had said.

"In my experience," she said in a low voice, somehow keeping that raw, scraped hollow thing inside of her at bay a little longer, "*destiny* is a word people use when they don't have a good reason for doing the thing they want to do, but they want permission to go ahead and do it anyway."

Reza pushed back from the table then, getting to his feet. Maggy didn't know why it surprised her—or maybe that wasn't the right word. It was more that when he moved, she *felt* it. It seemed to wrap tight around her and tug. There was a certain powerful smoothness to him. A different sort of danger. It made her belly fold in on itself and feel something like precarious.

She didn't want to keep sitting there like a target while he was moving around the room, so she got to her feet, too, hardly sparing a glance for the perfectly prepared roast that she hadn't so much as touched.

The king who'd told her she was a princess and, more than that, *his* moved from the seating area near the fire to the windows and stood there. She knew he couldn't really be gazing out at the mountains. It was too dark and she could see her own reflection from farther back in the room. He clasped his hands behind him in a way she found deeply royal even if she'd never given a moment's thought to what that might mean before.

Whatever a king was supposed to be, Reza looked the part. It only called more attention to the fact that she was about as far away from a princess as it was possible to get. She didn't need to consult her phone to understand that a stretchy dress from a low-market chain store was not what most European royals wore. Not even that endlessly trendy royal from England who was always on the front page of everything.

What she didn't understand was the way her stomach twisted at the thought she'd somehow…let Reza down.

You are pathological, she snapped at herself.

"You were promised to me at your birth," he said after a long moment. Maggy had the distinct impression he'd been watching her through the glass. And she was surprised at the gruffness in his voice. That and how it washed over her, like a caress. Like his hand against her face once more. She tried to blink that away. "Our fathers were, if not friends precisely, fond of each other and, more than that, committed to peace and prosperity in both our kingdoms. Combining our countries in marriage pleased them both—and made a great deal of sense in other ways, as well." Beyond him, the dark valley spread out toward the next set of hills, twinkling with village lights like grounded stars. But somehow, Maggy couldn't quite find them soothing. "I always knew I was to marry you. This meant that any youthful, adolescent shenanigans would affect you directly. I therefore kept such things to a minimum, so as to cause neither your father nor mine any embarrassment. Whatever life I wanted to lead, I always knew that there had to be room in it for you."

Maggy thought of her own adolescence. Empty and often painful. She'd thought of no one but herself because she'd had no one but herself. It wasn't selfishness if it was pure survival, surely. Because no one else had cared if she lived or died.

She had no idea how to reconcile those barren years with what he was telling her. The idea that anyone had ever cared about her, even in the most abstract way, simply didn't make sense.

"You must have hated me." Her voice was low. "I

would have hated it if I had to live my life based on some stranger."

Even as she said that, she knew it was a lie. That was true now. But there was a time Maggy would have given anything to think something—*anything*—she did or said or was mattered to another living soul.

Reza shook his head. In the glass, Maggy could see herself and his outline, as if the harsh beauty of his face was too much for mere glass to handle.

"You were mine," he said gruffly, and she told herself she didn't notice the way that seared into her. Like electricity. Like some kind of truth. "And I was under no illusions about the life I was expected to lead. I was bred to rule a country, not cater to my own self-interest. I assumed I would be lucky enough to rule it with a queen raised in a similar fashion, who would want the same things I did."

"What is that, exactly?" she asked, and there was some of that electricity in her voice, making it tighter than it should have been. "Because I wanted a roof over my head. A safe place to sleep. What does a king want from life that he doesn't already have every time he snaps his fingers?"

"My people safe, first and foremost," he told her, with another one of those shrugs that made her long for things she couldn't quite name. It was something about the width of his shoulders, the bold, masculine line of his back. "But beyond that, I want what any man wants, if for different reasons. Peace, prosperity, and heirs."

All this time, the conversation had been abstract. To Maggy, anyway. A princess who was to marry and become a queen to a man who was so indisputably a king. All part and parcel of the silly fairy tale this man kept spinning. He might as well have been talking about dancing candelabras or singing crabs for all the impact royalty was likely have on Maggy's life. Even after the aide had come back with the blood test results, she hadn't actually absorbed it.

Yet somehow, *heirs* was the word that smacked into her. It made her realize that whatever else was happening, Reza wasn't kidding around. About any of this. And that this wasn't a fairy tale. This was happening. To her. Right now.

Heirs.

His heirs.

Her heart was beating much too fast and much too hard. She crossed her arms over her chest and tried to hold herself together. And no matter that the empty place deep inside of her was…changing. Growing. Shifting. An earthquake from the inside out, and it seemed to throb, low and insistent, in her core.

"I've watched a lot of television shows where people carry on about heirs," Maggy managed to say. "I never thought it was a real thing anyone actually did. Meaning, I've literally never heard anyone use that word to describe their kids."

He turned to look at her then, and that was…not better. His gray gaze was dark. It seemed to punch straight through her.

"I will not be leaving my heirs a few pieces of chipped china and furniture of unknown provenance," Reza said softly, and yet there was somehow even more power in his voice than before. "And one does not generally refer to the princes and princesses of the Constantines as *kids*. Moreover, the Constantines are what

I will leave them. The House of Argos has held the throne for centuries."

She swallowed and was sure he could hear it. That was how dry her throat was just then. "I'm not sure I'm following you."

"I suspect you are following me perfectly well," he countered, and there was something different in his gaze then. Something almost lazy.

Maggy ignored the flush that moved over her. In her.

"You came to claim me because you thought I was this princess."

"And behold my prescience. You are."

She frowned at him—or more precisely, at the way that gleam in his gaze made her feel a different kind of itchy. Inside and out.

"You found me," she said quietly. "But now what? You want to whisk me off to some palace and make a queen out of me?"

He inclined his head. "I do."

"And where you come from, it's perfectly reasonable to talk about the heirs you need when you talk about things like marriage. To total strangers."

"Mine is a hereditary monarchy, Princess," Reza said in that same low, stirring way. "As such, I only have two jobs. One is to preserve the kingdom. The second is to pass it down to a child of my blood, as my ancestors have done since time immemorial."

"Why haven't you already married?" She studied him as he stood there, straight and tall and arrogant, making it clear he was subjecting himself to her questions because he chose to do so. Not because he had to. Maggy had no idea how he managed to make that so clear. She only knew that something in her thrilled to it. To him. "You've had twenty years to produce heirs with some other appropriate person."

"None of them were quite so perfect for me as you."

What amazed her, Maggy could admit, was how very much she wanted to believe that was a personal comment. A compliment of some kind. Was that how low she'd sunk? That she'd take anything—even this sheer madness—as evidence she didn't have to be quite as alone as she'd always been?

"And by *perfect*, you mean the blood in my veins."

He inclined his head again, though this time, there was something about his hard, stern mouth that got to her. Her heart kicked at her again. Harder this time.

"The blood in your veins is a factor, yes. As is the fact a marriage with a Santa Domini links our kingdoms in precisely the way our fathers envisioned. They were right about the benefits then. I am no less right about those same benefits now. Had all gone as planned, we would have married the moment you came of age."

There was no reason at all that should wind through her the way it did, more of that electricity and something sweet and melting besides. It shouldn't steal her breath, imagining that other life that had been stolen from her. Absurd wealth, yes, but also—and more important, to her mind—family. And perhaps in that alternate reality Maggy might have married this man the way he seemed to think she would have. Which would likely mean she'd already have his children, something she found both impossible to imagine and all too easy to conjure up.

That Maggy would have so much family she would never have to be alone again, unless she chose it.

But that Maggy had been killed in a car accident

twenty years ago. The fact Maggy had actually survived the crash didn't change that. She felt herself shiver
slightly. Very, very slightly, and she instantly tried to
hide it. Still, she thought he saw it.

"So the only difference between me in this scenario
and any other trophy wife is that you live in an actual
castle, not just a big, tacky house," she managed to say
through that same too-tight throat, but she knew she
wasn't fighting him any longer.

When exactly were you fighting him? a cynical little
voice asked, deep inside. *When you raced to get to this
hotel? At his beck and call?*

"I think you will find Constantine Castle to be something of an upgrade from your present circumstances,"
Reza said quietly, his gaze intent on her. "And that there
will be trophies to go around."

And Maggy wasn't a fool. She'd never had the opportunity to be a fool. She'd grown up too fast and much
too hard. Like any woman, especially one with limited
means, she'd had no choice but to make a study of men.
She knew rich men. She knew they did as they liked
and expected those they trampled over to thank them
for the privilege.

. She could only imagine that a king would be even
worse.

There was no such thing as fairy tales. She knew
that. She'd lived it.

But it seemed as if Reza was the closest she'd ever
come. Maggy could imagine a thousand ways she'd
come to regret what she was about to do, but at least
that would all be new. She'd done this. Poor, scared,
alone. She was tired of *this*.

If he said she was a princess, she'd become a princess. If he wanted a queen, she'd do that, too. Hell, heirs weren't an issue, either—if she ignored the *how* and concentrated on what came after that. A baby or two meant that no matter what happened with this man who watched her as if he was another one of the looming mountains outside and he could wait there forever, she could never be discarded again.

She could have everything she ever wanted. All those dreams she'd learned to despise in herself, thinking them a weakness. All those longings she'd tamped down and hidden away, refusing to give in to their lure in the harsh light of day. She could have all of it and a fairy tale, too.

All she had to do was dare to claim it.

"It sounds wonderful," she said, and she ignored the way her voice cracked. Maggy concentrated on the king before her with the hard rain eyes and the future she wanted, no matter the cost. "I can't wait to see it."

CHAPTER FIVE

WALKING AWAY FROM the only life she'd ever known should have been harder.

That was the thought that kept poking at Maggy. It lodged inside her, growing strange talons and digging into her with every breath. She'd always known who she was, or anyway, how she was defined in the community. The lost girl. The discarded girl. She'd been told who she was a thousand times, by well-meaning counselors and harried teachers and unimpressed employers alike. She'd always known exactly what her life entailed, whether she liked it or not. Surely learning that she was wrong about that, that everyone she'd ever known was wrong about that—about everything—should have been as much of a blow as a gift.

But in reality, it couldn't have been easier.

"We will leave in the morning," Reza told her that first night in his sprawling mountain lodge, a certain anticipation making his gray eyes gleam. Or maybe the anticipation was in her, not in him. She couldn't tell. "Do not worry about your possessions or the details of your life here. My people will handle it."

And Maggy had decided to surrender to this, hadn't she? She wanted the fairy tale, whatever it took. She didn't argue with him. She went and sat back down at the table. Then she thought, *what the hell*, and sampled the roast, assuming her appetite would catch up with her. She even took a sip or two of the wine, which was so different from any wine she'd ever tasted before that she couldn't quite believe both could be called by the same name.

"I don't think I can leave the country," she said at one point, glancing up to find Reza still over by the windows, watching her as if she baffled him. There was something else there, in that endlessly dark and gray gaze of his, but she didn't want to look too closely at that. Or the fact she could feel it like an echo inside of her all the same.

"Why not?" he asked, with a mildness she somehow didn't trust.

Maggy shrugged. "I never got a passport. International travel wasn't really on my list of goals these past few years. I've been more interested in other things. Like a steady job, a safe place to crash. You know."

She knew full well he didn't know. That was why she'd said it.

But of course, Reza was unconcerned with such petty things as reality.

"I took the liberty of having my government issue you a passport marking you as a citizen of the Constantines," he told her. "I trust you will find it sufficient to cross any and all borders."

Maggy had a lot of follow-up questions then. When had he had this passport made? What name was on the passport, for that matter? Why was he so certain and simultaneously unconcerned—about everything? But none of those questions mattered, in the long run. They had nothing to do with her goals here, which were fairy tales and her very own family, the end. She needed to keep her focus trained on the prize.

So she only aimed another smile at him, each one easier and smoother than the last. He returned to the table to join her and she kept right on eating, because the courses his staff kept bringing in were a far cry from the cups of noodles she prepared on her hot plate.

Maggy stuffed herself so full she thought she might burst. And she didn't think she'd mind if she did.

The next morning a fleet of sleek, gleaming black SUVs appeared outside the rickety old house where she'd lived these past few years. Maggy came down to meet them with the very few things she considered necessities in a backpack. In a sweatshirt that said STOWE across the front in a nod to a nearby ski resort, her favorite pair of battered jeans, and the boots that had always made her feel tougher than she really was. Blank-faced guards handed her into the SUV in the center of the little convoy. She climbed in and slid across buttery leather seats so soft she was afraid she'd destroy them somehow simply by touching them with her clumsy commoner denim.

But then she found herself inside an enclosed space with Reza, and that was far more alarming than any potential damage she might do to soft leather.

Her heart took up that low, wild beat again. Her blood surged through her in a way that seemed designed to do damage. She was shocked it didn't. And there was that melting, clenching thing, too, low in her belly, making it hard to sit still.

Reza sat next to her as if the spacious backseat was a throne. He took up too much of the available room—

or maybe it was that he seemed to claim all the air. He was wearing what she guessed was the royal version of casual. A button-down shirt that looked softer than the leather beneath her, crisp and white against his olive skin, and it amazed her on some distant level how that made her mouth water. He set down the papers he was scanning to look at her as she settled in the seat beside him.

His gaze was stern as it moved all over her, from her hair in a sloppy ponytail to the scuffed toes of her favorite boots.

Maggy stared back at him, her chin rising of its own accord, far more defiant than the moment called for. But she was seized with a desperate panic as the moment dragged out, even if she thought she'd rather die than let him see it.

Would he think better of this bizarre plan of his? In the cold light of the too-bright winter morning, would he take one look at her and realize that she could never be anything but the discarded piece of trash she'd always been? That there was nothing the least bit royal about her no matter what a blood test had said?

"Today is the last day you will walk around dressed like this in public," he told her, his voice a very calm, very clear command. "And I can only take it as my personal mission to convince you that it is better you do not dress like this in private, either."

"I'm American," she told him, because she preferred to combat nerves with her mouth whenever possible. "I like jeans."

"You are not American," he countered in that same cool way of his that made her whole body overheat. "You have never been American, despite appearances. You are one hundred percent Santa Dominian."

He rapped his knuckles against the window, making her flinch. But it was only his signal to his driver, she realized a moment later. He was giving his men an order, he wasn't having her thrown back into the life she'd decided to leave behind her.

The relief that washed over her then was so intense she was afraid it might flip over the SUV.

"Santa Domini means nothing to me," she murmured. She could only hope he hadn't seen her reaction, or if he had, she assured herself he wouldn't know what it meant. "It's as much a fairy tale to me as you are."

She shouldn't have said that. If she could have snatched the words back, she would have. Maggy glared down at her ratty old orange backpack and tried to pretend she couldn't feel his assessing gaze light up the side of her face, like an open flame.

But the truth was, she felt it everywhere. She felt *him* everywhere.

"I have no objection to jeans, per se," he said as the SUV started down the road, surprising her. "There is a time and place for them, of course. These are not the eighteen hundreds. What I object to is cheap fabric and unflattering, mass-produced cuts that do not flatter your form in any way."

She forgot she was trying to avoid looking at him and shifted to frown at him then. "But—"

Reza only held up a hand, in that way of his, as if he was holding an invisible scepter. "When I have outfitted you in a manner consistent with your actual station in life, if you truly wish to spend your time in the clothes you've brought with you, then we will revisit this conversation."

He didn't wait for her response. He returned to his

papers without sparing Maggy another glance. And it took her longer than it should have to really notice that he'd ended the conversation entirely on his terms, not on hers.

I think you can probably get used to that, she told herself as Deanville slid past her window. *That seems very king-like behavior.*

But the truth was, she couldn't bring herself to care about that as much as she should have. She was too focused on all the things she *wasn't* feeling about leaving the only home she'd ever known. Maggy knew every street, every hill, every tree on the way out of town. She'd been found on Route 132 in Strafford, which was how she'd gotten her surname, and she'd spent the longest stretch of time in a foster home in Deanville. These things—these places—should have left their marks on her. They must have. Yet she felt far more marked, and indelibly, by the man who sat beside her.

And when the convoy delivered them straight out onto the tarmac of a private airfield, not far from a sleek jet embossed with a very intricate and glossy coat of arms, Maggy stopped worrying about the separation anxiety she definitely wasn't feeling about leaving her old existence. Instead, she started panicking slightly about the fact she'd never been on a plane in her life.

"Are you well?" Reza asked as they stood on the tarmac, the sun making the cold bite of the winter air seem less harsh than it was. "You've gone unusually quiet."

"You don't know me well enough to know what's usual or unusual," Maggy pointed out.

His hard mouth almost quirked. "Answer the question, please."

She took her time looking at him. At his ruthless,

forbidding face that seemed to fill a thirst in her she hadn't known she had. Maggy had no idea what that meant. She wasn't sure she wanted to know. But she wasn't used to anyone paying such close attention to her.

Something she really didn't want to share with him.

"I'm terrific," she told him. "Never been better, in fact."

She expected him to throw something back at her, or glare in his kingly way. Reza did neither. His expression was too fierce and his mouth was that stern, unsmiling line. But then her breath caught in her throat, because he reached out and smoothed his hand over the length of her ponytail, not quite tugging it, and for a moment it was as if they were the only two people in all the world.

It made her heart flip over.

She was very much afraid that he could hear it.

One mad beat of her heart. Then another. And then Reza dropped his hand and touched her gently at the small of her back, indicating she should walk ahead of him toward the jet while his aides converged around him.

And it took her the whole way up the metal stairs and into the plane, waved in by smiling flight attendants, to catch her breath and get the wild drumming of her pulse under control.

Once on board, she had other things to think about, like the fact there was gold everywhere. Dark, gleaming wood. Thick, soft rugs at her feet. Especially when she was shown past what looked like a luxurious hotel living room into a fully outfitted bedroom suite. On a *plane*.

"Please don't hesitate to ring if you need anything, Your Highness," the flight attendant who'd escorted her said with a smile. "Anything at all."

And it wasn't until the uniformed man walked away that Maggy realized what had happened. That when the man had said *Your Highness*, he'd meant Maggy.

She had to close the door of her suite and sit on the wide, soft bed for a little while then. Until she found her breath again and got her head to stop spinning.

This is what you wanted, she told herself, trying to breathe in and out without hyperventilating. She ran her palms up and down her thighs, the feel of her same old jeans somehow even more disturbing. As if they could somehow snap her back to Deanville if she wasn't careful. Maggy promised herself she'd burn them at the first opportunity.

This is who you are now, she chanted to herself. *You need to figure out how to deal with it.*

But it took her a long while to pull herself together.

The flight was long and smooth. It was also one of the most pleasant experiences of Maggy's life. Every time she stepped outside her suite, there was a different selection of tempting foods laid out in the living room area. Sometimes Reza was out there on one of the sofas, but other times he was off in one of the other rooms in the jet. There was a guarded office, a conference room, bedrooms. An area featuring armchairs and tables where more guards sat, mixed in with a set of always busy-looking people that Maggy assumed were the king's top aides. Maybe his cabinet. None of them looked up when she walked past, stretching her legs, and yet she was sure she could feel their eyes on her back.

And when they finally landed, it was dark.

"Is this your kingdom?" she asked Reza when he escorted her off the plane. There was a strange, heavy salt scent to the air as they crossed another, smaller tarmac and climbed into one more waiting SUV. All the lights had halos around them and her head seemed to spin. She felt hollow straight through.

"Not quite," he replied, and she told herself it was her odd exhaustion that was making him sound like that. As deep and as dark as the night around them. "This island has been in my family for a very long time. It was a gift from an ancient Venetian doge for services rendered, or so the story goes. It will serve as a decent way station, I think."

Maggy felt muddled and thick from the long flight. She wanted to ask him what he meant by calling this a way station. She wanted to ask him if he'd take her to see the sea for the first time. It took her another beat to realize that the ocean itself was that scent in the air, like a rough magic threaded through the night. But she couldn't seem to make her body respond to any of the half-cooked thoughts whirling around and around in her head. She slumped against yet another soft leather seat back and didn't know where the SUV ended and the strange feelings inside of her began. And meanwhile, the world outside the window was nothing but dark in all directions. No towns, no cities. No lights. As if he'd carried her off the side of the world.

She didn't realize she'd fallen asleep until there were suddenly too many lights and a new sort of commotion woke her.

Maggy pushed herself to sitting position and it took her much too long to recognize that she'd fallen asleep with her head on Reza's wide shoulder. The scent in her nose now wasn't the sea. It was him. Faintly spiced, warm male. A far deeper and more treacherous magic and this one seemed to pool deep inside of her, making her core tighten, then ache. Her breath left her in a rush and her eyes flew to his—

To find him watching her in that way of his, his gray eyes dark. And that all too knowing silvery gleam in his gaze. As if he could tell that just then—one hand at his lean, hard side and the other on his muscled arm, the impression of his shoulder against her cheek—she wasn't thinking of him as a king at all.

Something rolled over her, intense and searing. She was suddenly aware of how terribly, inescapably *hot* she was. So hot she was surprised she wasn't glowing like those lights, with her own bright halo marking her as out of her depth and overheated as she felt.

"We have arrived at the villa," he told her quietly. It occurred to her to wonder how long he'd sat there, letting her sleep on him, before waking her. The idea that it might have been more than the moment or two it took to park wound tight inside of her, lit white-hot and bright. "Can you walk or shall I carry you?"

She couldn't tell if he was kidding. Not that he struck her as much of a kidder. The air between them seemed…taut. Charged. Maggy let go of him entirely and threw herself back across the seats, then told herself she didn't care if he could see her panic. As long as there was space between them. As long as she stopped touching him.

It made that unsmiling mouth of his soften slightly.

"I can walk," she said. Too quickly.

Her voice gave away too much. She could hear it. And more, she could see the way his eyes went dark, the gleam in them very silver and very, very male. It connected hard to something she hadn't known was there inside of her, making her core shiver, then melt.

Over and over again.

"As you wish, Princess," Reza murmured, laughter in his voice that she could see nowhere on his harsh face. "Welcome to the island."

And then he climbed out of the SUV, leaving her to sit there with only her too-loud breath for company. Wondering what might have happened if she'd said something else. If she hadn't let go.

If she'd moved toward him rather than away.

Reza stood out on the wide stone balcony that surrounded the master suite in the villa, paying no attention whatsoever to the frigid winter temperature as he let the crisp sea air wash all over him.

He needed to wash himself clean of this affliction.

Of this abominable *need* that was eating him alive from the inside out.

He didn't understand what was happening to him. Why the slightest, most innocuous touch from Maggy all but wrecked him. How was she managing it? How had she located the chinks in his armor when he'd had no idea it was armor in the first place? He'd thought this was simply who he was—unassailable in all ways—until now.

Was he more his father's son than he had ever imagined? Was it possible?

The cold night beat at him, but he didn't move inside.

This island had always been his family's retreat. Back when Reza was a boy, this was where his parents took him at least once a year so that the royal family could have some time away from the pressures of court and the endless scrutiny of the public. When he was older, he'd realized it was where his parents came to hash out their differences—meaning, his father's betrayals—in a place his father couldn't retreat. The one place his father's mistress wasn't available at a moment's notice, allowing his mother the chance to pretend the other woman didn't exist. Fittingly, this was where they'd taught him that he was never, ever to behave as if he was flesh and blood and a mortal like all the rest. Like them.

This was where he'd learned that there was no room in the king for any hint of the man.

It does not matter what you say, Reza, but what you do, his mother had told him again and again, that harsh look in her gaze not for him, he understood in retrospect, but aimed at him all the same. *Your subjects want to follow a king they can admire and support, not a flawed, weak little man whose clay feet trip him up whenever he tries to stand.*

His mother had been a remote parent and a distant queen. She'd believed her place was behind the king, silent and beautiful and ever supportive, and no matter the whispers about her husband's long-term dalliance or where his obsession with that woman had led him as the leader of a country. As far as Reza knew, she had never indicated in any kind of public setting that she even knew the other woman existed. *The people are interested in the king, never his consort*, she would tell her aides reprovingly when they'd broach the possibility of an interview or an article, perhaps talking about both of her husband's women. And then she'd proved that her devotion outstripped her rival's beyond a shadow of a doubt when she'd followed the king into the hereafter

within three years of the death she'd known full well
was no random heart attack. She had been a beacon of
correctness unto the grave, and all the better if she'd
been able to use it as a weapon. That was his mother.
Ferocious in her pain unto the end.

Reza had not brought Maggy, his feral princess, here
by accident.

But even now, even as he stood out in the cold and
tried to lecture himself back into the closed-off, hermet-
ically sealed state he had long preferred, Reza couldn't
quite manage it. He couldn't stop thinking about Maggy.

The fact he was thinking of her as *Maggy* at all,
instead of the more sophisticated, regal, and thus far
more appropriate *Magdalena*, was part of the problem.

She'd shuffled out of her house dressed like a Hal-
loween costume version of a young American woman,
all attitude and that stubborn chin. But then, her wide
caramel eyes had told him she was far more anxious
than she appeared. She'd looked more vulnerable in that
harsh morning light. Less hardened by the life she'd led
than she had the night before.

He hadn't known how to identify the feeling that had
worked in him then. He hadn't the slightest idea what
it was. It had taken him the entire ride to the airport,
reading and rereading the same three sentences on the
same damned document, to understand what it was.

Helpless.

He was Reza Argos. He was the king of the Constantines. He was not and never had been and never would
be anything like *helpless*. The very idea was laughable.

But then he'd proved that wasn't true at all when
he'd touched her again, running his hand over that
brash, blond hair that was nonetheless silky and smooth

against his palm. He'd stood too close to her out on that tarmac. She'd smelled vaguely of vanilla and coconut, and even that had slammed through him like a caress against the hardest part of him. And that same feeling had washed through him again.

He couldn't help himself. He couldn't stop.

He had no idea what the hell he was doing or when he'd become a slave to his feelings like his father. He only knew he couldn't allow it.

Reza was no untouched, untried boy. Yet here he stood on the other side of the planet, the cold wind from the Adriatic Sea pummeling him, and all he could think about was the way she'd looked at him back on a tarmac in the middle of nowhere in Vermont. What was happening to him?

Why was he *letting* this happen to him, and with the most unlikely creature imaginable? Did he care so little for his own pride—the promises he'd made himself that he would never, ever succumb to weakness like his father?

And that was before she'd fallen asleep on his shoulder.

It was a ten-minute drive from the airfield on the southern tip of the island to the magnificent villa that stood at its highest point, commanding views over the sea in all directions. And Reza had sat there perfectly still, unwilling to dislodge the soft weight of her.

Unwilling or unable. He couldn't decide which. He'd been lost somewhere in the heat of her body against his. The faint press of her against him. The way her head seemed crafted especially to fit right there on his shoulder—

"Sire."

His aide's voice came from behind him, snapping him out of the memory of her body next to his, and Reza didn't turn. He worried at what might be on his face. What he might reveal without realizing it. What might very well be shining off of him like a beacon, betraying every last thing he'd become. Showing that he'd turned into the very thing he hated.

"Is our guest settled?" he asked. He didn't like the effort it took to sound as calm as he usually did.

"Yes, sire. In the queen's suite, as you wished." His aide cleared his throat. "And everything is arranged for the morning, in accordance with your orders."

Reza turned then, nodding his acknowledgment and then following his aide back into the villa. He closed the doors against the winter chill, then stood in the great expanse of the bedroom that he'd once believed was the size of the world. He'd been allowed in here so rarely as a child. It had been his father's private retreat. He'd hidden away in here from the family he'd supposedly come to the island to spend time with in the first place.

As a small boy, Reza had wanted nothing more than to come in here. Now he viewed it as a monument to a past he had best start paying better attention to before he repeated it.

He hardly noticed when his aide left him to his thoughts.

The fact that he'd located the lost Santa Domini princess should have made him happier. He understood this. He'd not only found her, he'd rescued her from a life that was so far beneath her it astounded him. And more, he'd brought her here to this island to teach her not only how to step back into the life she'd been stolen from, but how to operate as his queen.

After all this time, he'd found his queen. The girl he'd been betrothed to when he was all of ten years old. The woman who represented a whole future he'd lost when that car had crashed in Montenegro when he was eighteen.

He'd mourned her—and the loss of the life they'd been meant to build together—for longer than he cared to admit.

But the trouble was, he wanted her. *Want* had never entered into it before, because it was irrelevant. Because he was not his damned father. His kingdom was what mattered. The promises their families had made and the contracts they'd signed were all that had mattered. He'd come of age expecting a queen who would take after his own mother and fade into the background, perfectly pedigreed and unquestionably correct, once she'd done her duty and provided him with an heir.

The trouble with Maggy was that all he could think about was taking her to his bed, and duty had nothing to do with it.

Which meant that for the first time in as long as he could remember, he wasn't doing his.

"What if I'm not a good king?" he'd dared to ask his parents on one of their visits here in a mild autumn. He'd still been so young. He hadn't understood the fierce chill between his mother and father as they'd all walked together. It was all he'd known. They'd strolled down the beach while sweet winds blew in from Venice to the west and off the Gulf of Trieste to the north.

"You will be," his father had told him, with that regal certainty in his deep voice that had straightened Reza's spine. His father had still been so much taller than Reza then, and Reza had been more than a little in awe of him. "Argos men have held the kingdom forever. You will do the same."

He had smiled when he'd looked down at Reza then, an unusual show of the emotion he usually saved for his extramarital relationship, or so the pictures Reza had been forced to destroy after his death suggested.

The queen had not smiled. Her cold eyes had seemed to burn. "You will have no choice."

Reza had never forgotten that.

Because having no choice but to put the kingdom first meant everything else fell into line behind it. Life was simple, in its way, and his father's terrible example had helped make it so. Reza was not burdened with the personal travails that took down so many other men in his position. He had no vices, because they would harm him and thus the kingdom. He had never felt trapped by the security details forever surrounding him and cutting him off from the rest of the world, he'd felt safe. No one touched him. No one had influence over him. He belonged only to his people and the two alpine valleys that had been there in his blood at birth.

And he was at an extreme disadvantage tonight because of it, as he stood in the middle of his bedroom floor, lost in unhelpful images of his future queen. One after the next, as if he had no control at all.

Because the startling truth was that he didn't have the slightest idea what to do with temptation. It had never been a factor.

Reza only knew he had to keep himself from surrendering to this—to her—whatever the cost.

CHAPTER SIX

REZA HADN'T BEEN KIDDING when he'd mentioned a spa, Maggy discovered the next morning.

She'd woken up after a strange night packed tight with odd dreams to find herself in a luxurious, sprawling ancient villa that somehow fused marvelous old Italian touches with surprisingly modern updates, from a perfect bathroom suite to its heated floors. More accurately, she'd been woken up by a cheerful attendant, who'd hurried her out of bed and into a soft robe, pressed an exquisitely made latte into her hands, and then led her through the achingly beautiful villa while she was still sipping at it.

Maggy was far too bleary-eyed to object. She had the hectic impression of graceful rooms filled with dancing morning light, and then she was being led through a warm, glassed-in area where a pretty pool gleamed bright blue in the sun. The attendant led her to the far side of the circular pool, then into an already hot sauna.

"Should you need anything at all, Your Highness, you need only press this button," the attendant told her, collecting Maggy's empty latte mug as she left and closed the heavy door behind her.

Maggy wasn't any more used to hearing herself

called that. *Your Highness.* She had to bite back an involuntary giggle. But then again, what part of any of this was she used to? She knew what a sauna was, but she'd never been in one before. She blinked as she looked around the wooden room. It seemed like an outward manifestation of how she felt already—hot and airless and finding it harder to breathe by the second.

But if this was what royals did, then by God, she would do it. She would do anything. *You* are *royal*, she reminded herself. *Your blood proves it.* She sat on the warm wooden slats as soothing new age music piped in, and wondered if maybe she was still sleeping. If maybe she'd wake up to find herself back in her narrow bed in her tiny room back in Vermont, late for work as usual. She reached down and pinched herself, viciously. On her thigh, then on her belly, but nothing happened. It hurt and it left her with two dull red marks, but that was it. She stayed put in this hot, cedar cell. Sweating wildly.

Even so, she couldn't discount the high possibility that this was a dream anyway. She'd had dreams like this before, in shocking, tactile detail. The difference was, Maggy intended to enjoy every minute no matter what. She was resolved. She tipped her head back, figured out how to breathe long and slow when the air felt nearly solid around her, and she let the deep heat soak into her.

When the lights and heat inside the sauna turned themselves off sometime later, she emerged, sleepy-eyed and wrapped in her robe again, to find that a personal spa had been assembled for her in the great, glassed-in space on the warm stones to the side of the pool. Attendants flocked around her, buffing and waxing whatever parts of her they could reach. She was manicured and pedicured. Her brows were shaped and her hair was set with color and then cut without a single word from her. She was served a steady stream of plates filled with colorful, astonishingly good food every time she made any kind of eye contact with anyone. She was massaged from head to toe and rubbed down with creams and rinses and who even knew what else, until she felt as if she'd been pummeled into the shape of an entirely new woman.

And when it was all done, her attendants wrapped her in a fluffy towel that could have enveloped a family of four and then led her back through the villa.

She'd been too dead on her feet the night before and much too bleary this morning as she'd been hustled down to the sauna area to really look around. But after a day of more pampering than she'd had in her whole life, she found she could hardly keep herself from happily soaking in the place as she followed the smiling women surrounding her.

Reza had called this *the villa*. But to Maggy, it was a palace. Polished marble stretching in all directions. Rooms filled with precious things beyond description. Couches that looked like works of art all their own, set on rugs that likely were. Gleaming pieces of desperately fancy furniture that were nicer than her entire previous life.

Everywhere she looked there were arches and windows, allowing her to see that the sea was *just there*. It was capped with white and surging deep blue and mighty in all directions, visible from every angle. Every room showed her a new view of the water, making it seem as if the villa itself was floating on the waves. Inside, the ceilings were high and set with intricate panels that she was sure probably had some fancy name she'd never learned. There was art on every wall, and Maggy didn't have to know anything about it to know what she was looking at was priceless. One or two paintings she even thought she might recognize, which she was aware meant they had to be so ridiculously famous someone who'd never looked at a single piece of art in a museum or anywhere else would know them at a glance.

She was in such a completely different world it made her head spin.

This is definitely a dream, that cynical voice inside warned her. *I wouldn't get too comfortable if I were you.*

But she wanted to be comfortable here, and no matter if she woke up tomorrow in her tiny room in Vermont. She wanted to be the princess Reza thought she was, with a family and a history at last. So she did nothing but follow her attendants back through the meandering wing that led to the set of rooms she'd been delivered to the night before. She ignored that voice deep inside. If this wasn't going to last, she wanted to enjoy every last bit of it. The smooth stone floors. The beautiful colors of everything she saw, from old-looking tables to tapestries on the ancient walls, to fresh flowers in every vase on almost every surface though it was still winter outside.

She walked through her private sitting room with its fireplace, cozy sofas, and shelves full of heavy-looking books arranged amid small statues. There were windows that doubled as doors leading out toward the sea, and it made her heart feel light that she could see so far. There was a smudge on the horizon that she was pretty sure was Italy. Or possibly Croatia. And that was according to the map on the sleek, very European smartphone an aide had handed her at some point earlier today.

"For your convenience, Your Highness," the man had murmured.

The phone had exactly one number programmed into it under the name *Reza Constantines*. Maggy had stared at it. But she hadn't dialed it.

She followed her little entourage into the vast, sprawling bedroom, set with delicate furniture that struck her as feminine and very thick rugs tossed across the stone floor. She'd crashed across the wide, four-poster bed last night in an utter daze as much from the flight as from her nap *on Reza*, and then she'd stared up at the magenta canopy until she'd drifted off approximately four seconds later. But now the bed was made up again as if for a magazine shoot and there were clothes laid out across its foot.

"His Majesty wishes you to meet him in his private salon," one of the attendants told her. "At your earliest convenience."

"I assume that means at *his* earliest convenience," Maggy murmured. She'd meant to sound dry, but she was far too relaxed. It came out much softer than it should have.

The women around her laughed, and that was its own head trip. Maggy was prickly, everybody said so. She couldn't remember the last time a group of people had laughed around her, unless it was *at* her.

"He is the king," one of the women said quietly. "We all serve at his pleasure."

And Maggy felt as if she ought to object to that,

on principle if nothing else, but somehow she couldn't quite bring herself to do it. *Later*, she told herself. *You can worry about* the king's pleasure *later—or maybe you'll just wake up.*

The women surrounded her again, and after a day of it she let them without another thought. She sat on the vanity stool and realized after a few moments that they were deliberately keeping her from looking in the mirror. She didn't fight it. This was her dream and she was going to eke every drop of this princess routine out of it before she was drop-kicked back to the real world.

Because there was always the chance that wanting this to be real would make it so.

One woman carefully made up her face while another blew out her hair. It took them some time. When they were done, they handed her a pile of soft, impossibly silky things it took her long, confused moments to realize were a bra and panties. Just of a far higher quality than the ones she'd bought herself in cotton value packs.

Even her feet looked like someone else's, she thought as she stepped into the deliriously silky panties behind the towel two attendants held up for her once she shed her robe. Tipped in a rich red now, buffed and sanded smooth and soft, they weren't *her* feet. *Her* feet were usually hard across the heels and aching. The panties fit perfectly, as did the matching bra, and she told herself she wasn't thinking about who could possibly have estimated her measurements so well.

She kept telling herself that even as that same, familiar heat that was all about Reza and his hard, stern mouth rolled over her, then pooled deep in her belly again.

But there was no time for blushing. Her attendants hurried her into the dress that waited for her at the foot of her bed, a dove-gray thing that didn't look very interesting when they held it up, but felt like a whisper once they pulled it over her head. The shoes they slipped on her feet were the same, so high she expected them to pinch and hurt, but instead she felt as if she was wearing bedroom slippers once she stood in them.

It explained a great deal about the things she'd seen famous people wear in magazines. Who could possibly have imagined all those crazy, acrobatic clothes were *comfortable*? No wonder Reza had been so dismissive about her clothes. It all made a lot more sense now.

She felt them fasten something around her neck, cool and slippery against her skin. Someone slid a ring onto her index finger, and then they were bustling her back out of the room. She could see that the sun was setting outside the windows, sinking in an orange blaze toward the sea, but she was dazzled by the lights inside the villa, too. They were everywhere, buttery and bright, making the hallway seem as if it was merry of its own accord.

Or maybe that was just her.

Her attendants hurried her down the hall, and it took her longer than it should have to make the obvious connection that her suite was only the next door down from Reza's—it was just that the rooms in the villa were very large and the hallway connecting them quite long. And in fact, the door in the far wall of her bedchamber that hadn't opened when she'd tried it last night must lead directly into his rooms—a notion that made every nerve ending in her body shiver to instant awareness.

But there was no time to process any of it, because

she was being led directly into the king's dazzling suite. His private salon was the size of a hotel ballroom, she thought wildly, looking all around her. The light here was as bright and glorious as the rest of the villa. It bounced off of all the inlaid gold in the different seating areas arranged in little clusters around the big room— here an elegant couch, there an impossibly graceful quartet of chairs. Even the walls themselves were lined with gold, interspersed with a deep crimson. It looked exactly the way Maggy would have imagined a king's room should look, had she ever had cause to think about such things.

And in the center of all that regal brightness stood Reza, in yet another perfectly crafted dark suit that made him look like a storm of a man, his gray eyes fixed to her as if this was the first time he'd ever seen her.

As if, she thought wildly, he'd been waiting his whole life to see her.

Maggy felt that gaze of his like a shudder, a wicked, rolling thing down deep inside of her. A new, dangerous heat bloomed there, then spread, washing over her limbs and making her pulse go liquid.

She was vaguely aware that the attendants left them. She didn't dare move—or she couldn't. And Reza only stood there for what seemed to her to be a long, long time, that stern gaze on her in a way that made her feel as if all the dizzy light in the room was trapped inside of her. A part of her.

She was certain he could see it. That he knew.

"I don't know what they did," she heard herself tell him. She had no idea what she was saying. How could she tell when she didn't sound anything like herself? "They wouldn't let me look."

He said nothing. He merely held out his hand.

Maggy didn't know why she didn't so much as hesitate.

The dream, she told herself, though her dreams had never been *quite* this vivid. *This is all part of the dream.*

The fairy-tale dream she hadn't allowed herself to truly indulge in for years.

She moved across the floor and took the hand he offered her, and only then—when a different blaze of sheer fire poured into her and made her heart kick at her—did she think to question why she'd thrown herself into it like that. Into him. Only then, when it was too late.

But Reza only led her over to a huge mirror left propped up against the wall in the farthest corner of the great room, looking as if it had stood exactly like that for centuries. It likely had. It, too, was edged in a heavy gold frame, as solid and certain as the king himself.

He positioned her in front of the glass and stood behind her. Much too close to her. One hand holding hers and the other a faint pressure at her waist. More of that delirious fire raced through her at the contact, making her legs feel weak. Maggy knew she should push herself away from him. Get his hands off of her, for a start. She knew she should do *something*.

But she couldn't seem to do anything but stare.

"Look at you," Reza murmured, his voice a rough velvet much too close to her ear and the birthmark he'd known was there from the start. "They did exactly as I asked. They made you who you are. Magdalena Santa Domini."

The woman in the huge, gold mirror was…not

Maggy. Or if she was, it was a version of herself that Maggy could hardly get her head around. A dream version she never would have dared imagine on her own. Never.

She knew it was her and yet…it couldn't possibly be her.

A princess, a small voice inside her whispered, with something like awe. *You look like a princess.*

They'd dyed her hair back to her natural color, a dark and lustrous chestnut, and they'd swept it back from her face. Still, the light picked up deep golds and russets that seemed to make her eyes glow. And her eyebrows looked elegant, in place of her usual unremarkable brows. Her whole face was smooth and she thought she looked different, and not only because of the subtle makeup they'd put on her. It took her a moment to realize she looked rested. Or not exhausted, anyway.

She'd never seen her own face so bright before.

The dress looked like something out of one of those glossy magazines she'd always pretended to loathe. The gray color was soft and interesting at once, making Maggy's pale skin seem to glow. It was a modest dress, she supposed, but it didn't seem that way. There was something about *how* it fell from a sophisticated neckline all the way to her knees, with only a slight indentation just beneath her breasts, that suggested a kind of restrained and high-class sex appeal without actually showing anything. The shoes did much the same thing, somehow managing to look elegant in a way Maggy didn't know shoes could. There was a gleaming diamond necklace around her neck and a chunky ring on her index finger featuring a collection of precious gems in a variety of colors, all of which caught the light and sparkled.

But more than all that, *she* looked like someone else. Completely different from the Maggy she'd seen in her own mirror yesterday morning before she'd headed out to meet Reza's convoy. If she hadn't known the reflection she was looking at was hers, she'd have easily and happily believed that it was some long-lost princess. And she hardly dared think it, but she really did look like that picture of the queen he'd shown her.

The queen. *Her mother.*

But she didn't want to think about that yet. Not yet. She took a breath and realized in the next instant that Reza was still holding her fingers in his as he stood behind her, his other hand at her waist. And suddenly she could think of nothing else. Except the tempting notion that if she leaned back the tiniest bit she could nestle herself directly against the wall of his chest.

She would never, ever know how she managed to keep herself from doing it.

"This is how you look after one day," Reza told her, his voice near her ear making her shiver. He was the one who stepped away then, something she couldn't read making his eyes silver. She fought to repress yet another shiver as she watched him in the mirror. "We will stay here several weeks. By the end of this time, I expect you will be able to acquit yourself quite well in the glare of whatever spotlight you might encounter."

"Yes," she said, because she had to say something. And she couldn't let herself say any of those things that clawed at her from that raw place, deep inside. She didn't want to think them. She wanted this. She wanted every last part of this. "I'm sure I will."

But even after he turned and headed across the room, Maggy stayed where she was before that great, tipped glass, staring at herself. Because she wasn't herself anymore.

She was the fairy-tale princess he'd made her into, just as he'd said he would, in the course of a single day.

And Maggy had absolutely no desire to ever wake up.

It was worse now she looked the part.

And much, much worse that he'd let himself hold her like that.

Reza told himself this mad obsession was beneath him. That he was in no position to lose himself in a woman like his father had done before him, particularly not this one. If she was to be his queen—and she was, of course, as their fathers had planned so many years ago—then the formalities needed to be observed above all else. The only thing he could think of that was worse than losing his head over an inappropriate mistress was doing the same thing over the woman who would have to bear his children. Where would it end? What destruction would he wreak? He couldn't imagine it. Or allow it.

He spent his days tending to matters of the crown from his office in the villa, surrounding himself with his advisers and running his country from afar. And if he insisted on an investigation into that long-ago accident and the following of twenty-year-old leads to figure out how a Santa Dominian child in a car accident in Montenegro had made it across the Atlantic Ocean to the United States, so be it. The Princess Magdalena was to be his queen. What had happened to her would be public record and, more than that, incorporated into the lore of the monarchy itself.

He filled her days with the very serious business of turning an abandoned American foster child into one of Europe's most celebrated royals.

He had her fitted for an entire new wardrobe that suited her position. He had Milanese courtiers fly in with one of a kind pieces for her to try on and choose between as she pleased, with the help and advice of his personal tailors. He flew in special jewelers from Paris to outfit her appropriately, so she might have a few pieces to wear until she regained her access to the Santa Dominian crown jewels, to say nothing of the Constantinian collection she would be expected to wear after their wedding.

And while all the outward trappings that would cement her as his betrothed in all the right ways were being attended to by the most fashionable people in the world, he brought in diction coaches to soften and shape her language. He couldn't teach her the Italian and German every Constantinian spoke fluently in so short a time, but he could work a bit on her English. Less rural American and more European, so it would sound better to the average Constantinian ear.

He brought in a former prima ballerina to teach his queen how to walk, how to stand, how to shake hands, and how to curtsy with varying degrees of deference. He made her sit with a selection of his aides and learn the rudiments of the kind of diplomacy she'd be expected to know inside and out at all formal functions. He had yet another aide talk her through the tangled history of Santa Domini and the Constantines, so she would be less likely to trip into any old, festering wounds that still lingered there, as such things tended to do between all ancient European nations. He had her consult with his own public affairs officers, to teach her how to handle cameras and reporters and the unsavory realities of public life in a tabloid world. He even brought in his formidable former nanny, now pushing eighty, to teach Maggy the same excruciatingly correct set of manners she'd taught him back in the day, at the table and everywhere else a royal might venture.

"A banquet is a performance," he heard Madame Rosso pronounce in her usual ringing tones from the formal dining room one afternoon, just as she had when he'd been a boy. "Your appetite has nothing to do with it. Indeed, you must worry about sating yourself on your own time. A banquet is an event at which you are royalty first and a hungry person never. Do you understand?"

"I understand," Maggy said. Sweetly enough that Reza paused outside the room, whatever errand he'd been on forgotten.

She was so understanding when asked anything these days. She always agreed, nodded, curtsied. She modulated her tone and softened her accent. It was as if she'd been possessed by an alien, Reza thought darkly—and the fact he should have been rejoicing over how easily she was taking to what she'd called *Princess School* in a rare flash of her old self one evening made him that much more annoyed with himself.

The truth, and he was all too aware of it, was that he was something far more dangerous than simply *annoyed with himself.*

Reza couldn't quite believe that he found himself missing the sharp-tongued bottle blonde who had looked at him with such blatant disrespect in Vermont. He told himself that of course he didn't. Not really. It was just that Maggy was immersing herself in her studies of all things royal and, in so doing, becoming the princess she'd always been meant to be. The real Maggy would come out the other side, he was sure of it.

Why on earth would you want her to come out the other side *of decent behavior?* he asked himself then, deeply irritated with his own frailties where this woman was concerned.

But he had no answer for that. The more appropriate she became, the harder he found it to resist her. It was as if the veneer of the princess he'd always wanted stretched over that fearless creature he'd met in Vermont made this woman into his own, personal, walking and talking downfall. No matter how steadfastly he refused to go there.

Meanwhile, he suspected he was a little too insistent about the dinners they shared every night. He told himself that these formal meals were a way to assess her progress. That they were necessary, and perhaps that was true. But he knew full well that wasn't why he found himself anticipating the dinner hour all day.

He was betraying himself and everything he stood for and he couldn't seem to stop.

One night he found her in the grand hall an hour or so before the bell was due to ring to announce dinner. She was counting out loud as she practiced waltzing by herself, her lovely face screwed up into a frown as she stared at her feet and held her arms in a rigid box in the air before her.

It was one thing to want her. That was bad enough.

But this...*melting* sensation in the region of his chest was something far worse than simply unacceptable. It was a different sort of danger entirely, he knew it. And it got worse the more she transformed before him. Tonight it very nearly ached.

Reza ordered himself to move on. To retire to his rooms and dress for dinner the way he knew he should, and maintain the level of formality between them that was the only thing keeping his sanity in check, he sometimes thought.

Instead, he walked into the ballroom.

Maggy was too busy counting to see him approach. "One, two, three, four. One two three four. *Onetwothree*—"

She stopped the moment she saw him. She seemed to freeze into place where she stood, those caramel eyes of hers wide on him, her arms still in the air as if she danced with a ghost.

And he was many things, most of them deeply unsavory at present and entirely too much his father's son, but he was no liar. He knew exactly what that heat was in her gaze. He felt the same thing storm through him, tying him into a thousand intricate knots that felt like fire.

"What are you doing?" she asked. He could tell from that strange tone in her voice that he must look particularly intense.

He should have cared about that. It should have set off every alarm inside of him, that he should betray himself at all, much less so obviously. But if it did, he couldn't bring himself to care.

If this was how his downfall started, he couldn't seem to mind. Not tonight. Not when she had transformed herself into every last thing he'd always, always wanted.

"Allow me to assist you," he said, his voice dark and low.

Reza didn't wait for her to respond. He had crossed the room by then, so he simply took her in his arms, ignoring the heat that blazed between them.

Well. It was more like he marinated in that heat. Soaked in it. Dared it to try to drown him.

He wrapped his fingers around hers. He liked, too much, her grip on his opposite shoulder. He held her at the correct distance and thought he deserved a medal or ten for refraining from pulling her up hard against his body the way he wanted to do.

And then he started to dance, sweeping her along with him. The fact that there was no music did not signify. There was her breath. There was his heartbeat, hard and deep and needy. Nothing else mattered.

Reza let himself admire her as they moved. His princess. His queen. Tonight her hair was piled on the top of her head, that dark, rich color he preferred, and she was wearing a shift dress that made her look very young and very chic at once. She was still slender, though she'd lost that hungry look over the past weeks. There was nothing at all to distract from her beauty now. Not one single thing.

And he liked having her in his arms almost too much to bear.

"It's hard to reconcile the woman I met in that coffee shop with you now," he said, because he couldn't seem to help himself. He couldn't keep from poking at the very thing he shouldn't touch. "You are so alarmingly agreeable."

"I'm the exact same person," Maggy replied, but he thought her response was too quick. Too pat. And he didn't like that she kept her gaze trained on his chin, as if she was deliberately keeping her eyes from him. Hiding, right there in his arms. "It's just that instead of trying to remember to pay my rent on time, I now have to remember which fork to use."

There was no reason so smooth and rehearsed a response should have bothered him. Reza told himself it didn't. This was what he'd wanted, after all. Indeed, this was what she deserved. She was a royal princess. She *should* appear this way, without any cracks and wholly unobjectionable. His odd nostalgia for the creature she'd become to survive what had happened to her demeaned them both, surely.

He was disgusted with himself. Still, he spun her around the room again and again because he couldn't bring himself to let go. He couldn't make himself do it.

You are a king, said a voice from deep inside of him, sounding very much like his mother's crisp, faintly starchy tones, in those dark days following what they'd all known was his father's suicide to avoid the mess he'd made of his life, his country. *Do you rule or are you ruled?*

He stopped then, abruptly. Maggy's momentum kept her going and she almost fell against him. He almost let her, to serve his own hunger—but at the last moment he righted her.

"I will instruct your dance instructor to pay more attention to your footwork," he heard himself say, his voice like a winter chill. "You cannot trip over foreign dignitaries without causing international incidents."

Her chin rose and she tugged at her hand to get him to release it. He only held it tighter.

"Given that I didn't know how to dance at all until a week or so ago, I think I'm doing fine." Her voice was even, but he was sure he heard a hint of that old fire beneath it.

How sad that he thrilled to it. But he did.

"It is not what you think that matters, Princess." His voice was too low, too telling. But all he could seem to do was stare at the tender place in the hollow of her neck, watching the way her pulse jumped. Reza told himself it could mean anything. That he shouldn't take it as a matching fire, no matter that he could see the echo of it in her gaze. "It is what I think."

He let her go this time when she tugged at her hand again. Maggy stepped back, her chin tilted at that mutinous angle he'd missed far more than he should have, and then, her challenging gaze on his, she executed a crisp and perfect curtsy.

It was perhaps the most eloquent *up yours* gesture he'd ever seen. Certainly directed at him.

"Bravo," he said. He wanted to laugh. But that wasn't the thing that wound tight inside of him, pulling him taut and making him ache. "But I must warn you not to attempt a repeat in front of any other monarch you might encounter. Particularly with all of your attitude on display. You might find yourself beheaded for the insult, and no matter that such things were outlawed centuries ago."

"If that was an insult, I must have learned how to do it wrong," she said, but her caramel eyes gleamed with that same hot challenge when they met his. "My deepest apologies if I offended you, Your Majesty."

And that was the last straw. His title in her mouth, crisp and pointed, as if it was another insult, even as it licked over him like something else entirely.

Reza didn't mean to move. He didn't know he did, but somehow the distance between them was gone, and worse, he had his hands wrapped around the smooth, entrancing place where her upper arms became her shoulders.

He was touching her skin, and not merely her hand. *At last.*

"Reza..." she whispered.

He ignored her. Because he was too close to her, he was *touching* her, and that changed everything.

All these games he'd been playing these last weeks fell away.

There was only this. There was only her.

He thought she said his name again, but it was as if it came from somewhere far away. Lost in the storm that washed through him. His thumbs dragged over her soft skin, back and forth as if he couldn't help himself. He watched, fascinated, as a fresh set of goose bumps rose and then swept across her throat, giving her away. Telling him everything he needed to know.

"You cannot taunt me with your brand-new manners and then take it back with my name, Princess," he told her, bending his head toward hers. "You cannot imagine that will work."

Her hands were flat against his chest, but she didn't push against him. Her fingers seemed to curl in, as if she was trying to find purchase against his jacket. As if she wanted to hold on to him.

And her full, lush mouth was *right there* within reach.

Reza stopped pretending he had any control left. He stopped pretending he could resist her when that resistance had grown more and more scant with every passing day.

He stopped pretending, full stop.

He damned himself fully, and then he took her mouth with his.

CHAPTER SEVEN

HIS MOUTH WAS as hard as it looked. Uncompromising and stern as it moved on hers, taking her and tasting her, encouraging her to do the same.

And when she did, when she met him, his taste filled her. Hot and ruthless and entirely Reza.

It was glorious. It was better than glorious.

This is no dream, something inside her whispered. *This is the fairy-tale kiss to end all fairy-tale kisses, and it's real.*

But for once, Maggy didn't care either way. She just wanted more.

She gave herself over to his demanding mouth. His kiss was heat and light, pouring into her and through her, kicking up fires wherever it touched. Her heart cartwheeled in her chest. Her head spun around and around. Her breasts seemed to swell with all the hunger that stormed through her, her nipples pulled to tight points, and between her legs she was nothing but a soft, molten ache.

His hands gripped her upper arms, firm and sure, and lifted her closer to him. And there wasn't a single thought in Maggy's entire being except *yes. More.* More of Reza. More of that stern, hard mouth. More of this wild, stirring electric hunger that tore through her, making her greedy and half-mad. Making her entirely his, as if this right here was where she truly belonged.

She wanted more.

Maggy surged up on her toes and she dug her fingers into the stone wall of his chest, and that was when he angled his mouth for a deeper, better fit.

And the world exploded.

All the heat and fire of these past weeks, all the sensation and need and longing, burst through her. He claimed her mouth, again and again, merciless and almost too hot to bear, and she couldn't seem to get close enough.

Maggy wanted more. She wanted everything.

He made a low noise she didn't recognize, but still it rolled through her and made her even warmer, as if there was some deep, feminine part of her that understood him in ways the rest of her couldn't.

She had always kept a part of her separate, no matter what, but here, now, in his arms, she melted. He kissed her again and again, and she met him with everything she was and everything inside of her and all the wildfire and yearning she'd been pretending wasn't there and Maggy knew, somehow, that there was no going back from this.

A princess was one thing. She could play that part, apparently. She even liked it.

But he kissed her as if she was the woman she'd always wanted to become.

As if she was truly his.

Very much as if he heard that dangerous thought inside her head—as if she'd shouted it out into the empty ballroom—Reza wrenched his mouth from hers. So fast and so unexpected that for a head-spinning moment, Maggy thought maybe she really had said it out loud.

Which would have been a disaster. She knew that. Having feelings for Reza could only complicate everything. Even this. Maybe especially this.

Would any of this have happened if you didn't *have feelings for him already?* an arch voice inside her asked. She ignored it.

His breath sawed out between them as if he'd been running, or maybe that was hers—she couldn't tell. But he didn't let go. His hands were strong and elegant at once, and he kept them wrapped tight around her upper arms.

Maggy knew she should have felt trapped. But she didn't. She felt safer than she could remember ever feeling before, and it didn't matter that the look on his face was anything but sweet.

"This cannot happen," he gritted out.

He was still holding her to him. His face, so harsh and fierce and stern and beautiful, was close to hers. And Maggy was plastered up against him, her breasts pressed to his chest, so hard she could feel her own nipples like twin points of fire where they brushed against him.

She should have been upset, surely. She should certainly have disliked his tone. She should have been… something. But instead she couldn't think of a single place she'd rather be than right here in his arms, no matter how or why or what intense reaction he was having to it.

"I thought you intended to marry me," she whispered, from that same, strange place she hadn't known was there, feminine and wise. She'd never flirted in her life. Why put something out there if she didn't care enough to mean it? But here, now, she tilted her head back and arched into him, smiling when his breath caught. "How will you manage that if we don't do this?"

He set her back from him then, and that felt like a much greater loss than it should have, surely. It felt as if he'd kicked her. For a moment she swayed as if she might topple over, so badly did every part of her want to be close to him again. Closer. The distance between them felt like a slap.

But yeah, that voice inside her poked at her. *Good thing you don't have any* feelings *for him.*

His gray gaze was so dark it looked nearly black. "Our marriage will be based on civility and respect," he grated at her, and he didn't sound like the Reza she knew at all. There was no distance there. No regal *certainty*. Something inside her prickled to awareness. "Not this...relentless hunger."

Maggy tilted her head to one side, then folded her arms over her chest, and who cared if her deportment instructor had forbidden her to do that. Repeatedly.

"I hate to break this to you, Reza," she said quietly. She realized as she spoke that she had no idea where her sense of calm came from. As if her body knew, way down deep inside, that she was safer here than she'd ever been anywhere else. Here, with him. No matter what was making him look at her that way. "But heirs are not made out of civility and respect. That sounds more like a handshake, which, unless it's different for kings, won't quite get the job done."

"This is who I am." His voice was even more ragged, his gray eyes were more storm than rain, and Maggy stared. That was temper on his face, she was sure of it.

Dark and furious. And with something else beneath that she understood instinctively, though she couldn't name it. She felt it inside her, like a new heat. "There is absolutely no place in my life for this kind of distraction."

"By *this kind of distraction*, do you mean a wife? Or a queen?" She studied him. "Or are you talking about a kiss?"

And then she watched him change, right there before her. She watched him beat back the storm and close himself off, one breath to the next. It was as if he rolled himself up tight into an armored ball. She watched his expression clear, then go cold. His gaze lightened, his mouth firmed. He stood straighter, somehow, and that intense, ruthless power that seemed to blaze straight out from inside him filled the whole of the ballroom.

This was the king of the Constantines in all his glory. But Maggy had kissed the man. She wanted him back. She wanted the storm.

She wanted to dance in it.

"You have taken to your role admirably," he told her, back to that stern, stuffy tone that she knew she should hate. She knew it. But instead it pulled taut inside of her, fire and need. "I anticipate we will be ready to introduce you to the world sooner rather than later."

"Do kings not kiss?" she asked mildly, in a provoking sort of tone her former employers and battalions of counselors would have used to prove her attitude was eternally bad. "I didn't realize that was a breach of royal protocol."

He looked at her with that arrogant astonishment she remembered from the coffee shop. But something had changed—inside her. She could see that same expression. She remembered how she'd felt about it the first time—or how she'd told herself she felt. But now it was like a lit flame, burning her from the inside out.

"I beg your pardon?"

It might have been phrased as a question, even if he used that scaldingly remote and royally outraged tone. It wasn't one.

Maggy shrugged. Deliberately. "You seem so…" She waved a hand at him, not quite as dismissive as his, but certainly a contender. "Upset. I thought maybe there was some royal proclamation forbidding the kingly lips from touching another's."

That muscle in his jaw clenched tight. "There is not."

"Then it's me that's the issue." She eyed him. "Is that what you're trying to tell me? That you have a problem with trailer trash after all? Even after all these weeks of playing Henry Higgins, just for me?"

Reza seemed to expand, hard and harsh, to fill the room, though he didn't move. Maggy could *feel* him everywhere. Pressing against her. Temper and divine right like a fog that stole inside and clogged the whole of the chamber.

"I will see you at dinner at the appointed time," he told her, his voice so cold she was surprised icicles didn't form. "We will discuss the history of the Constantines and the Santa Dominian line of succession."

She managed, somehow, to keep her expression blank. "That sounds thrilling."

His jaw looked tight enough to shatter. "We will never mention this unfortunate episode again, so allow me to make this clear now. You are not *trailer trash*. You are the daughter of a revered and ancient bloodline. And for the record, I do not have problems with anyone or anything. I solve problems or am otherwise above the fray, as is appropriate for a man in my position."

"Is that why you're so grumpy after a little kiss?" Maggy smiled at him when he glared at her, and she'd gotten a whole lot better at smiling since she'd come here. She was almost good at it now. "Because you're so above it?"

She thought he meant to say something. That perfect mouth of his moved and his dark gray eyes flashed, but he didn't speak. He merely inclined his head in that coolly dismissive way of his. Then he turned on his heel with military precision and marched from the room.

Maggy stood where he left her. She made herself breathe, deep and long, to get the shakiness out. Her mouth felt slightly swollen, sweetly battered from his, and she indulged herself, there in the middle of a fairy-tale ballroom on a faraway island, by pressing her fingers against her own lips. As if she could conjure up his kiss again that easily.

The truth was, everything had changed tonight. She thought he knew it, too, or why else would he have reacted that way? All this time, she'd told herself that she was happy to go along with this because it got her out of her hard, cold, empty grind and allowed her to live the sort of storybook life she'd tried so hard to stop letting herself dream because it was too painful every time she woke up. Because doing this meant she belonged somewhere, and she could never be rejected from a place she claimed with her blood. She'd told herself that was all that mattered.

But she'd been lying to herself. It had been as much about Reza as it had been about her remarkably stubborn princess dreams and the reality of that blood test. Maybe more.

She'd agreed to marry *him*, not a fairy tale. She'd left everything she knew because he'd come and found her. *Him*. Not some random person. Not one of the tabloid reporters who dogged the steps of every royal in Europe. Not the brother she was still coming to terms with having in the first place.

And she'd thrown herself headfirst into this crash course in becoming something other than trailer trash, which Maggy knew she'd been all her life no matter what he said to the contrary. No one in the foster care system had cared too much about her *ancient bloodline*. She hadn't done all this because she was particularly fired up about being a queen. Or even because the clothes were exquisite and she'd discovered things about herself she'd never have known before and would never have found out—like the fact emeralds didn't suit her, she preferred Louboutins to Jimmy Choos, and had an abiding appreciation for a very particular bath salt her attendants told her was handmade in one specific boutique in Bali. That was all its own delight, to be sure.

But deep down, if she was brutally honest with herself, she'd been trying her hardest to make herself into the kind of woman Reza wanted.

Maybe it wasn't even that deep down.

Every night she sat at the table in the formal dining room and turned herself inside out trying to make that ruthless mouth of his soften, just a little bit. Every night she trotted out pertinent facts and used the right utensils to show she was learning her numerous lessons. She sat with elegant posture and made the sort of easy and yet sophisticated conversation she'd been told—repeatedly—set a woman who would be queen apart from the masses. Educated and yet wry, compelling and yet not overly opinionated.

"The formal dinner table is no place for strong opinions," Madame Rosso told her again and again.

"Because heaven forbid it put a man off his food," Maggy had muttered once, glaring mulishly at the empty plate before her, several hours into a crash course on formal manners.

The king's former nanny had fixed her with a frank stare, all the way down the impressive length of her nose, the force of it making the white hair piled on top of her head seem to wobble.

"This is about diplomacy," she'd said in her crisp, clear-eyed way. "You are a royal princess. You will not be dining with people rounded up off the streets who might be in any doubt about the issues of the day. It is likely, in fact, that you will be seated with those who decide those issues. And when policy is served in the middle of a meal, it can only cause indigestion. A meal is the time one behaves as if the world is already perfect, war and strife do not exist, and everyone near you is a close, personal friend."

"Because no one needs to hear the opinion of a princess." Maggy had wrinkled up her nose. "I get it."

"Because the point of a princess is that you are a symbol," Madame Rosso had returned, her tone faintly chiding. "You are an amiable and benevolent reminder of what is for many a bygone time. It is called being gracious, Your Highness. In public, it is your greatest weapon. In private, of course, one expects you will have no trouble whatsoever making your opinions known however you choose and to whomever you wish."

And Maggy discovered that, in fact, she *wanted* to be gracious. She wanted to be a symbol of something positive as opposed to the poster child for neglect. She wanted to make this new role of hers her own in every possible way.

But most of all, she wanted to be Reza's.

Maggy could finally admit it, with her mouth still tingling from his mercilessly beautiful kiss. She wanted to be *his*.

She'd assumed that inhabiting the role of perfect princess was the way to do it, because that was what he'd said he needed from her, or wanted for her. The perfect princess, then the perfect queen. And all that entailed—heirs and grace and whatever else. But that was before he'd kissed her. That was before she'd seen that storm in him and wanted nothing more than to bathe in it.

That was before he'd claimed her mouth with his and brought her alive. Wickedly, deliciously, beautifully *alive*. More alive than she'd ever been before in all her life.

Which meant, she realized as she stood there in that ballroom filled with need and longing and *Reza* long after he'd left it, she needed to come up with a different plan.

Two nights later, after a series of such excruciatingly stiff meals she was surprised she hadn't turned to stone in the middle of them, Maggy decided it was time she tested the waters. He'd called what happened between them *a relentless hunger*. She wanted to see just how hungry he really was.

Because it turned out she was ravenous.

After another long, stiff dinner packed with a barrage of dry facts and the king's dark glower from across the exquisitely set table, they moved into one of the many salons that littered the villa. Reza chose a different one every night, but what happened in each was always the same. They would sit and talk about things even more innocuous than what had passed for dinner table conversation.

"This is ridiculous," she'd said on one of the first nights they'd done this, scowling at him. "I'm not going to tell you what I did in the summers while I was growing up. Why would you want to know?"

"This is called a conversation," he'd replied, his expression like granite, though she'd been sure she'd seen a hint of that silvery gleam in his gaze. Or maybe she'd just wanted it there, more than was probably healthy. "It is much like dancing. It is all about the appearance of being light and airy, the better to put the person you are speaking with at his ease."

"If the person I'm speaking with isn't at his ease after nine hundred courses and too much dessert, I don't think me sitting here making up pleasant lies about my summertime activities is going to help."

"You are not required to lie."

"Oh, okay." She'd glared at him, but she'd remembered to fold her hands in her lap so at least she looked like a lady while she did it. "I'd be happy to tell you about the summer I worked in the convenience store because I wanted to save up enough money to buy myself new shoes for school in the fall. My foster mother stole it from under my bed and spent it all on booze. Or wait, maybe the time the only job I could get was as a waitress in a sleazy motel restaurant, but the manager fired me because I wouldn't have sex with him. Or I know, the summer I got a great job in a cute boutique on Main Street, but they let me go because I didn't have a car and it took me so long to walk there every morning that I was always a sweaty mess when I arrived. That just wasn't the trendy boutique look they were going for, you see."

"You've made your point." His voice had been silken reproval, all the way through. She'd ignored it.

"What did you do in your summers?" she'd asked him. "Polish the crown jewels? Behead a few peasants for a little giggle? Use your scepter as a machete as the mood took you?"

"My summers were devoted to charity work," he'd said, surprising her more than she wanted to admit. "A different charity every summer from the time I was ten. Usually in a different country and for a different cause, and all of them quite hands-on. Many sick children, I'm afraid, though I also spent some time digging ditches. I was not raised to be the vicious and selfish monarch you seem to imagine." His brows rose. "Beheadings and machetes and the crown jewels do not figure strongly under my rule, you might be surprised to learn."

"I thought that was the point of being king," she'd said, but the edge had gone from the conversation. She'd seen that silver gleam in his gaze, the one that made her feel warm all over.

"The point of the kind of light, easy conversation we have after dinner is twofold," he'd told her after a moment. She'd become fixated on his hands then. The way he held one of them in the air as he lounged in his chair, looking as if he sat on a high throne instead of in an armchair. "First, it is happy. Sparkling. It allows you to guide the room in whichever direction you choose.

And second, it is more intimate. Guests will have eaten, perhaps have had too much to drink. It is highly likely this is where deeper topics will be discussed—but that won't happen if we all sit about in silence."

She'd looked at him. "I'm a diversion, then?"

He hadn't quite smiled. "My mother once held a room filled with men on the brink of war spellbound as she waxed rhapsodic about the balls she'd attended as a young woman. It was silly talk, but she made them laugh. It allowed my father to have a much needed casual aside with a man known at that time as the Butcher of the Balkans, and after that, the drums of war beat a little more quietly." He'd swirled something amber in his glass for a moment before fixing her with that fathomless gray stare. "Never underestimate the importance of that diversion, Princess."

Tonight, they settled into Maggy's favorite salon after their meal, which she decided was a good omen. It was an old study that felt more like a cozy library than a chilly sitting room. There was an ancient globe on a stand that had all the wrong names on countries with borders that had shifted a long time since. Hardbound books with gold-edged pages lined the walls. The fire was bright and warm tonight, holding the stormy winter weather outside at bay.

Maggy liked the rain against all the windows. It made her think of that hunger Reza had talked about. It made her feel it everywhere, roaring inside of her. Making her feel far braver than perhaps she should.

Reza was talking about something so light and so far removed from what she was thinking that she didn't pretend to follow it. He'd given her a glass of something as sweet as it was alcoholic, but she'd only tasted it once before putting it aside. She was after something else entirely tonight.

It took her a long moment to realize that Reza had stopped speaking. That the room had gone silent. That there was no sound at all save the fire crackling and spitting against the grate, and outside, the winter storm rattling the windows. That Reza's gaze was on hers, all that dark gray unreadable. If not outright forbidding.

Trouble was, it didn't intimidate her. She liked him granite and imposing. She thought the truth was, she liked *him*. Full stop.

"I apologize." He was quite obviously not sorry. That was clear from his tone, not to mention that frigid, regal expression on his face. "Am I boring you?"

Maggy stood then, trying to remember how to be graceful the way she'd been taught. She ran her hands down the front of her gown, a sweet fall of dark blue silk that brushed the floor despite the high shoes she wore. And any nerves she might have had now that she was really doing this—and she was really, truly doing this, no matter what—were swept away by the way Reza tracked the movement. As if he couldn't quite help himself. As if he wanted it to be *his* hands on her like that.

That was what she wanted to find out. If he did. If he wanted her as much as she wanted him.

If that kiss had been a mistake—or if it was the new beginning between them that it had felt like to her.

"I want to thank you," she told him.

He was lounging in yet another armchair, the way he always did. How he managed to give the impression of slumping without actually doing so was a marvel, she thought. A bit of royal magic. He'd opened the jacket of yet another perfect suit—and Maggy knew enough now to understand that the word for the kind of hand-tooled clothing he preferred was *bespoke*. That he had many such suits, all made to his precise specifications and all, like this one, a love song to his hard, solid, sculpted body.

She wanted to know the words to that song. Then she wanted to sing it.

Reza said nothing, and that was almost more alarming than all the cutting things he could have said. He only watched her as she moved toward him, though she could feel the weight of it, as if his gray gaze really was the hard, pounding rain that washed over the windows behind him. He remained silent when she came to stand before him, just inside the V of his outthrust legs.

"You've given me everything," she told him.

And even though she'd planned this to be light and airy, the way everyone kept teaching her these royal games of intrigue over waltzes and dinners and after dinner drinks were meant to be, it didn't sound that way when she said it. It occurred to her, once the words were out, that it was no less than the raw and simple truth.

Oh, well, she thought. *No use pretending now.*

She made herself continue. "I want to give you something in return."

"You will give me your hand in marriage soon enough." His voice was too low and a bit too rough, but he was watching her with a certain alertness that made her blood seem to quicken inside her veins. It encouraged her even as it moved in her like a deep, sweet caress. And most importantly, he didn't order her to step away from him. Or to take her seat again. "That is more than sufficient."

"I can't possibly give you any kind of gift you don't already have," she told him. Her heart was pounding inside her chest. Her eyes felt glassy. "So I thought instead I would give you something I've never given anyone else. Ever."

Something in his gray gaze changed then, like a new storm washing out the old. That hard mouth of his moved. "Princess. That isn't necessary."

But she had no intention of heeding that warning she heard in his voice. She wanted this too much. She wanted *him* too much. And she'd spent a lifetime refusing to allow herself to want things she couldn't have.

She didn't want to do it any longer. It felt like defeat, and that was a part of her old life. This was her new start. *He* was her new life.

Maggy wanted to taste every bit of it, starting with him.

She gathered up all her courage and every last bit of that greedy, ravenous hunger that stormed through her now and, if she was being as honest with herself as possible, had since he'd walked through the coffee shop door and she'd thought he was *extraordinary*. She still did. That made it easy to sink down on her knees before him, until she was kneeling up between his legs.

"Maggy."

She liked her name on his lips, and no matter the tone he used—just this side of a command. She liked the arrested, *aware* look on his harsh face and, even more, the way it shivered all through her, as if that silver gleam was inside her, too.

She shifted forward so she could put her hands on his thighs, then run them up toward his lap, her goal obvious.

Maggy thought of the coffee shop again, and how she'd thought he'd seemed like a man who was used to having people on their knees before him. Had she wanted to do this even then? Her mouth watered at the thought.

Reza didn't move. If anything, he got *more* still, as if he really did turn to stone beneath her hands. But it was a hot, masculine sort of stone. It made her belly seem to twist into a complicated knot, then sink down between her legs. Maggy tipped her head back so she could keep her eyes on his. Too much gray and too much silver besides, and when that muscle clenched in his jaw, she felt it in her core, molten and greedy.

She slid her hands up farther, reveling in the feel of his strong, corded thighs beneath her palms. All his power. All that heat. She sensed more than saw the way his hands gripped the arms of his chair.

"Maggy."

The way he said her name was supposed to stop her. She understood that. But he didn't actually order her to stop.

So she didn't.

She paused for the faintest moment at the top of his thighs, where she could see his hard length against his fly—growing larger and more fascinating the longer she sat there and looked at it. She slid her hands up farther still, only grazing the front of his fly in passing as she reached for his belt.

He jolted as if he would reach to stop her—but he didn't.

The sound of his buckle seemed louder than it should. Ruder and more delicious with only the snap of the fire behind it. Maggy felt herself flush, but she couldn't stop now. She was too close. Her breath kept tangling in her throat and between her legs, she felt a matching rush of sensation.

Molten heat, soft and wild, and all for him.

She pulled his trousers open, her heart punching at her hard. So hard it made her stomach flip over and over. Her hands trembled slightly. She didn't know which was worse, the longing that made her knees feel soft and weak beneath her or the panic that he might stop her at any moment when she was this close. When she was finally so close.

She reached into the opening she'd made and pulled out the hardest part of him, wrapping her fingers around the thick, hard length. She swallowed, hard, and looked up at him as she indulged herself, moving her hand all the way down to his root, his silken smoothness against her palm making her whole body shake with need.

His face was set, that muscle in his jaw something like ferocious. He was so fierce, so harsh, he should have scared her—but he didn't. He never had. She understood that glitter in his gaze now, the way she had the other night when he'd kissed her. She felt it racing through her, making her feel clumsy and needy and maddened with this same hunger.

And she knew that whatever else happened, however stony he became, he wanted her exactly as much as she wanted him.

The knowledge felt like safety. Like freedom. Like both at once, wrapped up together and indistinguishable from one another.

Maggy wrapped her free hand around him, too. Then she tipped herself forward, kept her gaze on his as she opened her mouth, and sucked him in deep.

CHAPTER EIGHT

REZA DIDN'T KNOW how he didn't embarrass himself on the spot.

Maggy's hot, clever mouth closed over him, the world exploded into bright red need and a mad rush of pure lust, and he was nearly lost.

Nearly.

She took him deeper. She wrapped her fingers around the base of him and she tested his length against her tongue. She pulled back and lavished attention on the broad head before sucking him back in again.

She'd said she'd never done this before, and he was amazed at how...primitive that made him. How possessive.

He thought her inexpert attempt to please him with her sheer enthusiasm and that hot, wet mouth of hers might actually kill him.

But if this was how he was going to die, Reza thought it might be worth it. He kept his hands fisted hard on the arms of his chair. He let her play with him, her dark hair swirling around her bare shoulders and moving over his thighs like heat. He watched in dark fascination and that same red-hot greed as she took him deeper. Then deeper still.

He felt her everywhere.

And he had never wanted anyone or anything more.

He knew that should have alarmed him, that razor's edge of desire that was a bit too close to desperation. He knew what indulging in this, in her, made him. He knew he should push her off, reclaim his control, insist on all the cold, clear boundaries that had to stand between them or everything else would shatter—

But he couldn't do it.

He didn't *want* to do it.

Reza wanted her. *Her.* He wanted his princess, his queen, the woman who had been promised to him at her birth. The girl he'd lost before she'd had a chance to grow up into his woman. The future that had been wrenched away from him when he'd only just become a man. He wanted the queen he'd mourned throughout his twenties.

He wanted the real, live, insanely beautiful woman who knelt before him and *thanked him* with every blazingly slick slide of her smart, hot mouth along the hardest, neediest part of him. Again and again and again.

And he had already damned himself when he'd kissed her in that ballroom. Why not enjoy the flames?

All the lies Reza had told himself since he'd seen that photograph with his own lost princess bride in the background, all the walls he'd built since then and tried to keep solid, all the thousands of ways he'd pretended he could maintain his boundaries against this woman who had been born to be his, the power she wielded over him because she was his lost Magdalena and because she was his Maggy besides—it all simply crumbled around him.

And Reza found he didn't much care, because in the

wreckage there was still her, his princess, knelt there between his legs with her mouth against him, driving him straight toward that cliff.

"No," he bit out, aware of the harshness of his voice only once he heard himself, the echo of his furious, ungovernable hunger rough in the quiet of the room.

Maggy froze, pulling her mouth free of him while her hands were still wrapped tight around him. But even that was too much. Reza muttered out something in Italian, a curse or a prayer and he didn't know which, reaching down to pull her off of him before he lost his last little shred of control. He eased her up from between his legs even as he moved out of the chair, sliding down to the floor to kneel there with her.

Then he took her face—her exquisite, impossible face, intelligent and lovely and *his*—between his hands.

"Reza," she whispered, her hands moving to curl around his wrists. "I want—"

"*I* want," he corrected her gruffly. "And believe me, Princess, I intend to have what I want. Everything I want."

And then he took her mouth with his, and let that bright red desire for her wash over him. He couldn't taste her deeply enough. He couldn't hold her close enough. He angled his jaw, tangling his tongue with hers. He indulged that sharp greed inside of him, letting one hand move to fist in her thick hair while the other learned that delicious arch of her back, then settled on the sweet curve of her bottom.

It wasn't enough. Reza feasted on her mouth the way he'd wanted to forever, and even more since that kiss in the ballroom. She shivered as she kissed him back, rubbing her breasts against his chest as if she was as desperate as he was. As needy. As impatient.

And everything had changed tonight.

The brakes were off. The walls were down.

There were so many reasons he shouldn't do this—but chief among them was the fact that with Maggy in his arms, her mouth beneath his again, and her lush, lean body pressed against him, he couldn't think of a single one of them.

To hell with the king of the Constantines. Tonight he was nobody but Reza.

With Maggy that felt like a revelation instead of a disaster.

He lost himself in her taste. The scent of her skin, vanilla and coconut, as if she was a touch of the tropics in the middle of the winter storm outside. The sheer, dizzying perfection of her mouth against his and the way her taste inflamed him and wrecked him, over and over again.

Reza lost himself in sensation. In her. In the perfection that was his lost princess, finally found. Finally exactly where she'd been meant to be all along.

He let his hands move over her again, restlessly testing her curves and making her moan into his mouth. He trailed a line of fire and need down the length of her elegant neck, learning every inch of her and where a lick or a graze of his teeth made her shudder. He bent to taste the plump, smooth thrust of her breasts above the bodice of her dress and in the mad fire of that he took her down with him to the soft, thick rug.

And then she was beneath him, her caramel eyes shining and her mouth faintly damp from his. *Finally.* Reza remembered her down on her knees in that coffee shop, staring at him as if he was an unwelcome intrusion. He remembered her soft and asleep on his shoulder in the back of the SUV, so vulnerable and so trusting at once. He could still feel her mouth all over the length of him, while the taste of her rocketed through him and made him something like thirsty.

She was his. Here, now she was entirely his. *At last.*

Her gaze was wide. Dark with the same need that moved in him. Her hair was a dark cloud around her, gleaming in the firelight, and it took everything he had to hold himself there for a moment, up on his elbows above her. As if he needed to etch this moment into his memory forever. Maggy reached up and pushed his jacket off his shoulders and he let her do it, tossing it aside as soon as possible. And then he hissed out a breath when she went further, reaching up beneath the tail of his shirt to get her hands on his skin.

It was like fire. It was better than fire. Her hands were a torment and a blessing as one traced its way up his spine and the other moved lower to test his backside against her palm.

He needed to be closer to her. He needed…everything.

"I need to be inside you," he gritted out, and he was too far gone to care that he sounded wrecked. Like a stranger to himself. Like a man with no brakes, no control, nothing.

Like a man, not a king.

It should have stopped him dead. But Maggy was clinging to him, her mouth to his.

"I need that, too," she whispered. "I need you, Reza."

And everything shifted then. It got hotter. Wilder. Deeper red and far more intense.

Reza reached between them and pulled her filmy,

silken dress up and out of his way with rather more intent than finesse. He didn't care that he'd lost all his ease and grace and caution, not when her smooth, sculpted legs were bared to his gaze. He ran his hand up, growling his appreciation of her taut thigh and continuing until he reached the tiny little scrap of silk and lace between her legs.

He held himself above her, his gaze hard and greedy on hers, as he stroked his way beneath that little scrap and found her scalding heat at last.

She shivered beneath him as he tested her with one finger. Two. So hot and soft. He thought she might kill him and he couldn't think, just then, of a better way to go than wrapped up tight in all her molten heat.

"Maggy—" he began, but he didn't know what he meant to say. Maybe he'd simply needed her name on his lips.

"Please." Her voice was stark. Greedy. Her gaze was dark and glassy at once, and she was writhing beneath him, every part of her a sweet, scalding invitation. "Please, Reza."

"Use your hands," he ordered her, low and sure. "Guide me in, Princess. Take me deep."

He felt the way she jolted against him at his words. He saw the fire dance over her face, making her gaze a gleaming thing, over-bright and needy.

Then her hands were on him again, a torment and a glory. She wrapped her fingers around his aching length, raising her hips to him as she did as he'd commanded and guided him toward her entrance, using one hand to rake her panties to one side. Reza bent to take her mouth as she lifted herself up, impaling herself on him. He slid one hand around to hold her bottom where he wanted her, and then he thrust into her. Deeper and then deeper still, too hungry, too greedy, to wait the extra seconds it would take to undress either one of them any further.

And when he was buried to the hilt, they both froze, their eyes locked to each other. His whole length snug inside of her, deep and hard.

The whole world narrowed down to this. Here. The two of them.

His princess. His queen. At last.

"Please…" she whispered. Again. And he thought he'd never heard a prettier sound than his tough little princess begging him.

Reza began to move.

It was throwing himself into an inferno, again and again and again. It was a wild taking. A deep, greedy possession.

It was perfect. *She* was perfect.

She wrapped herself around him and Reza couldn't get close enough. Deep enough. He couldn't taste her enough. Her wicked mouth. Her sweetly elegant neck. Her gorgeous, ripe little breasts.

He wondered if anything would ever be enough when it came to this woman. Even this.

Right here, right now, he didn't care.

And then suddenly, it was too much. He felt his control go liquid, and it took everything he had to haul himself back from that edge even as he maintained his hard, deep pace.

He reached between them and found the very center of her need. He rubbed her there, keeping his strokes deep and hard.

"Come for me," he growled against her neck.

And she obeyed him. She clenched against him and she shuddered all around him, then cried out his name as she fell.

And Reza followed her straight over the side of the world.

Outside the villa, the winter storm raged on through the night.

But Maggy was far more interested in the one she was caught up in with Reza, inside, where it was dry but not quite safe. Not when there were so many things to discover about him. And so many things he could do to her.

She wanted to do every single one of them.

When she came back into herself, there on the floor of the study, she felt wrecked—but in a beautiful, glorious way. As if her skin could hardly hold all the things she felt inside.

Reza lifted himself above her, his face dark. Unreadable.

And for a moment it was hard to tell where the rain outside ended and he began.

Then he lifted his hand and brought it to her face, stroking down her jaw. As if she was precious to him. As if he cared—

Maggy knew that was foolish. That she was only going to hurt herself, thinking such things about a man like him, so ruthless and mighty above all else.

She thought he would say something then. She thought he would go out of his way to remind her that he was a king and she was beneath him the way everyone else he encountered was beneath him. That he held all the power here, one way or another.

But he didn't say a word.

After a long moment lost in his endless gray gaze, Reza pulled out of her and rolled away. She hardly had time to process the loss of his silken and steel length within her, his hard body against her, his heat all around her, because he was standing then. He rose from the floor to his feet in an unconscious show of all that forbidding grace that made him who he was. He hauled up his trousers and fastened them, then looked down at her where she still lay there, spread out on the thick rug on the floor of the salon.

Boneless.

Something moved over his face, too quick for her to read, and then he held out his hand.

It reminded her of the coffee shop, and Maggy didn't know how she felt about that. Only that it seemed to trigger something raw and unwieldy inside of her, swamping her where she lay. She sat up, trying to fight it off, tugging her dress back down to cover her legs.

And Reza merely waited there, his hand extended, as if he could do so all night.

The only reason you're hesitating to take his hand is that you're too eager and you don't want him to know it, she told herself caustically.

She decided that was stupid. She'd already proved her eagerness with her mouth. What was the point of pretending otherwise now? She'd already given herself away entirely. There was no going back.

Maggy held out her hand and let him lift her to her feet. Then he hauled her against him. He kept tugging until she was off balance, and then he simply bent at the knees and swept her up into his arms.

"Reza," she began, high against his chest with that

unsmiling mouth of his *right there* and his harshly compelling face *so close*—

He didn't so much as glance at her as he started to move.

"Hush," he murmured as he shouldered his way out of the study and started down the long hall toward their rooms. "Not tonight."

Maggy took that as gospel.

He carried her through the dimly lit villa, and Maggy did nothing but wrap one arm around his neck and let him take her where he liked. She had only passing impressions of rooms with lights on and flickering candles in the sconces along the ancient walls. She saw the door to her own room as they passed it, and let a breath out then, resting her head against his strong shoulder.

Inside his suite, Reza moved quickly through the private salon where he'd stood with her before that tilted mirror. He carried her down another hall that was more like a paneled foyer, past what looked like an office and another, even more private study. She lifted her head from his shoulder when he entered yet another room, then kicked the door closed behind him.

There was a vast stone fireplace on one wall, taking over the whole of that side of the room with a fire dancing cheerfully in its grate. It was the only light in the bedchamber. She saw a few chairs and a sofa arranged before it, but then he was lifting her up and placing her on a vast, supremely kingly bed. Four stout, carved columns rose in each corner, but there was no canopy here to relieve the male stamp of it. Only acres of mattress and soft linens in dark, brooding colors.

And Maggy didn't care about any of that. She cared about the man who stood at the side of the wide, high bed, his glittering gaze fixed on her while the firelight played all over him and made him look more like a myth than a man.

He didn't speak.

And that look on his face was so intent, so fierce, that Maggy followed suit.

Reza undressed her carefully. His hard hands smoothed over her ankles and unbuckled the delicate straps of her shoes, then tugged them off. He found the fastening to her gown at its side and pulled the zipper down, then lifted her to sweep the dress away. His gaze glittered hot when he looked at her then, in nothing but the tiny panties she'd held to one side before, but he didn't haul her to him. He only hooked his fingers in the lacy sides of the panties and slid them down, then off.

When she was naked, he looked at her for a long, long while. He raked his fingers through her hair, almost as if he was arranging it to suit himself. Then he let his hands wander, testing her collarbone with one finger. Then finding her nipples with his thumbs while he lifted her breasts into his hard palms.

He leaned in then, putting his lips over one nipple and sucking until it hardened against his tongue. By the time he made his lazy way to her other nipple, she was shivering again, that same fire lit again inside of her and burning bright.

Reza stepped back then, and Maggy pushed herself up to her knees so she could watch him as he rid himself of his clothes with a certain ferocity that made that knot low in her belly pulse. Then glow.

When he was naked, Maggy heard herself let out a reverent sort of sigh that she could no more keep inside than she could have stopped herself from getting on her knees earlier.

He was beautiful. He was made of hard planes and delectable ridges, all lean muscle and corded, male power.

Reza crawled onto the bed with her, one arm around her middle to shift her into the center of the mattress.

"Reza…" she tried again, because the wild, raw hollow inside of her was growing, pushing everything else aside, caught in the storm of sensation. His thighs were a rough delight against hers. She could feel him again, hard and insistent, against the soft skin of her belly. And he was settled on his elbows above her, his fingers deep in her hair.

"Quiet, Princess," he murmured. "This is a time for action, not words."

And then he took her mouth with his, showing her exactly what he meant.

He tasted her everywhere. He spread fire and need everywhere he went. He explored her body, inch by inch, tasting her and touching her, then flipping her over so he could do the same to her other side. His mouth moved down the length of her spine, torturously slow, and she felt his hard mouth curve against her skin when he made her shudder.

By the time he turned her over again she was making no attempt to hide her moans, her pleading. His face was dark as he came over her, his eyes nearly black with passion.

And when he slid into her, she burst apart, sensation shattering her into a thousand pieces.

"Beautiful," he murmured as she shook and shook, her fingers pressed deep into his back. "You are so beautiful, my Magdalena."

Then he began to move.

Slow. Lazy.

Unbearably hot.

He rode her, sweet and easy, through her shattering, then kept on going, tossing her from one peak straight into a brand-new fire.

He played with her mouth, her breasts. He acted as if he had all the time in the world. And when she started to lift her hips to meet him again, when that tension wound around and around inside of her and made her cling to him and arch into his thrusts, he let himself go.

Reza gathered her close and pounded into her, every drag of his hips throwing her closer and closer and closer still, until she broke again, flying apart into scraps of fire and need and something far greater than either.

And she held him tight as he followed her, shouting out her name.

It took a long, long time for him to stir, and when he did, his gaze came to hers in the flickering light. Maggy had to bite her lip to keep back the things that threatened to spill over then. The truths she hadn't wanted to face but could hardly avoid now, naked with him like this.

She didn't know what he saw on her face. But he still didn't speak. He rolled them over again, and this time, he carried her to his bathroom. He set her down in a huge, glassed-in enclosure, and then he washed her, his expression serious.

When they were both squeaky clean, he took her back to that great big bed and climbed into it with her, arranging her so she was draped over his body, and Maggy thought it was the perfect time to say the things that sat there so heavy on her tongue.

But the rain still drummed against the windows and the silence seemed sweet.

Instead, she fell asleep, curled up on Reza's chest with the fire dancing all over them both.

They came together in the night, too many times to count. She would roll, or he would shift, and it was as if the barest slide of skin against skin was too much. The first time they slid against each other he spread her out beneath him and kissed his way down her belly before settling between her legs and licking her into sobbing bliss. Another time she woke with his heat all along her back and his thigh thrust between hers. She couldn't help herself. She'd arched against all that hard, muscled heat until he'd shifted her, thrusting into her as he held her in place.

She lost track of how many times they woke and found each other in the dark. She couldn't count the number of times she fell apart, only for him to catch her there when they both fell back to earth.

The last time they woke together it was gray outside, with a hint of light across the sea. The rain had finally stopped. Reza lifted her over him and settled her on his lap, thrusting into her once again as he sat up, gathering her astride him.

It was her turn to set the pace and she took it slow, every last part of her body so tuned to him now it was as if they were one.

One body. One mind.

One heart, she thought, though she knew she shouldn't.

And the higher she climbed, the brighter that flame between them, the more she knew. What that raw thing was that took up more and more of her every time they touched. What was eating her alive from the inside out.

"One more time," Reza urged her as the sweet tension pulled tight, as she worked herself against him, hard and deep within her with his mouth against her neck. "Just one more."

And this time they broke apart together, soft and shattering.

She slumped in his lap, her forehead pressed to his, and tried to catch her breath while inside her everything was too raw. Too big, too unwieldy, *too much*.

Maggy might not have felt any of these things before. But it was like the salt in the air outside that had meant the sea was near. She knew what it was.

"Are you with me?" Reza asked, his voice low and gruff and, somehow, the sweetest thing she'd ever heard, as his hands moved gently up and down her spine as if he was bringing her back to earth with the slide of his hands over her skin.

Maggy couldn't move. She couldn't open her eyes. And she couldn't care less.

"I'm with you," she said, her mouth close to his, her head tipped into his. As close to him as it was possible to get. "I love you."

It took her another breath, long and still shuddery, to realize what she'd said.

And still one more to feel that Reza had turned to stone beneath her.

She pushed back so she could look at his face, and her heart broke. She felt it crack apart and splinter, there and then. Because he looked like a statue. Remote and inaccessible and more forbidding than she'd ever seen him before.

"Reza," she whispered. "Forget I said that. Let's just pretend—"

"No." He sounded something far darker than merely *rough* then. Much darker and much, much worse. He lifted her off of him, setting her to the side as if she was terribly fragile and required care, but then he moved out of reach. Fast. When his gaze met hers, Maggy saw nothing but blank, hard slate. "No. You cannot. That is impossible. And unacceptable besides."

CHAPTER NINE

"You do not love me," Reza thundered at her, as if that could erase what she'd said. As if that could rewind this night. Shove it back in the bottle where he should have left it to begin with. "That is unacceptable on every level."

But there was an aching thing in his chest and he felt as if it might crack wide-open. And his body was as wrecked as if he'd gone out on a bender like a normal man might. Not that Reza needed drugs or alcohol when there was Maggy. She was infinitely more potent.

And he should never have let this happen. He knew exactly where it led. He'd been cleaning up the mess of it his whole adult life.

Maggy was still sitting in the middle of the vast bed where they'd hardly slept all night. Even now, he still wanted her. He stalked to his dressing room and threw on a pair of exercise trousers, letting them ride low on his hips. When he returned to the bedroom, she was standing by the side of the bed, buttoning herself into his shirt.

He didn't want to see how small and slender she was in his shirt. How long her legs were, naked and tempting, beneath the hem. When she was done buttoning it up, she lifted her chin and faced him, and he hated that she clearly needed to brace herself. Worse, she hugged herself around the middle as she studied him, too many things he didn't want to recognize clouding her pretty eyes and making him feel like the lowest bastard who had ever drawn breath.

Reza knew he was exactly that. But even so, he couldn't seem to ignore the part of him that urged him to go to her. To take her in his arms again. To make this right somehow, and no matter that she'd made a bad situation worse with the words she should never have said—but he couldn't do that.

"I didn't mean to say that," Maggy said, her voice quiet, though it seemed to punch into him all the same. "But that doesn't mean it isn't true."

"It cannot be true." He folded his arms over his chest and forced himself to stop admiring the way she looked in his damn shirt, as if he had as little control over himself as he'd exhibited this whole, long night. "This should never have happened." He jerked his chin at the bed between them. "Any of this."

He could see the instant she stopped feeling vulnerable—or decided to stop showing it, anyway. The exact moment that temper of hers kicked in. First there was that flash in her eyes. Then she frowned at him the way she hadn't done in some time, too busy smiling and folding her hands in her lap and learning how to exude good breeding with every breath.

"I have no idea what you're talking about." Her voice was even. Cool. "This is where all of this has been leading, surely. You didn't storm into my coffee shop in Vermont so we could end up polite and distant pen pals."

"I need a queen, not a lover," he threw her, and he

did nothing to make the hit of that any less harsh than it sounded. Standing there at the foot of the bed where he'd shown her exactly the opposite all night long. He couldn't even tell who he was more furious with—her or himself. "I have no time to dally, and certainly not with you."

For a moment, he thought he might have broken her, and a sea of self-loathing washed over him, nearly taking him from his feet.

But this was his Maggy. His tough survivor. She'd made it through twenty years of dire circumstances. She'd sailed through the past weeks. What was an unpleasant conversation at dawn? He'd seen her mouth tremble, he was sure of it, but she only pressed her lips into a firm line and kept her chin high.

Reza had the dark, uneasy notion that he was the only one at risk of falling apart here. Something that seemed far more imminent when she moved toward him, skirting the bed and coming closer than she should.

Close enough that he could smell her again. Vanilla and coconut and, beneath that, her. His Maggy. He knew her now. Her scent, her taste. He'd had his mouth and his hands on every last inch of her body. His body stirred anew, which should have been impossible after the night they'd had. But nothing was impossible when it came to Maggy. Nothing at all.

He was in so much trouble. He was far past *trouble* and into a full-blown crisis.

"You're going to have to explain to me why the fact we had sex is a problem," she said, still in that quiet way of hers, suggesting she was under control. But he could see that sheen in her eyes, telling him otherwise.

It made him feel worse. And more resolute at the same time. "Or why you freak out every time something happens between us. Shouldn't you want this?" She didn't wait for him to answer. "Why can't you have a queen *and* a lover?"

"This cannot happen," he bit out, his voice frigid, because the cold eating him from the inside out was the only thing he had. It was the only way he knew how to keep himself in one piece. "I am a king. I cannot allow anything to divert my attention from my responsibilities."

She shook her head, looking helpless for the first time in as long as he'd known her. "What are you talking about?"

"I have already told you." But it was harder now, wasn't it? He concentrated on keeping his hands to himself. And that scant bit of distance everything in him wanted to close. "I am a king. My focus must be on my people, not on the pleasures of the flesh. A king who loses his focus loses his way. Believe me."

"You're going to marry me." Her voice was fierce now, not cool at all, and there was a recalcitrant part of him that enjoyed that faint evidence that she was as shaken as he was. Reza didn't like to think what that made him. "You told me you want heirs. How did you think that would happen?"

"Not like this." He stepped back, putting distance between them the way he should have done from the start and keeping his damned hands to himself, no matter that he thought it might kill him. "I am a—"

"Stop saying that!"

He didn't know which one of them was more shocked when she shouted at him. She looked as surprised as he felt, though she couldn't have been. Reza wasn't certain anyone had ever raised a voice in his direction.

Why did it make him want to do nothing but gather her close to him again? What *was* this? Why was he still standing here, engaging in this conversation?

But he still couldn't move. He still couldn't leave her.

He was tearing himself apart.

"Stop it," she said again, her voice hoarse. "You're a king, yes. I know that. But you're also a man."

"That is the trouble," he grated out, unable to stop himself. Unable to keep himself in check the way he should. As if the tearing thing in him was a wrecking ball and he was splintering whether he liked it or not. "I must be more than a man. I must be above petty concerns. I am a creature of duty and honor, that is all. But you make me feel like a man and nothing more, Maggy, and I cannot have it."

Her face softened and that was worse. Much worse. "Reza—"

"Silence." His voice rang out, autocratic and regal. She stopped, making a faint sound, like a sob cut off before it could take root. But he was the king now. Not the man she could enchant and make into nothing more than her plaything. He had to be the goddamned king. "I should have delivered you to your brother the moment I found you. I should never have brought you here. I cannot allow *this* in my life."

"This?"

"You." He slashed a hand through the air. "I sit on a throne and hold the fate of a country in my hands. That must be my focus. That must be my *only* focus. My father split his focus and it cost him. He was blackmailed. Disgraced, if only privately. He nearly brought the country to its knees because he had a mistress he put before the crown. And his only excuse was *love*."

His voice was scathing, but she didn't back down. It was one more reason he couldn't have her. He couldn't risk it. "I don't know anything about your father, but you and I have been betrothed since I was born. You could have married someone else, but you didn't. Surely that means something."

"You died." His voice was so harsh. So cold. And he told himself he didn't care when she flinched. "And I moved on."

But Maggy had a spine of steel. She shook her head at him. "Clearly. That's what last night was about, I'm sure."

Reza ground his teeth together, and if his hands balled into fists and betrayed him, well. There was no way out of this. There was no fixing all the things he'd broken last night because he'd lost his hold on himself. There was only this, damage control and moving on.

He would not be his father, a disappointment to his wife, his son. A scandal on the throne, however hushed. A man who'd taken his own life and had left behind a son who had to clean up his mess. Reza had been twenty-four when he'd had to relocate his father's long-time mistress to one of the crown's far-off properties to keep her away from his mother and the royal court who'd despised her—and to keep her from blackmailing his father even after his death. He'd been paying for his father's mistakes—literally—ever since.

"I must marry and I must hold the throne," he told Maggy now, somehow keeping his voice in check. Somehow finding his control again. "These are the duties of every king of the Constantines across the ages.

You make me imagine that I am something more than the throne. You make me feel as if I am a man instead."

"You *are* a man." Her voice caught. "You are the best man I know."

"I am a king," he gritted out, and if his chest felt crushed, too bad. He didn't want to be the best man she knew. He didn't *want* this. He couldn't want anything like it, because he knew where it led. To a small cottage on the Isle of Skye, where a wretched old woman lived with the memories of a man who had never been hers, a man she'd tortured into taking his life, and the kingdom she'd been willing to ransom to serve her own ends. To his father's early grave, the circumstances of his death hushed up and hidden, and a cloud forever over his name and legacy. "Do you know what happens when a king believes he is a man? When he acts like he is no different from the rest? He becomes it. He thinks with his sex, his temper. He allows himself to be flattered, to be small. To think in tiny terms that benefit him, not his country."

He saw her swallow, hard. "Those are all bad things," she said quietly. "But there are other ways to be a man. It's not all sex and temper and war and pain."

"I have spent my entire life keeping myself apart from the masses for the good of my kingdom," he told her, fierce and rough. "I will not throw away what I have built on a woman. I refuse."

"Reza." His name in her mouth was a revelation, still. And he hated himself for it. "Don't you think there's another reason you feel so out of control? Maybe you feel the same things I do. Maybe this is your chance to be a king *and* a man, not one or the other. Maybe you lo—"

"Never." His voice was too harsh then. It was beyond

cold. It was nothing less than a slap—anything to keep her from saying that word. That impossible word. Love had no business here, with him. Love had nothing to do with the life he led, the kingdom he ruled. It had not one damned thing to do with that cracked feeling that was making his chest ache. "That will never happen. I will never allow it. *Never.*"

"Reza—"

But he couldn't allow her to stand there, naked beneath his shirt, all his temptations made flesh. It would be too easy to weaken, as he'd already proved. He had to end this. Now.

"I am summoning your brother," he told her, pulling the practicalities around him like a cloak. He moved around her, heading for the door, keeping his hands to himself no matter how little he wished to do so. "He will no doubt wish to carry you back to Santa Domini like the lost treasure you are. I hope that when I see you again at some or other event, we can be cordial."

"Cordial? Are you out of your mind? Reza, we—"

He looked over his shoulder. "There is no 'we.' I release you from our contract."

She looked lost, but she still stood tall. And made him feel tiny in comparison.

"What if I don't release you?"

He shrugged as if he didn't care about this. About her. "Then you will feel very foolish, I imagine, when I marry someone else. Which I will, Maggy. And soon."

And then he walked out of that bedroom before he changed his mind the way he longed to do. Before he decided she was right and he could be both a king and the kind of man he'd imagined he was last night, sunk deep inside her. Before he went to her and kissed her mouth and took her back to his bed, the way every part of him shouted he should do, right now.

Before he let her make him forget who he was all over again.

Cairo Santa Domini was due to arrive on the island only a handful of hours later.

Maggy realized that Reza must have summoned him immediately after leaving her in his bedchamber. It suggested that the man must have leapt up from whatever kingly thing he'd been doing and raced to fly here, all to meet a sister he'd believed dead for twenty years.

"His Majesty expects the Santa Dominian plane to land in two hours," one of her smiling attendants told her when she'd made it back to her own room, still dressed in Reza's shirt. The idea of wearing the dress he'd taken off of her with such sweet skill made her want to die. She'd decided it was far better to give the staff a little show, in case they'd missed Reza carrying her through the halls last night—

But it was better not to think about last night.

"Thank you," she replied. Because what else could she say?

Maggy didn't know what to expect from a brother. Especially not when he was a famous man in his own right. Another king, no less. And she certainly didn't know how to feel. About anything, after a night that had scraped her raw and a morning that had left her feeling nothing but beaten up and bloodied.

She made her way to the state-of-the-art shower in her expansive bathroom suite and locked herself in. She made the water so hot the steam billowed up in clouds and first she scrubbed herself, over and over, trying to get him off of her. His scent, his touch. The memory of his mouth against her skin. Then she sank down, her back against the wall so she could tuck her knees up beneath her chin, and she cried.

For so long she thought she'd wrung herself dry, and yet she still didn't feel any better.

When she was dressed, in a shift dress over soft leather boots and a lovely cashmere wrap she would have called *princess casual* if anyone had asked, she stood for too long at her own mirror. Remembering when he'd stood behind her.

You need to stop, that caustic voice inside her, the one that had kept her safe all this time, snapped at her. *You're only making this worse.*

She went out into the villa while her attendants saw to her packing. Maggy expected Reza to ignore her. To stay out of her way. Surely that was the least he could do.

Maggy was picking at a meal she thought she should eat, though she wasn't the least bit hungry, when Reza strode into the breakfast room.

She gaped at him. She didn't pretend otherwise. She didn't try to hide it.

And she hated herself for the little sliver of hope that wormed its way into her heart—

But this was Reza. He said nothing. He didn't take back any of the things he'd said in his bedchamber. His gray gaze raked over her as if he was looking for evidence she was still her—but then he looked away again as he helped himself to some of the food the staff had set out on a side table.

He was hungry, apparently. He was the king—and that was all he wanted to be, the goddamned king—and he couldn't have someone fix him a tray. Of course not. Of course he had to come here and torment her.

"Are you trying to torture me?" she asked him, through gritted teeth.

There was no sign of the man she knew on his set face when he turned to her. No hint of silver in his faintly astonished gaze. It was as if the Reza she knew had been replaced by a stranger.

"I cannot imagine what you mean."

Maggy pushed to her feet. "If you want to do this, I can't stop you. Believe me, I spent my whole life with my face pressed up to some or other glass, wishing I could have whatever was on the other side. I'm not doing it with you."

That muscle clenched in his jaw, which she might have seen as a sign of hope twenty-four hours ago. But that was before that scene in his bedroom. That was before he'd thrown her out, like once again, she was nothing but garbage.

She'd thought becoming a princess would change that, but it didn't. Maybe it was something in her that made her so easy to dispose of. So easy to toss aside.

"No one asked you to," he said, and she told herself she was imagining the bite in his voice. As if this was hard for him when she knew it couldn't be. Because if it was, why was he doing it?

"I'm not going to stand here and let you talk to me like a robot." She threw her linen napkin on the table and pretended it was something harder and she was aiming for his face. "You might be one. You clearly *want* to be one. And you can hide all you want. But I won't take part in it."

And yet, after all her tough talk, she just stood there.

She didn't *actually* beg him to reconsider. She didn't let him see her cry. But she might as well have.

He sat back in his chair, his mouth an unsmiling line that she wanted to taste. That was the trouble. She wanted him no matter what. No matter how little he wanted her.

"My investigators cannot be sure," he told her in his chilliest, most distant regal voice. "But they believe they've traced what happened to you."

Maggy wanted to hit him. And not with a linen napkin. But she wanted to hear this story, too. So she set her teeth and stood where she was.

"A man known to have been a member of the Santa Dominian military went on an unscheduled break not long after the car accident that killed your parents. Records trace him to London. Several weeks after that, a woman known to the British authorities after a botched drug smuggling attempt flew one-way to New York with a companion child. According to all records, the child named as that companion does not exist. The woman went underground soon after landing in New York City and was never heard from again. But three weeks later, you were discovered on that rural road in Vermont."

It shouldn't matter what the story was. She shouldn't care. "You think she was hired to throw me away across the Atlantic, far from anyone who was looking for me?"

She thought she saw a glimpse of the Reza she knew then—and it turned out, that was worse. The hint of compassion only made the cold that much more bitter when it claimed him all over again.

"I think if they wanted to throw you away, they would have left you in that car," he said softly. "I think someone took pity on an eight-year-old child. I suspect that woman was meant to care for you, not abandon you."

"Well." Maggy's voice was as cold as his. She could feel the chill of it. "That appears to be something I bring out in people. Over and over again."

Reza stared back at her and for a moment—only a moment—she was certain she could see something in his hard rain gaze. Something almost stricken. But it was gone in the next instant, leaving nothing but stone in its wake.

She told herself she was glad she felt empty inside as she walked from the room and left him there to his crown and his duty. Because the emptier she was inside, the less there was to hurt.

Maggy assured herself she was *relieved* when the Santa Dominian plane landed. During the ten minutes or so it took for the armored SUV to make it up from the airfield to the villa, she told herself what worked in her, leaving her feeling a little bit breathless, was happiness. Pure, unadulterated happiness. Because this was what she'd always wanted, wasn't it? A family. A home. And *without* having to make herself over into some Very Special Princess so she could marry a man she hardly knew.

You're just not used to all this happiness, she told herself stiffly. *That's why you feel like crying.*

Reza had never been anything but a diversion. He wasn't what she wanted. He'd been a means to an end, nothing more.

If she kept telling herself that, surely it would turn into truth.

And she was standing in the great open foyer when

the SUV carrying Cairo Santa Domini pulled up in the circular drive, her hands in fists at her sides. Alone, of course.

Because she was always alone.

Buck up, Princess, she told herself. *You always will be.*

She heard a faint noise then and glanced over to find Reza beside her. He wore an expression she couldn't decipher on his face and his eyes were much too dark.

"You don't have to be here," she told him, because she couldn't stay quiet. That made her focus too much on all that emptiness. "I'm sure you have very important king things to do. Things that men would never do, only kings."

Reza let out a small sound that she thought was a sigh of exasperation. Maybe she only wanted it to be. Then, his mouth in that flat line that still seemed to kick up all that longing inside of her, he inclined his head in that way of his. And something was wrong with her that she felt that like some kind of support. As if he was holding her when he wasn't.

When he'd made it so clear he wouldn't.

Still, something inside of her curled at that. Like a small flame. Like hope that this thing between them wasn't finished. Not yet.

Maggy jerked her head away from him, focusing on what was happening outside in the drive. She watched as if she was far, far away as a man climbed from the back of the SUV without waiting for it to stop fully or for the hovering attendants to open his door. He stopped once he was out, and didn't move again until a red-headed woman followed him from the vehicle, then stood beside him, slipping her hand into his.

And there was no denying who he was. Cairo Santa Domini, known as an exiled king and a playboy of epic proportions before he'd taken back his kingdom. Maggy had stared at his face on tabloid magazines for years. It was hard to believe he was here. And more, that a vial of blood made them family.

Whatever that meant.

The woman—Queen Brittany, Maggy knew from the internet, once a reality star and a stripper and now the most beloved queen in Europe—gazed up at the man Maggy was supposed to call her brother as if she was giving him strength.

Cairo moved again then, his strides long as he headed for the villa's glass entryway, and Maggy couldn't breathe. Her palms stung and on some distant level she knew she was digging her nails into them, but she couldn't bring herself to stop. She could hardly manage to breathe.

Beside her, Reza shifted. Then, impossibly, she felt his hand in the small of her back.

She wanted to scream at him. She wanted to ask him what the hell he was doing. But she didn't want to do anything that would take the comfort of that hand away, no matter how cruel it was. No matter how little it actually meant.

Because that was the trouble. It was nothing to him. *She* was nothing to him, no matter how much hope she might carry deep inside her.

Yet to her, that hand was everything.

It was how she managed to stand there, straight and silent, as Cairo Santa Domini and his queen came swiftly into the hall. It was how she managed to breathe, just enough, as Cairo's gaze moved from Reza to her.

Then stuck on her.

He came closer and closer, every step loud against the marble floor, and then he stopped.

Dead.

Queen Brittany murmured something, but Maggy didn't hear it. It was only when Reza replied that she realized it must have been some kind of greeting. But Cairo was silent, too busy staring at her, and Maggy found she could do nothing but stare back.

Her heart was catapulting against her chest. Her ribs ached at the assault, or maybe because she kept holding her breath.

Because he had the same eyes. The same eyes she saw in the mirror every day. Caramel colored and shaped the same. *The same eyes.*

He muttered something in what she thought was Italian.

"There was a blood test," Maggy said, bracing herself to be thrown away the way she always was. "I'll do another one if you don't believe it."

She felt Reza's hand tighten at her back, as if he wasn't throwing her away after all. Or as if he didn't want to. Her nails dug deeper into her palms.

"You look like a ghost," Cairo said, his voice rough and reverent at once. "You look just like our mother."

Maggy's breath left her in a rush. "I'm not a ghost."

"No," Cairo agreed. He dropped his queen's hand and he moved closer, then stopped again. His gaze moved all over her as if he couldn't believe she was real. As if he wanted her to be real and was afraid she wasn't, after all. Or maybe that was her and her pounding heart. "You are Magdalena. You could not possibly be anyone else."

"Call me Maggy," she whispered.

And Cairo Santa Domini smiled, so bright it seemed to haul the sun inside, lighting up the foyer and Maggy's heart besides.

"Ah, *sorrelina*," he murmured. "I always did."

And then he closed the space between them and hauled her into his arms, lifting her off the ground and holding her close. Maggy was startled. He spun her around and she caught Reza's gaze over Cairo's shoulder. Silver and gray. It punched into her.

She sneaked her arms around Cairo's shoulders, her gaze locked to Reza's, to hug her brother back.

And she told herself she didn't care when the man she loved inclined his head again, then turned away.

She concentrated on the good things. The man who set her down on her feet and returned to studying her face, his gaze as over-bright as hers felt.

Just like a brother. *Her brother.* Just like a dream.

Except this time, it wasn't a dream. It wasn't a fairy tale.

This man was her family. Which meant, at last and for good, she belonged.

And that left room for that little flicker of hope inside of her to burn bright, then glow.

CHAPTER TEN

THE THRONE ROOM in Constantine Castle was used only for special occasions these days. Coronations, of course. Special ceremonies and addresses. Mostly, it was cordoned off and used as part of the tours that the public could take through some of the less private parts of the castle.

There was absolutely no reason that Reza should have found himself there, standing before the throne like some petitioner of old.

It had been weeks since Maggy had left the villa. Weeks since the world had learned that the Santa Domini princess had lived through that car accident twenty years ago.

She was now the foremost obsession of the international tabloids, just as Reza had predicted.

And it did not help that he knew exactly what it had taken for her to smile so graciously at the cameras. How hard she had worked to appear so elegant and so beautiful, every inch of her as beautiful as her mother before her and so startlingly, obviously a Santa Domini that the fact it had taken twenty years to find her seemed like an outrage.

He told himself he only read these articles and

watched the news reports to see how and when he was mentioned. But he wasn't. And Reza did not care to speculate as to why the Santa Dominian palace did not share the fact that he had been the one to find her.

The palace said very little, in fact. It had released a statement upon her return, announcing that she was recovered after all this time and enjoying getting to know her brother and the life she'd forgotten. Cairo had given an address that had expressed his joy at having some part of his murdered family returned to him. And the world had been forced to content itself with the very few pictures the palace released over those first few days. Maggy and Cairo together, laughing at something that made their identical eyes shine. Maggy holding the Crown Prince Rafael, her young nephew, while Queen Brittany looked on.

All very heartwarming.

Yet Reza remained cold straight through.

Here in this throne room, all the ghosts of his bloodline seemed to congregate. He could feel their disapproval press against him, like the weight of the formal crown he wore only on specific occasions these days.

He stared at the throne itself.

It was only a chair, though it dated back to the fifteen hundreds. It was made of finely polished wood and it gleamed in the sunlight that poured in through the stained-glass windows and made the room into a kind of chapel. A place of power and resolve, or so Reza had been taught.

He didn't understand the part of him that wanted to burn it. Rip it apart with his hands. Make it into so much kindling—

But there was no point in this kind of maudlin self-indulgence. He had let her go, the way he should have done from the start. From the moment he'd understood that he couldn't keep his distance with her. That she made him as bad as his father.

He had made his choice.

Reza made himself turn away. He pushed his way out of the great doors, nodding at the guards who waited there. He heard them muttering into their earpieces as they followed him down the grand hall. Alerting the rest of the palace to his movements. All hail his very public life that he'd lived blamelessly all this time. Forever apologizing for his father's failures. Forever making up for his father's sins.

For the first time in his life, Reza felt as if he was drowning. As if his role here was holding his head beneath the water. As if he had no choice but to open up his mouth, suck in the sea, and sink.

Impatient with himself, he shook it off as he rounded a corner and headed for his offices. Or he tried to shake it off.

Either way, he was as controlled and expressionless as always when he walked into his office to find three of his aides and his personal secretary waiting for him.

"Sire," his secretary said, and the man's deferential tone set his teeth on edge, when it was no different than it had ever been before. "There has been a development."

"You will have to be more specific," Reza clipped out as he rounded his desk, all of the historic city laid out before him on the other side of the windows. The far-off snowcapped mountains. The gleaming alpine lakes in the distance.

But all he saw was her face.

He gritted his teeth, then focused on his staff.

"The princess, sire," his secretary continued. Carefully. "She's given her first interview."

He did not play games and ask which princess his secretary meant, though there was a part of him—the cowardly part he would excise with his own fingers if he could—that wanted to hide from whatever this was a while longer. Even inside his own head.

"I imagine it will be the first of many," he replied. Reza felt more than saw the glances his staff exchanged, and braced himself. "I assume you are bringing this particular interview to my attention for a reason?"

His secretary stood straighter. "She discusses her wedding plans, sire. In some detail."

And it took every bit of Reza's training in diplomacy to simply stand there as if nothing was the matter. As if this news did not affect him in the slightest.

If only that were true.

"Have my felicitations sent with the appropriate gift," he murmured, as if he'd already forgotten what they were talking about. Then he treated them all to the full force of his stare. "Surely such things are usually done automatically, without my input?"

"I fear I cannot do the interview justice, sire," his secretary murmured. The man thrust a tablet onto the desktop and hit the play arrow on its screen.

Reza did not want to watch this. He wanted to hurl the tablet through the window behind him. He wanted to institute beheadings and reopen the old dungeons, and he wanted to start with the staff standing before him.

He wanted anything but Maggy in front of him, laughing with one of those American television journalists with alarmingly bright white teeth.

She was too beautiful. It was worse on-screen, where her marvelous cheekbones seemed more pronounced and her lively eyes seemed warmer and more kind than he remembered. Her voice was the same, soft and faintly rough, and all he could think about was Maggy on her knees before him, sucking him deep into her mouth.

Damn her.

He'd known she would be the ruin of him. What he hadn't realized was that even when he'd removed the temptation of her from his life, he would remain ruined.

"And I'm told you plan to honor the Santa Domini royal family's traditions, despite all these years away?" the interviewer asked.

"Oh, yes," Maggy answered, sounding as if the interviewer were her best friend in the world. Reza made a mental note to give his public relations team bonuses, given the magic they'd worked with her. She looked nothing like the mouthy shopgirl he'd met. She looked like who she was—who she had always been. Magdalena Santa Domini. "I have been betrothed to the king of the Constantines since I was born. And I am happy to honor my commitments. After all, not every girl gets to wake up one morning to find she's actually a princess and, even better, she's meant for a king."

The interviewer laughed but made one of those fake noises of concern that would have annoyed Reza had he been able to do anything but stand there, frozen, that aching thing in his chest threatening to break free at last.

"But you only just found out who you are," the interviewer said. "How can you rush into something like this?"

"The king is the one who found me," Maggy said,

almost shyly, and Reza knew exactly why they'd held it back before now. For this moment. For maximum impact. He almost admired it—the Santa Dominis were nothing if not in complete control of their images. Why should Maggy be any different? "He knew who I was before I did. And we spent some time together as I adjusted to my new role." She smiled down at her lap, looking for all the world as if she was overcome with emotion. It set Reza's teeth on edge. Especially when she looked up again, now looking flushed. *Like a woman in love*, a voice inside him murmured. "I'm more than happy with my fate."

His hand shot out before he could control it, stopping the video. His heart kicked at him, making his ribs ache.

"If you continue, sire," his secretary said, even more carefully than before, "the princess claims the wedding will be in June."

"In June," Reza said. His voice sounded as if it was someone else's.

"Yes, sire."

"This June."

His secretary nodded.

Reza stared down at the tablet before him, frozen on Maggy.

He hardly knew himself any longer and it was her fault. He had spent his whole life keeping himself free of emotional entanglements, just as he'd been taught by both his mother's cold demands and his father's bad example. He was trying to rule a kingdom and Maggy was telling lies to the whole world, boxing him into corners he wouldn't be able to get out of without causing an international incident and destroying the relationship between the two kingdoms—

Reza paused then. He took a deep breath in, then let it go.

She had thrown down a gauntlet. He would pick it up.

Maggy might think she wanted the man. Reza knew better. It was high time he showed her what happened when she taunted both man *and* king.

"Have the helicopter ready in fifteen minutes." His voice was smooth. Even. As if there was none of that fire beneath it. As if he wasn't burning alive where he stood. "I believe it's time I called upon my lovely bride."

Maggy sensed him before she heard a sound.

She waited in one of the palace's grand salons, set aside for visiting heads of state and various monarchs, sitting like the picture-perfect princess Reza had made her. She'd been informed the moment his helicopter had entered Santa Dominian airspace. She'd been alerted when he'd landed.

But she didn't need anyone to come and whisper in her ear that Reza was in the palace. That he was being led straight to her. She could feel it deep in her belly. She could feel it in the electric shivers that traced patterns over her limbs and the butterflies that performed calisthenics inside of her.

And then at last he was there, striding into the grand salon as if it was his, and it all got worse.

Or better, depending on how she looked at it.

Reza moved through her brother's palace the same way he'd strode into that long-ago coffee shop. He looked elemental. Regal stone and royal temper, all the way through.

She made herself stay where she was, and no matter that he bore down upon her like a freight train.

The doors closed behind him, leaving them alone in this overwrought room of antiques with priceless artifacts scattered about on every surface. But all Maggy could see was Reza.

"I knew you'd come," she said softly when he was in front of her, standing there radiating fury and something else she couldn't quite decipher in another perfectly pressed suit. "I'm surprised it took you as long as it did."

"You should have told me you were psychic," he replied, his voice all edges and threat. Yet it rolled through her like a caress. Like his body moving over her and in her—but she had to focus. "It might have saved me the time and the trouble."

Back in the villa, that might have killed her. But she'd spent a few weeks here, in the company of her marvelously wicked sister-in-law and her sharp, funny brother, and she wasn't the same person she'd been then. Or she was more that person than she'd known how to be that awful morning after.

And she'd seen through him, at last.

"You weren't discarding me, Reza," she told him softly, not beating around the bush because she'd already lost twenty years of her real life. She didn't want to lose a moment more. "I know you might have told yourself that you were. But what you were really doing was running scared."

As she'd known he would, he turned to granite.

"I beg your pardon."

She smiled at that, and it wasn't one of her fake, princess smiles. She felt this one down deep. "I love it when you say that, so stuffy and *indignant*. But it's true. I think you know it."

"The king of the Constantines does not *run scared,* I think you will find." Reza's brows arched, but he was still right there in front of her. He hadn't walked away again. "By definition."

"Perhaps not." She raised her own brows, settling back against the sofa as if, this time, she was the one gracing a high throne with her presence. "But what about you, Reza?"

"What about me?" He frowned at her. "I don't follow."

Of course he didn't.

"You have the king thing down, I think we can all agree." And he was so much the king. Even now, standing in another man's palace, he radiated that fierce authority. Maggy could feel it deep in her belly. "Are you really going to pretend that you're not also a flesh and blood man with his own needs?"

"I am not pretending anything. But I do not have to give in to my baser instincts. I do not have to let whatever needs I might have control me."

She thought he was speaking more to himself than to her.

"But you're okay with letting your dead parents and their terrible marriage control you instead." He looked outraged, but she'd expected that. She pushed on. "I did some research into your parents these last weeks. I dug up all those rumors. The speculation that your father was so wrapped up in that woman he nearly brought the country to war. That he disgraced the crown, then took his own life. All those nasty whispers."

"They are not whispers, they are facts I have kept from the public for years." He sounded starched through, though she could see that muscle in his cheek, telling her the truth about his feelings. "And now that you know these unsavory truths, there is no need for these theatrics, is there?"

Maggy folded her hands in her lap even tighter, because she wanted to reach for him.

"I didn't have any parents," she said softly. "But I'm pretty sure the point of them is that they're supposed to protect *you*, Reza. Not make you responsible for *their* problems."

"You have no idea what you are talking about." His voice was dark. Low.

Tortured.

"If you say so," she replied in a tone that told him she disagreed. Quietly. Then inclined her head the way he liked to do. "Your Majesty. You must know best."

And she thought for a moment that she could hear his teeth grit.

The truth was, she knew him. That had been the truth she'd returned to again and again in this time away from him, nursing that flame of hope deep inside of her. She knew him because she *was* him, in all the ways that mattered. He was as alone as she'd always been. He hid it in his palaces and villas, his bespoke suits, and his ranting on about what the king could and could not do—but he was always alone. His life was a throne, nothing more.

It might shine a lot brighter than her little room in Vermont, but it was the same narrow bed and the same cold thing inside that never quite warmed. Maggy knew this better than anyone.

She knew *Reza* better than anyone, in part because he'd shown her the pain behind his mask that dreadful morning.

He had found her and rescued her from a life that had never been meant to be hers. This was her chance to rescue him in turn.

"Exactly what is it you think you are doing?" Reza asked her with soft menace, fierce danger all over his harsh face, but she couldn't allow herself to be intimidated. Not when it mattered this much. "Do you truly believe that you can announce a wedding date and I will simply honor it? Because you say so?"

"That was pretty much your original plan, if I remember it right." She shrugged. "Why shouldn't it work for me?"

"You should have told me you were barking mad," he gritted out. "I would have handled this whole thing differently."

"I'm not mad. I am mad *at* you," she retorted. She stood up then, letting her dress fall where it would. She'd chosen it carefully because it made her look like a queen and she knew it. She could see he knew it, too. "You made me into a princess. Now I want to be your queen. As promised."

His hands were clenched into fists at his sides. He looked like thunder. But he was here. He was *here*, and that was what kept her standing where she was, pretending her heart wasn't thumping and her stomach wasn't in knots.

"You cannot force me to marry you," he growled at her, as if that was the end of the matter. But he still didn't leave.

Maggy only smiled at him.

"First," she said, "it's not up to you whether you marry me or not. It's your destiny." She saw the moment he realized she was throwing his own words right back at him. It made those hard rain eyes go silver, and that was when she knew this would be okay. That it would work. That the flicker of light inside of her, hopeful and bright, had been guiding her in the right direction all along. "And second, you silly man, haven't you realized that we're made for each other? You took a scared, beaten-down woman and made her a princess."

"And you took a king and rendered him nothing but a man," he bit out, but she thought he sounded less furious than before.

She'd seen that gleam of silver and she wasn't afraid any longer. She'd already lost him, however briefly. She wasn't doing it again. Not ever again.

Maggy moved toward him, watching that muscle in his cheek flex as she did. She didn't stop when she drew near. She slid her hands up on his chest and she arched herself into him, never taking her eyes from his.

"I love you, Reza," she told him, from the very depths of her. "I love the king in you. I love how seriously you take your duties. I love how deeply it matters to you that you take care of your people. But it was the man who took care of me. And I love him more."

"Maggy…" he whispered, as if her name might break him in two. "I don't know how to do this. My father—"

"You are not your father," she told him, her gaze solemn on his. "And I have no desire to be your mistress. And, Reza, no one knows how to do it. I think that's the point."

And she watched him break. She saw his eyes flash silver and bright. She watched the ice crack and all that heat pour out of him as his arms came around her, and then he hauled her even closer.

Bringing Maggy home at last.

"You knew I would come to you," he growled at her, his mouth so close to hers. "You knew I couldn't resist."

Her eyes felt much too full. "I hoped."

"And if I marry you, then what?" he demanded. "When you strip away my control and I am rendered nothing but a man lost without you, what then?"

"Then I will come and find you wherever you're lost," she whispered. "Just as you came and found me. And I promise you, Reza, I won't let you stumble. I won't make you a worse king. I'll try my best to make you a better man."

His hands seemed uncertain as they moved up to smooth her hair back from her face, and she felt her tears spilling over when he leaned in and pressed a soft kiss on her forehead.

"I think I've loved you all my life," he told her, his voice a rough sort of velvet she'd never heard from him before. It washed through her, heat and love. "I loved you in the abstract. I mourned you. And then I saw you in that picture and I fell in love all over again."

He kissed her then, and it was a real kiss. Wild and dark and perfect, rolling through her and making her heart swell inside her chest. He kissed her again and again, as if they were making their vows here and now. As if they were fusing themselves into one.

When he pulled away again, it was her turn to reach up and cradle his face in her hands.

"When I was first found by the side of that road," she told him, "I dreamed of fairy tales. Kings and queens and palaces. Every night, for years, I would go to sleep and dream of fairy-tale stories filled with people I wanted so badly to believe were real." She smiled at him. She kissed him. "But maybe they were. Maybe they weren't dreams at all. Maybe they were the life I left behind me when that car crashed."

He whispered her name, drawing her closer.

"Reza." And her voice was a scrap of sound. "Don't you see? I've been dreaming of you my whole life. It's just that I forgot your name for a little while."

His smile then was the most beautiful thing she'd ever seen.

"I will endeavor to make certain you never do again."

"Marry me, Your Majesty," she whispered, tipping her head back and loving him with all she was, all she would be, all she'd ever dreamed she could be. Right here in his arms, at last. "Make me your queen."

That June, in a ceremony televised around the world and gushed over in all the tabloids, with her newfound family there to give her away and a brand-new country that had fallen in love with their king's lost princess, he did.

And they spent all their happily-ever-after together, making their fairy tale real.

Just as Maggy had always dreamed.

* * * * *

If you enjoyed this story, take a look at
these other great reads by Caitlin Crews
THE GUARDIAN'S VIRGIN WARD
THE RETURN OF THE DI SIONE WIFE
EXPECTING A ROYAL SCANDAL
Available now!

And why not explore these other
WEDLOCKED! stories?
BOUND BY HIS DESERT DIAMOND
by Andie Brock
A DIAMOND FOR DEL RIO'S HOUSEKEEPER
by Susan Stephens
Available now!

MILLS & BOON®

EXCLUSIVE EXTRACT

Raul Di Savo desires more than Lydia Hayward's
body—his seduction will stop his rival buying her!
Raul's expert touch awakens Lydia to irresistible
pleasure, but his game of revenge forces
Lydia to leave… until an unexpected
consequence binds them forever!

Read on for a sneak preview of
THE INNOCENT'S SECRET BABY

Somehow Lydia was back against the wall with Raul's
hands either side of her head.

She put her hands up to his chest and felt him solid
beneath her palms and she just felt him there a moment
and then looked up to his eyes.

His mouth moved in close and as it did she stared
right into his eyes.

She could feel heat hover between their mouths in a
slow tease before they first met.

Then they met.

And all that had been missing was suddenly there.

Yet, the gentle pressure his mouth exerted, though
blissful, caused a mire of sensations until the gentleness
of his kiss was no longer enough.

A slight inhale, a hitch in her breath and her lips
parted, just a little, and he slipped his tongue in.

The moan she made went straight to his groin.

At first taste she was his and he knew it for her hands

moved to the back of his head and he kissed her as hard back as her fingers demanded.

More so even.

His tongue was wicked and her fingers tightened in his thick hair and she could feel the wall cold and hard against her shoulders.

It was the middle of Rome just after six and even down a side street there was no real hiding from the crowds.

Lydia didn't care.

He slid one arm around her waist to move her body away from the wall and closer into his, so that her head could fall backwards.

If there was a bed, she would be on it.

If there was a room they would close the door.

Yet there wasn't and so he halted them, but only their lips.

Their bodies were heated and close and he looked her right in the eye. His mouth was wet from hers and his hair a little messed from her fingers.

Don't miss
THE INNOCENT'S SECRET BABY,
By Carol Marinelli

Available March 2017
www.millsandboon.co.uk

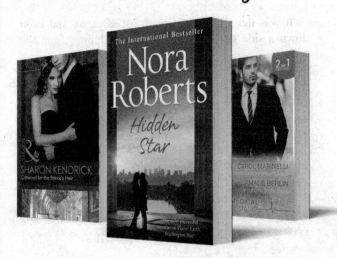

Join Britain's BIGGEST Romance Book Club

- **EXCLUSIVE offers** every month
- **FREE delivery direc** to your door
- **NEVER MISS a title**
- **EARN Bonus Book** points

Call Customer Services
0844 844 1358*

or visit
millsandboon.co.uk/subscription